SOMEWHERE
ALONG THE WAY

By the Author

Visit us at www.boldstrokesbooks.com

SOMEWHERE ALONG THE WAY

by

Kathleen Knowles

2019

SOMEWHERE ALONG THE WAY

ISBN 13: 978-1-63555-383-3

This Trade Paperback Original Is Published By
Bold Strokes Books, Inc.
P.O. Box 249
Valley Falls, NY 12185

First Edition: September 2019

Credits
Editor: Stacia Seaman
Production Design: Stacia Seaman
Cover Design by Tammy Seidick

Acknowledgments

Several people shared their memories of that time with me—Mary G, Marcus W, and Kent B. Kent and Marcus read the manuscript and helped me correct some factual errors. This wasn't an easy book to write, but it was an especially meaningful one.

For Jeanette as always

PROLOGUE

A nthony was there. He'd decided to move back to the City so he could be close to the best doctors for his long-term health. The people in the meeting looked expectantly at me. Some, like Anthony and my girlfriend, Trish, were smiling in an encouraging way. I paused and inhaled to calm myself. The point was to tell the truth; it didn't have to be anything fancy or profound, just honest.

I said, "My name is Max, and I'm an alcoholic and an addict."

The chorus of "Hello, Max" came back and that itself was reassuring. There was so much that was repetitive about AA, but it was a comfort to me now though it didn't used to be.

"My sobriety date is August 3, 1984. If you're new and you don't hear anything that helps you, keep coming back. If I only say one thing, that helps one person, then I've done my service.

"I'm going to follow the format: what it was like, what happened, and what it's like now."

Part I: What It Was Like

CHAPTER ONE

I looked through the tiny airplane window as we made the approach into San Francisco. The plane swerved so far out over the water, I thought we were going to land on the San Francisco Bay. As we approached, in the blackness, the lights of the suburbs looked like velvet with thousands of jewels scattered over it.

Chris crowded close to peer over my shoulder. He'd generously given me the window seat but now was as excited as I was to arrive at our destination.

"Look at that," he said and pointed at a freeway. His breath, smelling faintly of the orange juice in the screwdrivers he'd consumed, brushed my ear.

"Yeah, remember we had those back in Ohio?" I was irritable because I was tired and the drinks I'd consumed earlier had worn off and I didn't want to spend my limited supply of money on more airplane cocktails.

"You know what I mean, silly. We're here, finally," he said, in an awed tone.

Chris was my best friend and this trip was his idea. It wasn't a trip, even; we were moving to San Francisco to be free, to be gay, essentially. It was hard to be gay in Ohio. As undergrads, we were completely in the closet. In grad school, things were a little better but not much. We told select people one a time. We were together so much, a lot of people mistook us for a couple, and it was often safer to let them think so. Chris told me we had to move to San Francisco because we could really be gay there. He'd heard about Harvey Milk—a gay guy who'd actually been elected to city government in 1977. I suspected the bigger reason was Chris was as tired of Cleveland as I was and we were both tired of grad school.

"Because," Chris said, "it means that there were a lot of homos and they voted for him. I read that. So…what do you think?"

I didn't know what to think. I wasn't especially happy in Cleveland, so it didn't seem like a terrible idea.

We made our weary way out to the front of the airport, dragging our huge suitcases. We had find out how to get into downtown San Francisco. It was eleven o'clock at night, but the time difference made it feel like one in the morning to my jet-lagged brain and body.

Chris motioned me to follow him over to the bank of telephone booths near the baggage claim. As I watched, he awkwardly thumbed through the unwieldy phone book. It was enormous and chained to the shelf so that it was hard to open.

"Lee said he stayed at a residence hotel somewhere downtown but he didn't know where." Chris found the hotel listings and started reading them as I leaned on the shelf next to him, sagging with exhaustion.

"Just pick one, okay?"

"No, I want to find the one Lee stayed at. He said it was right on Polk Street and it was fun."

"What about Castro Street?" I asked. We were both vague on the geography of San Francisco.

"We'll find it tomorrow," Chris said.

I guessed it was okay to let him plan our actions because he had the original idea. He was usually the one with ideas and I was the one who went along. I was also just so tired I didn't care where we stayed as long as there was a bed. Chris scrutinized the SF Yellow Pages. Among the many things I admired and hated him for was he always looked perfect no matter what condition he was in. We'd started drinking in the airport and continued through most of the five-hour flight, but while I was bleary eyed and sagging, he seemed perfectly fine, his sandy hair slightly disheveled but in a sexy way.

"Aha," he said in triumph. "Here it is. Do you have some change?"

I dug out what I had. I half listened to his side of the phone call, just enough to know we had a place to sleep.

"It's right on Larkin Street, one block off Polk. Let's go ask how to get there."

In short order, we were on something called an Airporter and on our way down the freeway we'd flown over. It was lot like a Greyhound bus but nicer.

"Just think, Maxy, we're in San Francisco. *The* San Francisco!" He grabbed my arm and shook me lightly. That was his move when he was super excited. My own excitement was keeping me awake, at least.

We zoomed past water and freeway exits until we could see the skyscrapers of downtown. They looked like those in any city, but as we got closer, we could see a bridge.

"Is that the Golden Gate Bridge?" I asked Chris, but before he could answer, someone seated in front of me leaned into the aisle and looked at me and said, "Nah, that's the Bay Bridge." He didn't say it too disdainfully.

"Really?" Chris asked, curious and friendly when he realized the speaker was a handsome young man. "You live here?"

The other passenger was a guy with sideburns and a mustache and hazel eyes. My gaydar went off and evidently Chris's had as well. He had the look he gets when he's interested in someone; his eyes were wide and innocent and his smile chipper and ingenuous.

"I do. Just coming home from a weekend in New York."

"Oh cool, we just came from Cleveland. Like in Ohio."

The guy raised his eyebrows.

"Yes, I know where Cleveland is, after all, I changed planes there." He drilled a stare at Chris. "So your first time in SF?" he asked.

Then it hit me, he was cruising him. I glanced at Chris. He was smiling slightly as though he was thinking of something amusing.

"Yeah. Do you have any suggestions?" Chris asked, seeming clueless.

"Where are you staying?" the man asked, and I had to mentally roll my eyes.

Whenever I watched this dance, and I'd seen it many times, I always felt both envious and slightly irritated. It was so easy for gay boys. They knew instantaneously what or who they wanted and communicated it with what seemed no effort, almost telepathically. For me, when I tried to attract women, it was more complicated and much more fraught with uncertainty. Chris always said he could tell in the first minute, at the first eye contact if a man was interested.

"Well. That's just the thing. I got an address for this place on Larkin Street."

"What's your name? My name is Daniel," mustache man asked in friendly way.

"Chris. This is Max." He nodded at me.

"Chris, nice to meet you." Daniel didn't even spare me a glance. He kept right on grinning at Chris like a salesman. I knew what he was selling, and Chris was hooked. I had seen *that* before as well. I resigned myself to being abandoned in short order.

"I was named for the saint, I'm not one." I'd heard this before too, but he liked to try it on new people to gauge their reactions.

Daniel lowered his eyelids and paused a moment but only said, "Larkin Street? Larkin and what?"

"I don't know. The Airporter is dropping us on California Street."

"Oh great," Dan said brightly. "That's my stop. I live off Polk on Bush. I can show you where to go. Say, do you want to go get a drink?"

"Absolutely." Chris beamed. As tired as I was, that sounded good to me, but I wasn't sure if I was invited.

Dan said, "Let's get you checked in. What's the name of the place?"

"The Lattimer," Chris read from a scrap of paper.

"The Lattimer?" Daniel frowned, and his tone made it sound like the Lattimer was the pit of hell.

"Yep. What's wrong?" Why Chris had suddenly decided that this guy was our savior, I had no idea. I knew he loved it when boys wanted him. It happened often enough in Cleveland, but maybe it was different and better because we were in Frisco.

"Oh, honey, that place is crawling with hustlers. It's pickup central." Dan paused. "Unless that's what you want." His eyes narrowed. Well, that confirmed he was gay, as if we needed any more assurance.

"Um, no, I'm not into paying." Chris's flirtatious tone hardened.

"I think, then, you might want to try another place. I know a better one." Daniel had stopped flirting and he actually seemed kind.

"Maybe you could show us?" I said and he finally focused on me for a second.

"Yep, happy to."

"We don't know anything about Frisco," Chris said.

Dan smiled again, but less kindly. "Don't call it Frisco."

Before I could ask why, the bus driver called, "California and Polk."

The three of us exited and retrieved our luggage. The cold air woke me up. I looked around. Though it was after midnight, the street was busy. Lights winked from various places. I zipped my sweatshirt shut and shivered. This was July in California? Shit.

We faced Daniel like he was a tour guide, which I guess in a way he was.

"We'll walk a couple blocks to the Bedford Arms. I think you'll like it better than the Lattimer."

We set off down the street.

"Why not call it Frisco?" Chris asked. Daniel was leading the way and looked back over his shoulder.

"Only tourists call it Frisco. We call it SF or the City."

"We're kind of tourists. But we're moving here," Chris said, and Daniel perked up even more.

"Excellent. Well, you're starting in the right place, Polk Gulch. It's one of the gay neighborhoods, the real one as far as I'm concerned."

"I thought that was Castro Street?" I found his statement confusing.

"Oh yeah—*they* like to think so, but it all really started here."

Chris and I glanced at one another, confused. Who did he mean, "they"? I thought we were "we."

Daniel led us to the entrance of a brick building that might have been elegant at one time but now seemed a little seedy.

"Here we are."

As Daniel waited in the lobby, seated on the tattered leather couch smoking a cigarette, we checked into a room that turned out be basically okay—nothing special. Two single beds and a bathroom.

When we came down in the elevator, his face clouded a bit. I don't think he was expecting Chris to have me in tow. Well, I'd go along for a drink, but then I would leave them to their own devices. I knew what the score was, so to speak. I was too tired to go looking for company of my own. The thought crossed my mind but from my brief view of the pedestrians on the street, I didn't think I'd find any.

We headed up the street, and Daniel and Chris walked ahead, their heads together, chattering. I lagged behind to give them space. Two really young guys flew past us, shrieking. Yeah, I guess this was a gay neighborhood, since there were actual screaming queens. That made me smile. I'd have to tell Chris later to make him laugh.

"Here we are," he said, and we stood in front of a bar named

Suzy Q, but something told me it wasn't a dyke bar. My search for those places would have to come later. Daniel and Chris hadn't stopped talking since we'd left the hotel. At this point what I wanted was a drink. The walk in the cold night air had rendered me fully awake.

We slid onto barstools. It was Sunday night and the place was sort of full—all men, of course. I sighed.

"Whaddya have?" Daniel asked. He'd apparently decided I was okay, if mostly irrelevant.

"She likes brandy or beer." Chris answered for me, but he knew, so I didn't care. Daniel looked from Chris to me.

"Right, you're going to have to give me a little background here." He thought we were together—nothing unusual. "So? Which is it, both or which one?"

"Brandy," I said, hoping I could get a buzz faster.

We carried our drinks to a table. The place was a little drab looking, but that didn't concern me. Wow, my first San Francisco gay bar. I guess this was somewhat momentous. I didn't mind, I'd hung out in gay bars in Cleveland that were mostly men but somewhat mixed. We only had one dyke bar and it was a drag, not the fun kind. I mostly spent time in discos where the clientele was mixed, men and women. I was hoping and expecting San Francisco would have more lesbian bars, but I would have to find them. I'd need a female version of Daniel.

"So, tell me about you two." Daniel aimed this question at Chris, who glanced at me fondly. Even when he was about to embark on seduction, he still cared.

"We went to college together. Max is my best friend."

I took a sip of brandy and gave Daniel a little smirk. "And vice versa."

"Ah, yeah. I thought you were a couple." He seemed relieved. Yeah, Danny boy, you'll get into Chris's jeans, no problemo.

"We get that a lot," Chris said nonchalantly. He'd ordered a rum and Coke, his favorite. He always claimed the caffeine in the Coke helped him stay awake.

"What's Max short for?"

"Maxine."

"Oh honey. That's gotta be a dyke name."

"Um, yeah. So?" I said. That was obvious.

He put his hands up in a defensive way. "Whoa. Nothing to me. I'm just trying to keep things straight, so to speak."

He thought he was witty. I didn't like his attitude with me, but it was familiar. Gay guys could be dicks. Not Chris, but he was an exception.

Daniel turned his focus back to Chris and beamed, his teeth all bared. If he had fangs, he would have made a great vampire. He was ready to suck something, that's for sure. Chris was sitting back, his eyes a little droopy, but that wasn't because he was sleepy. I decided then and there to finish my drink and split.

I listened as the two boys bantered and flirted. I was okay with it, I just sat, smoked, and sipped my drink and soaked in the gay bar gestalt. I didn't much mind that there were no women, I was safe at least. I was in San Francisco, at last. The women were around somewhere and I'd find them.

"Hey, I'm going back to the Bedford," I said, interrupting their flow.

"You okay?" Chris asked as Daniel just stared.

"Oh, sure, I'm fine. I'll see you later." I patted his shoulder and said, "Thanks for the drink," to Daniel. He acknowledged me with the briefest possible nod, then turned back to Chris.

I was more alert after the drink, but when it wore off I would be sleepy. I spotted a marquee on the corner about two blocks from the hotel. It said Sukkers Liquors. It was amazing that something other than bars was open. I went inside.

A dark-haired, sallow-skinned man stood behind a counter, and he nodded at me indifferently, but I was struck by the fact that behind him were rows of shelves filled with nothing but booze, many in small bottles.

I stood in front of him as I scanned the alcohol display. What did you know, you didn't have to go to a state store to buy liquor. What a concept.

I spotted a pint bottle of brandy. That might come in handy. I giggled and the counterman squinted at me.

"I'll take the Christian Brothers pint," I said.

He rang it up and put it in a paper bag. I thanked him and took my little treasure back to the Bedford.

Inside the room, I took off my shoes and flopped on the bed, which proved to be somewhat hard. I considered having another drink but dismissed it. I really wanted to go to sleep and Chris wouldn't be back for a while, if he came back at all.

I undressed and thought about brushing my teeth but didn't feel like it and just got in bed and turned out the light that was on the table between the beds.

And I was wide awake. I suppose it was the excitement of finally arriving, and I thought about the events leading up to us making the decision to finally do it.

Both Chris and I had reasons to leave Cleveland. He claimed there were no more interesting men left for him to sleep with. I thought that was an exaggeration but not by much. He was a slut, that was for sure. I had my own reasons for wanting to leave Cleveland, not having to do with having no one left to sleep with. It was more like my reputation was so bad, no one would sleep with *me.* That was one of the many differences between dykes and faggots when it came to sex. You could do whatever and with whoever you wanted and wanted you and it was fine if you were gay, but not if you were a lesbian. Cleveland's dyke community was tiny, incestuous, and terminally gossipy and censorious. I was sick of it, really. They could go jump in Lake Erie as far as I was concerned. The kicker was everyone claimed to be feminists, that they were liberated, but it wasn't true. They all just wanted to get married or get married at least until someone better appeared. I always said, "Women are like buses, another one will be along in a minute." San Francisco offered a host of new possibilities, and I fell asleep thinking of them.

I woke up as the door opened and Chris stumbled into the room. He barked his shin on my bed frame and muttered, "Shit." I went back to sleep, though. I didn't feel like talking.

A few hours later, I woke up and knew it was for real. I was still on East Coast time. It was too early to disturb him—he was likely drunk when he returned last night and wouldn't appreciate it. He was usually good-natured, but not always.

I pulled on my clothes from the day before and went downstairs.

They had a coffeepot in the lobby and I grabbed a cup and put one of those little creamers in it. It still tasted awful. No matter, when Chris was awake, we could go out to breakfast.

I looked out the front door and it looked like it was going to rain, cloudy and gray. This pissed me off because I didn't want to be a tourist in the rain. I sat down at a scarred wooden table. Since it was only eight thirty, no one was around. No matter how late I went to sleep or how much I drank, I *always* woke up early. It was my curse.

There were pieces of a newspaper scattered on the table and I picked up one with a big ad on it. Macy's, it said, but to the left was a little vertical swatch of writing. At the top it said "Herb Caen." Over his name was a little picture of what I thought might be the San Francisco skyline, but it looked weird. I scanned down the print. It was short phrases separated by three dots. It was all gibberish to me but seemed to be about people and places in SF. I suppose I would someday understand the references. The other section was the sports news, and I had no interest in that.

I looked around and could find nothing else to read. I ought to have brought my book downstairs. I didn't want to leave without Chris. It wasn't that I was scared of being by myself; he would be mad if I left him behind. All of San Francisco was waiting out there for us, and I was ready to see it.

We had given ourselves a week to be just tourists before we'd have to find jobs and a place to live, in that order. One of Chris's Cleveland flings had been a guy from Berkeley visiting his folks in Cleveland and had given Chris the name of the biotech company he worked for in San Francisco and encouraged him to come out west and apply. That was Chris's place to start, and he promised if he was hired, he'd try to get me a job. Until then it was playtime, and I wanted to get started.

Chris and I never argued about much of anything. In the small college we attended, we were the only two gay people we knew, so we stuck together. We met our freshman year when I started seeing his roommate. I was in my straight phase. Chris had a couple girlfriends, but he was just going through the motions, like me. He decided he was Chris instead of Christopher and took a couple of theater courses where he met his first boyfriend, if you could call him that. Their relationship consisted of furtive sexual encounters behind the softball field—a real hassle when the weather turned wintry, and they soon broke up. Chris was terrified of being found out anyhow. I was the only one as far as I could see who knew about him. On the other hand, my gayness was largely theoretical in college.

While we were in grad school, we were roommates in Cleveland. There was where we both found out for real about being homo. He was the one person I could depend on, and he never let me down. We never let any of our lovers come between us either. We both knew when the lovers eventually left, we would still be there.

I went out the front door and looked up and down the street. It was Monday morning and there were a few folks about. I scrutinized them and some looked gay, some did not. The street didn't seem that different from any commercial district unless you took a good look at the passersby. I decided to scout out a breakfast place. I found a few—helpfully, there were menus in the windows.

I managed to kill an hour and decided to go back to our room and see if he was up. The shower was running when I walked in, a good sign.

As I waited, I picked up the book, one I had in fact borrowed from Chris, *Dancer from the Dance.* It was currently his bible. He wanted to find a Malone. If he could have convinced me, we would have gone to New York, but New York seemed daunting. We figured SF was just as good as far as being gay went but with better weather, or so we heard, but I hadn't yet seen evidence of it.

I'd read about being gay in New York, and Andrew Holleran made it sound pretty great if you were a guy. Why was it so much easier and more fun for them? I hoped San Francisco's dykes were a little looser than Cleveland's. Well, maybe I hoped they were a lot looser.

Chris walked out of the bathroom in a towel, drying his hair.

"You better have left me a dry towel, man," I said.

He looked at the towel in his hands.

"Oh," he said sheepishly. "I forgot. Here, use this one." And he handed it to me. It was only a little damp. I put it over a windowsill, hoping the chilly breeze would dry it some.

"How was Daniel?"

Chris sat on the bed and lit a cigarette. I did too. We usually took time to talk over the night before as soon as we could the next day.

"Well, the sex was great and we went at it for a while, but then he kicked me out and said he had to get up early in the morning. He works downtown."

I was confused. "Aren't we in downtown?"

Chris took a drag off his cigarette and said, "Nope, he said he works in the Financial District, that's over there." He gestured vaguely out the window.

"So he kicked you out, that's cold," I said, secretly happy he was with me. "Did he give you his phone number?"

"Yeah, so what? And no. 'Just once' is his philosophy."

"Huh, no big loss." I wasn't a fan of Daniel anyhow. I thought he was a jerk. I hoped he wasn't a typical of San Francisco fags.

"Nope, there's a whole city full of men out there."

After we found a better map in a bookstore cleverly called Books, Ink, we went to breakfast and plotted our strategy.

"First we need to go to Castro Street," Chris said with his usual finality.

When it came to logistics, I let him make the decisions. It was just easier that way and he was a great planner anyhow. He knew how to go to the Cleveland library and find out stuff about San Francisco. He'd also talked to Cleveland gay guys who had visited and then came back and reported, their eyes shining about how wonderful it was. Just because Milk got shot, one of them said, that didn't really make a difference. Gays were free and left alone to do what they wanted, openly and without hassle. To me, politics was boring anyhow whether the politician was gay or not.

We walked down Polk Street past a giant marquee sign that read "Mitchell Brothers O'Farrell Theatre Girls Live." Even in the so-called gay district, there was a huge straight porn place. Oh well, it was just San Francisco, I guess. We passed by a huge domed building that must have been some government thing and made it to Market Street. We turned the map around to get our directions.

"That way." I pointed and Chris frowned at me. He had a lousy sense of direction and didn't trust mine.

"See?" I put my finger on the map on Market Street and slid it up to Castro Street and then I pointed to the open area called Twin Peaks.

"It's right there," I said.

"Oh."

We found the subway stop, and in a short time we surfaced at the corner of Market and Castro Streets. I was beyond excited. We were in the Emerald City, just like Dorothy. We stood on the corner and looked down Castro Street. Then we hugged and Chris whispered, "We're here, at last." And as we stood there rubbernecking just like typical tourists, the sun came out and lit up our new city and made it glow.

CHAPTER TWO

Tell me again why we're doing this?" I asked Chris.

I was grouchy because we were climbing an enormous hill and jet lag was pummeling me along with what had started as a mild hangover but was morphing into something worse because of the time change. The breakfast that had been tasty hours before was now a heavy rock in my stomach.

"We're going up here to Noe Valley because Daniel told me about it and said we should see it."

"Why?" We could have taken a bus on Castro Street but there wasn't one coming and Chris could be impatient, hence we hiked up the mountain. I wondered if either of us had really understood just how hilly San Francisco was. Also, my smoky lungs were not used to this. That added to my misery along with my mild hangover and jet lag. Chris was unconcerned and unaffected, which galled me.

We made it to the summit at last, and Castro Street took a precipitous dip. All I could see were more hills. I hoped this was as far as we were going because I needed a nap before we went out that night.

The street signs advised us we were at Twenty-Fourth and Castro.

"So why did Daniel think we should come up here?" I hated it when Chris ignored me the first time and made me repeat myself.

"Max, my dear." He took my shoulders and turned me around to face him. "Have a little patience."

"Yeah," I said, grumpily. He should talk. I looked around and thought it was after all a pretty neighborhood, lots of nice little stores. Then I started looking at the passersby as we continued to walk.

There were couples: some men and some women. You'd never see this in Cleveland. You could just *tell* they were couples. They weren't making out, but they put their heads close together as they looked into store windows as they strolled down the street. We'd passed gay men holding hands on Castro Street, but this was different. I'd never seen anything like this. I had only experienced gay people being obvious in bars or discos or maybe some party. I was blown away. This was an entire city that homos felt at home in. I told Chris, and he laughed at my little quip.

"Yeah. That's one of the things Daniel told me last night. He said it wasn't just Castro or Polk Street. The way he put it was we're citizens like anyone else. Harvey Milk made that obvious. He wasn't just the gay supervisor, he supported unions, and his most famous law was the pooper scooper law. It's illegal for people to not pick up dog poop. Imagine that."

"I'm starting to understand better," I said. "Hey, can we go back to Castro Street?"

"Yep, I want a drink." *Me too.*

We walked back to Twenty-Fourth and Castro, and thank goodness we caught a bus over the hill. It was as though we were on a roller coaster. The bus crested the submit then plunged down abruptly. Since I was seated, I was in the proper frame of mind to appreciate the scene.

We arrived at the corner of Eighteenth Street in front of a bank called Hibernia. The bank was set back from the street and had a wall beside it along a concrete planter where a bunch of guys sat just hanging out. As we got off the bus, I noticed many of them gave Chris the once-over as we left the bus and walked past them. I started to laugh and tugged his arm to pull him across the street as he gazed over his shoulder at the boys cruising him.

"Come on, stud. Let's go get a drink." The place I wanted to go was right at the corner and had huge picture windows. It was called the Elephant Walk.

We sat at the bar and ordered drinks, a wine cooler for him and a beer for me.

The bartender brought our drinks over, and since it was not too crowded though busier than I thought it would be, he stopped to talk.

"So, where you from?"

"How do you know we're not from here?" Chris asked, archly. He just fell right into flirt mode, and if the last twelve hours was any indication, he might have to keep his switch permanently on. There were simply gay men everywhere, most of them young and good looking. I was happy for him, but I really needed to know where the girls were.

The bartender gave us a knowing look as he polished a glass.

"Your jeans," he said, causing us both to involuntarily look down, then at one another.

"What about our jeans?" Chris asked, his tone somewhere between plaintive and challenging.

"They look to me like Wranglers. No one here wears anything but Levi's. Local brand. Also you, just look like tourists—like a heterosexual couple, a mismatched one."

"We're not a couple." This time, I wasn't amused. We couldn't be mistaken for a couple in a gay area.

"No, I just said you *looked* like one. I know you're not."

"He's gay and so am I."

"Righto. I'm hip."

"So, our jeans aren't right. What else do we need to know?"

"The list is far too long. What kind of bars do you like?" He addressed this question to Chris. "Twinks? Clones? Drag? Leather? Latin? Hustlers? Black dudes? Country western?"

"Um, just good-looking guys."

I asked, "What are clones?"

The bartender snorted and said, "They're everywhere, haven't you noticed? And clones are Castro clones. Clean cut, well built, neat hair, macho. No queens."

"Oh, I see," Chris said, and he sounded a bit intimidated. He was always self-confident when we were out in Cleveland, but Cleveland was clearly different from San Francisco. Which we knew already, but it seemed much more complicated.

"What about women?" I asked the bartender, and he actually smiled at me in a genuine fashion.

"Maud's, Peg's, Amelia's, Scott's."

That list left me a little breathless, but I recovered enough to ask, "Where?"

"Not sure. I think Amelia's is in the Mission, Maud's is in the Haight. I don't know the addresses, sorry. Check at the Women's Building if you want to know more."

"Where's that?" A whole building? Full of women? What?

"A few blocks away down Eighteenth Street."

I wanted to go there right away, but that clashed with my idea of taking a disco nap before we went out that night.

"I want a regular gay bar. Like this one," Chris said, turning the bartender's focus back to him.

"Well, you've come to the right place."

I wanted to say, "What about me?" but I kept silent. I'd go out with Chris first, then figure out the dyke bar scene.

"When's the best time to come?"

"On a weeknight—in about three hours. We catch the commuter crowd on the way home. Happy hour."

Oh yeah, weekday. I patted Chris's arm and said, "Let's go."

"Hey, thanks for the info," Chris said to the bartender, leaving him a tip. The bartender raised his drink in a salute as we walked out the door.

"Can we head back to the room for a little bit?"

"You go ahead, I'll be back later."

I started to say something but thought better of it. We hugged by the stairs down to the subway, or Muni Metro, as it was apparently called, according to the sign.

I struggled not to feel abandoned and reminded myself that we weren't attached at the hip and Chris was just excited to be in San Francisco, as was I. I'd feel better when I had taken a nap.

I stopped in the hotel lobby at the pay phone and clumsily looked up addresses for the names of bars I could remember—Peg's and Maud's—and scribbled them down on scratch paper. I needed a little notebook or something so I wouldn't forget things. After looking up the streets on our map, I was reasonably certain I could find them. It helped that the map also showed bus lines.

I fell asleep and woke up to Chris shaking me and saying excitedly, "Get up, Max, we have to get ready to go out. I know where we're going."

I rubbed my eyes and asked, "Where?" Probably not to Maud's or Peg's.

He was pacing around the room smoking a cigarette, and he seemed oddly on edge.

"I-Beam. Andy told me it was the best dancing in the City every night of the week, the Stud was better on weekends. Oh, and it's mixed, so you won't be uncomfortable, *and* the dyke bar is just around the corner."

"Which one? And who's Andy?"

"I think he said Maud's, and Andy's just someone I met. He's much nicer than Daniel. We're going to meet at the I-Beam. He gave me some coke."

"Did you have sex with him?"

Chris stood in the bathroom fussing with his hair. "Yes, not that it's any of your business. Fabulous sex, to be precise. I need a haircut and I need to grow a mustache and we both need to go jeans shopping."

"Why do you need to grow a mustache?"

"All the hottest guys wear 'staches, and you remember what the bartender told us about our jeans. We need Levi's, Andy told me we can buy them anywhere. They're made here in San Francisco."

"Yeah, I was there when the bartender told us that, remember? Let me get ready."

"Right, sure." He lit another cigarette and paced some more while he waited for me.

We were back down on Market Street in short order, walking this time to the corner of Haight Street to catch a bus. It was around eight p.m. and Andy had helpfully told Chris that was a good time to show up at the I-Beam on weeknights. Work the next day and all. I wondered how in the hell people could work after drinking and dancing. I knew I couldn't. What was the secret?

We found a little sandwich shop on Cole Street so we could eat something and were soon in front of the black-fronted corner door of the I-Beam. A guy came strolling over to us, and he and Chris exchanged a hug and a kiss so long I thought they might run out of air, after which we made introductions. In San Francisco, it was apparently a piece of cake to meet people. Whenever and wherever, at least for Chris.

We went inside and were nearly knocked over by a wall of sound. A bouncer at the door collected a cover charge. I thought briefly of money but figured what the hell since this was part of touring SF.

Oddly, there were framed pictures of galaxies and planets right inside the entrance.

The main room had a stage at one end and the highest ceilings I'd ever seen in any disco, and it was as dark as a dungeon except for the disco balls. This place made the discos we used to frequent in Cleveland look a little like someone's overdecorated living room. It was also terrifically crowded for just a Monday night. I wandered if *anyone* in San Francisco worked or what the story was. It seemed like the party was permanently on. Like being able to buy booze at a corner store nearly any hour of the day or day of the week, you could go dancing on a Monday night. There were gay people everywhere in the City. I felt like I had come home.

Without a word, Chris and Andy hit the dance floor. Chris was a reasonably good dancer, but Andy was exceptional—fluid and inventive. No one could dance like gay men, I'd learned that a long time ago. It was something that went right along with their gayness, I suppose. The place was an oven, and I took off my sweatshirt and tied it around my waist and looked around. The dancers were mixed, and there were even heteros—I hadn't expected that—but there was only a scattering of female couples. I positioned myself where I could be seen and waited. I mostly liked to be asked even though I was butch. I'd gotten teased a lot about that in Cleveland, but I didn't care. I just hated rejection.

A couple of tunes later, Andy and Chris found me and said, "You wanna drink?" Boy, did I ever. I was hoping Chris would buy one for me.

"You get one free drink with your cover," Andy yelled into my ear.

"Oh boy." Well, that was good news anyhow.

I took the opportunity to go back to my wall-propping as I sipped my drink. Then, what do you know, a girl in leather pants walked over to me, slowly, smiling.

I'm not conceited about my looks but at the same time I didn't think I was a dog or anything. My best feature was my hair, thick and dark brown and wavy. I wore it just over my ears in kind of free-waving cloud, not long but not short. Also, I thought I had good legs even if they were currently encased in the incorrect and probably ill-fitting jeans.

"Hey," she said, "you like to dance?" Interesting way of putting it. I supposed the right answer was yes. I nodded and followed her out to the dance floor. She was taller than me by at least five inches, which I liked, and slender, which was fine, but at this point I was merely pleased have a woman spot me and ask me to dance. The current tune was Blondie's "Rapture."

She was good, loose and relaxed but not overtly sexual. I had to have a few more drinks in me to want to go forward with seduction.

"I've never seen you here before." She leaned close to my ear.

"I just got here. To San Francisco, I mean. I'm Max."

"Hi, Max, I'm Lily."

"Hi, Lily." That was a nice name. I'd gladly spend some time with Lily.

"So, you're new?" I'd just said that, but it was hard to make conversation amidst all the noise, so I didn't mind.

"Yep." The song flowed into a new tune, but I wanted to talk to Lily rather than dance. I motioned with my head and walked off the dance floor toward the room in front where the pool tables and pinball machines were. To my pleasure, she followed me.

"Sorry," I said, "I was hoping to have a little conversation, and it was impossible."

Lily leaned against a wall languidly and tilted her head. "Talking's fine. So where you from, Max?"

"Cleveland. Ohio."

"Oh, the Midwest." She made it sound like Siberia.

"Uh-huh. We just got here yesterday."

"We?"

"Me and my friend Chris. He's dancing."

She had a puzzled expression.

"He's gay. We're not together." It seemed like I was going to have to have this talk over and over. And over, with everyone we met.

Lily looked at me for a moment. "Sounds good. Say, you wanna get out of here?" What? Was she coming on to me already? San Francisco might be even better than I thought, but most of me went into a nervous frenzy. I wasn't ready. I'd only really been *out* out for about a year and a half. I'd had my flings in Cleveland, but honestly, as much as I wanted to be here, San Francisco and what I assumed were its ultrasophisticated lesbians intimidated me. I wanted to meet people, but I also wanted to control the speed and direction of every encounter.

I wanted to get laid, but I also wanted it to happen on my terms. Lily seemed nice, but who knew?

"And go where?" I asked in what I hoped was a blasé tone.

"Over to Maud's. It's just a few blocks away."

Aha, now we were talking.

"Sure. Let me just tell my friend."

I found Chris and told him what I was doing.

"See you later," he said to me, his eyes focused on Andy, who watched us talk with disinterest.

It was nice to get out of the nearly pitch-black, noisy, overheated I-Beam and into the windswept street. Lily had retrieved a nylon jacket from somewhere and we set off up Cole Street. I matched my stride to hers and she half turned and grinned at me.

"I'm sure glad I ran into you, Max from Cleveland. Not that many gals on Monday nights."

"I noticed. I went to the I-Beam because Chris wanted to go."

"He's your friend?"

"Yup, he's my best friend."

"I see. Well, that's nice." Her tone was neutral, but I got the sense she thought it was odd that my best friend was a guy.

"Are the bars in this town always open?" I asked to change the subject.

"Almost always. They have to close between two and six—city law, they can't sell liquor."

"But other than that?"

"Open." This was another bit of fascinating news. Bars were open nearly twenty-four hours a day. That was really something, although I didn't see myself needing an open bar at six in the morning.

In a few minutes, we arrived at a windowless wooden-fronted business. The sign was a sixties-esque graphic reading "Maud's" in red so it stood out. In front, there were a couple of motorcycles parked.

"Good thing, no cover on Monday night," Lily said cheerfully. I tingled all over and my mouth went dry. I was about to visit my first San Francisco lesbian bar.

Inside, there was a lovely old-fashioned Formica-topped mahogany bar. Neon beer signs ringed the wall—nothing too different from most bars. There was a jukebox and a pool table. I'm not sure what

I expected, but this was a pleasant, standard-issue sort of place. There was a lot of wood paneling, which made it a tad more aesthetically attractive to my eye. But I wasn't here to ogle oak paneling, I wanted to meet women. Lily sat down at the bar and I followed suit. The bartender was a tall, nice-looking brunette.

"Hey, Susan. This is Max, she's new in town. Can we have a couple of Michs?"

"Hi, Lil, hi, Max, nice to meet you." Susan served up the beers quickly and efficiently. The cold, crisp taste of beer was actually good after the cloying mixed drink I'd had at the I-Beam. I was never a big fan of cocktails anyhow, and if Lily was buying, beer was just fine.

"Tell us about yourself, Max. Are you visiting? Where you from?"

"I'm moving here, from Cleveland." On a slow night, you got more attention from the bartender, which in this case, I didn't mind at all. I was grateful for Lily's friendliness, but I didn't get any kind of sex hit from her. Susan the bartender, on the other hand, grinned at me knowingly. Of course, it could just be professional. Bartenders are huge flirts, they have to be, the better to sell drinks and get tips.

The jukebox was thankfully turned down enough so we could easily talk without having to yell. I told Lily and Susan about grad school and Cleveland's dyke community.

"We've got cliques here too," Lily said. "I guess that always happens. You'll find your group. That is, if you stick around. This isn't the only bar in town."

"Oh, yeah. I heard there were a couple more. Peg's?"

"Them." Lily tossed her head and rolled her eyes. "They're annoying. Tight asses. Now for dancing, we go to Amelia's down on Valencia." She looked meaningfully at Susan, who grinned.

"Maud's and Amelia's are both owned by the same woman. Rikki Streicher."

"Holy shit. A woman owns two bars." This was huge news to me. I'd never heard of that.

"Yeah," Susan said. "They're the two best dyke bars in SF."

"Right on," Lily said, and they high-fived across the bar as I looked on laughing.

Over to my right came the sound of a gravelly voice.

"Yeah, they're okay if you like pretty girls sipping on umbrella drinks. If you want to really drink with some real dykes, you gotta go to Scott's."

"Okay, Spike, that's your opinion," Susan said with an undercurrent of amusement in her voice like she'd heard this before, probably many times.

"Hi, my name is Max." I stuck out my hand. The Monday night lights in Maud's weren't turned way down, so I could get a good look at Spike. She was the shape of a fireplug—it went with her hoarse voice. I'd guess she was in her forties. She was a classic bar dyke, probably an alcoholic.

"Yeah, I heard." She sounded like she was from the Bronx and not the West Coast. "So you need somebody to show you around? Someone who knows her what she's doing?"

"Um, no, I don't think so."

Spike had delivered this offer with a salacious wink. It was all I could do not to visibly shudder. She wasn't my type. I'm a sort of soft butch, boyish and clean cut, clearly not her type but what did I know? Maybe she didn't have a type beyond whoever was willing to go with her.

I turned back to Susan and Lily, who were animatedly discussing softball. Well, that was a relief. I guess dykes everywhere were the same—softball players. I'd go to see games but I wouldn't play. I didn't like to do anything I wasn't good at, and I was lousy at softball.

I passed a pleasant hour with the two along with scattershot interruptions from Spike, then said goodbye after asking for directions back downtown. The jet lag was dragging on me again. I thought about going back to the I-Beam to find Chris, but I had a feeling he had other plans for the night. I would have hung around Maud's to see if I could scare up a little action for the night, but I was too tired.

I shivered on a street corner for a while before finally getting a Haight Street bus down to Market Street, then I walked the rest of the way up Polk Street. My God, summer in San Francisco was fucking cold. The wind blowing down Market practically knocked me over. At least it sobered me up and made me keep moving.

❖

The bed next to mine was empty the next morning. I asked at the desk and found I had a message. Chris had called, at least, and told me to meet him at Castro and Market at elevenish.

When I found him, we took ourselves to brunch at the Norse Cove and got caught up on our adventures.

Chris looked remarkably well for likely having been up most of the night screwing or whatever he did with Andy. Chris and I were up front with each other about everything, including sex, and I knew he was a top and he wouldn't bottom. So it was real surprise once we'd been served coffee and put our orders in that he emitted a big satisfied sigh and showed me a loopy grin and said, "Well, Maxy, I did it, and it was divine."

"You did? Why all of a sudden?" I knew he meant anal because we'd talked about it. It sounded painful to me.

He sighed and looked at the ceiling. "I don't know, being in San Fran, I thought maybe they know what they're doing. I've been thinking about it and I really liked Andy, so I thought what the hell." It blew me away that Chris had turned into a totally different person in San Francisco.

"And?"

"Oh my God, he was fantastic, he had some kind of super lube and he was very gentle and tender with me. I loved it, loved, loved, loved it."

"Nice." I drank my coffee and again was envious of how easy it was for Chris to have sex with somebody. I needed to find the female version of Andy. Someone friendly and cute and willing.

"Are you seeing him again?" I asked, mostly to be polite.

"Yeah, probably. He has to work today. He's a waiter."

I took out our map and we planned our tourist stops.

"But first," Chris said, "we have to go shopping."

We went to All American Boy, an extremely gay clothing store down the block, and bought new blue jeans. They were 501s with buttons instead of zippers.

I said to Chris, "Must take a little manual dexterity to get these off your trick."

He was admiring himself in the mirror and without looking at me said, "Just need to get most of the buttons undone."

"What about your underwear?"

"Oh, I won't wear any. Andy didn't have any briefs on. He asked me why I thought they were necessary."

"Hmm." I didn't care for the idea of no underwear, but I wasn't a guy.

"You look great," I told him. It was true, he wasn't overly muscled but he was well built and trim, and he put on a tank top with his new jeans and the All American Boy clerk whistled at him. Chris flicked his eyelashes.

"Let's go to the Laundromat and wash these so they don't look so new," Chris said.

"You'll want to put them in a dryer on high so they shrink to the right fit," the clerk added helpfully. I went along, but I sighed because laundry wasn't what I'd had in mind for my afternoon.

While we waited, we sat in the hard plastic chairs. Even as we talked, I was slightly irked that Chris's eyes kept darting all over the place. There was apparently no place on Castro Street where men didn't cruise each other. He would focus on me intermittently when I asked him questions, such as when he was going to apply for a job at California Genetics. I planned to get some shit job temporarily and then hoped he could get me an interview there, at least.

Chris leaned back and drank his soda, his eyes closed.

"I have to get a haircut and I have to grow a mustache. Andy said I ought to go to the gym too. It's the thing to do."

"What for?" I had never heard of that. I vaguely knew about Nautilus machines. There were some in the gym at our university. I had heard of bodybuilding because of Arnold Schwarzenegger.

"You're more attractive," he said, as though that was too obvious to have to be stated.

"Muscles and mustaches. Got it."

"Don't forget tight Levi's." Chris grinned. "Which we will have soon. What time are these done?" He craned his head around to look at the dryer we were using.

"Soon. Do you think someone might be interested in your personality or your brains?" I asked.

Chris laughed. "Maybe. But first things first. Does he have a big dick? Does he think mine's good enough?"

Back in Cleveland, Chris's boyfriends were a lot like him—

pleasant and at least had jobs or went to school. They might not have lasted a long time, but they were relationships. Here, the idea of a relationship seemed like a complete afterthought, coming far behind the possibility of sex, whenever or wherever or whoever. I didn't care that much, I just wanted him to have fun and be happy. That's all I wanted too. It looked like it might take a little longer for me.

The dryer buzzed at last and we were able to be on our way.

The rest of the week we wore our new jeans everywhere and did our sightseeing. Our newly washed Levi's were so tight, we struggled to put them on at first, but as the store clerk predicted, they stretched. By the end of the week, I felt like my jeans and me were one. I bought myself a new T-shirt from another Castro store called the Gilded Age. It read, "San Francisco, my favorite city, where the women are strong and the men are pretty."

The City *was* magical. Everywhere was another hill, another view of the ocean, always something we'd never seen before. I especially loved the Musée Mécanique underneath the Cliff House. It was like a Victorian funhouse. I couldn't decide if the central occupant, Laffing Sal, scared me or thrilled me. We rode the cable cars up and down the hill to Chinatown and North Beach. I vastly preferred that to walking.

Finally, it was Friday night and time to go out. This time, on Lily's invitation, I would meet her at Amelia's.

CHAPTER THREE

"Time to go out!" Chris said.

"Time to go out!" I replied.

When it's Friday or Saturday night, we have a ritual we follow to prepare. We agreed Monday's visit to the I-Beam and Maud's was just a rehearsal. It was Friday and time for the big show.

I took a swig out of my bottle of Christian Brothers and handed it to him. He only took a small sip.

"Echh. How can you drink this?" He made a face.

"I like it. That's how." It was more fun to drink from a nice brandy snifter, but I didn't have one handy.

Chris stood in front of the mirror and played with his hair. He'd gotten it cut two days before. Our hotel room had thoughtfully placed the sink and the mirror outside the bathroom so our preparations were more efficient. "Does this look okay or does it look like I just got my ears lowered?"

"It looks fine." It did, actually. Having the shagginess and the split ends chopped off was a good idea and it also made him look more clean cut, like a college student. The mustache would take some work.

Chris examined his face minutely. He smoothed his nascent mustache. "Uh-oh." He leaned toward the mirror, pulling his skin tight. "Shit. Fuck. I'm getting a pimple."

I stood beside him. "Where?"

"Here."

I could only see a little redness. "You can't see it. In the darkness, no one will ever know."

"Yeah, but what about the next day? In the morning?" Chris was paranoid about zits. He wasn't generally concerned about his looks—at least he hadn't been until we got to San Francisco. The Elephant Walk bartender's crack about our jeans really set him off. He'd also gone back the day before to get some different underwear. Something other than generic white briefs. Then the haircut.

I tried to tease him out of this onslaught of worry about his appearance.

"You know you're handsome. Don't worry. All the boys will love you." That was true in Cleveland. Here in SF, though, Chris clearly thought he had to compete at a higher level.

He put on his new jeans and laboriously buttoned them. They were so tight I worried about his circulation. Thanks to his new underwear, his penis was prominently displayed, as was his butt.

"You've got the goods," I told him.

"I do?" Chris turned around to look at his butt in the mirror. "I'm not that well built."

"Will you stop worrying? Did Andy or Daniel complain?"

"Nope. They didn't. I wonder how long it will take for my mustache to grow in?"

"Hey, man, what about me?" I wasn't as worried as Chris, but I was still concerned. After all, this was San Francisco. I was worried about competing too. Maud's crowd wasn't too scary or unlike the dykes I hung out with in Cleveland. I didn't know what to expect at Amelia's.

"Stand up," he told me. "Turn around." I complied. "You have a good ass too."

My jeans were snug but not skintight. I wouldn't be able to stand that. I'd elected to wear my new T-shirt since I didn't like any of the other shirts I'd brought with me. I thought they weren't fashionable enough, though I had no idea what would count as fashionable for SF lesbians.

Chris added, "I'm not a dyke, but I think we can say you have good breasts." That I agreed with. I'd gotten compliments. I was happy with them. They were just a tad too big to go braless, but they were nicely shaped. My breasts and my hair were my two best features, I figured.

"Lesbians aren't as shallow as gay guys," I said to Chris. "We do want to know someone's personality."

"Oh right, like that counts when you've picked someone up at the dance club and you're both a little drunk. Or a lot drunk." His tone was scornful.

"No, but later on when you get to know someone."

"Ha, I know you, Max, you don't stick around long enough to find out if you like someone's personality. You're always coming up with a reason why you're not going to see some girl again."

"Not always."

"Yes, always. Every time."

I was unwilling to concede he was right. Chris knew the customs of lesbian relationships well enough and he surely knew me. I'd complained to him about various women who, when I tried to get rid of them diplomatically, became whiny and bitchy. At least I didn't do that instant U-Haul thing we all joked about. I didn't date because it seemed like a waste of time. I don't know why, but women I found irresistible and exciting when I took them home invariably were much less so in daylight. That was the reason why I needed a new pool of talent. I was done with Cleveland lesbians. They were done with me too. Burned bridges and all.

"I just know it will be different here," I said.

Chris was back to fussing with his hair and answered me while looking in the mirror. "Yeah, I think we already know it's different."

"I'm ready to go. Are you done primping yet?"

He took one last look and said, "Don't be such a nag. Yeah, I'm ready." We were meeting Andy on Castro Street or, as he told Chris, "in the Castro" for a drink, and they would go to the Stud and Andy would tell me how to get to Amelia's. All I knew was it was on Valencia Street and I was meeting Lily there.

This time we went to the Midnight Sun. This was as dark as the I-Beam, but at least they had films projected on the wall.

Andy said, "I call this place the Midnight Scum because of, you know, the clientele." He smirked. I looked around but they seemed fine to me. In fact, everyone looked alike except for natural variation in body types and hair color. Tall or short, thin or chunky but not too many of the latter. Blond, brunette, redhead. Tank tops, tight Levi's, and facial hair.

I told Andy my observation.

"Oh, you are talking about the Castro clone." He said it

dismissively, yet that was how he looked too. He had medium brown hair, brown eyes, and a well-trimmed mustache.

"That's what I want," Chris said, "I want to be a Castro clone."

"You're well on your way, handsome." Andy kissed him again. I was aware that Chris wasn't expecting he would go home with Andy necessarily that night.

"Why should I?" he'd asked me rhetorically, "When the possibilities are virtually endless." I couldn't argue with that.

Andy gave me directions to Amelia's, and I went to the bus stop at the corner to wait for the 33 Stanyan bus to take me down Eighteenth Street from the Castro to the Mission. The bar, Andy said, was between Nineteenth and Twentieth Streets. It seemed simple. I looked at my watch. It was about nine thirty, just the right time to go to Amelia's. I didn't mind being a little early when I went out. It gave me time to have a couple of drinks and loosen up and sort of just check out the scene and watch everyone arrive.

Ah, the possibilities that came with every time I went out to a disco. It was the delicious unknown. The prospect of love—at least of the temporary variety. The tantalizing question of who it would be. The darkness punctuated by the colored lights, the heartbeat of disco music. What would the night bring? Who would materialize out of the darkness as though she was created by it? I wanted to find out.

I saw the place from the intersection where the bus let me off. This, I had also found, was the same intersection as the Women's Building. I had visited once. There were a plethora of offerings via posters and notes for groups, for events, for classes. What struck me was the bulletin board where I could look for housing. We were going to have to get going with that search soon. We couldn't stay at the Bedford Arms forever. It was by the week and was fairly cheap, but still…

But I wasn't thinking of an apartment at that moment. It was Friday night and I was going out dancing.

There was the usual row of motorcycles parked out front, and in the lights over the door, I could see the women standing around. My heart started to pound and my pulse throbbed. Finally, I arrived. And the women by the door slid discreet looks at me as I went through.

Inside was smaller than I expected and already crowded. The bar was on the right side of the room, the dance floor on the left.

I was waiting for a bartender when I felt a tap on my shoulder. I knew without looking it was Lily.

"Hey, you found it." She hugged me.

"Oh yeah, Andy, Chris's friend told me about the bus and all."

"Well, are you ready to party?" Her grin was lascivious.

"Way past ready. Should we get a drink?"

"Absolutely." Lily leaned over the bar and yelled, "Margie, over here." She looked cute with her butt stuck out, but not sleeping-with-cute.

"What do you want?" she asked me.

"Shot of brandy," I said automatically. "Christian Brothers with water back."

"Ooh," Lily murmured. "The girl's serious."

We leaned back against the bar with our drinks. I sternly counseled myself to sip slowly. I didn't want to get too drunk too quickly, and money was never far from my mind. The sweet burn in my throat and the quick rush to my head calmed my nerves. I had to get in the proper frame of mind to be sociable. One more gulp and I was there. Lily looked around the bar, presumably for women she knew. I just looked. The San Francisco lesbians seemed similar to Cleveland dykes, maybe just a bit better looking, or maybe I imagined that. They all had an air of self-confidence, or so it seemed.

I was startled by Lily hugging someone right next to me.

"Annie, this is Max. She just moved here from Cleveland."

I stuck my hand out and Annie shook it firmly.

"Hiya."

"What's going on?" Lily asked Annie.

"Oh, not much. I had a shitty week and I need some amusement."

"Female variety?"

"What do you think?" Annie was blond and well built. A California girl, I concluded. Hmm. I told myself to be patient. She wasn't in any case paying any attention to me, which irked me.

"Hey, who are those pictures?" I asked. I was curious but I mostly wanted to make conversation, try to connect.

They both looked around to where I pointed. On the dance floor were giant blown-up black-and-white photos of women I didn't recognize.

"That one's Marlene Dietrich, I'm pretty sure," Annie said.

"Isn't that one Amelia Earhart?" Lily pointed at the picture of a cute short-haired woman in flying gear standing by an airplane.

"Oh yeah. Right." Annie laughed as though that was obvious.

Lily said, "I don't know about the other two."

I barely even knew about Amelia Earhart and I guessed the other one was probably a movie star, but I didn't know.

We all fell silent. The music was turned up past where you could talk anyhow. The song playing, Donna Summer's "Hot Stuff," reminded me of last summer and Trina. I think it was playing when we started to dance, and she went home with me that night.

Lily said in my ear, "You want to get high?"

"Yep." I followed them out to the alley next to the front door. We passed around a joint and finally, Annie turned her attention to me.

"So how do you like San Fran so far?"

"Okay. It's fucking cold, though."

They laughed. "Everyone says that. It's foggy in the summer."

"No shit. But I have to say it's okay that it's not hot. It's about ninety degrees in Cleveland right now." I shivered in my T-shirt and wished I'd remembered to bring my sweatshirt out instead of checking it.

"Just drink more," Lily said, taking a big toke and talking as she tried to exhale slowly.

"Or find a nice warm woman," Annie said.

"That sounds like a great idea," I said, grinning, and then gazed around at the other denizens in the alley mainly doing the same thing we were. Some things don't change no matter what city you're in.

I went in and got another brandy and lit a cigarette as I continued to watch the dancers. Lily and Annie went off to dance, so I was on my own. I didn't mind—less chance of anyone thinking I was with either of them. I wanted to appear maximally available.

"Do you want to dance?" a homely short dyke asked me.

What the hell, why not? It's better to be doing something than just standing there. I remembered that Chris had passed on another piece of advice from Andy. This one concerned cruising. Never say yes to the first guy who comes up to talk to you, only the second or the third.

"Sure." I swallowed the rest of my drink, stubbed out my cigarette in the ashtray on the shelf that ran the length of the wall, and followed her to the floor. What the hell. She wasn't one of the chicks I'd been eying, but she'd do for the moment. It was just a dance.

I ditched her with a regretful smile the moment the song ended. I walked over to Lily and Annie, who had been joined by a leather-jacketed, tough-looking dyke. Probably never took that jacket off. Leather wasn't a big thing in Cleveland. They introduced me to her. Sheila was her name.

My quick size-up said she was okay looking. So far, Annie was the one who struck me. Something about blondes…but it was early yet.

Amelia's was getting rowdy. I was actually impressed at how crowded it was. Short, ugly girl asked me to dance again but I said no. It was tough when the wrong people asked me. I tried to talk to Sheila but she basically ignored me. Fuck her then. I spotted a couple of other likely prospects. Once I got someone to ask me to dance, I could often take it to the next level. I might not have been the best-looking girl in the club, but I did okay.

I got another drink. I had no idea where Annie and Lily had disappeared to, but I didn't care. It was nice to make acquaintances, but this was about getting laid. There was someone there and I just had to be patient. I could sense the short girl still looking at me. No way. I should have never danced with her. I had an accommodating side that surfaced at inopportune times, but I still had my standards.

I spotted a handsome semi-butch type in a tank top across the dance floor. She was alone and smoking. Just my type, I thought sardonically. She was actually well put together; I could see muscles. I liked that, though I had none myself. I went over and stood next to her and pretended to watch the dance floor. I caught her eye and said, "Hi." She looked at me for a couple of seconds too long, then said, "Hey."

Not very friendly, but I wasn't deterred.

"This is my first time here. I just moved from Cleveland." *There, I gave you a big opening, what are you going to do with it?*

"Oh yeah?" A little bit of interest. I could use this new-girl-in-town thing to my advantage, I hoped.

"Yep." And I flashed my best "I'm harmless" grin and took a drag from my smoke.

She pulled out a cigarette herself and I lit it for her.

She leaned in and spoke into my ear. "You want to go outside for a few?" I nodded and we threaded our way out the door.

In the lights of the alley, I was able to get a better look at her. She was on the heavier side but not overly so. I liked her features, like I thought, surfer girl—maybe dissipated surfer girl.

"How do you like the City so far?"

"Oh, it's great. Pretty and all." Pretty if you didn't look too close. It was also filthy. When I thought it was going to rain, it was only clouds in the morning. Outside our hotel, the street was covered in greasy drippings, litter and things I couldn't identify and would rather not know. Then there was the Golden Gate Bridge. The City was a study in contrasts.

"Yeah, it's a terrific place." She was as tongue tied as I was, sheesh.

"So where do you live and what do you do?" I asked and added, "Not that I really know the city yet."

"Oh, I'm an auto parts store manager and I live not far from here."

My ears pricked up at that. Good, if we were going home, it wouldn't be a hassle.

"I'm downtown off Polk Street in a residence hotel."

She blew out a cloud of smoke and looked at me speculatively. "Huh. How's that?"

"Oh, it's fine. I'll look for a place to live soon." I didn't want to get into the whole Chris thing while I was trying to get laid.

I took a chance. "You want to dance?"

She grinned then, and it changed her whole face. I liked her more and more.

We threw out our butts and went to find a spot on the packed dance floor. She put her hands on my hips to keep us in time. *Here we go.*

She actually twirled me and pulled me into her. The touch of her warm, well-padded body jolted me. I began to tingle all over. I liked that she was assertive, even a little rough. All good signs. We went and got more drinks and went back to dancing.

We were glued together, gyrating, and I whispered in her ear, "Want to get out of here?"

"Sure, where to?" she asked and nuzzled my ear a little. I brushed my lips over her jaw.

"How about your place?"

"Eh. Can't. I've got a roommate."

I was momentarily flummoxed. How we were going to consummate this little flirtation? I liked going to my pickup's place so I could make a quick getaway in the morning, Avoid too much conversation. I thought fast. Chris would likely be gone all night, so it was probably okay.

"We can go over to my place."

"Terrific. Let's go."

"How about one more drink?" I asked. I was fairly buzzed but I needed just a bit more to be ready for this.

"Okay." We sipped our drinks and made eyes at one another without trying to talk over the noise of the bar.

The night air was certainly sobering as we navigated the bus, then the Muni Metro and the walk up Polk Street from Market. I guessed it was after twelve, and there were vaguely menacing figures around but my new friend projected a suitably tough air, and I imitated her. We heard one shouted "Hey, dyke" from somewhere and we just walked faster.

Once in the room, I was barely even drunk anymore and nervous plus excited. It was getting to the point of no return, and I was psyched and scared in that gratifying way that anticipation of sex called up in me.

I invited her to sit on the bed.

She looked around suspiciously. "Who else is here?"

"My friend Chris, but he's not coming back tonight. He's gay." As if that explained everything. Maybe it did. I hoped it would soothe whatever doubts she was feeling.

"Have a drink." I had broken out my brandy bottle and took a good healthy swig.

"No thanks." She sat next to me playing with my hair and stroking my shoulders as I drank. It felt good. I shivered from arousal and nerves.

I set the pint back on the end table and turned toward her. Her mouth crashed into mine. My lips were already wet from the brandy and hers were just damp. We grappled and slid on the bed. She was a greedy kisser but I didn't mind, it made me think she'd be equally voracious in other ways. I could only hope she'd let me dominate. Sometimes the greedy types wouldn't.

We lost our clothes and I was virtually smothered in hot willing female flesh. She suddenly seemed a lot bigger than me. We groped and stroked and grabbed and panted. I finally got her on her back and her legs spread and I dove in. That's my thing—oral, the fastest way to nirvana. In the dark, submerged in a pussy, that's where I want to be. I reveled in her scent, pungent and strong. Her strong thighs squeezed my ears but I didn't care, I was in control and I was going to give this chick the orgasm of her life. She was easy, it turned out, and they weren't always. It didn't take hours of licking and sucking to make it happen. She came in a crash and I thought my head would implode.

"Christ," my partner in crime exclaimed. "Shit. That was something." She lay on her back panting, and in the light from the street, I saw the wetness on her thighs.

"Amen," I said, satisfied as I watched her recovery.

"You're next." She growled and pushed my shoulder to make me lie down. I giggled to cover up my nerves. This was always the moment of truth for me. My deep dark secret was I couldn't come with my lovers. I could only reach orgasm by my own hand. It could cause awkward moments, unless the girl of the evening was too drunk to notice. My new friend didn't seem to be more than pleasantly tipsy.

She was aggressive, though. Faster than I thought possible she was devouring me. I made the right moves and the right noises, but it was no good. I let her go on for a few minutes, then tapped her head.

She looked up. "Are you okay? I don't think it's happened yet."

"I'm good," I said gently, "Come up here." She crawled up to the pillow and settled heavily beside me. We fell asleep in a sweaty tangle.

❖

It was the door opening and a muttered curse that woke me up.

It was Chris. "Oops, crap."

He stumbled around the bed. I opened one eye. I was aware there was someone crammed into my single bed with me. Oh yeah, last night. I was also aware my head hurt and my mouth was dry.

"Sorry," Chris whispered.

"It's okay," I croaked, and my bed partner stirred.

I slid out from under the covers and looked at him in the gray light from the window. "Why are you here?"

"Because, I, um, live here?" His tone was unfriendly.

The body in my bed groaned. I spared her a glance. Oh boy. Time for sleeping beauty to wake up and split. In spite of my fogginess, I had an inspiration: Chris would be my excuse.

"I know that, I just didn't think you'd be back till later."

"Obviously."

"It's fine but what time is it?"

"It's six." What's-her-name turned over and the bed shook. What *was* her name? I'd forgotten, not the first time that had happened to me.

"Six? Why are you back so early?"

He sighed, kicked off his sneakers, and leaned back on his pillow.

"Andy's lover came home unexpectedly, and he was not pleased to see me." This was a sort of mini chain reaction. It was even sort of funny.

"His lover?" This was news.

"So, I got booted and here I am. Who's this? Are you going to introduce me?"

I mouthed, "I don't know." And Chris snickered.

I shook my head to shush him.

"Hey you." I shook the woman's shoulder. "Hey, sorry to wake you up, but my roommate's here. Sorry, you have to go."

"What?" She didn't sound too happy. I guess I could understand.

She opened her eyes looked at me and frowned. It didn't improve her looks.

Chris smoked and regarded the two of us nonchalantly, then he wrinkled his nose. The smell of pussy, I imagined. Not his favorite scent.

"I apologize for the early hour. But Chris came back early."

She hiked herself up on her elbows, carefully keeping the messed-up covers over her tits. She needn't have bothered.

"I need to find my clothes," she said. "And, you know, put them on."

Chris popped off the bed, slipped on his shoes, and said, "Hey, no rush. I'll go get us some coffees and I'll take my time."

As he closed the door gently, he winked at me.

"I'm sorry," I said again. "I wasn't expecting he'd come back so early and…"

"Right, right," she said. I was going to have to come up with something to make this seem less of a really abrupt kiss-off.

"I'm Max, by the way. We somehow forgot to introduce ourselves last night." I put on an apologetic winning smile. "What's your name?"

"Tammy," she said. "Nice to meet you." She yawned as she slowly put her clothes on.

"Yeah, nice to meet you. Hey, last night was great." I raised my eyebrows.

She didn't smile. "Really?"

"Really," I assured her, with all my teeth showing.

"Well. Good then." She didn't look convinced.

While she was in the bathroom, I put my own clothes on and Chris returned juggling three cups of the hotel's coffee, which was on twenty-four hours a day and tasted like it.

"You're staying up? Not going back to sleep?" I asked him.

"Yeah, may as well. What about your paramour?" That was Chris's term for my various sex partners.

"She's on her way home."

"What, no breakfast? You're such a bitch."

"No. I'm not."

Tammy emerged from the bathroom looking not too disheveled. I handed her a coffee. She took a sip and wrinkled her nose.

"Bad."

"Yeah. Sorry." There was a moment of silence. I introduced the two.

"So, I've sort of got to get ready to go out in bit."

She glanced at Chris, who had a Marlboro in one hand and coffee in the other and a blank expression.

"Yeah, I kind of guessed that. No problem." Her voice was resigned. "Here's my phone number. In case." She knew I wouldn't call.

She left without another word besides "Bye."

When the door shut, Chris waited for a moment, then said, "You dog."

I flopped on my bed and drank my awful coffee. "Guess so, but that one wasn't going to last."

"They never do, do they? Funny how good someone can look in a bar and somehow not so much the next day?" He grinned at me and I knew he was yanking my chain, but I didn't care.

"Yup. It's sure an odd thing."

CHAPTER FOUR

Two weeks later, Chris stood in front of the mirror in our room, this time dressed in a blue suit. His nascent mustache was coming along, and he carefully smoothed it with his finger. Then he put his nose right up to the mirror and glared at himself. He turned around and said, "Look at this spot—is this another zit?"

I dutifully pulled myself off my bed and went to peer where he pointed. "No, it's just a little red is all. You look fine. You'll do fine." I meant it. Chris, though he was acting like a beauty queen at that moment, was in fact a straight-A student when we were undergrads. He was going to an interview at California Genetics, and we were optimistic. My assignment for the day was to start looking for a place for us to live. The Bedford Arms was getting a bit old. Also expensive. I was going to the Women's Building, and I would go to Maud's in the afternoon and chat up the bartender.

Chris combed his hair again and then turned around to face me. I gave him the thumbs-up.

At the Women's Building, I pulled a couple of numbers of offers of rooms to rent. It occurred to me that having Chris in tow might make it more difficult to find a place to live. I went back to the Castro and put an application in the rental office, though I didn't know if we could afford a two-bedroom on our own.

Maud's was certainly not empty, but it was very quiet. I ordered a beer that I could sip slowly and make it last. We were going to the I-Beam later, where I would want to have a few drinks.

I was going to have to find some kind of a job soon as well, because I didn't know when or if I could apply to the same company as Chris. My little pile of money was being eaten up quickly. Chris would carry me for a short time, but I didn't want to ask him. We had started bringing food into our room that we bought at the grocery store so we didn't have to eat out all the time, but crackers, fruit, and baloney sandwiches were really getting old, and I found a cockroach snooping around the drawer where we stored our tiny food stash.

The Maud's day bartender was Shirley, and she was certainly friendly enough. When I made my request, she told me to write my number down and she'd ask around. We had to get our phone messages at the front desk of the Bedford, and I wasn't that confident we were receiving all of them. Some of the help seemed a little flaky. The guy on days was a skinny, sick-looking fellow with a cigarette dangling from his lip essentially all the time. He seemed to be gay but only because he didn't leer at me like the night clerk did. Fortunately, I was usually with Chris as we came and went, except the night I came in with Tammy, and we scuttled past him so fast I doubt if he even saw us.

I left Maud's and wandered down the street. I looked for a restaurant where I could pick up some shifts to keep me afloat. I put in an application at a couple places. It wasn't a cheery prospect, but I can do what I have to do. I just wouldn't tell my mom. She would flip and say something reproving about a National Merit Scholar waiting tables. You'd think someone who'd had to divorce an alcoholic husband and scrape a living in an insurance company would have an appreciation of necessity but she thought things ought to be better for me. It would be further proof that my so-called "lifestyle" was bad. I would call my mom when I had a "real" job.

I was uncertain what to do next, so I decided to go back to the Bedford and wait for Chris. I flopped on my bed and after a moment pulled my brandy bottle out, took a drink, and started reading my book.

Chris sailed through the door, his tie off and looking a little breathless. "Hello, Max," he yelled.

"Good news?"

"The best! I'm starting next Monday." This was a relief, but it didn't surprise me. Chris was able to put on whatever persona he needed to adopt, and he was a natural at the earnest diligent scientist. Our professors in grad school thought he was phenomenal and, I'm sure, had given him great recommendations. I hadn't asked them for any. Some difficulties made me think I ought not to put them on the spot.

"Where is this place?"

"It's in Pacific Heights."

"Where's that?"

"About a half-hour bus ride. I don't know, near a hospital. Let's go celebrate. Tell me what you've been up to."

I told him and he hugged me and said, "Max, honey, we are on our way."

We went to a diner for some actual food that was cooked and didn't have cockroach footprints all over it, then we went to the I-Beam. I stayed for a few minutes and then walked to Maud's. It was close to the end of the workday, and sure enough there were a few more people around.

I saw the short woman from Amelia's at the jukebox, but I studiously avoided her. I sat at the bar and talked to Shirley when she was available, but I was uncomfortable and at a loss. I wondered if I should go back to the I-Beam, where at least I knew Chris, though he'd probably already picked somebody up. I swiveled on my barstool and looked around the room. The space was nice, that was for sure, with its wood paneling and small, intimate size. I was contemplating another brandy, and then a whole bunch of women waltzed through the door, noisy and happy.

"N Judah just arrived," Shirley said, grinning. "Time for happy hour." I looked closer and saw that a lot of the newcomers were wearing skirts or pantsuits. They were professionals. I envied them, but that wasn't for me. In a lab, no one cares what you wear. I felt a hand on my shoulder and turned and it was Lily.

I was relieved to see her. She was in a dark skirt and light blouse and looked good.

"Hey, girl. What's happening? Shirley?" She waved at the bartender, who brought her a drink.

"Hi, there. You look good enough to eat." Lily smirked but all she said was, "You have fun with Tammy the other night?"

I blushed. "Yeah. I did." I decided brazening it out was the best approach.

"She wasn't too sure. You know, since you booted her out so quick. And she was weirded out by that guy who showed up."

Well, huh. I ought not to be surprised that there was as much gossip with the Amelia's/Maud's crowd as there was in Cleveland. Dykes are dykes.

"It was nothing personal. And you know Chris is my friend I came here with."

"Right. I know." She twirled her swizzle stick around and wrinkled her nose.

I asked, "You wanna go over to the I-Beam?"

"Maybe in a while. I have to get a buzz on to want to dance."

I was already there. I was on my third drink, and now that I knew someone in the bar, I didn't feel quite as lonely and conspicuous. I still needed to meet more women. Lily had leapt off her barstool and went off in the crowd.

The short dyke from Amelia's came over and stood awkwardly in front of me, a quizzical expression on her face.

"Hi. Didn't we meet at Amelia's the other day?" she asked tentatively.

I took drag on my cigarette before I answered, and I adopted as blasé a tone as I could manage. "Yeah. I think we did."

"I'm Mari."

"Max." We shook hands rather solemnly. The stool next to me was open. What the hell. "Have a seat," I told her.

"Thanks." She was still not my type, but I didn't have anything better to do. Lily either would or would not want to split for the I-Beam.

"So, you like to come here?" That was a not as lame a line as "Do you come here often?" but it was close.

"Sure. I'm new to San Francisco, so I'm just checking everything out."

"Oh? Where you from?"

I told her my little story. I was becoming very practiced at it. Meantime, I was considering what I wanted to do. She had that interested look, the innocent bright eyes and the way she leaned toward me. I could have her if I wanted to. The question was did I want her? Not especially, but what else did I have to do at the moment but essentially drink by myself?

Mari beamed at me. "Want another?" she asked, pointing at my empty glass.

Does a bear shit in the woods?

A couple hours later, it was dark outside as Mari and I staggered out the door together and she dragged me over to the N Judah Muni train.

"I like Maud's 'cause it's real convenient to come after work, and I live right on Duboce Street, so I can just go home."

She was becoming a little slurry, but so was I. Slurry and blurry. I gathered I was going to Mari's place and fuck her. At least this time we weren't going to be in my room at the Bedford. With whatever power of thought that remained in me, I realized that I could make my getaway in the morning easily. She would have to go to work. Super.

All was proceeding swimmingly but man, she was a screamer. I mean from the moment I had my hand on her, she gasped, she thrashed, she moaned, then she yelled. It was only because my fingers were up her that I actually knew when she came because I felt it.

For a small woman, she was strong. She flipped me over and began to finger me like her life depended on it.

"Are you okay, honey? Does this feel good? Should I do it harder? Do you want me to do something else? Are you close?" The screams had morphed into nonstop questions when she started doing me. I wanted to tell her to please shut the fuck up, but I didn't. I tried to concentrate on reaching orgasm. She went down on me, and even in my foggy state, I knew that wasn't going to make it happen. She had all the finesse of a teenage boy. I thought she might swallow me whole. I tapped on her head finally.

"What?" she asked. "Is it good? Can I do something else? Should I keep going?" Even though she was drunk, she was not so befuddled that she didn't know I hadn't come. I followed my usual MO. I pulled her into my arms and put her head on my shoulder and kissed her.

"It's not happening for me tonight. I must be too drunk. It's okay."

She raised her head. "I'm so sorry. Is it me? Am I bad?" Oh brother, she just couldn't leave well enough alone.

I stroked her hair and said, "No, no nothing like that. It's not you. You're fine. In fact..." I rolled over on top of her and bit her neck lightly. "I think you're ready for more." This stopped the conversation, anyhow, and the screeching started up again. I hoped her walls weren't too thin.

❖

When I wobbled into the lobby of the Bedford the next morning, I stopped at the desk and there was a message from one of the restaurants I had applied to—Bert's. It was on Haight Street and they were wondering if I could come interview that day. Holy crap. I called them back and the guy who came to the phone said, "Can you come in at ten thirty?" It was already nine. I said yes automatically, then raced upstairs. Thank goodness my hangover wasn't too bad. I was just a bit frayed around the edges, I could power through this.

Chris was in bed sound asleep, so I tried to tiptoe around, but he woke up anyway.

"Where'd you disappear to last night?"

"I'll chat later, I have to go to an interview."

"Oh, good. Later then." And with that he turned over and went back to sleep.

I made it on time and it turned out to be a breakfast and lunch place, so I would have my evenings off. Once the manager, Harry, had verified all my details, he wanted me to start the next day. Dynamite. I talked him into giving me a few days because I had to find a place to live. The breakfast part might be a little harsh, but I was used to getting up for my classes. I could cut back, and it was only for a little while anyhow. I met up with Chris later and we went out to celebrate. He was looking a little out of it, uncharacteristically.

"Andy gave me the kiss-off last night and I was pissed. But I met some dark-haired muscle type who took me South of Market."

"What's that mean?"

Chris grimaced. "There are a lot of leather bars. It's like being in a zoo. Those guys are really not into social niceties, but some of them are so hot. They called me a twink, though, which means I'm not masculine enough. They also called me a clone."

"Well, you kind of are a clone?"

"Yeah, but the way he said it pissed me off. Someone gave me a white pill, and whew, Max, I was super high and floaty. The guy called it a seven fourteen. When we had sex, it felt incredible. You'd like it, I think. I don't believe I want to get into leather, though. Those guys kind of scared me."

"Maybe I'd like it. Try and find some. Say, the bartender at Maud's told me to go look around the neighborhood where we want to live and see if there are For Rent signs in the windows. I haven't gotten a single call from the messages I left. Unless that nitwit at the front desk isn't giving me my messages."

"That's possible. Where do we want to live? Castro?"

"How about where we can find a place with two rooms. I'm not sharing a bedroom with you anymore."

"So you're no picnic either, man." We grinned at each other.

The next day we started our search in the Castro, but we tried two places and were turned down. Just one room available, the guys said. I strongly suspected once they saw me, it was a no go, but I couldn't prove it. We only needed a couple rooms for a while until we could afford our own apartment, or flat, as they seemed to be called. I didn't know what the difference was.

We widened our search to the other neighborhoods close by, which I didn't know the names of. It was discouraging, to say the least. Chris suggested we hang out at the Bedford for one night and start the next morning because he was going to work on Monday and I'd have to take care of it myself. I agreed, since he'd managed to score some weed and we could just hang out together. It had been a whirlwind of activity since we'd gotten to SF and it seemed like a better idea just to stay in.

I had told him about my encounter with Mari while we were cruising around looking for rooms to rent. Although we were depressed at the thought of staying in our room at the Bedford, it wasn't as though it was forever, and besides, anything can be endured when you have booze and weed.

"So, girlfriend, what the heck's the matter with you—going with girls you don't even really like? What's that about?"

"I don't know. Sometimes I just want to have sex. It gets me off when they get off. It's not like I hate them or anything. And you aren't all that picky yourself."

Chris ignored my dig and asked, "What about you? Getting off, I mean."

I was feeling loose, and besides, I almost always told him everything and I had not so far admitted to this, so I copped to the truth. Since he asked, I just blurted it out.

"I can't come with, you know, someone else."

"Jesus fucking Christ." He was appalled. "Never?"

"Not so far. Except if I do it myself. Which I can't exactly when you're here."

"Well, I'll leave for a while if that's what you want, but that doesn't exactly solve your problem."

"I think I'll find someone eventually. I know she's out there. In the meantime, I'm fine. I like sex, I mean it's not that I don't like it."

"Sure. I know some are better than others, but it's just great to do it. Like you're winning a prize or something."

"I know. If a girl looks at me in a certain way and I just know she's up for it, I'm like, okay. I'm ready. Then when she does have an orgasm or two or three, it's like wow, look at me."

Chris laughed and said, "Yeah, you stud you. Well, there's sure a lot of gay people in San Francisco. There must be someone here for you."

And we went on to other subjects and we got silly and giggly, trying to flip bottle caps. Chris could do imitations of TV actors and movie stars, and he would put me in hysterics.

Later after we went to bed, as I fell asleep I wondered if I would meet someone. I didn't want to settle down and I certainly didn't want to be monogamous. Honestly, if I could get someone to go home with, it made my night. The sex was almost beside the point. I sometimes couldn't remember much the next day. I figured if someone actually was able to make me come, I'd remember that.

❖

We slowly got moving the next day and kept up the ever-widening circles of our search. A couple places we wrote down the addresses for because no one was home. It was exhausting, and I was pretty much ready to hang it up for the day.

"Just one more," Chris said. We walked up a street that ran behind Market Street and past a gigantic gray building surrounded by a fence and barbed wire.

"What the hell is this?" I asked, mostly rhetorically.

"Let's ask someone," Chris said. He was way more gregarious than me. He had no problem walking up to a random man in the street and asking the question.

"That's the Mint. Where they make the money, man."

"Oh. Wow." Chris stared at it as though he wanted to see if we could get in and, if he was just charming enough, they would give us some money.

"Come on, let's just take one circuit of a couple blocks and see if there's anything."

We turned onto street called Webster, and in the middle of the block was a row of three identical maroon and white buildings, the middle of which had a For Rent sign in the front window. We looked at each other and silently climbed the front steps, and Chris knocked on the door.

Some minutes went by and we nearly left, but finally the door opened a crack. We could see only a shaggy head of hair and one eye. They seemed to belong to a woman.

"Yeah?"

"Hi there. Sorry to bother you, but we've come to see about the rental—how many rooms?" I said in my brightest most innocuous tone.

"Uh, two, but can ya give me a second?"

"Oh sure—" The door slammed before I even finished the word.

Chris and I just glanced at one another, said nothing and bounced on our heels. The "second" stretched into about ten minutes. Finally, the door opened a second time, all the way, to reveal a diminutive, sleepy-looking woman.

"Hey. Marilyn," she said by way of introduction, and I told her our names. She led us down a hallway past what seemed to be an occupied bedroom and a closed door. The hallway terminated in a sparsely furnished living room with a kitchen beyond and another room.

"You said two bedrooms?" Marilyn asked vaguely.

We nodded and I said, "Yep. One for me and one for him." I pointed to Chris, who grinned.

"Right. Yeah, okay. I live here with my girlfriend. Two people moved out at the same time. So..." She shrugged. I couldn't tell if Marilyn was stoned or just sleepy.

"Can we see the rest of the house?" I asked, growing impatient.

She didn't say anything but ambled toward the kitchen, and we followed.

"Bathroom." She pointed to a room off the kitchen where I could see a sink and a bathtub. No toilet.

"Come on back here." There was door in the back of the kitchen that Marilyn opened. It was a kind of closed-in porch. It was full of junk, and in the corner was another door and behind it was a toilet. The whole space had unfinished walls, the beams showing with drywall between. This was strange and I said so aloud.

Marilyn grimaced. "Oh yeah. It's the old California split. It comes in handy sometimes, though."

Then she said, "Let me show you the rooms," and we walked back to the living room. Marilyn stopped, picked up an album from the floor, put it on the turntable, and dropped the cover back on the floor. The cover was a garish yellow and read *B-52's*.

I was curious, so I examined it. Marilyn opened the door to the room off the living room. Inside, it looked like someone had thrown a monumental temper tantrum rather than moved out. There was junk everywhere, and it smelled musty.

"That's one." Marilyn had to raise her voice to be heard over the music.

"This is the other." She opened the door. It still looked like someone lived there.

"What's the rent?"

"Two hundred each, plus utilities." I caught Chris's eye and he nodded.

"Um, when will the other room be open?"

"Next week, I think. What do you say?" This was astonishingly fast and free of requirements.

"We need to talk about it. But we'll let you know soon. Are you okay with a little pot smoking and alcohol?"

Marilyn snorted as though that was a silly question. Maybe it was.

"If you can pay the rent and don't destroy the place, it's cool."

She wrote out her phone number on a scrap of paper. Chris and I thanked her and left.

Back out on the sidewalk, we chattered as we made our way down Church Street toward the Muni Metro station.

"She seems kind of out of it," Chris said.

"We woke her up."

"She got it that we were gay and she just came right out and said she was."

"I know. It seems too easy." Chris was sometimes a little too cautious when it came to new things other than picking up men.

"You want it to be hard?" My tone was a little demanding, but it seemed fine to me, and I wanted to be done with this apartment search.

When we caught our train, Chris pulled out our map.

"It's right next to the bus line I have to take to go up to Cal Genetics."

"Bert's is three blocks away," I said.

"Let's do it," Chris said. "Now, how about a drink?"

"Yes. The Special?"

"Why not. I'm not going to pick anyone up tonight. I have to go shopping tomorrow. The Special will just have a bunch of old drunk queens, so I won't even be tempted."

The Special was a couple blocks from the Bedford Arms and seemed to always be full of aging alcoholic gay dudes. That was how one of them described it himself when we first visited. He was oblivious to the fact that he was one as well.

CHAPTER FIVE

I was so tired after the first few days at Bert's, I almost quit. It wasn't mentally challenging work, and it was obvious to me after the first day that Bert's didn't care if you drank their booze—they served beer and wine—and whether or not they cared, the staff also indulged in quite a few other substances including weed and coke.

Chris came home from the biotech company with a mixture of stories. The research, which revolved around immunological-based therapies for cancer, interested him. Their aim was to create antibodies with a poison molecule, specifically ricin, attached that could latch onto and theoretically kill cancer cells.

On the other hand, the married couple who ran the antibody research lab, Sarah and Richard, were, in Chris's words, eccentric.

Chris said, "However, you can play them off each other, and I already told them about you. They are going to need more people. The head of the company wants FDA approval in five years. That's really fast, so they are throwing money at it. Just give me a little time."

I was anxious because, really, restaurant work drove me crazy. I knew I was overqualified for it. I had almost finished my master's degree in biology, for crap's sake. It didn't take that much brainpower to serve food, not at Bert's. It wasn't a thought process so much as an endurance challenge. The breakfast shift started at seven a.m. Three days a week, I worked through the lunch shift. I went home at four in the afternoon, which gave me a nice, long evening where I could head out to Maud's. I needed to save money, though, so that meant drinking at home with Chris when he came home from work or with Marilyn and Tory.

Chris and I had happily said goodbye to the Bedford Arms and splurged on a taxi to take us and our stuff over to the flat on Webster Street. Then we went down to the Salvation Army to buy furniture. Chris was going to buy most of it, including my bed, and I was going to pay him back in installments.

Marilyn's girlfriend, Tory, was a night manager at a downtown hotel, and it couldn't have been much fancier than the Bedford because Tory didn't bother to dress up in girl clothes. She was boyish and cute. If she wasn't taken, I might have tried her, though I knew that was likely not a good idea. I wasn't ready to start a relationship, but if I did, I wanted one like theirs. If we couldn't be like gay guys, we didn't have to be as prudish as those dykes I knew in Cleveland who were coupled. They tended to look down on those of us who weren't, or maybe they were worried about their girlfriends getting snapped up by someone else. That happened a lot too.

One day, a big box for Chris arrived in the mail and the three of us gathered around to watch him open it. I already knew what it was, but it was fun to see his excitement.

A lot of the boys loved Judy or Bette Davis or Midler or Cher or Barbra, but not Chris. In his choice of diva to worship, he was a maverick. He was besotted by Elizabeth Taylor and had been since he was a little boy. His love of Liz had been a major source of friction with his father, who rightly suspected it was a big flashing sign that Chis wasn't like the other boys. Chris and his mother went to every Liz Taylor movie reissue together, and his mom collected the many movie magazines that featured stories about her, which they read aloud to one another.

Chris opened his box, and out came all his VHS tapes of her movies, his copy of her biography, and his most treasured bit of memorabilia—a signed note from her thanking him for the elaborate birthday card he'd sent her when he was a teenager.

We three lesbians looked at all this with an air of bemusement. I was not that much of a movie fan in any case, and if I did go to a movie it was usually sci-fi, like *Star Wars*.

Tory was a few years younger than us, barely twenty, and said, "I think of Elizabeth Taylor as sort of my mom's generation."

Chris spread all his stuff out on the floor, the better to admire it, and said, "She started in the movies when she was twelve in 1944 in

National Velvet, so yeah, she's the older generation, but she's a movie star so she never ages, not really. She's always going to be the greatest movie star."

I'd heard this before, but it made me smile because it was like listening to one of your favorite records over again. It was Chris and I loved him, so I loved him talking about Liz Taylor.

Marilyn and Tory were quiet through the Liz rap. They were New Wavers, and that was what they were into to the exclusion of anything else.

"Who wants to get high?" Marilyn asked. That at least was something we all had in common. Tory had to go to work in two hours, but that never mattered to her. Marilyn oddly didn't seem to have any sort of job. The way she talked about her wealthy parents made me think that she was supported by them. That would make me resentful, if it was me.

Marilyn brought out the plastic baggie and dumped its contents on the cover of a Ramones album. She started rolling joints, and it was amazing how good she was at it. I could manage to roll a serviceable joint, but Marilyn turned them out with machinelike efficiency. She lit one and took a toke, then handed it me and went to start up the stereo with, inevitably, the Ramones. I like rock, but they were way too harsh for me. We passed the joint around and Chris started talking about Liz Taylor again as he got stoned.

After a while, Marilyn and Tory simply ignored him and talked to each other. I picked up the Ramones album cover and read it, though I wasn't especially interested.

"You want a drink?" I asked Chris. The girls didn't drink. They got stoned and dabbled in hallucinogens, but they didn't like booze.

"Why not? I'm thinking of going out."

"Don't you have to work tomorrow?"

"Oh, sure, but I won't stay out late." It annoyed me that he could party and not suffer the consequences I did if I went out on a weekday. Also, he didn't have to spend the night with someone to get laid. He told me they would just go to the guy's car and get a blow job.

I opened two beers. I had to work in the morning, but I figured I'd just take it easy.

"Where you going?" I asked Chris, though I knew the answer.

"Where else? I-Beam."

Tory broke off talking to Marilyn and said, "I hate that disco shit. It's not even music, it's a corporate noise to make money off gays."

Chris was usually not quick to anger at anything, but for some reason, this bothered him.

"Well, honey, disco doesn't like you either. Talk about noise, that would be the Ramones. That isn't real music. They can't even play their instruments."

"At least they're real, not fakes."

"Cool it, baby." Marilyn rubbed her back. Tory fell quiet. I just looked at Chris and shrugged and watched Marilyn and Tory touch each other. They were *both* kind of cute. Then I admonished myself to leave it alone.

Chris stood up and drained his beer.

"I'm going to change and then I'm out of here." He disappeared to put on his tight Levi's and wifebeater undershirt. He wore much more conservative clothes to work, though not suits and ties. It was a lab, after all.

I watched Tory and Marilyn for a while and concluded it was really Tory who was the cute one. Marilyn was okay, but Tory's hazel eyes and strong body gave me a little frisson.

"Hey, how's Bert's?" Marilyn asked, still rubbing Tory's back.

I yawned and said, "It's okay. It's only temporary."

"Can you bring home some food?"

"Maybe." I would have to befriend one or more of the cooks.

Chris reappeared. "I'm going for a new look," he said.

"You look just the same as always," I said, eying him.

"Ah, I'll show you." He unbuttoned his jeans and peeled them down to reveal he was wearing a jockstrap instead of underwear.

Marilyn and Tory gawked. I laughed.

"And what's different?" I asked.

"Oh, can't you see? The jock holds my dick nice and high and tight and brings everything forward so…" He pulled his pants up and rebuttoned them. He waved grandly as though he'd unveiled a work of art.

"I guess I can see the difference. I don't often stare at your crotch."

He grinned and then said, "One of my friends at the I-Beam told me about it. For cruising, you know."

"It seems everything you do is for that." I was impatient because it struck me that Chris really didn't say or do anything else lately that didn't somehow relate to going out and getting a guy. He was going to work during the day, but even then he would sometimes go right over to the Castro after work and not come back for hours. I missed him, so I was a bit testy. I didn't expect him to spend a lot of time with me, but he was completely unavailable and I was lonely. I needed more friends than just him or Marilyn and Tory. There wasn't anyone at Bert's. I guessed I could go to Maud's, but unless I drank I was too shy to talk to anyone. And if I drank, I couldn't predict how much I would drink, and I had to get up too early in the morning.

"All right, girls," Chris said. "See you later."

"Don't call us girls," Marilyn said. "Bye."

"Bye. Have fun," I said, dejected.

I went to my room and flopped down on the bed. It was just a mattress on the floor. I'd go buy a frame when I had more money. I had a little light to read by, so that's what I did. I thought maybe a TV would be nice. There wasn't one in the house. Marilyn and Tory didn't believe in TV.

I went and got another beer, and eventually I fell asleep.

❖

The first time one of the cooks, Troy, offered me a line I didn't take it, mostly because I wasn't sure how it would affect me and I was new and still trying to be a good girl, which I was mostly. But no one else there was "good," and I wanted to fit in.

I'm a rule follower, which for a gay person tends to bring on a lot of cognitive dissonance that never gets better—it just gets worse. It also made me not want to be so quick to conform in other ways, but I needed the job for some unspecified time interval.

I brought a couple joints into work with me, and Troy and I took a break out in the back to smoke them.

He said, "This is okay, but how about something with a little more zing?"

"Sure," I said impulsively. I didn't think it would hurt. I had grown used to my work.

He pulled a vial and a teeny spoon from his pocket. He scooped up the coke and sniffed—both nostrils. He then took a giant breath in and rubbed his nose. then handed the gear to me and I imitated his actions exactly.

Within a few seconds I felt a giant rush, like my brain was being washed by a big ocean wave and I was surfing it magnificently. Everything was suddenly sharper and brighter and I was absolutely ready for anything. It was a terrific feeling, like I was floating on a cloud of exhilaration.

"Wow, thanks, man."

"Yeah, you bet. Now go in there and wow those customers."

For the next half hour, I was a paragon of efficiency and cheeriness. I didn't mind the picky eaters, the substitution requestors, or the cranky kids. But slowly, the good feelings wore off, and I wanted to go lie down somewhere or I wanted another hit.

It was the middle of lunch, and Troy was jamming away in the kitchen and I knew he couldn't get away. When I got a break, I poured myself a cup of coffee. It helped. Somewhat.

At the end of the shift, I was dragging. I asked Troy, "Can we do that again?" He threw me a big smirk. This time we went into one of the bathrooms.

I asked, "Do you think I could take some leftover food home?"

"Yep. I'll show you what's available in the walk-in. Do you want to go get a drink?"

Alarm bells went off and I said, "Maybe some other time."

It occurred to me the free hits of coke and maybe the food might not be so free. For the next couple of days, Troy's beady black eyes started lighting up every time he saw me. I didn't ask him for anything else again, not food and not coke.

❖

It was the softball playoffs and we all went to the Mission playground on Sunday afternoon to watch. As far as I was concerned, it was a good excuse to drink in the afternoon. I brought a cooler with the ingredients for screwdrivers so I could mostly just look like I was drinking orange juice. I truly am not a fan of beer. Now that I had an actual paycheck, I could buy some decent booze. It was a good thing Tory and Marilyn didn't like to drink—I didn't have to worry about them pilfering my stash. I didn't care if Chris did, but he was always out anyhow. He'd promised me we'd go to the movies soon, and he was still working on the family Robinson about hiring me at the lab.

I hoped it would happen soon. Once old Troy figured out I wasn't going to go out with him, he not only no longer offered me coke, he snarled at me all the time.

Sitting on bleachers made my butt hurt, but I didn't care after a few screwdrivers. It was at least not hot as it would have been in Cleveland. It was in fact overcast and cool. The game was between Peg's Place and Maud's, and the two factions of fans exchanged good-natured insults.

"Hey, you Peg's girls sure you're okay with getting dirty? Someone might have to slide into home and get her ass all dusty."

"Oh, we have more important things to worry about—like getting beat up by cops."

The Maud's fans looked at each other and fell quiet.

"What are they talking about?" I asked the woman sitting next to me who I recognized but whose name I didn't know. Before she could answer, Spike interrupted. I had spotted her but I wouldn't make eye contact with her, and I hoped she'd leave me alone.

"Oh, they're all full of themselves now that they've been in the papers. They're not real dykes anyhow." That didn't tell me much of anything. I pointedly directed my attention to the Peg's Place woman, who looked at me and rolled her eyes at Spike.

She said, "I'm Alice, by the way," and shook my hand. I told her my name, and once I focused on her, I realized Alice wasn't bad looking. She wore nice sandals and capri pants, a mite odd but I liked the effect, and she had a small cute nose, freckles, and a friendly tone. Also, I thought she might just be the ticket for me to keep Spike at bay.

"We were raided by SF's finest in March two years ago, and people went to the hospital." She told me the whole story, and it sounded terrible. Here in San Francisco, we were *still* not safe. That was depressing.

Alice continued, "We have a dress code at the bar. Some people don't want to conform." She glanced at Spike and I understood. Spike was wearing a baseball cap, which isn't exactly wrong for a softball game. She also was wearing baggy blue jeans. I automatically wondered if they were Levi's.

Alice beamed at me and said, "You ought to come by next week, but you can't wear jeans." And I got a hit of interest from her.

"I've got some black corduroys. And maybe a button-down shirt," I responded, turning on my flirtatious persona.

"Perfect," Alice said, her face registering pleasure and welcome. We grinned foolishly at one another until a combination of shouts and groans rose around us. Peg's had scored.

When Alice stood up and excused herself, Spike came over and sat on my other side. I almost moved, but I was feeling the screwdrivers and that kept me rooted to my seat.

"Are ya having a good time?" Spike asked me. I think she was flirting, but she sounded sly rather than sexy.

"Yup."

"Pretty sure we're going to still win. You ought to come over to the bar after. It'll be a blast."

"I'll think about it." I wasn't going to. If anything, I hoped I would go somewhere with Alice, just maybe not to Peg's since my outfit wasn't right.

Alice returned and I asked her if she wanted a drink. She'd been sipping in a ladylike fashion on a light beer. I held up my bottle of screwdrivers.

She looked from me to it and narrowed her eyes. Oops, what happened?

"No, thanks," she said. We all watched the rest of the game, and sure enough Maud's won, though I didn't care. I was pretty buzzed and Alice's freckles were swimming across my vision.

We stood up and gathered our stuff, and I lost my balance and nearly fell over the bleacher into the seat behind.

"Whoa there. You okay?" Alice gripped my arm and gave it a firm tug.

"Yeah. Sure. So guess I'll go." I was hoping for the invite, but all she said was, "Nice to meet you. See you around."

I stood there feeling foolish.

From somewhere behind me, Spike asked, "Do you need a ride?"

And I realized I did, but I didn't want to accept one from her. Who knew what sort of strings would be attached? But I stumbled again trying to negotiate the steps.

"Come on." Spike gripped my arm harder than Alice did. I seemed to be going with her.

I told her where I lived, and off we went as she kept up a rapid patter of info about Maud's and why it was so much better than Peg's until we arrived at my apartment.

"Take care," Spike said as I clumsily pulled my little ice chest out of her back seat and tried to walk in a straight line up the front stairs. She'd not tried to hit on me, though I could tell she wanted to.

❖

"Come into the office," Bert's manager Harry said to me as we were preparing to open for lunch. Just his tone sent a wave of nausea through me. He was an odd guy. He pretended to be indifferent to almost everything except the food we served, then all of a sudden, he would criticize a small variation in procedure. Like the knife blades faced outward when they should face inward.

I followed him into the broom closet he called the office, quarters entirely too close for my taste.

"Sit down." I obeyed.

"You're not a bad waitress." I hated being called "waitress," but I said nothing.

"But there have been complaints."

"Who? About what?" I asked, as Troy's ugly face popped into my head.

"Never mind. I don't want you to get mad." Get mad and do what?

"You've been known to steal food."

What an asshole. "Everyone steals food."

"Nope, not true." It *was* true.

I slumped in the folding chair and glowered at Harry.

"You can finish out your shift today and I'll give your back pay in cash. Don't bother reporting tomorrow."

"That's it? I'm fired?" I was incredulous. I knew it was because Troy was mad at me and no other reason.

"Sorry," Harry muttered, not looking at me.

At the end of my shift at three, I walked home and stopped at the corner store, and instead of buying a pint of Christian Brothers, I bought a quart. I could probably get a joint off Marilyn or Tory if they were around.

There went my plans for buying a bed frame and a TV.

The house was quiet. Marilyn wasn't around, Tory was asleep, and

Chris was at work. It was just me and my anger and disappointment. I tamped down the fear with a big glass of brandy. It was soothing.

I sat down on the couch with the bottle and glass in front of me, lit a cigarette, and looked around. This living room was so ugly, I decided. It was just one broken-spring chair and the ugly, ratty couch I was sitting on. The coffee table had seen better days as well, but fuck it. I couldn't even put the record player on because I would wake up Tory. I went to my bedroom and found a book I'd been reading, *Some Girls.* It was about lesbians, and that was about the only thing I could find positive to say about it.

I must have fallen asleep, because I woke up when Chris shook me.

"Max. Wake up. I've got great news."

His voice was abnormally loud. I shook my head and forced my eyes open. My mouth tasted like cigarettes and brandy—in other words, horrible. I swallowed and asked, "What time is it?"

"It's nine."

"You're just getting home."

Through my slitted eyes, Chris looked impatient and…a little guilty.

"Yes, Mother, I stopped at the Midnight Sun for happy hour and I, um, got delayed."

"You picked someone up or someone picked you up."

"Never mind that. Are you awake, because Sarah wants you to come for an interview. They want to hire you, it's only a formality. They have to do an interview for human resources."

My head was spinning from brandy, but also because I was trying to wrap my mind around what Chris was saying.

"They do? When?"

"Next week. Can you do it?"

"Just hang on and let me go pee and get some water." I walked out to our back porch toilet and realized I hadn't eaten anything since noon and I was nauseated. I washed my face and drank some water.

When I came back I was slightly more sentient. Chris sat on the couch with his legs crossed, smoking a joint and squinting at me triumphantly.

When I sat down, he hugged me and said, "Maxy girl, this is it. We're going to work together. What do you think?"

"I'm happy. I have to find something to wear."

"We'll go shopping."

I rubbed my face and said, "This is great because I got fired from Bert's today."

"That explains this." Chris gestured to the quarter-empty brandy bottle.

"I was pissed. It was fucking Troy, I know it." I was still burned up about the whole situation.

"Never mind them. You're going to be fine."

"I know." I mustered a somewhat sickly smile. I was grateful. Chris would never let me down. If he had sex six times a day every day, that didn't matter a bit to him and me, as long as he was my friend.

"They want to see you on Monday, so we can go downtown on Saturday and find you something decent to wear. Are you okay?"

I didn't look at him, but I nodded.

"You are going to have to watch this." Chris gestured at the brandy bottle and glass. "You really can't mess up at the lab." He was uncharacteristically serious. I knew he was right, but it was kind of the pot and kettle situation to me. He drank as much as, if not more than, I did.

I said, "Sure. Okay. Hey, can we buy a TV? I can pay you back when I get my first paycheck."

Chris shook his head, resigned, but he said, "Yeah. Okay."

CHAPTER SIX

C hris and I rode the 22 Fillmore bus line to work together.
"Boy, am I glad you're here," he said as we waited. "This time of day, the bus is filled with teenagers on their way to school and they say stuff to me—especially the boys. With you here, we can pretend we're together. Just like in the old days."

I was nervous, of course. I had purposely not had anything to drink on Sunday night, so I was okay physically, though the skirt and flat shoes I wore felt weird.

Chris shepherded me into a brick building next to a hospital and into the elevator. When he was in his mother hen mode, he was sweet if a little irritating.

We got off the elevator, turned right into large laboratory, and I followed him to a set of offices on the other side of the lab. He called out greetings as we walked through. There were a lot of people there for the early morning.

He knocked on one of the office doors, and a woman with a feathery shag cut looked up from something on her desk.

"Hi, Sarah, here's Maxine Cooper."

"Hi, Chris. Thanks very much. Please come in."

Chris left, grinning at me over his shoulder.

"Please sit down. I'm Sarah, by the way."

"Hi, Sarah, thanks for interviewing me." I tugged at my skirt compulsively as I sat down and reminded myself to keep my legs together.

"Oh, we're happy to. Chris speaks so highly of you, and we just love Chris."

"I've known him a long time, and yes, he's great."

"You went to college together, and let's see…" She consulted a piece of paper I assumed was my résumé.

"You worked for the same professor at Cuyahoga Community College."

"Yes. He ran a business on the side doing fish research for the Army Corps of Engineers."

"You primarily worked in the lab?"

"Yes."

She went on to ask me a lot of questions about my background.

I watched Sarah fidget as she talked, rambled really.

"We like our group to be like a family, you know. We like to try and do things together, it makes the science better, we think, when everyone gets along."

She looked at me waiting for a comment, I guess.

"I see," was all I could muster, but I remembered to smile.

"Now Chris, he's the best. And he spoke very highly of you. He said you're likely smarter than almost anyone else. You got the highest grade on your entrance exam to grad school. But tell me about your experience." That grade, I recalled, didn't mean a whole lot when our advisor Andy White decided I wasn't what he wanted in his company or as his grad student. I talked him out of firing me, but it was harsh.

I told her what I thought was necessary. I left out the part where the man who was our professor *and* employer almost fired me because I'd screwed something up that almost cost us a contract with the Corps. I didn't think it was really my fault, but he did.

Sarah excused herself and left the office.

I sat in the wooden chair and tried to not to jump out of my skin.

She returned after a little while.

"We want to offer you a job in our protein chemistry group. Can you start tomorrow?"

I wasn't sure I heard correctly, so I stuttered a bit. "Yeah—yes. I can, sure."

"Let's take a look around the lab and meet everyone."

"Where's Chris?" I didn't see him.

"Oh, I sent him downstairs to the other lab so he could learn a protein extraction procedure I want him to do up here."

I trailed behind her and thought of myself at the bench. I hoped that Sarah was more the hands-off type and would just give assignments and let me work, but I sort of suspected she wouldn't be.

"This is Maria." We stood in a glassware washing room and spoke to the Chinese woman who clearly worked there, since she wore a lab coat plus rubber gloves.

"Maria used to be a doctor in China," Sarah said, and it sounded like she thought Maria fared better washing glassware here in the US than she had been as a doctor in communist China. Maybe that was wishful thinking on Sarah's part. Maria and I grinned vaguely at each other.

There were people here and there, hard at work at their benches. We stopped in at an office on the other side of the lab where a tall thin man sat behind a desk that was covered with huge piles of papers with books mixed in.

"Rich, this is Max, Chris's friend."

He looked up from what he was doing and his face said he was annoyed, but he quickly rearranged it to a semblance of a friendly grin. "Hi, nice to meet you. Sarah taking care of you?"

"Oh sure."

"Great. Good to hear."

Sarah whisked me away. It was clear why she managed the lab. Richard was not a people person. "You can go across the street and finish up your paperwork with HR and then I'll see you tomorrow."

We shook hands, and not too long after, I was back out on the street waiting for the bus home.

❖

We sat in a diner called the Church Street Station at the corner of Church and Market. It advertised itself as a twenty-four-hour place, and that might come in handy sometime.

Chris ordered a cocktail and I ordered a beer, mindful of needing to get up early the next day. We clinked glasses.

"To Cal Genetics and to us," he said. "What do you think of Sarah?" he asked, grinning evilly.

"She's okay, I guess. I can't say yet."

"She can be a real bitch. Maybe when she's on the rag. I don't know."

He sucked his drink straw. In spite of his comment, I knew he'd charm the pants off her and get along with her better than anyone else no matter how much she pissed him off. I didn't have that gift. If I didn't like someone, I couldn't hide it.

"I'll watch out for that."

"Richard is above it all, and that's how he likes it. The man can barely remember anyone's name, he's such a space cadet. He treats Sarah like a slave. But he likes me."

Of course. I said nothing.

"So what are you going to do this weekend to celebrate?"

"Maybe go to Amelia's. What about you?"

The waitress showed up to take our orders, and she had to be over fifty. She sure fit in with the diner scene.

"What would you like, honey?" I gave her my order—roast chicken.

"So, we're both working at the same place," I said.

Christ grinned and ate some bread. "Uh-huh. It's going to be good. I feel like we're settled now."

"Me too."

"Next stop, true love or at least great sex." He raised his rum and Coke.

I mirrored his grin but stayed silent. I was willing to settle for great sex if not true love. I wasn't entirely sure I could get either, but I was willing to keep trying.

❖

That conversation with Chris was on my mind when I went to Amelia's on Saturday night. Ah, the endless possibilities of a crowded disco on Saturday night. Who would show up? Who would I dance with? Who would I take home? Hey, I could do that now. I actually had a home with a room to myself. If it was someone I liked, I could even spend some time with her the next day. That was the challenge, though. I never knew exactly who I would end up with, depending on how much I drank.

I sauntered through the door and took up a spot along the wall, determined to delay my first drink for as long as possible. I had already smoked a joint with my housemates and took a couple swigs of brandy, so I was primed and ready. I had also bought a new shirt—a tight V-neck T-shirt. I figured I looked pretty darn good. The Eagles tune "One of These Nights" played in my brain.

I smoked and surveyed the crowd. It was early yet, only ten. Then I spotted Tammy across the dance floor. *Be cool. It's not going to be a problem. She probably doesn't want to talk to you. Or dance with you. Or sleep with you again.*

I braced myself as she came toward me. She didn't look pissed.

"How's it going?" That was an innocuous enough greeting.

"Good. You?" I exhaled smoke, suave and in control.

"Fine. You want to dance?" Oh crap, was she going to try and pick me up again?

I said as smoothly as I could, "Nope, not right now."

"Not right now or not ever?" That ticked me off.

"How should I know?"

"You're a little full of yourself, aren't you?"

That stung. "Not really. Sorry you think that. Look, I just don't want to dance right now. Not with anybody. Okay?"

"Sure." She turned and walked away. I didn't want to be, but I was embarrassed. This was as bad as Cleveland. Some girls just couldn't take a hint. It was time for a drink, so I headed over to the bar, ordered a double, and drank half of it. The warmth and the smoky flavor and burn in my throat felt great.

Lily showed up at my elbow, looking as chipper as ever. "Hi, girl. What's the haps?"

"Don't know. You?"

"Me? I'm on the move tonight. These women better look out."

I gave Lily a little sexy half grin. "Oh?" I raised my eyebrows. "You're available."

"I'm not only available, I'm the best you're gonna get."

Was she talking to me or just in general? I'd pegged Lily as friend material only that first night at I-Beam, but I was starting to change my mind. I wanted to be cool in case I was wrong. It was so hard to tell with women sometimes.

"In that case, who's a likely candidate?"

Lily took a good long look around the room. "Nobody. Yet."

"The night is young. Someone is sure to show up. You know the saying, 'Girls are like streetcars, another one will be along in a minute.' I'm not looking for Ms Right, though."

Lily laughed, then sipped her drink and regarded me curiously and, I thought, with interest.

"No?"

"I'm okay with Ms Right Now." And put on my best nonchalant relaxed smile.

"You're terrible. But you may have something there. This is no place to find love. All these women"—she swept her arm in a large gesture—"they think they're going to find the love of their life. That's a laugh."

"I'm not looking for that. I'm too young to settle down."

"Then you have the right idea, Maxy baby. Here's to you." We toasted each other. I caught her in a hard eye contact. I thought of it as my tractor beam. *You don't know it, girl, but if I want you. you're going to get picked up without you even realizing what's happening. I can catch you in my magic beam and draw you in. Voilà, you can't get away.* It had worked often enough. I had only a few moves, but they were good ones, or at least good enough to get me who I wanted. Most of the time.

Lily watched the dancers for a while, tapping her foot. I watched her, sending telepathic messages. She turned to me and asked me to dance, so off we went. She was a good dancer, intuitive but not too show-offy. I hadn't really noticed before, like I'd not noticed a lot about Lily, her feathery light brown hair and lively grin. Maybe she had buck teeth and sometimes talked too loud. So what? She was worth a shot, and I was going to go for it.

❖

I rolled over and opened my eyes. As I came awake ever so slowly, it dawned on me that if I moved too fast, I would instantly throw up. There was someone next to me, and I carefully turned over to see who it was. Lily. Huh. I shuddered because I couldn't remember exactly how this had happened. Since I wanted to stay still and not wake her up, never mind not losing my cookies, I remained in bed as I tried to think.

It was hard. The disconnected images of the dance floor at Amelia's, a slow dance, me eating her out. Her making love to me. So we did it, I was pretty sure. The slickness on my thighs said so.

She stirred slightly. I froze. I had to get up if only to pee—not, I hoped, to throw up. The dim light from my window said it was still very early. I stood up inch by inch. My mouth tasted like an ashtray and my head pounded. This was awful. I didn't really get bad hangovers. Not like this. Usually.

The back porch toilet was freezing. Christ, it was only September. What the hell was wrong with San Francisco's weather? The fog hadn't lifted until late August. Then it was pretty and clear, and it still was, just a tad cooler. The problem with this bathroom was it was completely unheated. Marilyn told me it had been added as an afterthought sometime in the 1930s. The only heat in the whole house was in the living room. I was not looking forward to winter, though Marilyn said it didn't go below freezing, as though that would help.

As I sat there, I put my head down and just breathed in long, slow inhales, and the nausea dissipated. Next, I needed water. In the kitchen I ran the tap for a while to clear out the taste of metal pipes and then gulped half a glass. It almost came back up, but no, it was going to be okay. I needed my stomach to quiet so I could take some aspirin to solve my other problem—my throbbing headache.

Back in my bedroom, Lily lay with an arm over her eyes. I got back in bed carefully, but she groaned. She was awake. Was I ready for this? Well, ready or not...

I stubbornly ignored my discomfort and put a hand on her shoulder. "Hi there."

She took her arm away and looked at me with, what? Confusion? Dismay? Maybe she was just hungover like I was.

"Max. How much did we drink last night?" Her voice was rough, but her tone was amused regret. Okay, so far so good.

"Don't know. A lot, I think."

"How'd we get here? This is your house, right?"

"Yep, and taxi." I had a quick flash of us falling into the back seat of a cab, giggly and then groping and kissing as we rode home.

"It's all kind of coming back to me. Hoo, boy. I feel like hell."

"Me too, but I think I may have something to help."

She looked at me skeptically. "Like what?"

"Like this." I produced a joint from the box next to the bed. "This is our medicine."

"Now?" She was incredulous. She found her wristwatch—I sort of remembered her taking it off—and peered at it. "It's seven thirty in the morning."

I shrugged noncommitally.

"I'll be back." She dragged on her T shirt and jeans.

I lay quietly, sipping my glass of water, and considered how I wanted this scenario to go. I wanted to get high and then I would seduce her again. Maybe that would soothe her a bit. It would certainly make me feel better.

"You're serious," Lily said. "Well, I feel bad enough that I'm willing to try it."

"Dynamite." I beamed and lit the joint.

In a jiffy, we were giggling again.

"When we met, I didn't know you liked me," Lily said. "Then the way you looked at me when we danced. Different than before. I thought, well why not."

"Well, last night it just occurred to me that I'd overlooked you. I put you in the friend category when we met at the I-Beam and then, I don't know. I just didn't think about it."

I lit a cigarette, ignoring the bad taste. My stomach had settled down and my head wasn't pounding. I was looking over Lily's slender body—she'd taken off her pants, conveniently enough. She had the covers up to her armpits but all she had on was a T-shirt.

I reached over and rubbed her thigh and cocked an eyebrow. She smiled vaguely and then said in a dreamy voice, "I thought we were just friends too but then you, I don't know, you changed."

I handed her the jay and worked on formulating some logical explanation for my new behavior.

She handed it back to me and said, "Enough for me."

I took a drag and held it in until I started to cough. "Ya know, I usually just grab someone who's halfway decent and, well, willing, but I like you and I thought I might try it with someone I already know and kind of like."

"Kind of?" Lily was not impressed by that qualifier.

I stubbed the jay out in the ashtray and turned to embrace her. I nuzzled her neck and nipped the skin under her chin slightly.

I turned her face toward me and kissed her. "More than kind of." I kissed her firmly with a little bit of tongue. She went limp in my arms and I took that as a yes. I quickly grew dizzier than I already was and gave her a quick orgasm. That was a thrill as always, her body trembling and her sighs echoed in my own. I held her until we both fell back to sleep.

Sometime later, sounds outside the bedroom door woke me up and I groggily reached for the nearest clothes. Lily awoke as well and I whispered, "Stay here."

I crept out to the living room. My roommates, all three of them, sat in the kitchen with cereal and coffee.

"Hi there. Any more coffee?"

"Sure. Help yourself," Chris said. Odd that he was home. He most often didn't show up until later in the day on Saturday or Sunday, and always looking profoundly pleased with himself.

I poured two cups and Chris looked at me with a question in his eyes.

"I'll be back in a little bit."

In the bedroom, Lily was getting dressed.

"Here's some coffee. Are you going?" I was apprehensive and a little disappointed.

"I thought I might. Thanks," she said, accepting the cup I offered. I drew the bedspread up and we sat on top with our coffees. Neither of us said anything for a few minutes until the caffeine started to take hold.

"Would you like to stick around awhile?" I asked.

"If you're not busy." Did I look busy?

"I'm not. We could, um, do something?" I heard myself say.

"Like what for instance?" She sounded mildly suspicious.

I paused, racking my brain. Since Chris had lent me money to buy my own TV, I usually got high and watched TV, but something told me I ought to come up with a better alternative than that.

"A movie? Or downtown or Castro Street and just window shop."

Lily smiled suddenly. "Sure. That sounds good. But could we eat something? I'm starved."

I was not the greatest host. I was not used to women sticking around. I needed to get with the program.

"Come on." I grabbed her coffee-free hand and helped her stand. *Got to get a bed frame soon.*

When we walked into the kitchen, we were treated to the deep scrutiny of three sets of eyes.

"Hi, everyone, this is Lily." They chorused hellos and made room for me to pull in an extra chair at the kitchen table, and introductions were made.

"Cheerios okay?" I asked, holding up the box.

"Great." We sat in a not too awkward silence. The girls talked to each other and Chris just stared into space for so long I thought he'd lost the power of speech.

Finally, he turned to Lily and said, "I know you. You were at the I-Beam months ago. When we first went." He tilted his head at me.

"That's right. I didn't think you'd remember me."

"Yeah, yeah. I remember. So, what are you two up to?" He arched his eyebrows and his voice took on a teasing tone.

"We're not sure, but we might go to the movies," I said. I had my hand on Lily's thigh, though, and wondered how she'd feel about going back to bed. I rubbed my hand on her warm leg, and it heated me up.

"To see what?"

"Let's look at the paper." We did have a household newspaper subscription that we split three ways. We split a lot of stuff three ways. The arithmetic was a pain, but it was fair.

The paper didn't yield any good choices. I motioned to Lily with my head and she followed me back into my bedroom. I kissed her and stroked her shoulders and arms. She relaxed and we slithered back in bed where I made love to her again and she attempted to make love to me, but I stopped her.

"Let's just be still." We fell back to sleep again, and when I woke up she was gone but I could hear the rumble voices in the living room. I got up and put my clothes on for the third time.

The roommates were getting high, but Lily wasn't.

When I sat down next to her, she grinned and said, "How do you feel? I think I need to go."

I took a drag off the joint Chris handed me and said, "I feel good." That wasn't quite true but close enough.

Lily looked funny—sort of like she didn't know what to say. She was quiet as the three of us passed around the weed. She didn't smoke anything.

"I'm going to take off," she said, standing up.

"Do I have your number?"

My roommates snickered.

"No, let me write it down for you."

I found some paper and a pen and we wrote our numbers down and exchanged them.

"Have a good day," I said, pitching my tone to be cheerful, though I was anything but. I wanted Lily to stick around but she wasn't going to. I walked her to the front door, where she let me kiss her again.

"Bye, Max, I'll call you." And she was gone.

I sat back down with the group after I retrieved my bottle of brandy. What the fuck, it was almost noon.

"Anyone want a drink?" I said, knowing no one shared my tastes. Which was fine since it meant more for me.

❖

On my lunch break the next day, I dialed Lily's number and left her a message. It was the middle of the day and I doubted she'd be home. I think she worked downtown in an office somewhere. The details were still fuzzy to me. I couldn't tell for sure what Lily thought about us or about me. I just knew I wanted to see her again. This exercise of picking someone up I already knew and liked was a surprising source of happiness to me. If I was going to have a girlfriend, I thought she might be a good choice. Friendly, low key, and amiable. Also, she was a great lay—she liked what I could provide and she didn't bug me about doing me. I thought I might just let her try again. Who knew? Maybe she was the one.

"Hey, girl." Chris plopped down next to me, startling me out of my thoughts. "Whatcha doing?"

The remains of my lunch were on the table next to me. "Not much. How about you?"

"Nothing. Sarah's waiting for results on my last run. It's not going to be done for another hour. I'm hanging. So you and Lily, eh?"

"I don't know for sure. Maybe."

"Well, that's new and different. You actually like her?"

"I actually do. I don't know if she likes me." I sighed.

"She probably does. Come on, Max, cheer up."

"I'll try. Hey, what are you going to do this weekend?"

"I got an invite to the Hurray for Hollywood party at the Trocadero."

"Oh yeah?" I got a jolt of sadness. I was going to ask him to go out if Lily wasn't available. "What's that?"

"It's a big deal. Something like a thousand guys. Big show. Disco boys. The whole thing. Eric told me it's a blast."

Who was Eric?

"Sounds fun."

"What's the matter, Max?" He put an arm around me, and I felt like I was about to start crying and I felt stupid.

"Nothing. I just miss you."

"Oh, honey, I'm sorry. In a couple weeks, we'll go out, just you and me. It will be great, just like the old days." He squeezed my shoulder and kissed me on the cheek. It was like I was five and my dad just promised me a special outing. It wasn't like that, but it felt like it.

"Sure, that would be great." I hoped I could get hold of Lily. I needed something to do. I didn't want to just go to Maud's and hang around and wait for someone interesting to show up.

"Oops. Got to get back to work." Chris left me sitting by myself in the empty lunch room.

When I heard from Lily that evening, she was curiously noncommittal.

"Hey. Glad you called. Want to do something on Saturday?"

"Sure. That would be fine."

"How about dinner?" Food followed by sex, I hoped. This was an actual date, I realized. It scared me more than a little, but why not?

"Okay." She could be a little more enthusiastic, but what the hell.

On Saturday, we met at a little restaurant on Haight Street near her apartment. I had dressed carefully, and I counseled myself not to have too many drinks. Just one or two glasses of wine with dinner. Very civilized.

"What kind of week did you have?" I asked after we were seated as I looked for a waiter. I wanted to pay attention to her, but I also wanted to order a drink as soon as possible.

"Oh, it was all right. Nothing special. You?"

The waiter appeared and I decided I wanted a vodka martini because it seemed glamorous. Lily ordered white wine. Once we got our drinks and I could take a few swallows, I started to loosen up. The martini was bitter, but it was potent. This dating thing was nerve-wracking—no wonder I didn't do it. It was like being onstage or something. I kept drinking though I knew I was probably drinking too fast. Lily wasn't that voluble and I struggled to ask her questions to keep a conversation.

We made it through dinner and I ordered another vodka martini. I didn't much like the taste of the first one, but it numbed me enough to ignore the taste and down the second one. We asked for the check, and as we stood up, I think I swayed a bit. I certainly felt far drunker than I should have on two drinks. I'd only smoked a little dope before I left the house to meet Lily. I should have smoked more.

"Whoa, there. You okay?" she asked, concerned.

"Yeah, yeah, I'm fine. Where to now? I'd like to see your place." I smirked and hoped she took the hint.

"All right."

The three-block walk sobered me up a bit, which was both good and bad. Good because I felt better, bad because all my nerves sobered up too, and they were shooting anxiety pulses.

Lily's place was up a flight of stairs. It was small and cozy, right across the street from Golden Gate Park. It made me wonder vaguely about walks in the park with Lily. That seemed like something we ought to do.

Lily sat me down on the couch.

"You got anything to drink?" I asked. I was desperate to return to a comfortably buzzed state ASAP.

From the kitchen she said, "Yeah, I think I have some wine. Is that okay?"

It wasn't my favorite thing, but it would have to do. I needed to get back to cruising altitude.

She brought me a glass and I swilled it, drawing a puzzled look from Lily. She sat on the couch with a glass of water, of all things, which she sipped daintily and didn't say a word. I edged closer to her and draped an arm on the back of the couch behind her. I leaned in for a kiss, but she stopped me with a hand on my breastbone.

"What's wrong?" I asked, dismayed.

"I don't think this is a good idea."

The fumes of the wine were in the back of my throat, making me feel a bit nauseated, but I ignored that as I drew back a little and asked, "Why not?"

"I'm not sure we should sleep together."

"Why not?" I was sounding repetitive. I was irritated and somewhat scared. Things had been weird during dinner but were even worse now. Lily wouldn't meet my eye and she was talking to her knees. Her cute little breasts were calling me from under her blouse, nipples erect.

"I think you maybe ought to go home, Max. I'm feeling a little out of it myself."

She looked regretful, but me changing her mind didn't seem possible. I slumped back on the couch and hiccupped. I mumbled an apology. How could I suddenly be this drunk?

"Well. Then. Okay."

"Do you want me to call you a cab?"

"Ah. No. I'm fine. So long." I stood up and nearly fell over. She caught my arm.

"I'll call you a cab," she said firmly.

When she led me outside and sort of shoved me into the back of the cab, I was super dizzy. She gave my address to the cabbie and even gave him some money.

I managed to get out of the cab in front of my house and unlock the door after a couple of tries. It was dark and quiet. No one home. I didn't bother undressing. I flopped on my mattress and the whirlies started. Shit. I knew this was not a good sign. I just made it to the bathroom in time.

The next morning, I kind of came to and knew I was sick. My head ached and my nose was stuffed. I think I had a fever. I lay in bed convincing myself to just get up and get some water. It took some time. Then I found some aspirin. What would solve this? A couple tokes? I still had the leftover joint. No, I wasn't in the mood for any weed. I eyed the brandy in the corner. Maybe just a little sip. My stomach was okay. Just enough to take the edge off being sick.

Lily. Christ. What went wrong there? She was fine until she wasn't. I would call her later. This was such a stupid situation. Here was someone I liked, and she rejected me. What had I done? This was why I fucking never dated anyone, it was too much to handle. Women were inscrutable. I stayed in bed drinking my brandy. I don't know if I felt better or not. I tried eating a piece of toast, and that helped and I went back to bed. I could hear Marilyn and Tory talking through my closed door. I just sat there and smoked a cigarette. It occurred to me that I probably felt so drunk the night before because I was starting to getting sick with the flu or whatever this was. That was it, that's what did me in.

I must have passed out for a while because I woke up in the early evening.

I heard Chris's voice. I didn't really want to talk to anyone but I needed to eat something. I hung out with him long enough to have toast, then I went back to bed. He was sympathetic but distracted.

I stayed home from work the next day, and that experience made me decide daytime TV was a form of hell. I managed to stay away from the brandy and was more or less okay by late in the day. I didn't call Lily until the next day.

When she picked up, I pitched my voice to sound breezy and cheerful, but she did not seem happy to hear from me.

"Turns out I had the flu or something." I lit a Newport and waited for her to say something.

When she finally did, it was only, "Hope you feel better."

"Thanks, I do. So like, do you want to go out again? We could go to Maud's if you want. Or dancing at Amelia's."

"Max, you're a nice person but I don't think we ought to see each other."

"What? Why not?" Again the whiny-sounding question popped out before I could stop myself.

"I just don't think so." What the fuck?

"But you won't tell me why?"

There was a long pause. "You drink way too much."

"I told you I had the flu. That was the problem."

"I'm not sure that's the whole reason. I sat there and watched you down three vodka martinis in an hour. Then wine at my place. You were a wreck. That's just too much for me."

"I only had two martinis and a little bit of wine."

"No, that's not true. You had three, two before dinner and one after. Look, this conversation isn't going anywhere, I'm going to hang up now."

"Lily—" She was gone.

Fuck. This was just great. Where did she get off telling me I drank too much? She was a drinker too. Screw it. She wasn't that good looking or interesting. I had made this call from my bedroom for privacy, so the door was closed. I threw the phone across the room and looked at the ceiling.

"I need a drink," I said aloud to no one in particular. I checked my brandy bottle, and it was nearly empty. I groaned but hauled myself up and out the door to the corner store up the hill and bought a fifth. What the hell. I was gainfully employed and I could afford it.

CHAPTER SEVEN

"Y ou need to let it go, Max. She's not worth your time or effort. Come on, let's go get a drink."

We walked down Castro from the Muni Metro station after work. I was grousing about Lily shining me on.

"Do I drink too much?" I asked Chris.

"Nah. Sometimes, not really. Besides, you had the flu, so that meant the alcohol hit you super hard."

"Yeah. I guess so." It still bothered me that I couldn't remember how many martinis I'd had. "I'm not used to martinis either."

"Nope, that's not your drink."

"Boy, is it not. Never again." I was mildly reassured by Chris's words.

"Hey, what's going on here?" Chris asked.

There was a little knot of guys standing in front of Star Pharmacy, our destination, reading something in the window. When we were able to get close enough to see, it proved to be a bunch of Polaroid pictures of purple spots on someone's feet and legs.

The note on the side of the pictures read, "I'm Bobbi Campbell and I've got gay cancer."

This was a strange thing to see in the window of Star Pharmacy. I scrutinized Chris's face as he looked at the photos and read the note.

At last he said, "Vince's roommate is from New York and he shows Vince all these articles about gay guys in New York dying of cancer. Maybe this is that too." He said this calmly but I knew Chris. He was thinking about it. Hard.

"Probably nothing to worry about," he said, finally.

We crossed the street to the Elephant Walk.

❖

I stared at the rack of test tubes on my bench. They were numbered, but I couldn't remember the last one I'd pipetted reagent A into. If I couldn't figure it out, I'd have to start over. And Sarah told me they needed the results by two o'clock. My vision was somewhat fuzzy and my hand was shaking.

I'd gone to happy hour at Maud's the night before. It turned into a longer night than I'd intended. I was not super hungover, but I knew I'd been drinking.

I peered into the test tube to try and gauge the level of fluid. The last tube was number six. I went on pipetting, then I waited for fifteen minutes, then added the dye and put each tube into the reader. Little beams of light would show how much protein was present in each sample and send me a printout.

I pulled the printout. The first five tubes were controls, the last fifteen were the samples Chris had given me at eleven a.m. from his column separation fractions. He was testing an antibody to see how well it would bind to the proteins of the cell capsule.

Something was wrong. There was nothing in the first three fractions. I'd made a mistake somewhere. I had that sour, sick feeling. I could sense the blood vessels in my temple throbbing. I stared at the printout. What had I done wrong? I didn't have time to redo it. I'd have to tell Sarah and Chris that I failed. With mounting dread, I walked over to Chris's lab bench.

"What's the news?" he asked cheerily, but then he saw my face. "Uh-oh. None of the fractions show adherence?"

"Worse. I don't know for sure."

"Well, you just need to rerun them," he said. "Sarah will have to wait until tomorrow."

"I don't have them. I used all the samples up to run the test," I said to him morosely. I'd cost him a bunch of hours of work. His body sagged and he stared at me for a moment.

"Crap. Okay. Well, let's go tell Sarah. I'll rerun it with a new column and you'll have to retest."

We walked over to Sarah's office together, and I thought I might pass out but Chris was great. He did all the talking and tried to minimize my error. Sarah looked from me to him, eyes narrowed, saying nothing.

"Well. Fine, but we need it done tomorrow latest. Richard is waiting."

"Oh yeah. We'll be ready," Chris said with much more confidence than I felt. He would have to stay until late in the night to finish.

I told him, "I'll come in early tomorrow and get it done."

He just patted my shoulder and nodded.

I left him there and went home. I was wrung out from anxiety and I needed a drink. I poured myself a short glass of brandy and downed it. I sat in the living room but I got restless so went in and turned on my TV, mindlessly watching the news as I drank. I replayed the lab test, the conversation with Chris and then with Sarah. It was useless but I couldn't stop thinking about it.

I snapped awake in the middle of the night. What the hell time was it? Then I remembered I had to get up to go in early so I could have the results by the time Sarah showed up. I'd forgotten to eat. I found something to eat in the kitchen, cereal and bread. I was too out of it to even make toast. I wolfed it down and went back to bed. The clock said it was one thirty. I set my alarm for five a.m. I was restless and I couldn't seem to find a comfortable way to sleep. I took a few mouthfuls of brandy and a bunch of water and finally fell back to sleep.

The alarm was a shock. I couldn't deal with taking a bath, so I washed my hair in the sink. Boy, was this ever not the way to start the day. I would have to concentrate super hard to make it through the spec test.

At least the bus wasn't crowded at that early hour. The teenagers weren't around—it was too early for school. I got off on Fillmore Street to go to a café and get some coffee and a bagel. I hoped it would help me feel better, it did but only a little. Pull your socks up, I told myself, you can do this. Just concentrate. I took a deep breath and started setting up the test on my bench. I found Chris's fractions in the refrigerator. I wondered how long it took him. My hand started to shake as I measured the reagents, and I grabbed it with left hand to steady it. I was stuck between the time pressure and trying to hurry and not making a mistake that would invalidate the test.

I completed the mixtures and ran the test samples through the spec. I tapped on the lid nervously while I waited. The printout of the results came out: the numbers looked good. I took Chris's notes on what was what and went to see Sarah.

She looked everything over and said, "Looks good. Thank you."

"I was wondering if I could leave early today since I came in early."

Sarah glared at me for several seconds. "Fine," she said, grudgingly.

I didn't care what she thought. I was just relieved that I made it through.

"You know, Max, maybe you ought to take up running the acrylamide gels for a while. Just to take a break." I knew the subtext of what she was saying. The protein analysis of column fractions was just too important. It couldn't be fucked up. Chris tested the final products, and his column fractions told the story of which purification process yielded the best binding antibodies. This was what would take us to the next level.

The gels only checked the level of the toxin in the raw material. It was not nearly as crucial. In fact, Maria the dishwasher ran gels sometimes. I was being demoted. I was almost too wrung out to even care, but a gnawing worm of self-doubt wiggled in my brain.

It was November, which meant, in practice, there would be about ten days of rain followed by a few days of sunshine, then the cycle would repeat. The bedrooms in our flat were freezing, ditto the toilet. I could warm myself up in the bathroom by running a hot bath and steaming the room up. As a consequence, if I spent any time in my unheated bedroom, I had to stay in bed to keep warm. My multiple trips to the toilet every night were excruciating. The ice-cold porch and freezing toilet seat coupled with my various stages of fogginess and fatigue were miserable. I thought about moving, but the idea of finding a new home was overwhelming. Chris didn't seem to mind, but then again he was rarely around. I didn't miss much about Cleveland, but I missed the central heating.

It was time at last for our long-promised evening together. He said he had a surprise for me. It was pouring rain so we were staying home. We made ready with some hot food from Safeway and plenty of booze. And better yet, Marilyn and Tory were away. We'd have the living room to ourselves and we could stay warm and play whatever music we desired.

Chris mixed a rum and Coke for himself and poured me a glass of brandy. We toasted. "To us," I said, and I meant it.

"Tell me what you've been up to. I never see you," I said, trying to not sound plaintive.

"Oh, this and that," he said vaguely. "I did have to go down to the Department of Public Health last week. It seems I've got the clap." He took a big gulp of his drink.

"The clap?" I thought I knew what he meant, but I wasn't sure.

"Yep. Rectal gonorrhea."

"Yuck." I wrinkled my nose. "What do you have to do to get rid of it?"

"Penicillin for the next three weeks. The clinic at DPH is like this big social scene. Everyone has to go down and get tested so they can keep track. I even got someone's number. I'm seeing him next week."

I shook my head. "Is everything an opportunity to find a trick?"

Chris grinned. "It sure seems so. There are handsome and willing boys everywhere. Simply everywhere. It's a sexual candy store. I'll take one of those and one of those. That one over there." He pointed in different directions. "It's fantastic."

"So how did you get rectal gonorrhea?"

"I think I got it at the baths."

"What are the baths?"

He lit a Marlboro and snickered. "Literally what they sound like. They have steam rooms, swimming pools. You go in and pay and get a key to a room, you lock up your clothes. Everyone walks around in towels and cruises each other. It's a blast."

"Except for the part where you got the clap," I said.

I was irritated at his cavalier attitude. Chris had not only changed physically in the months since we moved to SF, he was not the same person. He'd definitely gained a lot of muscle from going to the gym all the time. In some way, he seemed older. His face, which used to be boyishly round and innocent, had developed cheekbones. He had a certain hardness of expression, almost intensity. He was not as playful as he'd once been, and in the past, he would have freaked out at getting an STD. Not now. He laughed it off like it was nothing to be concerned with.

He leaned back on the couch and put his hands behind his head.

"It's not a big deal. The guy I talked to at the STD clinic, the one who gave me his number, told me it happens to him all time and he just takes penicillin and doesn't fuck for a couple of weeks."

"Chris? Do you want to fall in love?"

He snorted. "Me? Love? I get all the love I need."

"Not sex, silly. Love. Remember back in Cleveland you told me you wanted to find somebody to spend the rest of your life with."

"Max, baby, that's not a realistic goal. Not here. The name of the game is do as many great-looking guys as possible. I mean, it might happen, I'm not ruling it out, but I'm not sweating it. There's too much fun to have. And what about you, Miss Round Heels? I don't see you settling down anytime soon."

"I haven't met anyone." I ran the list of women I'd slept with in the past few months. Nonstarters. Maybe Lily, but she was out of the picture.

"Maybe you need to try harder. Go do something else besides picking up someone at Amelia's."

"I don't care. If it happens, it happens." I was lying and Chris probably knew that, but he just looked at me.

He sat up abruptly and put his cigarette out. "Oh man, I almost forgot. My surprise. I want to give it to you now before we drink too much more. With this little gem, Max, you won't have to drink as much to get the same effect."

He reached into the change pocket of his Levi's and showed me two largish white pills in his palm.

I remembered he'd mentioned these before and felt a surge of anticipation.

He dropped one in my hand.

"So what's going to happen?"

"Oh girl, you're going to feel great. All loosey goosey and relaxed. They're great for sex—especially anal. And it's like you're drunk, but better. You just fall asleep, no hangover. So don't drink anything more. Just take this."

I grinned and downed it with some water. We'd not eaten anything yet, so I figured it would take effect faster.

Chris kept chattering away about this and that guy. The guy at the gym, the clerk at the mail store on Castro, three different bartenders. Some doctor he saw at the hospital next to where we worked. Someone on the 22 Fillmore bus, even. It still bugged me that it was so fucking easy for him. I could go to Amelia's or Maud's. I suppose I could try a different bar. I remembered the girls from Peg's at the softball game. The location, way out on Geary, seemed like too big a hassle to go, but that was not insurmountable. I decided to go there soon. And that place Scott's that old Spike mentioned, where the real dykes drank, she said. I resolved to try that bar soon. Broaden my horizons, so to speak; spread my wings.

I felt the rush in my head first, then it spread to my body. I was relaxed and floaty. My joints were way softer. I pictured being in bed with some girl. It would be dreamlike, we'd be swimming while entwined. It was so nice, I never wanted it to end.

Chris looked the way I felt. He had a beatific smile on his face and his eyes were closed.

He slowly unwound himself from the couch and stood up carefully. "I'll go put on some music, some of mine, not Marilyn's." He'd acquired his own receiver and turntable.

I just sat in my warm soup of Quaalude euphoria. The next thing I heard was the Pointer Sisters, "Slow Hand." Perfect. I could just substitute the word "woman" for "man." This was a damn sexy song. If only there was a nice girl next to me on the couch instead of Chris. He'd sat back down and the two of us were virtually motionless, lost in our separate fantasies, listening to the music as it filtered through our Quaalude high. I took tiny sips of brandy, just to help things along.

The record scratching woke me up. It was such a weird sound. Next I heard Chris curse. I opened my eyes and tried to fully come to. Oh yeah. Seven fourteens. My mouth was dry.

Chris came back from his bedroom. "Fuck, I passed out. The album's ruined now." He stretched. "You okay, Max?"

"Yeah," I said, though it took some effort to speak.

"We ought to have something to eat. I think there's some cheese." Chris knit his brows.

"Yep, there is." I wasn't hungry, exactly, but I knew I needed to eat or I would feel like shit the next day. I followed him into the kitchen, where he clumsily made us some grilled cheese sandwiches.

❖

It was time for the Cal Genetics Christmas party, and they'd rented a banquet room in the Hyatt hotel downtown. Chris and I made ready to go. Our preparations consisted of admiring each other's outfits, smoking a little grass, and having one cocktail each.

"Just a little pick-me-up so I can face these people," Chris said.

It was one of those things, I guess, that goes with work—you have to socialize with your colleagues whether you want to or not.

Chris wore twill pants and a crisp white dress shirt. He'd helped me pick out some girly khakis and blouse.

He smoothed my collar and said, "Don't want you to be too dykey." What he said didn't bother me—it was certainly true. We might have been out at the lab but there was no sense rubbing everyone's faces in it. Chris definitely acted differently when we were at work. He was toned down, I guess. He wasn't a screaming queen by any means, but he made sure to cultivate a neutral personality. He was witty and sweet and everyone loved him, so it was not a problem.

I'd managed to keep a low profile at work since my disaster with the column fractions, but I had to be careful. I tried to make sure I didn't drink much during the week. I ordered myself not to drink too much at the Christmas party.

We took the Metro downtown, and I have to say that striding into the banquet room with Chris, all dressed up and just a tad buzzed, was a trip. The Christmas decorations sparkled and everyone was nicely dressed. Even Richard, who generally looked like an unmade bed, had cleaned up pretty well.

They didn't have any hard liquor, just beer and wine, which was disappointing. Almost as soon as we arrived, Chris was off chatting everyone up. I stood by the drinks table, uncomfortable and at a loss, and asked for a glass of white wine. Yuck. I downed half of it. A 714 would have been helpful; then I wouldn't have cared about anything. I finished the wine and asked for another glass.

Sarah materialized out of nowhere. "Hi, there. How's it going?"

"Good. I just got here. This is nice." I fidgeted with my wineglass.

"Yeah. It is, isn't it? They try and make it a good party. The food's okay too. Then later we can dance." I wonder if Sarah was sounding as inane to herself as she sounded to me. I took another sip of wine and tried to think of something else to say.

Sarah had her own glass of red wine, and it seemed she was struggling with our enforced sociability as much as I was. She stared off into space. We'd never so much as exchanged a single iota of personal information at work. The only thing I knew about her was she was married to Richard. I'm not sure there was anything about myself I wanted to tell her.

"Excuse me," she said and left. I wandered around, wineglass in hand, smiling randomly at people. I talked to people sometimes at work, if they talked to me first. I found Chris in a group, where he was holding forth about something. I slid in next to him and focused on what he was saying.

He gestured with his glass and made eye contact with each person. He was talking about movies, a particular love of his.

"Oh, you know Mary Tyler Moore got best actress for *Ordinary People* because no one thought America's sweetheart could be such a cold bitch."

The wine he'd drunk made his gay side surface a tad.

I stood by his side, not knowing what to say.

He noticed I was there, as I hoped he would.

"Everyone, this is Max. She's in the scale-up lab with me."

I looked around at the people in the circle. I recognized some of them. It made sense that Chris would know everyone.

I got the quick once-over glance and a quick "hi" from everyone, but it was Chris who held their attention. I listened for a few minutes, but no one paid me any attention so I left. I've always had very hard time in social situations where I don't know people. In bars I could just drink and then wait for someone to ask me to dance. I scanned the room for people I did know and there was Maria, sitting at a table looking around benevolently. Maria barely spoke English, but I decided to give her a try.

I sat down next to her with a fresh glass of wine.

"Hi there. Are you having fun?" I asked with an excess of exuberance. Maria nodded and grinned.

"How many people do you know here?"

Her expression said she didn't understand what I asked. I tried to rephrase it.

"Who do you know? You know me, right? And Chris? And Sarah?" I pointed at myself and then at each of them.

Maria nodded vigorously and said, "Sarah. Chris. Max." Then she asked me, "Max? Is boy's name?"

I giggled lightly. "Oh no, short for Maxine."

"Oh. Maxine."

"Right." I smiled at Maria and then decided to go get another drink. I was definitely feeling the first three, but I didn't know what else to do besides have another drink. Fortunately, they announced dinner would begin and please take a seat. I made sure I sat at the same table as Chris.

The food gave us something to talk about at least for a few minutes. The woman to my left said to me, "So you're Chris's friend?"

I guess that wasn't a bad way to be known.

"Yep. Max."

"Mary, HR." We awkwardly shook hands.

"Where do you live?" she asked between bites.

"We live on Webster Street in the City."

"You and Chris?" She seemed surprised.

"Yes."

"But I thought he was, you know, gay."

I arranged my expression as one of kind bemusement. "Yes, he is. I am too."

"Oh. Oh, What a dumb question. I just thought…oh, never mind." She blushed.

"Don't worry. It's okay. Back in Cleveland, some people thought we were married."

That at least made her laugh. "Oh no. Really? So, you've known him a long time?"

And I told her the whole story. It's a good thing when I can focus on one person and get a conversation going. We were soon chattering away. The waiters poured us more wine. I began, at last, to feel somewhat at ease. Mary's initial dumb misinterpretation of Chris's and my relationship granted me a temporary advantage that let me coast through my shyness and into some rapport with her.

Mary was keeping up with me on drinks, and she became ever more animated and started to touch my arm with alarming frequency. We made it through dessert, and as far as I was concerned, we could be the only two people in the world, let alone in the room.

There were a few after-dinner speeches from company mucky-mucks, but Mary and I kept grinning at each other and rolling our eyes at the clichés they spouted.

They announced the dancing would begin. And sure enough, they set up a DJ booth on the stage and lowered the lights. The very first song was by our apartment's favorite group: the B-52's "Planet Claire."

I was flush with success at participating in the party and making a new friend, and I grandly asked Mary to dance. She was game and off we went. I caught Chris, who was actually dancing with Sarah, throw me a look that may have been envy or maybe it was a warning. Mary and I were in the zone. Look at me: the dyke who gets the prettiest girl in the room to dance. Well, she may not have been *the* prettiest, but she was damn close. I twirled and dipped her at the end. And thank God, didn't drop her. We staggered back to our seats, laughing loudly. Since the music made it noisy, we scooted our chairs together to talk, in that odd intimacy a noisy room will confer.

I lost track of events, but I think I may have tried to kiss Mary. I came to with Chris shaking my shoulder rather roughly.

"Max, come on, we have to go." He seemed to be angry with me. What?

He actually thrust a cup of coffee in my hand and I automatically drank it. I forced my eyes open. The ballroom lights were on and they made me blink.

"We'll take a cab," Chris said. Over his shoulder, to someone else he said, "No, she's fine. I'll take care of her." He led me out to the street where the blast of cold air temporarily revived me.

PART II: WHAT HAPPENED

CHAPTER ONE

When I woke up the next day, I was fully dressed and lying on top of my bedspread and I was cold, especially my feet. Chris must have taken off my shoes.

In the kitchen, he sat at the table with his coffee and the newspaper. He glared at me when I walked in.

"Good morning to you too," I said. What was his problem?

"Good morning," Chris muttered and went back to his paper.

I poured myself a cup, lit a cigarette, and sat down, determined to just wait him out and not start asking questions. He could tell me what was bugging him.

"You had a lot to drink last night," he said. Well, duh.

"Yep, it was a party."

"You were all over Mary from HR. Everyone noticed."

"So what about her? She was flirting with *me*." My defensiveness sounded bad to me, but I was mad.

"That's not the point. Sarah noticed, and she said something to me."

"So what? It's none of her business."

"That may be what you think, but she's our boss. This isn't going to help you at work."

I was incensed now. This wasn't what I expected from my best friend. He was supposed to be on my side.

"I think you're exaggerating."

"I'm not. Sarah's already said stuff to me that I don't repeat to you. You're not her favorite and she keeps coming back to me."

"Well? So what?" I didn't want to make trouble for him, but what Sarah said wasn't within my control.

"I just want to stay in her good graces."

"I know, Chris. You like to get along. It was just the Christmas party, and I'll be careful at work."

❖

The winter was so dreary it made me want to drink at home, but that got pretty dull pretty quickly. I decided I needed a change of scene and it was time to try Peg's Place out in the Avenues, as they called the numbered streets on the western end of the City. I still hit Maud's every so often, and my encounters with Lily were awkward but not too bad. We mostly said "Hi" and "How are you?" and left it at that. I couldn't seem to break into any of the cliques and concluded they were just a drag. I'd only come originally with Lily because I was curious and because Maud's was close to the I-Beam.

I stood in the bathroom combing my hair. I kept the door open because privacy wasn't the most essential thing at the point. I wanted to hear the Eagle's "Life in the Fast Lane" as I prepared to go out. It revved me up along with a couple of small drinks.

Shit, I said my reflection, *you're twenty-six years old and you're not a dog, you ought to be able to find someone. Someone who doesn't want to be exclusive. Some good-time girl.* I grinned. *Like me.* I wasn't a flashy dresser. I wore jeans and a nice button-down shirt. Just the basics. That's who am. Basic.

Chris appeared behind me. He was obviously on his way out too. He was wearing a tight tank top, the requisite tight Levi's, and a Members Only jacket.

"If I were a gay guy, I'd snap you right up." I spoke to the mirror.

"If I were a lesbian, you wouldn't have a chance." He came in and kissed my cheek.

"Have fun and don't do anything I wouldn't do." He beamed. "When faced with temptation…"

"My policy is to yield," we finished together.

"That leaves me a lot of choices."

He laughed.

I wished I'd had one more drink. The bus ride out to Peg's was so long I had lost my high by the time I got there. Well, I was going to fix that problem quick.

The place was not jumping. It was sort of quiet, actually. The women who were there truly looked like just couples, but there was one likely prospect at the bar. Hmm. I was mostly glad it wasn't noisy, but I was nervous because it meant I would have to make conversation. I couldn't pose against a wall or at the jukebox and look available until someone approached me. A drink or two would let me strike up an acquaintance.

She was blond, sort of clean cut and all-American. She had a mullet, but I wasn't too turned off by that. She was speaking with the bartender in a manner that suggested they were well acquainted.

I sat on the barstool next to her, and when she turned to me, I flashed a big wide grin and said, "Hello." Shit, was I overenthusiastic?

"Hi, yourself," the blonde said. I ordered another double brandy. The thing I liked most about brandy, besides its effect, was it was served in a brandy snifter, an elegantly shaped glass that I could hold in my palm and swish the liquid around and literally sniff. Sophisticated. So much more so than sucking on a bottle of beer. The strange blonde had a glass of clear liquid before her, and as the bartender left to take care of me, I noticed she looked at her watch. Twice. I wondered if she was meeting someone. I hoped not.

"What time is it?" I asked her to be friendly.

She looked startled and a little embarrassed.

"Oh, I'm waiting for my friend. She wanted one drink before we go to the movie down the street."

Drat. "My friend" was usually code for "my girlfriend." Though why anyone needed to employ that euphemism in a dyke bar in San Francisco was beyond me. She wasn't sticking around. Well, I could follow through with my New Year's resolution and get her phone number and ask her out.

"I'm Max." I stuck my hand out.

"Laurie," she said, shaking my hand. Her palm was pleasantly smooth and warm.

"What are you drinking, Laurie?" I asked, preparing to buy both of us another. My glass was empty.

"Just water."

That brought me up short. In a bar and drinking water? I would have guessed vodka. Or gin, though that was less likely. There was no olive in her glass.

"Water?" I asked stupidly.

"Yeah, I'm allergic to alcohol. Cindy wanted to meet here, though. What's that you got there?" She pointed at my snifter.

"Brandy," I said, all at once feeling self-conscious.

"I see." Her face was expressionless. She looked over her shoulder at the door to the bar, as though contemplating escape.

"What do you do, Laurie?" I asked, desperate for some way to make conversation.

"Insurance adjuster. I work downtown. You?"

"I'm a scientist," I said grandly. "Biotech company over in Pacific Heights."

"Wow. That's great." Good, she was impressed. I told her all about antibodies and ricin and clinical trials between swallows of brandy.

After about twenty minutes, Laurie said, "Looks like Cindy's not going to show up. I should go."

"Oh, no," I said. "Why not just stay for one more—just a little while longer. Let's go over and sit at a table." We moved from the bar to a little table in the corner, much nicer and more intimate.

I was gabby now that I had a sufficient amount to drink. I was unnerved that she wasn't drinking but I still had the hots for her.

"I live down in the lower Haight," I told her. Chris and I had learned that was what our neighborhood was called, and it was important to identify where one lived in San Francisco. "What about you?"

We could also say Western Addition, but I'd found that drew perplexed and cautious looks since it was known as the area where black people lived.

"Laurel Heights," Laurie said.

I giggled. "Laurie. Laurel Heights."

"Yeah." Probably not the first time she'd heard that.

I edged my chair closer to hers as though I was having a hard time hearing her.

"So, what do you like to do? Apart from going to movies?" I asked. I pitched my voice a little lower, a little sexier. It was hard for me to ignore that I was talking to a woman who wasn't drinking. I felt as though I was on the other side of glass wall. Although she gave me attention via her direct gaze, it was somewhat like we were communicating through a filter. She didn't exude warmth and didn't look like a gal on the make. She was clearly being polite, so I chose my words carefully.

"Don't know. Lots of stuff. I like fiction. I also like to run." Oh, right, a health nut. She also wasn't smoking, and she avoided my smoke in a subtle way.

"That's cool. I don't have much time for reading, but I used to read a lot." This sounded lame. I could tell I was losing her.

"Oh God, Laurie. I'm sorry." There was someone standing behind Laurie, who turned and craned her neck.

"Hi, I was worried about you."

"I'm gonna blame it on the bus. I waited for forty-five minutes. I took a cab. It was so good of you to wait for me." This was Cindy, I supposed.

Laurie said, "I'm fine. This is Max. She's been keeping me company while I wait."

I said hello and shook Cindy's hand and gave her a medium smile. I was about to lose contact with Laurie. This had ended the pickup scenario for sure. I would actually have to get her number and ask her out.

Laurie said, "Should we go to the later show? You can have your drink. There's no rush."

Cindy glanced at me and said, "Sure, why not." One of the other bartenders came over and took orders, and I asked for another. The three of us settled in. Mostly they talked to each other and I was iced out. Swell. I'm not the pushy type, so I stayed quiet and tried to listen attentively, but it bugged me.

They made ready to leave and I said to Laurie, "It's been great to talk to you and I hope we can get together sometime." I said this as neutrally as possible. I of course had nothing to write a phone number on, and it didn't seem workable to go to the bar to acquire pen and paper. I wanted to see what she'd say.

Laurie tilted her head and said, "It was nice to talk to you too. Max. Maybe we'll run into each other sometime. Take care of yourself." They left. I stayed at the table, feeling quite conspicuous. No one came over to say anything to me. I thought about another drink, but in the end, I went home with a curious sense of disappointment. Was I losing my touch? Or was she turned off because she didn't drink? I couldn't relate very well to someone who wasn't drinking. She might have been judging me. She'd not said anything, but I got an inkling and it bothered me.

❖

In February, I managed to transfer to another part of Cal Genetics—the quality control or QC group. I was no longer under Sarah and Richard and it was a relief, in some ways. Mary from HR left the company, so that lingering sense of embarrassment I felt whenever I saw her lifted. I had mostly wanted to get away from Sarah, so I accomplished that.

The QC director, Howard, was no fan of Sarah's, and he must have dismissed whatever she had to say about me. He gave me an actual tryout: he gave me a kit to test for lipopolysaccharide contamination and told me to run it. I can read directions, fortunately, and it was a simple-minded enough task. It was a success and I was in.

The downside of this move, however, was QC was going to be under pressure since we were about to begin the first stage of gaining FDA approval for the cancer-killing antibody conjugate. They would try the treatment on some actual patients. Howard often said that we were the last stop before the actual people, so the pressure would be on. Chris was in the new scale-up group, and he and his cohorts would make batches of antibody ricin conjugate and we would check that they worked before they were shipped off to the hospitals. It seemed straightforward in theory. The fun was set to begin in April.

Through the rainy winter days after New Year's, Chris and I huddled in the flat, drinking and playing cards, and I liked this much more than the long nights at the bars. It was cheaper. Sometimes we went to the movies. I didn't care, I was never bored in Chris's company. If he'd been a cute girl, I'd have had it made.

"I'm not feeling that good," he said one day.

"Oh, is that why you're not out and about?" I asked.

"Partially. The crummy weather too. I just can't deal with getting around in the rain."

"I hear you."

"What about you?" He played a card and said, "Gin."

"Me? What do you mean what about me?"

He shuffled the cards. "I mean, what about your love life? I haven't seen any girls skulking out of your room on Sunday morning."

"Yeah, About that," I said glumly. I told him about Laurie. "I'm kind of done with whole pickup thing. I'm not that good at it anyhow."

"You girls make it so complicated. You see someone you like, you go have sex, and if that's it, no big deal. Or maybe you do it again."

"If only it were that simple."

"Say, I'm kind of not feeling well. I think I'll to go to bed." He didn't look well. His color was odd—he didn't have that normal rosy glow he usually had.

"Yeah. Get some rest. Do you want me to go get you anything at Safeway?"

"I'm not hungry. Maybe some Pepto-Bismol."

When I returned from my errand, I walked into the house to the sound of Chris throwing up. That never happened to him no matter how much he drank.

He appeared in the kitchen looking even worse than he had a half hour before. I handed him Pepto and he took it without a word. I went to my bedroom and watched TV, sipping on a little brandy. It occurred to me I ought not get drunk in case I needed to help Chris.

I'd dozed off and woke up with him standing over me.

"Can you borrow Tory's car and take me to the hospital? I think I have a fever and I feel so awful, I can barely stand."

I helped him sit on the couch and talked to Marilyn since Tory was asleep. She went along, and between the two of us we supported Chris, who flopped in the back seat of Tory's Toyota with a bowl from the kitchen in case he upchucked.

"Nothing's coming up, though," he said and groaned.

It was late afternoon and the emergency room at the Ralph K. Davies Medical Center wasn't busy, thank goodness.

"I have to take the car back. Tory's going to wake up and have to work."

"Thanks so much." I sat in the waiting room with Chris, not saying anything but just looking at him.

A handsome gay nurse came out and called for him. I saw his expression brighten just a hair. I smiled to myself. Chris was irrepressible.

"Can she come too?" he asked the dark-haired, well-built fellow.

"Related?" His face said he knew the answer.

"Well. No. I'm his friend," I said, with a slightly pleading expression.

"I'll come find you as soon as he sees the doctor," he said sympathetically.

There wasn't a bloody thing to read in the waiting room but fashion magazines. I went outside the ER entrance to smoke.

After more than an hour, the hunky nurse reappeared and said, "You can come with me. It's not really kosher but you're the only one here, so I'm bending the rules."

Chris was in a curtained cubicle with an IV in his arm.

"You'll never guess," he whispered. "It's hepatitis. I have to stay in the hospital for a couple days. But I'll be okay."

I took his hand. "You're just one happy way station for germs, aren't you, man. First gonorrhea, now this."

Chris lay back on his tiny hospital pillow and sighed. "The doctor gave me a lecture about unprotected sex. After I told him that I wasn't a junkie and I didn't use needles, he made me talk about my sex life. I *think* he's gay, so it's all right. But he said hep is super common with gay men because well, you know, we have sex all the time. With everyone. His name's Ostrow and he asked me if he could take some of my blood for a research study he's doing. Of course I said yes."

"Well. Okay. You have to stay in the hospital. When will you get well?"

Chris's eyes clouded. "You know, the doctor said I might be okay in a few weeks but I have a twenty percent chance of developing liver cancer. There's no treatment." He got quiet. I didn't know what to say.

Chris said, in his normal voice, "Can you go tell Albert where I am on Monday?" He referred to his supervisor.

"Of course. And I'll come back tomorrow."

Chris came home in the middle of the week and he looked like a squash. Even his eyeballs were yellow.

"I can't drink. Worse, I can't have sex for six weeks at least or I'll infect someone else. Probably did that already anyhow."

"When can you go back to work?"

"No idea. I'll let them know."

❖

It was a long six weeks before Chris was well enough to go back to work in early May. He obeyed Dr. Ostrow and stayed home and didn't cruise or trick with anyone.

He moaned, "I truly might die of lack of sex."

"If that were possible, I'd be dead already," I told him. We were sitting in his bedroom. I kept him supplied with movie magazines and plenty of sodas.

"I can't drink either." He didn't seem as upset about this as he was about lack of sex.

Tory popped her head in the door. Since she was home during the day, she often would run errands for Chris, and as a consequence I got to know her better.

In fact, she told me one day before she went to work, "Mar and I are trying an open relationship." I received this information with interest. I took another look at Tory. Marilyn didn't appeal to me, but Tory was a different story. She had light brown hair, a sturdy build, and a beautiful smile. Her stepping up to help with Chris's care didn't hurt. We had limited opportunities to interact, since she left for work around six in the evening and I wasn't home until fiveish. But I made the most of it, hanging out with her and mildly flirting.

A week or so after Chris went back to work he told me he was staying late since he'd been sick for so long, he felt obligated.

When I came home, thinking vaguely of what to eat for dinner, I was startled when Tory walked into the kitchen.

"Hi there, I've got the night off. Want me to cook us something?" She was one of the cooks at the house, Chris was the other. Neither Marilyn nor I really had to do anything but wash dishes.

"Sure. Anything. Is Marilyn going to join us?" I asked.

"Oh no, she went up north to see her mom. What about Chris?"

"He's working late. It's just us, I guess." This realization hit me, and I think Tory was cognizant of the meaning of "just us" because she gave me a look, inscrutable but a look just the same.

"Wanna get high?" I offered.

Tory looked over her shoulder at me as she opened the fridge. "Absolutely."

I lit a joint and handed it to her and poured myself a drink.

She'd made some kind of baked chicken with a glaze and

vegetables. We'd barely started to eat when the tension exploded for both of us and we raced to bed.

We did it in my bed, which was still a mattress on the floor, which she made mention of, though not unkindly.

"It serves the purpose," she said, as I parted her legs and plunged my fingers into her, eliciting a nice gasp.

I bent over her and said, "I've been thinking about this since you made your announcement."

"You have?" she said, a little raggedly. My touch was having the desired effect. Once she was truly wet, I replaced my fingers with my tongue.

"Wow," was her verdict after two orgasms in quick succession. I just grinned.

I let her take me with her hand for a short interval.

"Is this okay?" she asked.

"Yeah, it's great." I was only mildly buzzed and it did indeed feel very nice, but I knew I was never going to come. "I have a hard time getting there. It's not you."

"Well, tell me if you want to stop or do something different." She was sweet and cute and I should have been able to come, but it wasn't happening.

We heard the front door open and close and then a shouted hello.

"Anyone home?" It was Marilyn. I was awash in fear. Tory jumped up and threw on her clothes. So did I, but it didn't matter, we were busted.

We were in the midst of a tense, chain-smoking three-way discussion when Chris arrived around nine that evening.

"Are there leftovers? I smelled something really great when I opened the door."

"Sure. Stove," Tory said tersely.

Chris made up a plate for himself and sat down at the table.

He looked around at the three of us, picked up on the vibe, and asked, "What's going on, girls? You look like someone's pet died, and we don't have any pets."

Marilyn was rocking in her chair with a cigarette in her hand. Tory was staring at the table. I was wondering if I ought to pour another glass of brandy. No one said a word. Chris chewed and waited.

"Well, if you must know, she fucked my girlfriend." Marilyn flicked her head at me.

This was infuriating. What happened to the "open relationship"?

Tory said through her teeth, "It was your idea to see other people."

"I never thought it would be Max. That's classless."

"Hey," I said. "It's not my fault."

Chris watched the verbal tennis game as he ate.

"We didn't do anything in our bed," Tory said, as though that would mollify Marilyn.

"Whoopee shit. You think that gets you off the hook?"

Tory said, "Honey, I'm sorry. I didn't think you'd mind."

"You didn't think I'd mind?" Marilyn almost shouted.

"I think we might want to leave these two to work this out," Chris said. "Come on, Max."

We went to his room.

"Have you never heard the saying, 'Don't shit where you eat'?"

"That's disgusting," I said peevishly, though I took his point and didn't want to admit it.

"Not as disgusting as you making it with our roommate who's the lover of our *other* roommate. You have the *worst* judgment."

"This from a guy who lets anyone with a pulse screw him." I was not in the mood for him judging me. Mr. STD himself.

"We're not talking about me, sweetheart, and I keep it out of the house. You just created the biggest dyke drama of all, the triangle. You are probably going to get us kicked out of here."

I could think of nothing to say. We smoked a joint and I went to bed, and sure enough, when I got up the next morning, there was a note under my door inviting me to pack up and split.

CHAPTER TWO

It's the biggest day on the calendar for homos," Chris said, "There is no way you cannot get laid."

He was talking about the Lesbian Gay Freedom Day Parade and Celebration. We were going together. Whatever happened, happened, but we would start the day watching the parade, just him and me.

Chris and I had moved out of Webster Street, and we found a small two-bedroom flat in the Duboce Triangle on Sanchez Street. The move was a hassle, but I ended up buying a new bed, and even Chris thought it was much better that we didn't have to deal with other people.

We were in a waiting game at work because the clinical trial had been delayed. Chris and his cohorts produced batch after batch of product, and QC tested them. It was okay with me that there was no particular anxiety around work. I was looking forward to the parade—party time, of course. Maud's had a group marching and I could have joined, but I opted to watch with Chris.

He was gleeful, almost vibrating with anticipation. He grinned and told me the population of the Castro would swell by many thousands since lots of guys from everywhere wanted to come to gay mecca.

"I can experience sex with a Southern accent or a French accent. You name it." He leered.

"As if you need any more choice. Geez."

"Max, don't be nasty." He grabbed my arm and pointed out a lesbian walking up Castro Street as we stood near the intersection at Eighteenth Street.

"Look, how about her?"

"Will you stop?" I said, but I was amused.

"Hey, let's go to Star Pharmacy. We'll need some sunscreen."

"Oh sure. You're positive there will be sun?"

"Yes, everyone tells me the sun always shines on parade day."

The sunshine prediction was true, and I didn't mind admitting that. I had, with some effort, refrained from drinking too much on Saturday night. The prospect of getting up at eight or nine to stand in the sun all day convinced me to moderate. Chris's friend's experiences and advice directed our day, and that was fine with me; I was overjoyed we were there. We'd missed the 1981 parade because we'd arrived in the City in July. We heard enough about it and saw pictures in various gay newspapers to convince us both it was not to be missed.

Consequently, Chris and I were waiting for the Muni train at the extraordinary, for Sunday morning, hour of ten a.m.

"Jack said the best place to watch is farther downtown, less crowded. We can take the Metro back to Civic Center when the parade's over. And he said if we get there early enough, we can get a curbside spot and a good view. You're too short to see over the crowd."

I shoved him but I laughed. It was actually a nice feeling not to be headachy and dragged out. I would cut loose that night. If all went well, I'd have a new friend to drink with. It would be an interesting experiment to make friends in broad daylight. I convinced myself it was possible. After all, we were in San Francisco and at the parade, so it ought to be a snap with the number of people everyone told us to expect.

We took up our spots near New Montgomery and Market Streets. There were already people around, but not many. I stood guard while Chris went off to find a place to buy us some coffee and breakfast that we could consume standing on a curb.

I made myself make eye contact and say hello to people who began to fill in the spaces on either side of us. It wasn't hard. There was a certain electricity in the air, a glow of excitement that emanated from the parade-goers. It was infectious, and within a few minutes I was chatting with a dyke couple from Cincinnati, Ohio, who were flying high over just being in San Francisco and being able to hold hands and cuddle. It gave me a little stab of wistfulness. I don't know when I'd decided a relationship was what I wanted too, but once I did, the lack of success I had in acquiring a girlfriend gnawed at me. Well, today was another day, and a special one at that.

Chris handed me a coffee. The time passed swiftly as more and more people arrived. They flooded out of the Muni and BART station. It was almost time to start.

We heard rather than saw them—motorcycles. Lots of them. Then they passed. The banner carried by the passenger on one of the first bikes read, "Dykes on Bikes."

There were not just a few, there were hundreds. Big butch lesbians, corset-wearing femmes. They were, well, a sight. Being out, in both senses of the term. I had a sudden realization: I was part of a huge community that was bigger than any bar. I think it hit me at last, what being gay in San Francisco truly meant.

The parade streamed by. There was so much to see I could scarcely take it in. Along with the other spectators I gazed in slack-jawed awe. I clapped and yelled and so did Chris. He sometimes professes a certain jadedness, an "I've seen and done it all" coolness. But he didn't this morning. He was like a little boy, exuberant and loud. It made me smile.

I turned to say that to him. He grinned knowingly and nodded. As we returned our focus to the street, three women moved in to stand directly in front of us. How rude! was my first reaction and I became angry.

I said to Chris, "The nerve."

He shrugged. "I can still see. But if it bugs you, tell them."

"You need to help me," I said, irked at him as well. "It will work better with two of us."

"No," Chris said. "They'll just cop an attitude if some gay dude says anything. They're your people. They'll listen to you."

I huffed, not wanting to do it by myself, but there was no alternative. My view of the parade was blocked and standing on the curb didn't help.

I took a breath, tapped the woman closest to me on the shoulder, and said, "Excuse me."

She turned around and I was presented with a set of black eyes, or else eyes so brown that I couldn't see her pupils. She had a mass of floppy silky black hair.

"Yes?" she said, not unfriendly but not friendly either.

"We've been standing here for hours and you just got here and stood in front of us. I can't see the parade."

The strange woman didn't say or do anything for a few seconds but merely stared at me with the same neutral expression, then she broke into a smile and said, "Well. What are we to do about that?"

What was this "we" thing? I grew more annoyed.

"Well. You and your friends could move," I said and after a moment added, "Please."

I braced myself for the objection. She whispered something to the two women who were with her and then turned back to me. "Okay." And with that, the three of them stepped back onto the curb, in line with us, gently jostling Chris and me and the people on their other side to make room.

The black-haired woman stood right next to me.

"Okay now?" she asked good-naturedly. The noise of the parade and the crowd almost drowned her voice out, and I leaned close to respond to her.

"Yes. Thanks." Our eyes locked. She had a knowing grin, an "I've got a secret" grin that also invited me to ask what she was thinking. She was quite good looking. To go with her black hair, her skin tone was somewhere between a dark gold and taupe. Chris had taught me about fancy names for colors. Clad in cut-off jean shorts and a sleeveless white shirt, she was a lesbian wet dream. Taking the entire picture of her into my consciousness was like a being hit by a strong electric current. I couldn't say anything else at that moment.

"My name's Adrian. What's yours?"

"Max. Hi, Adrian."

"Hi, Max. So how long have you been here?"

"Since ten a.m." It was two p.m.

"Wow, no wonder you were pissed. I would be too. These two made us late." She gestured toward her two companions, who I noticed were draped over one another as though separation would cause them to expire. They didn't say anything but favored us with sexy smiles, and one licked the other's earlobe. Then they went back to watching the parade. I wanted to do that myself, but I couldn't seem to tear myself away from Adrian.

If I had seen her in Amelia's I would have never had the guts to walk up to her to ask her to dance. And I couldn't imagine a universe where she would have said anything to me. Yet here she was focused on me like I was the only important thing she could see at that moment, never mind the spectacle in front of us. A huge bar float bearing a dozen naked muscle boys gyrating to loud disco music came by and Adrian had to move very close to me as she asked her next question: "Is this your first parade?"

"Yes, it is." I got a small hit of mint toothpaste and, since I was eye level with her chin, a view of her nice white teeth.

She waited until the noisy disco float proceeded down the street. "Are you here by yourself?"

"Oh no. I'm here with my friend Chris." I turned and touched his arm.

He looked as though he'd been awakened from a nap. Must have been the last float that did it.

"This is Adrian."

They shook hands. I noticed that Adrian hadn't shaken hands with me and it made me mad. I was mesmerized by her looks and wanted to touch that remarkable skin if only via a quick handshake. I was shaken, confused. I suddenly wanted a drink if only to quiet the storm of emotions that welled up: lust, curiosity, and something more. I wanted a connection with Adrian.

We watched the parade in silence for a time. The sun was powerful, and though it wasn't especially hot, it was taking its toll on me. I wondered if it was too soon to ask Adrian if she wanted a drink. Who knew when the parade would end? I enjoyed it, but the sensual assault of all the sound and colors and so many people plus my awareness of Adrian made me dizzy and disoriented as though I was already drunk.

I realized that Chris had struck up a conversation with a man at his side. I knew from his tone and his expression that he'd discovered his next trick, and from what I could tell, the young stranger was game.

"Do you live here in the City?" I asked Adrian, mostly just to keep her talking to me.

"I do. In the Mission. Guerrero Street. You?"

"We"—I pointed to Chris—"live in the Duboce Triangle."

"Oh. Interesting." This time her smile was inquisitive.

"Why interesting?"

"Because your roommate is a guy. At least I assume he's just your roommate. There I go. I'm assuming, which I don't like to do. My motto is 'Don't assume anything.'"

I liked her self-deprecation.

"No, you're right. We go way back. College."

"That's nice. Really." She beamed. "I'm a little sick of separatists."

"Oh. Them." I knew what she meant from having heard many conversations in Peg's or Maud's. I laughed ruefully. I tended to not talk about Chris much if I knew the woman I was chatting up in the bar was a separatist.

"Yep. Them." And with that, I began to relax with Adrian. She was so disarming it was easy for me to put my anxieties aside and enjoy the moment.

We stayed put for the next two hours, and the parade finally ended with one final ear-shattering disco float.

"Where are you off to?" I asked.

"They"—she pointed to her two friends—"want to go home for a while. We're going out tonight. Amelia's."

"What about you?"

Adrian tilted her head and grinned. "I'm open."

"Want to go walk around Civic Center?"

"Sure."

I turned to Chris. He was necking with his new friend.

"I'm going up to Civic Center with Adrian," I told him.

"What do you want to do?" he asked his friend, who shrugged what seemed to be a passive assent.

"Okay. Let's go." The four of us joined the throngs down in the Metro station to ride two stops to the Civic Center.

I took Adrian's hand so we wouldn't be separated. I didn't think she'd mind. I was ready to jump out of my skin, I was so excited.

The escalator at Market and Eighth Street was vertigo inducing, and I gripped Adrian's hand harder. She squeezed my hand back. We wandered through the hordes of people, Chris and his buddy close behind. There was a giant stage in front of City Hall. At that moment, someone was making a speech.

Adrian looked up at the stage with an awestruck expression. I had to admit it was a dramatic scene. The dome of the San Francisco City Hall loomed behind the stage and the plaza was crowded, but I was interested in nothing at that moment except her.

"You want a drink?" she asked me.

"Yeah, that sounds good."

I told Chris where we were going.

He said, "Yeah. I think I'll see you later. Have fun."

"You too." I rolled my eyes toward the man with him.

He suddenly hugged me. "Take care, Max." It was a bit unusual for him.

I hugged him back and repeated, "You too."

❖

We went from the Civic Center Plaza to the Mission for something to eat and talked nonstop. I was enthralled by Adrian, by her looks, certainly, and her effortless conversation, but mostly by her attention to me. She lit my cigarettes gallantly and listened to me with grave attention.

She was a Bay Area native although she'd grown up in Daly City. "Where's that?" I asked.

She laughed then said, "Literally nowhere. It's just south of the City but another world. It's the ugliest, dullest, most suburban suburb you ever saw. The only difference between it and other suburbs is a lot of Filipinos live there. My dad's Filipino and my mom's Guatemalan."

"Is that how you got that skin color?"

"Yup. I look like a cup of bad diner coffee."

"No, I like it." I wasn't lying. I'd truly never seen anyone with that skin tone. I knew white people, maybe Italians who were a little darker skinned, and I knew black people who came in various shades, but Adrian's color was unique.

She looked shy but pleased.

We walked around on Valencia Street while we waited for it to be late enough to go to Amelia's.

Adrian said, "We'll hit it a little early. On parade day, it'll be packed." She turned to look me in the eye. I thought vaguely I might have seen her there sometime, but I couldn't remember, and if she was with someone, I would have left her alone.

"Then when it gets too crowded, we'll leave." She favored me with a meaningful look. I shivered.

"Here's Osento." She pointed to a Victorian duplex that I'd noticed but didn't know what it was.

"Women's bathhouse. We ought to go sometime."

"Okay."

Then we passed by two storefronts close together. One read, Old

Wives' Tales, the other, Artemis. I hadn't even made it up the street this far from Amelia's.

"Books and coffee." Adrian grinned. "All lesbian."

"Really?"

"Yeah. This is the lesbian neighborhood. You didn't know that?"

"Nope. I don't get out much, I guess." That was mostly true.

It was time, finally, to hit the bar. Adrian was correct, there were already lots of women milling about outside, and it was only dusk.

We eased our way to the bar and this time I bought her a drink—vodka and 7Up.

We turned and clinked glasses. She smiled slightly.

"To another memorable gay day."

We drank. I couldn't remember ever savoring a swallow of brandy as much as I did at the moment with Adrian and our gazes meeting over the rims of our glasses.

❖

I woke up slowly, opening one eye at a time. I became aware that I was in the vise grip of a headache and I couldn't swallow, my mouth was so dry. Bit by bit, my memory kicked into gear, rendering hazy images.

We were in Amelia's, dancing. I had never danced better in my life, I thought. We had more drinks, then at some point, we groped our way down the street. I recalled Adrian said she only lived four blocks away from Amelia's and I'd said to her, "That's handy."

"Yeah, it is, isn't it?" she replied in a sexy whispery tone.

Then…nothing.

I turned over as carefully as I could. There she was. Adrian. Had we? I didn't know, and it made my head hurt worse as my mind struggled to put memory in motion.

If only I didn't feel so crappy, I'd wake her up and…

She opened one eye and grinned. "Hey, you."

"Hi. Um. Where's your bathroom?"

"Out the door and turn right."

My limbs felt encased in cement, as did my head. I palmed some water into my mouth, then staggered back to Adrian's bed. The flat was silent, so I hoped there was no one else around because I couldn't deal with putting on any clothes. I didn't even remember taking them off. We were both naked, so that seemed to imply something had happened.

Adrian observed me getting back in bed without saying anything.

I closed my eyes, trying to will myself to feel better. It didn't work.

I felt a cool palm on my forehead.

"You okay?"

Was I?

"It depends on what you mean by okay," I said through my cotton mouth. If cotton tasted like a combination of cigarettes and metal shavings.

"You need some TLC," Adrian said. "Don't move. I'll be right back."

She needn't have worried, I had exhausted any moving energy I had going to the bathroom.

"Not to worry." I watched her naked back as she swung her legs over the side of the bed. Though the headache was making my vision blur, I still craved to touch that body. It annoyed me that I couldn't recall if I had, how much I'd touched, or if she had an orgasm.

While she was gone, I took an inventory. My pussy wasn't wet or sore, so that said we'd not done it. Even through this hangover, I wanted to. Desperately. Even though it was morning, the room was dark enough. I was wondering how that would go when she came back, closed her bedroom door, and took off her robe. She sat that remarkable body on the edge of the bed, two inches from me, and produced a large glass of water in one hand and opened her palm to reveal three small white pills.

"You're dehydrated, so you need to drink this whole glass and I will bring you another. Take these. You're not sick to your stomach, are you?"

No, surprisingly I wasn't. I only had an upset stomach that one time because of the flu.

I shook my head and she grinned as she watched me take the pills and down the glass of water.

"What are the pills? Aspirin?"

"Yep."

She came back with another glass of water. I drank that.

"Now just lie still for a while." She slid into bed next me and put her arms around me, and every nerve I had jumped to attention. I could feel her nipples against my back.

I turned over and looked at her. She was smiling sweetly.

"What happened last night?" I asked.

Adrian laughed lightly, "Oh, a lot of drinks, some dancing."

"Nothing else?"

"Nope, unless you count your putting one hand on my left breast before you passed out."

I was chagrined. "Really? I passed out on you?"

"You did. It was cute, but I was disappointed."

"I'm so sorry. I wanted to, but…" I was totally ashamed. "I don't usually pass out until I've made a girl happy."

"Oh, I'm sure that's true. Don't worry. I wasn't in great shape myself." She lay back down and embraced me again and we lay quietly for a while.

The water and the aspirin were slowly kicking in and my headache faded into background noise as my sex drive awakened. How would this go? I wasn't usually a person for morning sex. Usually I was in the process of leaving, I thought sarcastically.

"How are you doing?" Adrian asked.

I considered carefully before answering. "Not bad. Better, thanks."

I locked eyes with her and gave her a little smile I hoped was a sexy little smile.

She looked at me for a long moment. I dared to put a hand on the breast nearest me and her nipple hardened and tickled my palm. I squeezed her slightly. She didn't change expression but she closed her eyes and blew out a little breath.

She turned on her side, stroked my hip, then my stomach. She leaned over and put her lips on my mine. I nearly recoiled because I was afraid my breath was bad, but she wouldn't release me for a long moment.

Then she took her mouth away from mine but only long enough to say, "All right, let's see what you're all about."

Holy shit, I was fired up to make love to her but I was soon on my back, she was on top of me, and I was helpless. Maybe my hangover weakened me, but I was evidently not able to take over the momentum of sex in my usual fashion. In the back of my mind, I readied my standard excuses for my lack of orgasm. But for some reason, I didn't tense up, even though I was cold sober. I found the touch of other women clumsy at times, and if it wasn't, I always knew I could not achieve the desired result. That had become a self-fulfilling prophecy.

Adrian had an extraordinary touch that fell exactly midway between assertive and gentle. Even more miraculous, I *wanted* her to touch me. This unbelievably attractive woman was making love to me, and I was willing to submit. She didn't ask me any anxious questions about how this or that felt or whether some move or another was working or not. She was clearly concentrating on giving me pleasure, and that itself was arousing. I went limp and when I sensed the first mild signs of pending orgasm, I didn't tense, I waited. I waited and nothing happened. She stopped stroking me and lay back, keeping a hand on my breast.

"I think you need a break," she whispered. I was bereft, abandoned. But I breathed and nodded.

I rolled over and said, "I really want you."

"Then have me," she said and grinned. That was more like it. I can't come myself but I sure can do the trick for other women. And in this odd sober but hungover state, I was as eager as I'd ever been when I was drunk. She was a terrific partner, sensuous and eager. There was no hesitation and I quickly got her off. The feel and sound of her orgasm thrilled me and kicked my arousal onto a higher plane.

She rolled me over and picked up where she left off and I came abruptly, surprising the heck out of me. She left her fingers in place but stopped moving them as I struggled to catch my breath. She waited for a few moments and then began again. My second orgasm was as strong as the first. I swear the tops of my feet tingled.

We fell back asleep and woke in the late afternoon. I could tell because the sun was finally out.

Adrian said, "Well. I'm very sorry that our little get-acquainted party has to end. I've got some things to do, I'll call you later."

It was excruciating to have to leave her but I enjoyed the bus ride home with my thighs slick with come and the images of sex playing in my brain.

Chris was home when I arrived, lying on our couch. I told him the whole story, including my miraculous breakthrough.

"Wow, look at you. Finally you understand the joy of sex."

"Yeah, I think I do." The real question was when would I get a replay?

"Did you have a good parade day?" I asked.

He smiled dreamily and nodded.

"That guy, what's his name?"

"Andrew. I think he might be a keeper."

"Really?" I was astonished. I thought racking up the numbers was the name of the game for Chris.

"Yeah. He's different. He's sort of innocent, if you believe that."

"Not sure I do," I said, laughing, wondering how any gay guy in San Francisco could be called "innocent."

"He's more like innocent emotionally, not sexually. I don't know, he doesn't have that cynical edge like everyone else I meet. Like me too, I suppose. Except with him it all feels new."

"Adrian is, well, I can't describe her very well except that she's beautiful and, well, like I said, I actually had an orgasm, a bunch of them."

Chris grinned lasciviously at me. "I bet you'd like a few more too. She's very cute. That is what I call a romantic meeting. You asked her to move at the parade. That's a good story."

I grinned. "Yeah, it is, isn't it? I would love to see her again. Very much."

But Adrian didn't call me that night. I decided to wait until the next evening to call her.

Her tone was light, she seemed happy to hear from me. "Oh. Dear. Sorry. Yes. I was busy but hey, why don't we get together tomorrow?"

Chapter Three

The clinical trials were finally about to start. I struggled to concentrate at work since my mind wanted to fully occupy itself with either my memories of my previous night with Adrian or the anticipation of the one to come.

Somehow, Adrian possessed the clues to the mystery of my sexuality. When we were together, she was such a physical presence, but she was otherwise so elusive. It was a conundrum I vaguely wanted to solve, but meanwhile, I would take what I could get, which was, when I managed to see her, incredible mind-destroying sex.

At any time of the day or night, at work on the bus, wherever, if I thought about Adrian, I creamed my jeans. My body literally prepared itself to orgasm as though she was right there touching me. It was maddening and wonderful. When I heard her voice on the phone, I would get weak in the knees. But she was difficult to depend on. She wouldn't call when she said she would. We'd have a magical night together and then I wouldn't hear from her for a week.

Chris startled me out of one of these reveries one afternoon. I was at my desk supposedly working when he appeared at my side.

"Sarah told us to be ready for Thursday. She said, 'Once you guys give the green light, it'll ship to Washington.'"

"Wow. I guess we better make sure it passes all the assays."

"Yep. But it will." He patted my shoulder. Chris's self-assurance always buoyed my own rather shakier confidence. This had been true in our school days and was still true.

I wondered about Adrian. It had been a couple days since I'd last seen her. She was always vague about when we would next see each other. I was entirely at her mercy and it bugged me, but what could I do?

At that instant, I wanted a drink, but it was the middle of a workday. I forced myself to go into the lab and check through all the supplies to make sure we were ready to test the first batch of clinical trial antibody. While I worked, the song "Tainted Love" on the lab radio made me think of Adrian.

At home, I lay on my bed, watched the phone, and willed it to ring. I sipped my glass of vodka.

After parade day, I decided that brandy was just too hard on my system and switched to vodka. I read somewhere that, as a clear liquor, it had fewer additives. It seemed to work well. I mixed it with some Crystal Geyser sparkling water, so it was practically healthy.

"I'll call you," Adrian had said on Sunday morning and it was already fucking Wednesday. I was beside myself with anxiety.

I dialed Adrian's number, and miraculously, she picked up. That didn't happen often. She'd call back when I called her. Eventually.

"Hi there," I said brightly.

"Oh. Max, hi. I thought it was someone else."

"Nope." I said, all cheerful and laid back, "Just me. Hey, can I come over? Are you busy?"

She hesitated and then said, "Kind of but sure, why not? Should be done soon."

Yahoo. I threw some clothes and toothbrush in a bag and hightailed it over to her place. One of the mysterious things about Adrian was what kind of work she did.

"Sales," she told me when I asked but that was all, no elaboration.

She opened the door and kissed me quickly. I followed her down the hall to her living room. She had one of those long, narrow flats where the bedrooms were up front. She had no roommate, though, which was why we always slept together at her place. She'd come over to my apartment and was friendly with Chris, but she obviously preferred having control over *where* we met as well as when.

There on her couch sat a strange man. I managed to conceal my surprise and dismay. She left me there and went to the kitchen.

"Hello, I'm Max," I said to him. He wasn't exactly seedy looking but he clearly wasn't gay. He was a bit slovenly, his jeans were ragged, and he wore a stained sweatshirt.

Adrian came back and handed him some money.

"Go ahead. Count it."

"I will," he said, "Though I trust you."

"I know, but still…"

I didn't know what to say or where to look, so I did nothing. I was creeped out by this dude. The way he looked at me and then at Adrian boded no good.

"All here. So enjoy," he said brightly. He stared at me.

"Why are you looking at me?" It incensed me, I could tell what he was thinking.

"Nothing. No reason. Sorry."

"Right, see you next time," Adrian said firmly.

Seeming reluctant, he stood up, muttered a "See ya," and left. Creep.

Adrian sat down next to me on the couch, gave me a distracted kiss, and then inhaled.

"Who was that?"

"Nobody special. He's kind of a jerk. Thanks for helping me to get rid of him."

"He was in your living room and you handed him a wad of money." It was annoying to have to try and drag this information out of her.

"If you must know, he came over to sell me five hundred Valium."

"Five hundred?" I was aghast as well as impressed. Hmm. I'd never tried Valium, though I knew about it.

"Yep. Now I have to turn them over fast, and then once that's done, I can get some more."

"So, by sales you meant you're a drug dealer," I said, feeling idiotic.

"Yes, that is what I meant. Now you know."

"Now I know." I sounded like an echo. What did I think was the dilemma? I didn't know.

"Do you hate me?" Adrian kissed my neck. She likely knew the answer to that. She was well aware that I was enslaved to her because of sex. I was, wasn't I? I clearly was willing to endure any amount of uncertainty about her if she would still fuck me.

"So are you going to sample the merchandise?" I asked her.

"I usually do. That's the other thing, I wasn't sure how you'd feel about that."

"It's fine. If you let me sample it along with you." I grinned.

"But of course." She beamed. "But you, just to be safe, stop with the vodka. I have another idea." She went to the kitchen and returned with a bottle of white wine and two glasses.

Adrian sang, "Valium and white wine."

"Where's that from?" I asked.

"I made it up." I doubted that but let it go. Adrian often sang snippets of songs as a sort of emotional shorthand. It amused me. Sometimes. Such as when she sang to me, "Nothing would be finer than to be in your vagina in the mo-orning," when we were having sex.

She sat down on the couch, close to me. She poured us two glasses. I tamped down my dislike of white wine. If Adrian thought it was appropriate to wash down Valium, that's what I would do. In the end it was kind of irrelevant. Alcohol was alcohol *and* I wanted the effect of it plus Valium, that famous anti-anxiety drug. I knew when it came to drugs and alcohol that the whole was greater than the sum of the parts. I knew this from trying Quaaludes with Chris. What was the old Dow Chemical advertising tagline? "Better living through chemistry."

Grinning exuberantly at one another, we each took our little blue pills and swallowed some wine.

"Ahhh," Adrian said and smacked her lips. "Just wait."

"I know. I've done Quaaludes."

"Okey dokey. Those are good too, but sometimes hard to judge how much alcohol is too much."

"Oh, right." I recalled that I'd had about fifteen minutes of feeling really really good then I passed out. I didn't want to pass out this time. I had that mad craving for Adrian that I always got in her presence, and overindulgence would fuck up what I had planned. I forced myself to forgo my tendency to drain my glass and sipped.

"I was super curious about what it is you do and how you make money. I'm glad I know now."

Adrian's dark eyes flashed. "I'm glad you're cool with it. I was worried. That's why it took so long for me to tell you. I wasn't sure how you would take it and I'm starting to like you. A lot." She smiled bashfully.

Oh good. That was wonderful.

"I like you too. Very much." Just how much, she didn't have to know just yet.

"Oh, I picked up on that. 'Something in the way she moves.'"

"No, it's fine. That you do what you do," I said. And it truly was. Who the fuck was I to judge?

She kissed me. "Good."

Then she leaned back to scrutinize me. "How are you feeling?"

"Like I haven't got a care in the world."

"Outstanding." We necked a little bit. It was a sense of lightness, subtle at first then stronger. My head didn't get as woozy as it did with the Quaalude. And it was as she said it would be. I felt calm without a single thing to bother me.

Adrian crawled on top of me and pressed me into the couch. I was quiescent. It seemed like the most natural thing in the world as she removed my jeans and underwear and went down on me. I almost was floating above us, watching us. The orgasm when it came seemed long, drawn out, unfurling in a lazy, relaxed way. Whatever residual nervousness I had when Adrian made love to me—and there was still a mite—was completely gone.

"That was…" I said at last. But I couldn't finish my sentence. Nor did it seem important. I stroked Adrian's black hair as she rested her head on my stomach.

I was grateful, peaceful and happy.

The alarm clock ringing had to be the worst noise I'd ever heard in my life. It was like someone was drilling into my skull via the sound in my ear.

I jumped out of bed, though. Adrian groaned.

"I have to go to work," I told her, a little panicky. Somehow I'd remembered to ask her set an alarm. Who knows when we finally went to sleep. I recalled more wine, another Valium, and a lot more sex.

What time was it? And how long was it going to take me to get from the Mission up to Pacific Heights? I hadn't a clue.

In the shower, my knees were weak and I remembered we hadn't gotten around to eating anything. I needed to remedy that before I tackled Muni.

I found some bread in the kitchen and stuffed it into my face as I put my clothes on. At least it was Monday and I wouldn't have to face any pointed questions from my coworkers as to why I was wearing the same clothes as the day before.

Then as the hot shower and the bread helped get my brain working, it spat out the information that today we had to start all the QC tests for the clinical trial product.

Fortunately, I wasn't in too bad a state. I'd get some coffee before I went to the lab. We probably wouldn't start lab tests right away; my boss would have a meeting first. At least I hoped I wouldn't have to start lab operations before I got a chance to eat something else and generally finish waking up. My head was wooly and my mouth was dry, but otherwise things seemed to be in working order.

I wasn't super late to work—only about fifteen minutes.

"Come on, Max, Howard is waiting for you." This was Ellen. She was irreverent and fun to be around, but this morning she was keyed up.

We went to the conference room.

Howard was standing in front of the wipe board. He'd listed all the assays and who would do them.

"We're getting material at ten o'clock and we have to finish by four so they can ship overnight by Federal Express. Things have to pass. I'm sure you know that."

"They don't have backup lots?" Ellen asked.

"They do, but it's only in case of emergency. I know it's not our fault if stuff doesn't pass. But I don't want anything to go wrong that they can blame us for."

Ellen and I glanced at each other.

"All right. Here are the assignments."

Mine was the binding assay. I had to label the antibody portion of the conjugate with a radioactive tag and then add the solution to some cells, incubate them for a few hours, and then wash all the media and extra hot tag away and count everything in a scintillation counter. The amount of the radioactivity would tell us how well the product would bind to its target cancer cells. In theory, it wasn't a difficult test, and I'd done it plenty of times over the past months. There were lots of steps and it took several hours.

I went down to the hospital and got some crummy cafeteria food and more coffee. I was holding up but I was tired.

In the lab, I set up my bench and mixed and labeled all my solutions ahead of time so that all I had to do was wait. I sat at my desk and occupied my mind with pleasant memories of Valium, white wine, and sex with Adrian.

I must have dozed off because I woke up with a start as Ellen shook me.

"Showtime, Max." I jumped out of my chair too fast and it made me dizzy.

I threw on my lab coat and squared my shoulders. Ellen walked into the lab carrying a bunch of sterile 10 milliliter vials. They were labeled with two lot numbers and the same dates.

I took a vial of each lot number over to my bench. I had to use a plastic shield to mix them with the radioactive tag and some buffer. I worked at concentrating on each step and each movement. I then had to dilute the solution from full strength down to less than 5%. My vision got blurry and I had to struggle to read the dilutions. Good thing I did them in the same order every time, lowest to highest.

I brought in the plates full of cells. This was where it became tricky because the cell culture plates were hard to label and I couldn't use tape because I had try and keep everything clean in the incubator. I had used a Sharpie to write on the bottom of the plate, but sometimes that got smeared and I had to rely on my memory. Lab work is not forgiving of mistakes, and especially in quality control, you had to do it the same way exactly every time if you wanted to get reliable results. I was proud of my technique. I'd honed it to near perfection in the time I'd been in the QC group, but I was definitely not at my best today, so it would require extra attention.

I finished the cell labeling step, now it was a blessed few hours of waiting while the tags adhered to the cells. Or not.

That was the break I was looking for. I returned to my desk and put my head down. The office was deserted but who knew for how long. I was too keyed up to doze, so I opened my lab notebook and pretended to write in it. The morning's coffee had worn off and I was sleepy. I couldn't actually fall asleep, though; that would be very bad form.

More coffee was what I needed. I went to the kitchen and poured myself a cup of the hours-old brew. It was nasty. I tried to shake the pain out of my shoulders, but it was impossible. I wondered if I dared to take any aspirin. I drank some more coffee hoping it would help.

I went back to the lab and made sure I had everything I needed for the next steps. It was too early for lunch, but I went to the cafeteria anyhow and chowed down on a sandwich, took a quick trip outside for some air.

It was autumn, September or what San Franciscans call summer, people told me. It was sunny and a little warm. I physically woke up somewhat. But when I went back indoors, that drifted away and I was heading toward the post-lunch coma. I had one more hour of incubation. There were things I could have been doing but I just didn't have the energy. My only aim was to get through the rest of this assay, report my results, and then coast the rest of the afternoon until I could go home. I thought about seeing Adrian, but maybe not tonight. Whenever I was with her, it always turned into a long night. I needed to catch up on my sleep. I yawned involuntarily.

Back at my desk I opened a technical journal in front of me to look busy, I kept staring at the timer whenever my eyes were open but they always wanted to close. At last, at one thirty or so the timer dinged. Showtime. Again.

Fighting through my fatigue, I set my plates on the bench and labeled my counting vials. I picked up the second plate and—crap—I couldn't read the notes on the plate's lid. I struggled to make my mind work and remember how I'd loaded the wells I the plate. High to low? That had to be it. I added the cell culture media, but my hand started to shake and I splashed some. It was the stupid coffee. I took a breath and prayed it wouldn't muck up the results too much for that tube.

Done. At last. I loaded the vials into the counter, and it was another twenty-five-minute wait. Ellen came over to stand next to me.

"Howard said two thirty he's supposed to call Tony, then Abe." Tony was the production supervisor and Abe was the clinical trial coordinator.

"I'll be ready." I sounded more confident than I felt. "How about you?"

"Passed. So did Amy's sterility test."

I watched the LED on the scintillation counter show each number. It was silly because I wouldn't be able to tell until the machine spat out the printout. I squeezed my fists, willing the scintillation counter to work faster, which, of course, it couldn't.

I grabbed the printer paper and took it my desk so I could compare it to my notebook where I listed what each sample was.

My head ached and I stopped breathing. The results made no sense. The controls were not where they should have been. *Shit. Holy shit.* I went back to the lab and found the plate lids. How was this supposed to go? I couldn't remember what I did. Increasingly frantic, I looked at the list and then at the lid. But I couldn't figure out what I had put where. The numbers on the scintillation counter printout were useless.

In a stew of dread, I went to Howard's office. He stared at me stonily while I lamely tried to explain.

"You have no idea what went wrong?" he asked. "Not that it matters, if we don't have the results, we can't release the lots. All right. So. Yeah."

He was the guy who would have to tell everyone we couldn't ship out product that night. His expression as he looked at me said it all even if he wasn't the kind of person to berate me or yell.

In a very small voice, I asked, "Do you want me to start over?"

"No," he said, coldly. "There's not enough time. They have to ship by five p.m."

"Do you want me to stay while you call?"

He looked at me. "No, that's not necessary. You can repeat the binding assay tomorrow so we can release."

I cleaned up my lab bench. My arms were heavy. I moved mechanically, my mind thrumming. I had screwed up so badly I wasn't sure what would happen next. I noodled around the office until five p.m. hit and I could go home. I went to find Chris to ride the bus with me. I told him what happened and he shook his head sadly.

"Oh man. They're not going to be happy," he said.

I hung on to the pole as the bus careened down Fillmore Street.

"Were you at Adrian's last night?" he asked, looking at me, eyes narrow.

"Yep." I didn't want to confess to Chris who Adrian really was. "We were partying a little and, you know, one thing led to another and I didn't go to sleep until late."

Chris just stared at me for a long time until he said, "Don't fuck things up at Cal Genetics. It could come back on me. Just be careful, Max. I'm only telling you this for your own good."

That was bullshit. He didn't want to get in trouble. Chris always wanted to be the good boy and he hated to have anyone mad at him.

After we ate dinner I went to my room and drank vodka and watched TV, trying not to think about my terrible day or what might happen next.

❖

I reran the binding assay and nothing more was said. Except Howard switched tests for Ellen and me and I would perform the sterility testing, a simple-minded exercise. But I didn't protest, it wasn't worth it.

Through the rest of autumn, I started spending more time over at Adrian's apartment. She was gone for long stretches of time, taking care of business, I assumed. I didn't want to ask a lot of questions. It was enough that when she was around, we had a good time. Sex and drugs and rock and roll, I would say to myself and smile. A lot of all three.

I loved the fact that Adrian was okay with me hanging around in her flat even if she wasn't there. It helped convince me I was part of a real couple, and I was thrilled. I didn't long for the old days of cruising in bars and one-night stands. Adrian was everything I needed or wanted. If she was gone on mysterious business, I missed her, but I told myself it didn't bother me. It was just her.

I didn't even think twice when the phone rang one night when she was gone. I picked it up and said hello.

"Uh, er. Is Adrian around?" The voice was female and sounded surprised and confused.

"No, she's not, can I take a message?"

"Just tell her Rhonda called."

"Does she have—" Click. She hung up. That was rude.

Later, I told Adrian that Rhonda had called.

"What did you say?"

"I just said you weren't here, I asked her to leave a message. She hung up on me."

"Don't answer the phone, just let the machine pick it up."

"I don't mind, I can"—I started to say but I stopped talking when I saw Adrian's expression.

"I said, don't answer my phone. Ever." Her tone was furious. It couldn't be the drug stuff, I knew all about that. What?

"Okay. I won't. Don't be mad." I really hadn't meant to pick a fight. I was hoping for some more Valium. I'd had a long day and we'd just got word there was another site added to the clinical trial and to be ready to test another product release. I wanted to relax big time.

I asked Adrian, "What are we doing tonight?"

"Nothing, as far as I know." She still sounded a little pissed-off.

"I mean…I wondered…if you know…" I sounded lame, but I really wanted to know.

"Oh yeah. I got what you need. Not to worry but just so we're clear, you're going to have to promise you'll do things my way. Everything's fine as long as you do things my way." She put an arm around me. I don't think she was joking even though her tone was humorous.

"Yeah. Of course. Always." It sounded a bit like a threat was lurking there.

We were seated on the couch and I reached over to pull her head toward me so I could kiss her. She didn't seem as warm as she usually was. I became even more nervous.

When I broke the kiss, I said in as heartfelt a tone as I could muster, "Adrian, You know you can trust me. Always."

She peered at me as though weighing whether I was telling the truth.

"Yes, I know. Don't worry." She wasn't exactly cold, but she didn't seemed convinced.

She reached into her pocket and brought out a little enamel box. I recognized it as the one she kept her own drugs in. I watched her put it on the coffee table.

She grinned then and said, "Why don't you go pour us some wine."

I jumped up to obey and when I came back, she opened the box and held it out to me.

"Go ahead, girlfriend," she said. I grabbed the little blue pill and downed it, followed by a healthy swallow of chardonnay. I started to relax even before the Valium hit my brain.

The mysterious Rhonda showed up a few days later to buy drugs, and amidst the strained and overly casual small talk, I detected something was off about her. For one thing, she seemed very nervous and it didn't seem to be about buying the pills. For another, Rhonda's eyes tracked Adrian's movements around the room. She never took her gaze off Adrian, not for even one little second. It was unnerving to see another woman do the same thing I did. There was something going on.

After business was concluded, she left.

I confronted Adrian. "Who is that?"

"What do you mean who is that?" Adrian said, faux indignant.

"Are you sleeping with her?"

"It's nothing," Adrian said, not looking at me. "We never said we'd be monogamous."

"I thought it was given."

"Interesting you would make that assumption," Adrian said coldly. "She's not important. It's good customer service for a good customer is all. I like Rhonda. I want to keep her coming back for more."

"More drugs or more you?" I was dangerously close to crying.

"Look, I'll end it, okay? It really has nothing to do with you."

"Okay." I stopped sniffling, feeling like a dope. I noticed, though, she never promised to not do it again.

CHAPTER FOUR

When I told Chris about it, he shook his head.

"Max, this is not good for you. This is not like you. Dump that bitch."

"I'm not ready to do that," I said. "I want to wait and see." What I didn't say was between the easy orgasms and ready supply of Valium, I was unable to let go of Adrian. Being deprived of either would kill me, I was sure. I wouldn't tell Chris that, I couldn't handle his judging me.

I changed the subject.

"What's up with you and Andrew?"

"Oh, we're fine. He's just had the flu for the last three weeks. He feels awful, poor baby. His doctor isn't sure what's wrong with him."

"That's too bad. Means no sex for a while. Poor you."

"That's what that means. Thanks for reminding me." Then I was sorry. Andrew obviously meant more to Chris than just good sex.

"So next week, the trial is on again. Are you ready?" he asked me.

"Yeah. I'm ready. Psyched, as a matter of fact." I meant it, though I still had some lingering doubt. I didn't want to screw up again and I prayed I wouldn't, but buried under my outward confidence was the fear that was exactly what I would do.

After my encounter with Rhonda, Adrian was as sweet as could be. She was still AWOL a lot of the time and I gritted my teeth and kept my mouth shut. We had sex every time we were together.

I no longer smoked much pot since I had discovered Valium was so much more efficient. I had to be careful, though, not to drink too much on top of the Valium or I would pass out too soon. Like during sex.

I didn't know this had happened until Adrian told me. One night we were doing it and I fell asleep when I was going down on her.

"I knew something was wrong because your tongue stopped moving," she said. She was more amused than annoyed, but I was chagrined.

She continued, "I rolled you over on your side and finished myself off."

"Oh. That's why I woke up with the blanket on me but almost halfway down the bed. I'm sorry."

"Don't worry, it happens."

"Yep." I was still embarrassed. But not enough to stop doing Valium and white wine.

Adrian had me try all manner of substances with her. One day she came home and said, "This isn't something I'm going to sell, but Arnold told me about it." Arnold was the name of her skanky drug source. I wasn't sure I would take Arnold's recommendation on anything.

I must have looked dubious because she laughed and said, "It doesn't need a prescription or anything. You can just buy it over the counter." She grinned when she saw my expression.

From her bag, she brought out a box of little metal canisters that looked exactly like the tanks of carbon dioxide we used at work.

"What's this?" I asked.

"Whippets. They're for whipped cream. It's nitrous—laughing gas. Like the dentist gives you."

"Oh." I said, intrigued. "But how...?"

"Patience, my pretty, I will demonstrate."

Adrian had a certain flair for things. She used her Swiss Army knife mini ice pick arm to puncture the top of a whippet and then quickly snapped a rubber balloon onto it. We listened to the hiss of the gas and watched the balloon fill up. When it was full, Adrian drew the canister out, replaced it with her mouth, and inhaled. Her face went slack and her eyes closed. She slumped on the couch and literally began to laugh.

"Oh wow, baby, what a rush."

I let her do one for me. When the cool gas hit my lungs, the rush swooped into my brain and boom, instant euphoria. We spent the rest of the afternoon on the couch, inhaling the entire box of whippets and laughing like maniacs.

A few weeks later, Adrian sat me down and said, "I've got

something I might want to add to my wares, but I think you and I ought to try it first."

"I don't want to try anything new tonight. We have the product release again tomorrow."

Because Adrian didn't have a regular job, she was entirely ignorant of the concept of workdays.

"Come on, it'll be fine. I have to get back to Arnold tomorrow since he's got another buyer, but he wants to sell it to me—all of it. I have to give him an answer." I had heard these sorts of specious arguments from her before.

I was certainly interested. I was always up for a new sensation. Even during the week.

"Okay, but let's do it now."

Adrian handed me a blue and red pill.

"What's it called?"

"Tuinal," she said. "For sleep. If nothing else, you'll get a good night's sleep. That will help you tomorrow, right?"

I swallowed it, washing it down with vodka.

"Yeah that'll help."

It didn't, or not really. For one thing, I didn't get high from it so much as just slide into unconsciousness way too fast. I had some truly bad dreams and I almost slept through my alarm.

As I crawled out of bed, Adrian groaned.

"Motherfucker. That was like a sledgehammer."

"Yeah." I moaned. "I feel like my head weighs about fifty pounds."

No amount of coffee had the tiniest effect. I was dragging, that was for sure. At least I was assigned to the sterility test, the one I had originally performed for audition for the QC group. Unlike the binding assay, it ought to be a piece of cake despite my dopeover.

Never doing Tuinals again, I told myself. They were worse than Quaaludes—about five minutes of wooziness followed by oblivion.

Four hours later, I was sitting in Howard's office, shaking.

"What happened this time?" he asked.

"I don't know," I said, sullenly, hating myself. "I swore I did it by the book."

"Wrong book, I guess."

"I'll do it again," I said desperately. "It'll work." I had no such assurance. I couldn't be sure of anything anymore.

"No, you won't. Ellen will do the retest," Howard said.

The next day, Howard brought me in and told me I was on probation for one month. At the end of the month, he'd evaluate me again. No more Mr. Nice Guy.

"If you're not able to perform your job, I'm going to have to fire you." He could do that, I knew. Cal Genetics was a private company and California was a right-to-work state. He didn't need a reason to fire me, he could just do it. He was doing me a favor by putting me on probation. I had to straighten up, so to speak. I snickered to myself even though nothing was funny. If I knew what I was doing wrong that would have helped, but I didn't. I could only keep trying and hope for the best.

"You're on probation?" Chris asked rhetorically. "That sucks. Big time."

"Yes, it sure does." I was mopey. I couldn't go over to Adrian's and drown my sorrows. She was "busy." Busy doing what exactly, I didn't ask.

I needed a drink. But Chris was off to Andrew's since he was still ailing. There I was alone again, naturally. Who sang that? I couldn't remember.

It was just me and my bottle of vodka and TV. Chris had had cable installed, so our reception was good.

I sat in the armchair and poured a big glass of vodka. I drained half of it. It hit my stomach then whooshed back up to my head. The first drink was always the best. By the third drink, nothing mattered. I found something to watch. *Hill Street Blues.* Cops. I lost myself in their problems. The captain, Furillo was his name, made reference to the fact that he used to drink but he didn't anymore. Easy for him. I saluted the TV with my glass of vodka. He was sleeping with a gorgeous district attorney. I wondered distantly what it would be like to not drink. It seemed like a horrible way to live.

❖

I tried to ignore the possibility that I would be fired. It was in the realm of the unimaginable and I struggled to not think about it. I had other things on my mind, anyhow.

After Rhonda, I took care not to complain to Adrian much lest she stop giving me Valium. Or 'ludes. She'd added them to her list of products. Also Darvon, Percodan, codeine number three. A veritable cornucopia of happy pills.

They resided in an old-fashioned cookie jar, a rotund bear who was in one of the kitchen cabinets. Adrian, for all her flakiness with me, kept track of the numbers of the stash with accountant-like precision. I didn't dare steal any because she would know. I had to ask for what I wanted and she had to give it to me. I could visualize all the pills tucked into ziplock bags in the fat belly of the bear.

Howard called me into his office about two months after the last lab test fiasco and told me. I was suffused with dread because I already knew what was coming. I had made another error, not a really dire one, so I had my fingers crossed he'd let it go. But no.

"This isn't working out, Max. We're letting you go."

I sat there across from him, silent, just staring. I didn't even mount a protest. I suppose it was inevitable. He had me leave the same day. I got six weeks of severance pay.

On my way home, though, I was in oddly good mood. No more worrying about assays and messing them up. No more Fillmore bus rides with all the noisy teenagers that made my head hurt worse than it already did. I was free.

"What are you going to do now?" Chris asked me.

"Look for another job. What else would I do?" I said. I was unaccountably annoyed with him. He wasn't around, and if he was, his attitude with me was strange. He was sorry that I was fired but he also thought somehow it reflected back to him. He tried to talk me out of seeing Adrian but I shut him down. I started spending even more time at her flat so I wouldn't have to talk to him.

How I was going to make my half of the rent was my biggest problem. I needed to conserve my last paycheck.

I approached Chris with a proposal.

"Can I skip this month's rent and pay you back when I get a job?"

We were sitting on our couch at opposite ends. Chris wrinkled his forehead and stared at the ceiling in frustration.

He didn't say anything for a long time, then he sighed and said, "Okay, Max, okay. But you have to give me the money for next month."

"I will, I promise," I said. But even as I said it I wasn't sure I believed it. That would likely mean I would have to call my dad, and I wanted nothing to do with that mean old drunk. I only talked to him if I had to. My mom had no money since she'd divorced him, so asking her was out.

But it occurred to me that if I didn't have a job, I could drink whenever I wanted to. That cheered me up.

I dutifully read the newspaper want ads every day, but it was kind of pointless. I was no closer to finding a job then I was when I got fired. What the hell was I going to say anyhow? I'd have to figure something out. Chris was going to ask me for the rent pretty soon and I didn't have it. I still couldn't bring myself to call my dad and probably have to listen to him lecture me about responsibility.

The days were so boring—rainy and grim. The first of the year came and went. I decided it was not worthwhile trying to find a job until after the holidays. I'd done the holiday employment thing before and I couldn't bring myself to do it again.

I spent less time with Adrian. She had made it clear I had to give her space. Screw her, but if that was the price of still seeing her, I'd have to cope. Chris was hardly ever around, and if he was, he was a drag. Andrew was still sick; in fact, he was in the hospital.

"They don't know what's wrong with him. He's got these weird infections I've never heard of." When he was home, Chris would sometimes have a drink with me, but all he could talk about was poor sick Andrew.

The first week of January 1983 was upon me and I *had* to find a job. Soon. There wasn't much in the newspaper. I called Adrian and left her a message. We hadn't seen each other for a few days and I was out of Valium, so I needed to sweet-talk her into giving me some more.

Chris called to say he wouldn't be home till late, he was going to the hospital.

I sat in front of the TV, sipping vodka and waiting for Adrian to call back and Chris to come home. I must have passed out because the next thing I knew, Chris was shaking me. I struggled to wake up.

He picked up my vodka and drank straight from the bottle. He looked terrible. In my head two things were going on. One was "Get your own booze" and the other was wondering what was wrong. Fortunately, the second train of thought was the one that I voiced. I could see he was crying.

"What's wrong?"

"Andrew's dead."

"Dead? How can he be dead?" This wasn't registering with me.

"He stopped breathing. His lungs were full of those crazy protozoans. They couldn't help him." Chris recited this mechanically.

"I'm sorry," I said. And I was. I put my arms around him and he alternately sobbed and babbled about Andrew. I could tell he was exhausted and feeling sick.

The next day, Chris called in sick, but he just sat and stared at the TV. I was at a loss for words. I just sat with him. Adrian called back finally and said, "Yes, come over."

"I have to go."

"Uh-huh. Say, are you planning to pay your rent and the back rent you owe me?"

This was just the question I'd been dreading.

"I can't just yet, Chris, but I'm going in to apply for a job tomorrow." This wasn't true, but I had to say something.

"Max, I think you ought to leave. You need to find a new place to live. I'm tired of your shit."

I was shocked. "Chris, I'll find a way. Please. but I'll figure something out. Give me until next month. Please."

He glared at me and coughed. He looked terrible, and I wasn't sure it was only Andrew's death. He looked sick.

"Okay, but only one more month, okay? I'm really not in the mood to deal with you."

❖

I forced myself to apply for some jobs, but it didn't do any good. The newspaper sucked. I couldn't face having to work at a restaurant. I told Chris the following month that I couldn't make rent or pay him back.

It killed me, but I pleaded with him to give me more time.

"No. I'm done. Just pack up and leave. You're irresponsible and you're a drunk. I'm tired of it all. I'm just tired, period. You're still my friend but I can't keep carrying you."

Although I was horribly hurt, I couldn't summon the energy to argue with him. I went and pulled together what I could. I'd have to plead with Adrian to let me stay with her. Maybe he'd change his mind later and let me come back.

I didn't have the money to spare but I took a cab to Adrian's flat anyway. When she opened the door and saw me standing there with a suitcase, her face darkened.

"Chris threw me out," I said. "Can I please stay with you?"

She turned away and I followed her.

"Adrian. Please. Just for a little while, until I find a job." I was worse than pathetic, I was a total loser.

She rubbed that beautiful face of hers in exasperation.

"Yeah, okay, but we're not exclusive, okay? You can't complain when I bring home other women or try to control me."

"Yeah. Sure. Right. Of course. I just need a place to crash for a while. That's all. I can help you with stuff. Do whatever you need."

"Fine. You can sleep on the couch." That was not what I had in mind. I still thought she was hot. I hadn't stopped wanting her. Other things…got in the way. I also had to get her to part with some Valium.

"Whatever you want. I'm not going to dictate anything," I said fervently.

As much as I hated asking, I needed to.

"Uh, Adrian, can I get some blues? I don't have any money. Maybe trade?"

She looked at me, then smirked.

"Yeah, that'd be fine. The thing is, Rhonda's coming over later but I'm not sure I can, you know, wait."

I didn't say anything but moved toward her, kissed her tenderly, unzipped her jeans, and lowered her to the couch. At least, Rhonda would get sloppy seconds. That thought comforted me. She was still sweet, God help me. I got the tingles when she came but I knew not to ask for anything else back. I had already asked for something so I had to be careful.

She put herself back together and went to the kitchen and came back and dropped three Valium in my palm. I'd have to make them last. Or maybe I had another alternative. There were only so many places she could hide the cookie jar in the kitchen. All I needed was an opportunity. Since I was going to be here presumably by myself it ought not to be hard. Maybe she wouldn't miss the pills if I was careful.

Rhonda arrived, gave me some smug glances, and the two of them wound themselves together on the couch. I sat and made casual small talk with them until they disappeared into Adrian's bedroom.

No sweat. I camped out in the living room and had my own little party, starting with giving myself an orgasm.

A couple days later, Adrian said. "I've figured out how you can help me. I did this gig a while back before I met you, but they know me now, so I can't do it again but you could."

"Do what?" I asked.

"You have to sign up for Medicaid and go to this doctor on Haight Street and get drugs. Legally."

Oh. Hmm. Well, it didn't sound that bad. I had to go apply for welfare and food stamps too, so why not. I hoped she'd let me keep some of the drugs for myself and not insist on selling them all.

Clearly, being unemployed was a full-time job. Each of the social services I wanted to sign up for took up a full day. The social workers I talked to weren't unkind, but they had gone through these conversations with people like me so many times their job satisfaction, whatever it might have started at, had long since disappeared. I kept my anxiety tamped down enough so that I was polite to them. I'm sure that helped me get through the process. Not that many of my peers in those offices talking to the social workers had much patience or politeness left.

One day, I had to show up in person at the welfare office, and I sat there for five hours. The boredom made me fall into a conversation with a middle-aged black dude sitting next to me. His number was not far from mine, but both our numbers were far from the number showing who was being helped at that second.

"Yeah, girl, this is the biggest drag in the world, I'm telling you. Gov'mint don't want you to have what's coming to you. I heard Mr. Reagan talk about the welfare queens. He talking about the black folks. You got to know their code. You know what I'm saying?"

"Yeah, well, we're not all black."

"I hear that. Just look around." He gestured at the waiting area. It was true, there was a rainbow's variety of people. We all had a common look, though: tired and bored.

My new friend, whose name was Jake, said, "You know about the plasma people, don't you?"

"No, who are they?"

"Girl, you got to go check that out. You can sell your own plasma twice a week for twelve bucks a pop, if you ain't scared of needles. You're young and healthy, they happy to get your plasma."

"Needles don't bother me." I agreed with the young part, but I wasn't sure about the healthy. My blood was likely 20% alcohol.

"There you go. They over on Howard Street. Not far from detox. Ha ha. Those people at detox, they're good customers." He laughed at his joke.

Jake and I moved on to talk about music and TV, and so we passed the time until I was called. I put the idea of selling plasma into the back of my mind.

"Hey, thanks, man. See you." I shook hands with him and plopped myself down in a chair next to a desk commanded by a social worker who looked as dragged out as I felt.

I finally received my Medicaid card in August. Adrian gave me the name and phone number of the pill doctor, and I duly obtained an appointment the following month. Adrian coached me on what to say. "Say you're nervous all the time and you have back pain. Those are the best symptoms. You can get some good painkillers and more Valium. We can get good prices for both."

"I *am* actually nervous and my back hurts. What about me?"

"Don't worry, we'll take care of you." Adrian laughed and kissed my cheek. I hoped that was true. She'd ditched Rhonda and we were back sleeping together. If I wasn't broke, I'd be in good shape.

At Dr. Harper's dingy office on Haight Street, I sat and waited for a long time, again. The other patients looked a lot like my compatriots from welfare and food stamps.

Dr. Harper proved to be an older disheveled man who asked me questions in a manner that told me all I needed to know about the nature of his practice. Disinterested. I left with my two prescriptions and went to the nearest drugstore to get them filled. While I waited in line for the pharmacy, I could swear I saw the same people who'd been in Dr. Harper's office, but maybe I was paranoid. I wondered if I could just go back home and chill out or if I ought to go to the plasma place. It would be worth it to snag twelve bucks. That would take care of a pint of vodka and couple packs of Newports, plus it would cover my bus fare.

But when I arrived, the line was around the block. Looked like it was a popular pastime for the other down-and-outers. Like me. I checked with someone at the end of the line, a scraggly woman with a backpack.

"Yeah, it's better if you get here when they open at eight," she advised me.

I made my way home, where I scraped together enough change to buy a half pint, which wasn't nearly enough to last the night. I had my trusty stash of drugs, but it wasn't really mine since Adrian wanted to turn a profit on them.

But she had told me not to worry, "we" would take of me.

She left me alone that night, and that was just fine. I set myself up in the living room, arraying my vodka and the two pills I planned to take. One each of Valium and the codeine. I admired them for a few minutes, then I swallowed them with some water followed by vodka, turned on the TV and sat back, and waited for the magic to happen.

Of course, the next morning it was raining. Just the perfect day to have to take Muni downtown. During rush hour. I had awakened, cotton mouthed and headachey but not too destroyed. I must have passed out on the couch early. I didn't have any time to eat if I wanted to arrive at the plasma center at opening.

The scene at the plasma center was inescapably dreary, and not just because it was raining. They opened the door finally and let us in. The nurses who ran the center were nicer than social workers I'd recently dealt with. It was all pretty routine. They checked my blood pressure and hematocrit and I passed. The needles they used were enormous, though. I made myself not look. They fed saline into me as they withdrew the blood. The whole thing was over with in a half hour.

I left the plasma center thinking I'd go home and eat. I didn't want to waste my precious twelve bucks on restaurant food. I stopped at a corner store and bought a pint of vodka.

As I continued to walk up Seventh Street toward Market and the Muni station, I began to feel really light-headed. Fuck. I needed to sit down before I passed out. My vision swam and my knees started to give way as I ducked into a small diner-like place just because the chairs were beckoning me.

I sat down just in time before I fell down. Maybe some water would do the trick. I looked around to see if there was a server. Nope. There was an older woman at the cash register. One customer was there with her back to me.

I waved to get the attention of the woman at the counter. She said "excuse me" to her customer and walked over to me.

"You're going to need to leave."

"Could I just get a glass of water?" I asked, not believing she'd throw me out.

"Nope, you have to leave. Before I call the cops."

The blackness behind my eyeballs was threatening to take over and my head felt like it was going to fall off. I felt nauseated but not like I was about to throw up. I was dangerously close to passing out.

"It's okay. She's with me," I heard a voice say. It was a familiar voice.

"I don't serve drunks in here. They're a hassle." This I knew was the owner of the restaurant.

"Are you drunk?" the familiar voice asked and I opened my eyes with a lot of struggle.

I knew who it was. I just couldn't place her name or where I knew her from. Her face peering at me with an expression I interpreted as sympathetic was nice. *She's blonde. Cute.*

I croaked, "No. I just gave blood. I need to eat."

"Yeah. You do. Here drink some of this." She shoved the go cup of coffee at me.

I sipped, but it was really hot. I noticed that I'd slapped my pint of vodka in its paper bag on the table.

She left and came back with a donut, and I saw her eyes flick toward my vodka.

"Don't they give you something to eat when you donate blood?" She sat down across from me.

I took a bite of the donut and almost immediately began to feel better, so I could at last focus on my savior. I knew her face.

"I'm Laurie," she said. "You're Max, right?"

"Right. I'm Max." Why was she here and why did she buy me a donut?

I took another bite of the donut. "The plasma center doesn't hand out any donuts or juice. Not like a Red Cross blood donation. They pay you, though."

"Oh, yeah. The plasma center," Laurie said as though she was describing a den of iniquity. She probably noticed the customers in line and made judgments about them.

I vaguely remember the circumstances of our meeting, and I was embarrassed she was seeing me in this state. I must appear really bedraggled. I was damp from being in the rain and probably pale. I *felt* pale.

I finished the donut. "Where do I know you from?"

"Peg's Place. A few months back. I was waiting for my friend. We talked. You don't remember?"

"Oh right. What are you doing here?" I asked and it came out way more hostile than I meant it.

"I work a few blocks away at an insurance office. I came over to grab a cup of coffee."

"Oh." I was in a ratty raincoat, nearly passing out from hunger in Skid Row. My bottle of booze sat in front of us. Swell.

"You looked like you could use a hand, so..." She shrugged, but she was looking at me closely in a way that made me uneasy. I recalled her attitude when we met at Peg's Place. It wasn't pity exactly, but she seemed as though she was concerned about me. I sort of liked and was curious about that, but I pushed the feeling away. I decided I didn't actually care for the way she was looking at me, like she understood far more about me than I did. Far more than she possibly could have gleaned in our brief meetings.

"Thanks for the donut. Saved my life."

"How often do you sell your blood?" she asked.

I was offended. What did she mean by that?

"This is the first time. I just need some extra cash."

"Uh-huh." She fell silent and continued to stare at me. She was thinking of something.

"You don't have to live this way, you know." She nodded at the pint of vodka sitting on the table by my elbow.

"What's that mean?" I was becoming angry. This sounded like the beginning of a lecture. This was not worth one donut.

"I'm just saying. I know what you're going through. I have to go back to work, I'm late, but here's my number. Call me if you need help. If you want to get sober, I can help you. Here." She forced the piece of paper into my hand. "Take care, Max. Seriously, call me anytime if you just want to talk."

She had some nerve. What kind of assumptions was this chick making about me? Did she think I had a drinking problem? She likely had one if she didn't drink but didn't need to put that on me. Cute or not, donut or not, I was pissed.

"Thanks for the donut and coffee." I wouldn't have accepted them if I'd known what strings were attached.

Sober? Why did she say that? I wasn't drunk. Just a little hungover maybe. I jammed the piece of paper into the pocket of my raincoat and made my weary way back to Adrian's flat.

CHAPTER FIVE

The phone rang and I listened to the answering machine pick up, then I lunged to grab the receiver. It was the messenger service I'd called from a newspaper ad finally calling back.

Yes, I would love to come downtown and talk to them. Thank goodness I'd not had anything to drink yet. I pulled myself together and went to the interview, and just like that I had a job, of a sort. The pay was shit, the work would be mindless, but I didn't care.

It didn't take long for me to master the routine of Legal Partners work and even less time to integrate into the office routine, which suited me just fine after all.

I arrived at eight a.m. and Jay, the manager, greeted me with a couple lines of coke.

He always said the same thing, "Things go better with coke."

And I always laughed and said, "Better than coffee."

He used coke to keep his process servers in line. Fortunately, I wasn't a process server, I was a messenger, and he was just being nice.

Legal Partners provided services to the multiple law firms in downtown San Francisco. There were the process servers who also did courier work, using their cars if needed. Then there was me and another guy, Rob, who took care of picking up and filing legal papers each morning, then returning the copies and retrieving more from the law offices each afternoon.

Suitably jazzed up from a couple of lines, Rob and I collected all the paperwork and walked across Market and Seventh Streets to the UN Plaza and then on to San Francisco City Hall clerk's office. The location of our office was certainly convenient to the courts in the Civic Center. Most of our filings were for cases in the municipal and superior courts of San Francisco. A few we would have to walk across the street to the State Building and a couple more blocks to the US district court in the Federal Building.

Hundreds of homeless people camped out on the UN Plaza and Civic Center Plaza that we had to traverse to reach City Hall. I never knew what we would encounter.

We walked past a guy throwing up and I quickly averted my eyes. Another homeless dude came up to us and said, "Hey, General Custer. Got a cigarette?" I think he was Native American. Rob had long blond hair. Rob laughed and gave him one.

"Giants game last night?" I asked Rob.

He nodded. He told me that the only way to survive night games at Candlestick Park was to drink. The baseball stadium had been thoughtfully built on a small peninsula called Candlestick Point sticking out in the Bay so as to afford maximum exposure to the ocean winds and summer fog.

We entered the county clerk's office. Standing next to Rob at a counter, sorting our legal papers, I could smell the beer he'd drunk, and it nauseated me.

I wasn't doing so well myself. A couple lines of coke and a bracing walk across the plazas generally woke me up at least. I had a pounding headache, though. Adrian had been home the night before, and so we partied hearty. I no longer even cared about fucking her. Most of the time.

I'd not eaten any breakfast and my stomach felt funny, so I went downstairs to the snack counter and bought a box of Junior Mints. I popped them as we sorted our filings.

I went to the window of my favorite clerk, Marty. He was an acerbic older guy who always had a cigarette burning next to his elbow. He reviewed the original documents before he stamped them with the date and handed me the copies. Each slam of his stamp echoed in my head and increased my pain.

"Hey, Marty, can you please pad that?" He smirked at me. That's how I told him I was hungover. He slid his copy of the *SF Chronicle* newspaper underneath the papers. It helped. A little.

Rob and I hoofed it back to the office and sorted everything into oversize folders labeled with the law offices' names and addresses.

"You got a joint?" I asked him. He nodded.

We went to the alley behind the office and smoked. Across Seventh Street was another whole population of derelicts. They were a combination of overflow from Skid Row at Sixth and Howard Streets, which was only three blocks away, and the customers of the Greyhound bus terminal directly across the street. We were typically set upon by people asking for money cigarettes, dope, whatever.

I ate a sandwich and we prepared to go out for deliveries. I felt only marginally better. The coke had long since worn off, and I didn't want to ask Jay for more. A little marijuana buzz was better than nothing, but not by much. The thought of Chris popped into my head and I wondered how he was doing. I was only a little pissed at him for booting me out. I guess I deserved it. I still didn't have enough money for half the rent. I didn't have enough to give Adrian more than a few bucks for food. She seemed fine with it, and I didn't say anything. Why stir up trouble when I didn't have to? When some woman came over to sleep with her, I felt slight stirrings of jealousy, but as I promised, I never said a thing. Rhonda had been replaced with Cindy, who was replaced with Maggie. Sleeping on the couch was getting old, though.

I had arranged my stops in the most efficient pattern so I didn't have to backtrack, but I could still look forward to a couple hours of walking. The first office I went to, Logan and Prince, I was in and out in a flash. Their receptionist was not one of the friendly ones.

As I rode the elevator down from their office on the twenty-ninth floor of the Russ Building, I tried to ignore the unspoken but quite obvious disdain of the well-dressed professional people who shared the elevator with me. I was a messenger and to them a being to ignore, a necessary evil. I tried to forget that I possessed an education and an intellect equal to or better than theirs. This was not obvious since I wore tattered blue jeans, an old sweater, and scuffed sneakers, whereas the women all wore power suits with big shoulders and the men wore expensive ties and pinstripes.

At the grand oak-paneled offices of the Major, Trewlawney, Forest & Briggs law office way up on the penthouse of the Flood Building, I stopped to rest because their receptionist, Anne, was nice to me. This wasn't always the case either. Some of the front-desk people were as snooty as the lawyers and bankers and securities traders who snubbed me in the elevator.

"Hi, Max, how's it going? Good to see you." Anne was a gorgeous black woman. I wondered how she felt in the overwhelmingly white world of the Financial District, but I never asked.

"Can I sit for minute?"

"Let me see." She checked her calendar or something and then said, "Yeah, it's okay. You want some tea?"

"Sure." Thus I could, in some law offices, get a little respite from my labors and a friendly word.

It didn't last long, though. I was off in ten minutes. And when the elevator dropped me into the building lobby, I could see out the huge glass doors that it had begun to rain.

❖

Adrian said, "Some guy called you."

"Who? Chris?" I was seated on my end of the couch, cradled by a dent that was the shape of my ass. In front of me on the coffee table I'd arrayed my cigarettes, lighter, ashtray, pint of vodka, and glass. I had a bottle of Crystal Geyser water. I'd lately begun chasing the vodka with it, thinking to dilute the vodka so I could drink more for a longer period of time. I'd not talked to Chris in months. I didn't want to call him because he was mad at me and I was mad at him and it would be hard to talk. I missed him terribly.

"No, not him. I don't know. Some guy. Here's his number." She had indeed only written a number down and not a name.

"Thanks," I said, wondering not for the first time if I should find a new place to live. I had not the motivation or money to do so, however.

I dialed the number and to the male voice that answered, I said, "This is Max Cooper. Someone from this number called me."

"Oh. Yeah. That was me. I'm Tony, friend of Chris's."

My hand tightened on the phone.

"Hi, Tony," I said, my voice tight. A sort of unformed dread floated in my mind. If Chris wasn't calling me himself, what did that mean? I thought guiltily it had been about eight months since I had last talked to him after Andrew died and he'd kicked me out.

"Hi, Max, Chris asked me to call you." His tone was odd, not angry but not super friendly. Resigned, I guess I'd call it. "He's in the hospital. Ralph K. Davies."

"What's the matter with him? Is he okay?" I thought accident or gay bashing and I was terrified.

"He's stable for now. He's got pneumocystis and he's on a respirator. He just wanted you to know."

He wanted me to know. Did that mean he wanted to see me? He knew I wasn't a fan of hospitals. When he was in Ralph K. Davies for hepatitis B, I only visited him once. What the fuck was pneumocystis?

"When can he go home?" I asked. Better I see him at home, I decided.

"Don't know. His doctors don't know if he's going to get well."

I wasn't sure if I heard correctly.

"Not get well? What do you mean?" I took a gulp of vodka. It burned my throat but then the alcohol rush welled up into my brain.

"He's got it."

"What's it?" I was becoming angry at this Tony guy's attitude.

"AIDS."

"I still don't understand, you said he has something called pneumocystis."

"Yeah. That's part of it. Look, he just told me to tell you. Or rather he wrote a note, since he can't talk. On a respirator and all. I think he wants to see you. He may not make it. They're trying to treat him, but see, this isn't usually curable."

"What?" None of this made any sense to me. Tony made it sound like Chris was going to die, but I didn't feel up to asking him that question. Nor could I face going to the hospital.

"It's not usually curable," he repeated. "His lungs are filled up with bugs and he can't breathe, okay?" Tony began to cry.

I was at a loss. The reality that Chris might die slowly penetrated the fog in my mind though I wanted to push it away.

"Okay, okay. What room is he in?"

Tony, still sniffling, told me and I memorized it. He said goodbye and hung up. I sat motionless for a while, my thoughts whirling. How could Chris be dying? This seemed utterly impossible.

❖

The next day after work, Thursday, I went to the Castro and picked up a copy of the *Bay Area Reporter*. This was the day it came out each week. They might have some more information on this AIDS thing.

Sure enough, there was an article. I flashed back to a couple of years before and the posting about gay cancer in the Star Pharmacy. Chris's words came back to me. *Nothing to worry about.* Was this related to that? It didn't seem possible.

He was almost unrecognizable. He had a mask over his face. He'd lost so much weight he looked like a starving person. His color was gray, so unlike his normal ruddy complexion. I flashed on how upset he'd get when he got a pimple. His cheeks were hollow and his skin was dull. This must be what a dying person looked like.

Nothing looked or seemed real to me. I sat down in the hospital chair and just looked at him. His eyes were closed. The machine was breathing for him. I spread the newspaper out on my lap and read it again.

A nurse came in, said hello to me briefly, and made some adjustments to the machines he was hooked up to. I said nothing.

A man appeared at the door, and it made me look up from staring at Chris.

He was good looking, about my age, gay of course. It must be Tony. He went directly to Chris and stroked his hair and his hand and said, "Sweetheart? It's me. How are you?"

Chris, naturally, didn't answer. Nothing changed.

"You Max?" Tony asked me.

"Yes. You're Tony."

"Right," he said. "You came."

"Yep. Does he know we're here?" My words coming out of me felt like the last bit of toothpaste being forced from a nearly empty tube. Sludgy and strangled.

"The doctor says he might or he might not. I prefer to think some part of him knows."

"How long has he been sick?"

"With the pneumo? About three weeks, but he started feeling sick a couple months ago. He would have this terrible sweating at night and he had a fever all the time. Like all day, every day."

I remembered then when he kicked me out of the apartment. He didn't look well and he must have been starting to get sick. Was this part of that? That had been a long time ago, it seemed to me. I was confused.

"I finally was able to get him to go to the doctor. He went back to see Ostrow."

"That's the doctor who treated him for hepatitis B a couple years ago."

"Yes, they talked about that. Dr. Ostrow gave him the news that he probably had AIDS. But he already suspected that."

We turned as one to look at Chris. In the silence, the various monitors chirped and the respirator hummed.

"What does that mean?"

"His immune system doesn't work. His T cells are almost zero. He has no defense against infections—like the pneumonia, especially this pneumonia. It's caused by his lungs filling up with protozoa."

"I see." I took a breath. I knew the answer but I asked the question anyhow.

"Is he going to die?" I forced myself to meet Tony's gaze.

"Yeah." His tears welled up. He wasn't just anybody, he loved Chris. All those guys, one after another, this one had fallen in love with him and now he was losing him.

"Did you know Andrew?" I asked.

"I actually met Chris right around the time Andrew passed away. I went to the hospital with Chris to see him."

"What happens now?"

Tony wiped his eyes and sniffed. "Nothing. We wait."

"Okay, thanks for letting me know."

Suddenly I had the urge to leave. I could no longer stand next to Tony and stare at the person on the bed who was once my closest friend. What had happened? He kicked me out of our apartment. That's what he did.

He could have called me. It wasn't my fault I didn't know he was sick.

❖

I had no idea what time I'd gone to sleep. I was late and didn't take a shower but washed my hair in the sink, leaning over the pile of dirty dishes. Adrian wasn't any better a housekeeper than me. She had not been home, I was fairly sure. I cursed her for not doing the dishes. I didn't remember even eating anything the night before. I stuffed bread in my face as I dressed. My headache was so bad, my hair hurt. I took some aspirin after I swallowed the bread. I didn't have any Valium, thanks to Adrian having disappeared.

It was February and rain was crashing down, making my commute abjectly slow and excruciating. Stuffed in the Muni with hundreds of other rain-soaked commuters, I hung on to the bar, staring out the window as the blurred tunnel sped past.

Chris was going to die and I hadn't even spoken to him in months. These two facts clashed in my mind fighting for primacy to claim which was worse.

Rob looked at me when I walked in the door. "What's up? You look like hell."

"Friend of mine is going to die."

"Oh no."

"Hey, have you got any…?" I mimed smoking a joint.

"Ah, no. sadly. I'm dry."

We went up front to see Jay. He grinned ruefully and spread his hands.

"No nose candy today. Sorry. My dealer is AWOL."

When he said that, I thought of Adrian. My dealer slash girlfriend was undependable too.

Rob and I loaded up and put on our ponchos. That was the only way to keep all that paper dry. We could wear our messenger bags underneath the ponchos.

We trudged over to the clerk's office. At least in the downpour, UN plaza inhabitants were hunkering down in whatever shelter they could find and didn't bother us as we walked across to City Hall.

I readied myself to go downtown and make my deliveries. Every time I closed my eyes, I saw Chris in his hospital bed, silent, sick, lost to me.

The rain was coming down hard and fast. I actually was perversely happy it was raining so bad—I felt so awful physically, and it went well with my sorrow over Chris. I walked from office to office. Even the usually snooty receptionists were sympathetic about my plight. The poncho wasn't any good at keeping my feet dry. My sneakers squished rainwater in the elevators, and my toes were numb.

SOMEWHERE ALONG THE WAY

Anne greeted me with raised eyebrows when I arrived at the Major, Trewlawney, Forest & Briggs offices.

"Girl, you look like a drowned rat. Sit down. I'll get you some tea."

I was glad to obey. While Anne was gone, I looked around at the lobby. There were some goofy paintings on the walls. I couldn't tell if they were originals or copies. I wondered what it would be like to work in such a place. It wouldn't likely be that great. I wasn't the kind of person who would work in the Financial District. I wouldn't fit in. I was a lab person, or at least I used to be.

Chris is dying. I couldn't distract myself from this salient fact.

I was looking at the floor; my neck was too tired to hold my head up. The fresh air had at least beat back my headache to a dull ache.

"Excuse me. What are you doing here?" I looked up and a three-piece-suited snarling gray-haired guy was standing over me.

"I'm your legal messenger. I'm just resting for a minute."

"Oh. Where's Anne?" His annoyance and worse, his contempt, were palpable.

"Uh…" It didn't seem like a great idea to answer that question. I didn't want to meet his eyes, so I was looking away, saw Anne come around the corner, and saw her face fall. She tucked my cup of tea behind the receptionist desk out of sight.

"Mr. Forrest?" Uh-oh, he was one of the big four. Yikes.

He whirled around. "Anne, I was looking for you. I cannot find the Pershing file, and Lydia is nowhere to be found."

"Certainly, let me put the answering machine on for a minute and I'll come right in and help you."

He walked over close to her and started whispering. I knew he was talking about me. I watched Anne's face grow more and more dismayed. Crap. I'd gotten her in trouble by being this ugly pile of wet messenger in their pristine lobby.

He stalked back to the office area.

"I'm sorry," I said.

"Just drink your tea. He'll be fine. He's just in a tizzy about his damn file."

That at least made me smile.

"I have to go," she told me, and I understood that to mean that I ought to leave as soon as possible.

My bag of legal papers seemed to weigh a ton as I looped it over my shoulder. I put on my wet poncho, and within a few minutes I was walking through the never-ending rain to my next stop. My heart weighed as much as my messenger bag.

❖

When I got home from work, Adrian was there and no one was with her.

"Chris is in the hospital and he's not going to make it," I said with no preamble.

She leaned back on the couch and drew on her cigarette, her head tilted back. "That right?" she asked as she exhaled.

"Yeah," I said. "I don't really know exactly what's going on. He's got something called AIDS and his lungs are full of bugs and he can't breathe." I took some refuge in the dispassionate recital of facts, but I truly wanted her to comfort me.

"That sucks," Adrian said. "Come here."

I moved toward her, and her embrace felt wonderful. For the first time in a while she was present and focused solely on me. I settled into her arms. She kissed my forehead and hair. We stayed that way without talking for some time.

The phone rang and roused us out of our stupor. Adrian and I looked at each other as I heard Tony's voice harsh and rife with sadness.

"Max? Hey, I wanted to let you know that Chris passed this afternoon. I got in touch with his mom and she's on her way. I can let you know later about his funeral. It's kind of dependent on what Aggie wants." He was on a first-name basis with Chris's mom, that was something.

Adrian tightened her arms and I wept into her shoulder for a little while. Then I disengaged and poured myself a drink.

True to his word, Tony called again and left a message with the details of the service. I listened to it a couple times. I didn't have the nerve to show up for this. I'd met Aggie once and I didn't want to have to talk to her about Chris. I didn't want to talk to anybody. I couldn't do a thing about anything. The only person I wanted to comfort me was Adrian. She was the only one I could bear to be around. We were almost back to being the same as we were the summer when we first met. We started to make love again regularly, she slipped me tabs of Valium, and for a few weeks, there were no random chicks showing up. I tried hard not to think of Chris, but his face, his words, kept popping into my consciousness. When I'd had enough to drink, this would not stop exactly but would sort of dissolve into a formless cloud of disconnected thoughts.

❖

A couple weeks after Chris passed away, Adrian said, "Come on, Max, let's go have some fun. You have to go to Amelia's with me."

It touched me, I guess, that Adrian was worried about me. Naturally, I couldn't tell if going out dancing at Amelia's would end up with us going home together. She didn't say and I didn't ask. What I decided was it didn't matter to me because I could pick someone else up at Amelia's. That didn't seem like it would be too hard. I wanted Adrian, but if I couldn't have her, then it was on to someone else. Adrian's solicitousness toward me was nice, but I had to be realistic and not assume it would continue. Adrian was mercurial and always cagey about her actions.

"Max, baby, we need to go have fun, especially you. I know you're sad about Chris, but life goes on and so should you, starting with tonight. We'll go to Amelia's and party with all the girls, right?"

"Yeah, you're absolutely right. I need a night out."

"That's the spirit! That's my girl." I didn't know if she meant I was her girl literally. There was no Rhonda or anyone else at the moment, so that was something. But what this all meant, I'd just have to find out.

❖

More than usual, I wanted to get a good head start on the night, and Adrian came through with a gram of coke. This ought to keep us moving and awake for quite a while. We snorted a couple of lines at home around nine thirty and had a couple drinks. The more I thought about going out, the better I felt. Even if I didn't end up with Adrian, it would be okay, I told myself stubbornly.

When we arrived at Amelia's, it was happening. We moved through the throngs of animated women to get some drinks. I recognized a lot of women from Maud's, including Lily, who waved at me. I waved back and endured a little stab of regret. Oh well, women were like buses. Or streetcars.

It occurred to me that I had never actually gone out with Adrian other than the night of the day we met. It somehow had struck me that I wanted to keep her under wraps, keep her to myself. Of course, that didn't work out at all. Her profession, such as it was, kept her meeting a variety of people, like Rhonda, for example. As I stood next to her, I glanced at her profile illuminated by the flashing lights, then I looked around the dance floor, and sure enough, heads were turning. Swell. I wasn't going to be ending my night with Adrian. We might technically live together but we didn't *live* together in the way I understood the word to mean. I was sharing her space on the strength of whatever fondness she had for me. Our relationship was ill defined. She didn't need me for anything in the manner I needed her—for mind-blowing orgasms and drugs.

She sometimes said to me, "Max I don't know what I'd do without you." It sounded good but it made no sense. Fuck her, I would just find someone else tonight. Ought not to be difficult. I didn't want to make her jealous exactly, just show her I didn't need her as much as she might think. I lit another cigarette and didn't exactly pose but tried to project as much as possible that I was available. I looked for and made eye contact with whomever I could. Sure enough, a tough-looking redhead in leather chaps sauntered over. And headed directly to Adrian, who smiled her slow, knowing grin and went to dance. As I mentally collapsed, I struggled to not show it and to not stare at them as they moved closer and then farther apart and exchanged whispers. Then the redhead threw me a speculative look. What was that about? I abruptly wheeled and shouldered my way to the bar where I ordered two vodkas, shotgunned one, and took the other with me back to the dance floor. I wanted another line of coke but I wasn't sure how to get Adrian's attention. Then I saw her giving me the come-here motion with her arm.

"Max, this is Shel. Shel, Max."

"Hi, Shel," I whisper-shouted in her ear.

"We're going to get in line for the bathroom." Adrian flicked her lovely dark eyebrows up. Aha.

We made desultory small talk as we waited and I finished my

vodka. The prospect of a couple lines cheered me right up. Then I noticed Shel's hand sneaking up from Adrian's thigh to her butt. Well, Adrian asked me along to snort some blow, so she must want me.

The stall wasn't made for two, let alone three, so that meant we were squashed together. Shel and I gave Adrian space so she could lay out our lines on her pocket mirror. While we watched, Shel fondled my butt and pulled me into a sensuous kiss. It gave me a little rush of naughtiness. Adrian noticed but she didn't react. We took our turns snorting up the coke and then spent a few more minutes locked in a three-way embrace, kissing and groping. There was an impatient knock on the door and a rough voice said, "Women are waiting to pee. Finish up in there." We made our exit past the glares of the girls in line.

Back on the dance floor, we stuck together. Whatever was going on, I was determined not to be shut out, and so far so good. We snuck in one more hit of coke but Shel said, "This bathroom scene is a drag. Can we get out of here?"

Adrian beamed. "Absolutely. Let's go."

Shel followed us on her motorcycle back to Adrian's place. I thought I knew what was going to happen and I was game for it. Whatever way I could have Adrian I would take her, even if that meant another woman along for the ride.

Adrian sat down at the kitchen table and pulled Shel into her lap as she awkwardly poured out some more coke, this time on the big mirror. Shel was about three inches taller than Adrian. I watched them, trying to control my jealousy. I was happy that Shel had to remove herself from Adrian's lap so she could do her lines. Adrian had set up humongous rails, and after my turn, I got a such a huge rush I thought the top of my head was going to pop off. The two of them started necking again and I watched as the coke residue slid down the back of my throat and made me cough. Shel must be really into Adrian more than me. Adrian turned to look at me, though, and reached out her hand. All right then.

We maneuvered ourselves into the bedroom and into bed. Shel moved aggressively on Adrian, but my ever-slippery girl wasn't going to be topped that easily. She instead turned to me and relegated Shel to touching her as she made love to me. When I came, it was a surreal feeling through the coke high, and honestly it wasn't much of an orgasm. I was mostly charged up from the mental clarity of coke, which sharpens the edges of reality. I wanted Adrian, but as soon as I was done, Shel was back on top, but this time, Adrian succumbed and I was the second fiddle. I caressed Adrian where I could reach her, which wasn't easy because Shel was all over her and she loomed even bigger in bed than she had in Amelia's.

The rest of the night was a tangle of arms, legs, and slurping sounds. We stopped once for some water and ended up doing the rest of the coke. I don't know when we finally collapsed, but I remember waking up with my throat on fire and a headache to see Shel and Adrian all tangled up. I left the bed, put on some clothes, and went to crash on the couch.

When we all were awake at last, there was the predictable strained small talk, and to my relief, Adrian gave Shel the boot as soon as was practical. But once that was done, Adrian didn't want to talk and disappeared back into her room, leaving me alone. Chris popped into my mind. I thought about describing the previous night to him and making a funny story about it. I almost but not quite succeeded in making it a funny story to myself.

Adrian, when she emerged, was noncommittal.

"So, does this mean we're back together?"

"We weren't exactly together, Max, so no."

"When you feel like it you have a three-way with me?"

"Maybe. Something wrong?" Adrian was maddeningly distant.

"No. Nothing. I guess."

It was close enough to five p.m., so I went over to the corner store and picked up a bottle from Ahmed.

Chapter Six

I started reading the gay rags regularly, as though somehow my acquiring knowledge would make cheer me up and help me get over Chris, but it never did. In fact, the night after I read an article saying the number of gay men in San Francisco who were afflicted by AIDS was increasing, I had a terrible nightmare. In my dream, a graph with a blood-red line climbed from zero up to infinity, and I knew when I woke up what it meant. There would be more and more men who would die just like Chris had.

I absolutely couldn't stop all my thoughts of him even if I wanted to, no matter how much I drank. And I drank every night until I passed out. Then I woke up and went to work. Part of me wanted to go out and have fun, but the other part asked what the point was. I could get drunk more cheaply by myself at home in the living room. When I had had enough drinks, Chris's death didn't hurt as much and I could tell myself it was just too bad what happened. I couldn't have done anything about it anyhow. Also, I could avoid asking myself questions about why I was staying with Adrian when we didn't actually have a relationship, we were essentially distant roommates. I dreaded the day she would ask me to leave. She never said anything about it, she never said much of anything at all to me. We occasionally had dinner together and got high.

I put my own party together for myself on the living room couch. There was no more Valium forthcoming from Adrian, so just vodka would have to suffice. She'd moved the stash out the bear cookie jar—I looked—and into her bedroom somewhere. If I tried to find it, she'd know.

I poured one drink and downed it and then another right away. I waited for the feeling to happen. I tried a third big glass of vodka and nothing changed. I stretched out on the couch, trying to get comfortable, to no avail. I sat up again and stuck my hands between the cushions. My fingers touched something hard. I tried to grab it but it only worked its way deeper. I stood up and flipped the cushion onto the floor. On top of the couch's canvas frame cover was Adrian's little enamel pillbox. I froze, disbelieving at first. Then I picked it up and opened it. Inside were four Quaaludes. My first thought was *Eureka* and my second thought was *When did she get 'ludes and why didn't she share?* Well, she'd stopped giving me drugs months ago.

I put the cushion back on the couch, sat on it, and cradled the box in my hand, staring at it. I was saved. I sort of remembered Adrian asking me suspiciously if I'd seen the pillbox and at the time I could answer honestly, "No." So here it was in my hand.

All was not lost. My little party of one was about to get way more fun.

First question was should I save this and return everything to Adrian? Fuck that. She was always so annoying the way she doled out the pills. Nope, she lost that box and it was going to stay lost.

Next question was should I save any of the 714s? Take one and hoard the rest?

Nah, my best friend was dead, I deserved to get fucked up.

I went to get a glass of water. I stared at the white pill again, then I threw two of them in my mouth and washed them down.

I lit a cigarette and waited. With the vodka I'd already drunk, this ought not to take long. Nothing happened. This was fucked up. Screw it, I took the other two. That ought to do it. I had nowhere to go anyhow.

Then the happy, floaty feeling started at the base of my skull and tentacles of pleasure slithered around my whole brain. My limbs went slack. It was nirvana, I was in an invisible warm bath. I took some more sips of vodka.

Yippee. I began to feel sleepy. I shook another Newport out of the pack and fired it. I wanted to keep watching TV, but it was becoming impossible. Just needed to close my eyes for a minute.

In fact, when I closed my eyes, I saw Chris as he used to look before we moved to San Francisco. He seemed to be trying to tell me something, but I couldn't make out what it was, I couldn't hear anything. I was falling into a black hole, I was dying too. Just like Chris.

❖

When I woke up the next morning, the first thing I saw a metal railing. I squinted because the room was too bright. The light was like an icepick piercing my brain through my eyes. I slowly surfaced into consciousness. I was in a hospital bed and had an IV stuck in my arm. Fragments of memory floated through my mind. Well. I wasn't dead, that was for sure, though I wished I was. I was in a hospital room. What the fuck? I sat up as carefully as I could. I was light-headed but I had to pee so bad, I had to chance getting to the bathroom. I found the valve for the IV and closed it, then gingerly pulled the needle out. Sitting up made me feel worse. I stopped to let my blood pump a little before I slid off the bed at the foot.

My throat was so sore, it made me think I was sick with some kind of bug. But I didn't have a runny nose. That was the only positive thing about my current state that I could identify. My limbs were hard to move, as though I was swimming in cement. I was so dizzy I'd thought I'd keel over. I finally made it to and from the bathroom, crawled back into bed, and forced myself to lie still. Had I ever eaten anything last night? I didn't remember. My stomach felt totally empty. If I'd thrown up, I couldn't remember when. Or where.

I was aware of someone coming into the room, I cracked my eyes open. It was a woman in a white uniform. Oh. A nurse. The first thing she did was pick up the IV tube and frown at it. I opened my mouth and started to ask, "What am I..." but I couldn't speak.

At last, I managed to croak one word. "Water."

The nurse turned to look at me and scowled. I wonder how she would have reacted if I'd peed in the bed?

"You shouldn't have taken out your IV. You could have called me."

Oh. The call button. I was too out of it to remember. But really, I was too thirsty to have this conversation.

I tried again. "Some water. Please."

She poured some into a plastic cup and handed it to me and helped me drink. I sank back with the effort. She put the needle back into my arm and retaped it.

"What am I doing here?" I asked.

The nurse, whose expression was reproving and not very friendly, said, "You don't remember?"

Well, if I did, I wouldn't need to ask. Bitch.

"Your friends brought you in last night because they couldn't wake you up. We pumped your stomach."

That must be why my throat hurt so bad and why I was dizzy. And thirsty.

"They said they didn't know how much you'd drunk or how many pills you took. They were concerned." I wondered who "they' was besides Adrian. She'd brought someone home. Well, I'd put a crimp in *that* scenario. A very small part of me was guilty. What the hell. I needed to get out of here.

"So when can I go home?" I asked Nurse Sunshine. She wasn't looking at me, she was taking my pulse.

"I have to wait for the on-call physician to discharge you."

"Fine. When does he get here?" I asked. My stomach rumbled, a good sign, I supposed.

"He'll be around as soon as he can. Can I get you some juice or something else?"

I had drained my cup of water. "Yeah sure, juice is fine."

She disappeared, leaving me with another cup of water and my still jumbled thoughts. Chris was still dead, that much was clear. This wasn't the worst hangover I'd ever had. The IV bag read Ringer's Solution. That was saline, I knew. Hydrating me.

I spotted a phone in the corner. What time was it? Could I call Adrian? Fuck it, I didn't care, I only wanted to leave the hospital as soon as possible.

"Hello?" It was Adrian, her voice scratchy.

"Hi. It's Max."

"Yeah. Max, good, you're okay. They told us last night that you'd be fine, but you had to stay for observation."

"Look, can you come get me? I don't have money for a cab or anything."

I heard Adrian muttering to someone else. Her trick was still there.

"Okay. Susie's got a car, so we'll pick you up. Give us some time to wake up and get dressed, but we'll be there."

"All right. Thanks." I hung up. Well. I was going to meet whoever Adrian had screwed. Swell.

There wasn't a damn thing to do but wait. I lay in the hugely uncomfortable hospital bed and stared at the walls, then the ceiling. The nurse came back and offered me some Jell-O. Boy, did that sound unappealing, but I said yes and went back to my brooding as I ate it.

Something had happened last night. I didn't remember a thing. I'd had a hard time sometimes remembering why I had brought some woman home, but I'd never been so completely out of it that I couldn't remember anything. I had an inkling I might hear more detail from Adrian and whoever.

As weak and dizzy as I felt, I was itching to leave, but all I could do was wait. It was infuriating. My thoughts kept wanting to go back to Chris and the last few months. He'd kicked me out of our apartment, the twit. I was still pissed about that. But then he'd gotten sick and I should have been there for him, but I couldn't deal. Then all of sudden he'd died and I couldn't even make it to his funeral. I was an asshole.

A tall guy in a white coat swept into the room. He didn't say a word but scanned the clipboard at the end of my bed. This would be the doctor. I told myself to be cool so that he'd release me.

"Hmm. Yes. Well, then. How are you feeling?"

"Okay. So-so. But mostly okay. When can I go home?"

"Let's check you over. Do you know what happened to you?"

All these nosy questions.

He put his stethoscope on my chest and took my pulse again.

"Not sure. The nurse said you pumped my stomach."

"Right. Just to be on the safe side. They said you took Quaaludes but they didn't know how many or how much you drank. But they could only estimate. You were unresponsive. So we cleaned you out." He shined a light in my eyes. "The tox screen said you had Quaaludes mixed with alcohol in your system. Is this an unusual occurrence for you?" he asked, his tone deceptively mild. "Do you usually mix downers with alcohol?"

He was extremely nosy.

"No. I don't," I said firmly. I'm wasn't about to spill my guts to this strange dude. Doctor or not.

He looked hard at me. "Well, I suggest you not mix pills and alcohol. Your breathing becomes depressed and it could stop altogether, and guess where that leaves you?"

I didn't answer but I knew what he meant.

"Dead." He pulled up the sheet and blanket. "I'll write your discharge order. Take it easy for a couple days, don't go to work."

"Okay. Thanks."

In about a half hour, I was sitting down in the lobby of Ralph K. Davies. And I tried to read the magazines as I waited for Adrian. It took another forty-five minutes, and they finally showed up. I didn't recognize the other woman. They must have had sex before coming to pick me up. Fuckers.

"Hi, Max. This is Susie." She was a nondescript brunette. I wondered what the attraction for Adrian was. I was vaguely aware that I probably looked like shit in my clothes from the night before. I probably smelled, too.

Susie grinned at me and said brightly, "Hi, Max. You look a lot better today than you did last night. You're not passed out."

"Thanks. Can we go?" I addressed this question to Adrian.

"Right away. Susie was nice about coming over here to get you." Adrian's message was clear—be nice. I wasn't in the mood to be nice, but I struggled to be civil.

Susie left us alone once we arrived at Adrian's. They exchanged a sloppy kiss and some whispered conversation at the front door.

Adrian sat next to me on the couch. I looked down and there was a huge cigarette burn in the rug. Oops. I must have done that. The smell of singed carpet wafted up my nose, along with stale vodka and the full ashtray before me on the table. And there was Adrian's little enamel pillbox sitting right next to my glass.

"Max, you scared the fuck out of me. I couldn't wake you up. Susie and I got here around one and here you were passed out on the couch with the cigarette in your hand. Thank God it went out. You could have burned the place down with you passed out here."

"I guess I fell asleep."

"Bullshit, I see you found my 'ludes."

I was ashamed. She wasn't supposed to find that out. But I wasn't going to apologize or admit to anything.

"It was between the cushions."

"I don't know how many were left, but you took them all. You could have died."

"There were only four, and I wasn't going to die." I sounded whiny. Adrian, however, seemed genuinely upset, but I didn't trust her.

"You have to slow down, Max. This isn't good for you."

I leapt up and started pacing in the living room. I didn't want or need Adrian's judgment.

"Yeah, like you're one to talk."

"I admit I like to get fucked up, but you're on a whole other level."

"Right. So you say." I suspected she might be correct, but I didn't care.

"You passed out when you were smoking. You had to get your stomach pumped."

"I know, but I am not going to do that again." I looked at her directly, willing her to believe me. I believed myself. Last night was a flukey situation, not to be repeated. I knew that much.

"If you can't ease up on the partying, I'm going to ask you to leave."

There it was—the blackmail. Fuck her.

"I will. Are we still good?"

"Depends on what you mean. I still care about you. I'll still sleep with you. I'm not giving you any more drugs."

That sucked.

"What if I can pay?"

Adrian sighed. "No, not even then. You have no control. You never really did, and now you're worse. I can't be part of you killing yourself. You may not think it, but I care about you. When you're not wasted, you're a good person, funny. Sexy."

"I'm not going to kill myself." What a stupid thing to say. I got angrier.

"So you say," Adrian replied sadly.

"I promise no more fires, no more trips to Ralph K. Davies. I have nowhere to go, you have to let me stay here, Adrian."

"Like I said, it depends."

I waited until she left, not saying where she was going, as usual. Likely to see Susie. My chance at having sex with her had disappeared. She was still likely too irritated with me to do it anyway. I'd have to be on my best behavior for a while to get back on her good side. I spent the rest of the day watching bad TV and trying not to think of

Chris or Adrian without the benefit of a single drink. I felt like my skin was being peeled off my body. It was excruciating, but I had to prove something to myself, if not to Adrian.

I lasted until Wednesday and stopped at the store on the way home. I could drink without passing out, and if I just could show Adrian, that would help.

She came home while I was sitting there, and she glared at me.

"See? Just a couple drinks." I said cheerfully. The truth was I'd had about three, and it wasn't working the way it was supposed to.

"I'm back to take a shower and change. I'm going out with Susie."

"Adrian. I'm trying to make it work. Will you spend some time with me?" I knew she knew I meant could we have sex.

"You know, Max, I have to see."

"Geez, Adrian, what more do you want from me? Here I am, I'm not drunk or passed out."

She stared at me for a lengthy moment, then said, "Okay, let's go out on Thursday."

"Great."

She left with a hurried "See you later."

What the hell. I finished the bottle, but at the end I couldn't feel anything except sleepy.

❖

We sat at the Spaghetti Factory on Eighteenth Street, and it seemed to me at least as though we were a normal couple out on a date. I carefully and slowly drank the glass of wine she'd ordered for me and waited in vain for it to work its will on me.

We chatted in a not-too strained fashion. I told her about the lawyers at work.

She said, "I'm thinking of getting out of the business. It's too much trouble. I just don't know what else I would do."

"You can do anything, you know. You're really bright."

"Thanks. You too, Max. This messenger thing is way beneath you."

"I know." It hurt to hear her say it out loud, but I knew it was true. I couldn't envision how to get another biotech job, though. It felt impossible, like becoming a rock star or an actress.

Back at the flat, we sat and made out on the couch, and we were getting fairly heated when Adrian stopped.

"I can't. I can't do it anymore. It's gone."

I doubt I'd ever felt as disappointed in my life. I kissed her some more and said, desperately trying not to sound desperate, "Come on, A. Let's keep going, maybe you can get into it once I, you know…"

My experience was I could rev her up very well.

She sat on the couch, tilted her head back, and sighed. "I'd like to, but it's not happening. I'm sorry, I really am."

I struggled to keep my temper.

"Okay. If that's how it is. I'm all right." I was *not* all right at all.

"Thanks. I think I'll just go to bed now."

I sat for a few minutes, then I put my coat on and went out to the corner store. Ahmed never failed me. He stayed open until eleven at night. I bought a pint of vodka.

I remember my relief when I opened the seal, unscrewed the cap, filled my oversize shot glass, and downed it. That was the last thing I remember until I woke up.

Paralyzed. I was probably sensitive since my stomach-pumping experience three days before. I looked at my watch. Ugh. I was going to have to call in sick. This wasn't going to go over well with Rob. He'd have to do all my work and his too. I couldn't move, though.

To top it off, Adrian emerged from her bedroom and didn't say anything to me. she didn't have to.

I dreaded her coming home that day. I know what our conversation was going to be. Worse, I was broke, and if I wanted any more booze, I'd have to ask her for money. That wouldn't work, I was positive. I started to paw through all my pants pockets, even my coat pockets. I came up about fifty cents short. Crap. Ahmed was nice, but he wasn't going to sell me a bottle of vodka I couldn't pay for. I dug through my raincoat again and came up with a wrinkled scrap of paper. I almost threw it aside, but something made me uncrumple it and read it.

Laurie M. 555-1314.

What the hell? Who was Laurie? I hadn't been anywhere to meet any girls for a long time. I read it again. A picture of a nice-looking blonde surfaced, bit by bit. Right. I had given plasma and was about to pass out in the diner, and she bought me a donut. I had left my pint of vodka sitting there on the table, and she'd looked at it, then at me: *You don't have to live this way. Call me if you need help. If you want to get sober, I can help you.*

Stop drinking—that was out of the question. It was a silly notion. Laurie didn't know me or know what she was talking about. But I didn't throw the paper away. I smoothed it out and left it on the coffee table. No, I wasn't in trouble and I didn't need a lecture about drinking. Fuck it.

I went back through all my things, but there was no more change. Then I had an inspiration. The sofa cushions. They'd yielded treasure before, why not now?

I threw my blanket, sheet, and pillow, along with the cushions, on the floor.

Aha, there was a dime. Only forty more cents. *Come on.*

I went into Adrian's bedroom and right off was treated to a stab of longing and regret when I passed her bed. We'd had some fine times there. Where the fuck did she keep her change? *Dresser.*

"What are you doing?" Holy shit, it was Adrian.

"Uh." I paused to try and come up with a logical explanation for why I was in her bedroom. "I, um, lost my comb. So I wanted to borrow yours."

"Max, give me a fucking break."

"Adrian, can I borrow some money from you? Just a buck. I can pay you back in a couple days."

"What for? You want something to eat? I'll get you something to eat. Come on, Max. For what?"

"I need to get some vodka and I'm just a little short."

"No."

"Adrian. Please."

She crossed her arms. "No. You're a fucking mess, Max. If you don't get yourself straightened out, you have to leave."

Even though I didn't want to plead, I didn't want to whine, I had to. I had not a shred of self-respect left.

"You have to help me. My best friend just died, I've had some tough times lately. I just need something to tide me over. How about just one Valium?"

Adrian stared at me silently for what seemed like forever.

"Max, don't you see? You've got a problem."

"If I have a problem, you have a problem, girlfriend. You have no right to lecture me. You got some nerve, all the times we got fucked up together."

Adrian looked sad, but I could tell she was unmoved.

"You have to stop drinking or I'm going to kick you out. Period."

I turned away and put on my raincoat. It was, as a matter of fact, fucking raining. It was March, for Christ's sake. Again, I went to the corner store.

"Hello, Max, what can I do for you? Vodka? Pint."

"Half pint, and I don't have the money, Ahmed, I swear I'll pay you back next week."

"Max, I know you're a good customer, but I can't do it. Sorry."

I didn't say another word, I just left. Fuck.

I walked back to Adrian's. I wanted to die. I wanted a drink worse than I wanted to die. What the hell was I going to do?

I retrieved Laurie's phone number and went over to the phone alcove. I looked at the number. *Maybe I have a drinking problem, maybe not. There's nothing else I can do. Adrian probably means what she says. I'm nothing to her anyhow.* Chris was gone. Dead and gone. I began to cry.

Adrian walked up behind me and put her arms around me. I turned and let her hold me and kept right on sobbing.

"I'm sorry, Max, you've had it rough for a while. I'm not the girlfriend you want. But believe it or not, I want the best for you."

I struggled to calm down. "I'm going to call someone."

"That's good. You do that."

I picked up the phone and dialed Laurie's number. The answering machine with her outlandishly cheerful voice advised me to leave a message. My sentences were disjointed, I wondered if I even made any sense. I felt abysmally stupid calling this woman out of the blue just because she said it was okay and I should if I ever wanted to stop drinking.

I sat back down on the couch, and Adrian brought me a cup of tea and sat next to me. We didn't say a word. In a couple hours the phone rang. We waited to hear the machine pick up. It was Laurie. I snatched the phone before she finished her message.

"It's Max."

"Hi, Max. I'm glad you called. Are you okay?"

"No—no." My voice was shaking. *God damn it.* "I'm not. That's why I called you."

"That's good you called. It's going to be all right. You're going to be all right even though you might not think so at the moment. Listen, I'm going to come over and talk to you and bring a friend with me. Is that okay?"

What choice did I have? I couldn't think of a good reason to say no.

"Sure. Yeah." I gave her the address.

"About forty-five minutes."

Adrian listened to the whole exchange and said, "I'm going to split. Good luck. I'll see you later."

I opened the front door and there stood Laurie, as promised, with a friend.

"Hi, Max, this is Talia."

"Hi, Talia. Hi, Laurie. Please come in." The whole scene had a surreal feel to it. This was sure not a social occasion. I didn't know what the hell it was. There was one stranger and one almost-stranger. I didn't know what they were going to do or say. I was squeezed in a vise: I was going to get booted if I drank again, but I didn't know how to stop. Laurie had asked me months ago to call her if I wanted to stop drinking. What I wanted was to stop hurting and feeling like a piece of shit, mentally, physically. I wanted to be myself again. I'd lost myself somewhere along the way. How these women could help with that, I had no clue. But I had nothing to lose by listening to them. I'm a scientist—why not just see what they had to say? I wasn't positive I wanted to stop drinking.

Laurie and Talia sat together on the couch, so I pulled the armchair over.

"Do you want anything to drink?" I asked, wincing at the absurdity of this question.

Laurie grinned, "No, thanks, I'm fine."

Talia shook her head. Then they glanced at each other with looks I couldn't interpret.

Laurie said, "Why don't you tell us what's going on."

It was still hard to string together coherent sentences, but I did my best. I did admit to the hospital and stomach pumping, which killed me to say aloud. And why did hearing myself describe it made it sound so much worse? But, somehow, I hoped the two women seated before me would not be judgmental. I couldn't deal with that right now.

They listened without comment, only nodding a few times.

"I—we"—Laurie pointed to Talia—"get where you're coming from."

Talia said, "I was fifty-one-fiftied twice for attempted suicide. When I was drinking."

Laurie said, "I had two DUIs, and the second one, SFPD threw me in the drunk tank overnight. I'd apparently mouthed off to the cop."

That impressed me. I'd never heard anyone say things like that. Immediately, though, I said, "I don't want to commit suicide and I've never been arrested." It irked me I sounded so defensive.

"We're telling you this stuff because we want you to know we've had similar experiences when we drank."

"Oh." I said. *When do we get to the part where you help me?*

"Do you want to drink now?" Laurie asked.

"Yep. I sure do."

"And if you do, what will happen?"

"I don't understand the question," I said. "I just told you."

I didn't like Laurie's expression. I remembered it from our first meeting at Peg's Place. Like she knew all about me. It wasn't a disdainful look, though, just a knowing one, and it still annoyed me.

"If you start drinking now, Max, will you stop after two drinks or will you keep drinking?"

This was a loaded question. There was what I wanted to say but there was what I suspected was the truth. Since they'd been honest with me, I'd go with the truth.

"I will keep drinking."

"Until?" Talia asked.

"I don't know. Until I've had enough," I said. "Or I pass out."

"I would start drinking and not stop," Laurie said. "I had no way to stop. I had no endpoint. I'd pass out, or worse, I would black out and sometimes wake up somewhere with no memory of how I got there. For me, there was no such thing as enough."

"Wow." Again, this was astounding stuff to hear said out loud.

Talia said, "If you start drinking, can you predict with any certainty what will happen to you?"

I took a long time before I answered, but I was starting to see what they were getting at.

"No. I can't."

They nodded at me and Laurie said, "Would you like to have a different kind of life?"

"I think I would." I was exhausted. Truthfully, the thought of vodka at that moment was unwelcome.

"If you want, you can come to a meeting with us," Laurie said. "There's one in a half hour. If you think you want to explore a way to live without alcohol."

"What kind of a meeting?" I asked. I thought they'd just tell me what to do.

"Alcoholics Anonymous," Talia said.

What the fuck? What did that mean?

"We would like you to come with us, but only if that's what you want."

What I wanted? What *did* I want? Not to feel horrible and out of control. That's what I wanted.

"Yeah. I'll go with you." What was the harm? Laurie and Talia were gentle and non-threatening. I could check it out.

"Terrific, let's go get some burritos first." Laurie beamed.

"I'm broke," I said, ashamed.

"Don't worry about it," Laurie said. "We'll buy you a burrito."

And that simple kindness at last convinced me these women might be able to help me.

CHAPTER SEVEN

We devoured burritos at a little taquería on Valencia Street and were soon seated on some folding chairs in a nondescript room in the Women's Building, of all places. I was back to being uneasy, uncomfortable, and skeptical. There was a table off to the side of the room with a coffee urn and some plates of what looked like cookies.

This was the answer to my drinking problem? Bad coffee—I assumed—and stale cookies?

There were ashtrays on every other chair. The table in front showed a bunch of books and pamphlets and a couple wicker baskets.

Talia and Laurie greeted various women as they drifted in, and they introduced me, but all they said was "This is Max." No further information. Not that I was an alcoholic. Nothing.

We sat down on the hard chairs under the harsh fluorescent lights. I squirmed. I wanted a drink, or something, anything to make me feel better.

At the front of the room were large posters with titles "The Twelve Steps" and "The Twelve Traditions." Was this like a seminar? None of the women in the room looked like alcoholics, whatever the fuck alcoholics were supposed to look like. Like grubby old men with bottles in paper bags. Like the dudes down in Skid Row.

When I was a teenager, I'd watched a horrible movie, *Days of Wine and Roses*. Jack Lemmon and Lee Remick were alcoholics. Lee Remick dies at the end. It was a dumb movie. My mind was wondering all over the place and I'd not noticed the meeting started.

"At this time would any newcomers please raise your hands and introduce yourself. A newcomer is usually defined as anyone in her first thirty days of sobriety or someone just out of a recovery program. Do we have any newcomers?"

Uh-oh. That was probably me and I'd have to speak. I didn't want to. I listened as several women said their names followed by "I'm an alcoholic" followed by "newcomer." *Oh no, this isn't happening. I didn't agree to this.* I kept my hand down and slumped in my chair, looking at the floor.

The rest of it was a blur. People were talking, clapping. Then at the end I had to stand up and we stood in a circle and prayed. Over the course of the hour, I was feeling more and more exhausted yet agitated at the same time. I either wanted to get in bed and sleep or jump out of my skin. Laurie thrust a bunch of papers into my hands and told me to take a look at them.

Talia and Laurie didn't say much afterward. They didn't even say anything about me not raising my hand and saying I was a newcomer, which I'd expected they would.

They took me back to Adrian's and both of them hugged me and said, "Please try not to drink. If you want to drink, call one of us. Get some sleep. Don't try to figure everything out right now. Just work on not drinking."

Laurie squeezed my arm. "I'll call you tomorrow evening or you can call me."

I took off my clothes and lay down on the couch. It was only nine p.m., but I didn't want to try to watch TV. I didn't think I could concentrate anyhow. Tomorrow I had to go back to work; I couldn't risk calling in sick again. I flip-flopped on the sofa. This was impossible.

When I was a kid, my mother would give me hot chocolate if I was restless and couldn't sleep. I went to the kitchen and searched and yes, there was a box of Hershey chocolate. I clumsily heated some milk and mixed in the powder.

I sat at the kitchen table, absurdly feeling like a five-year-old, and drank the hot chocolate. I didn't comprehend why Laurie and Talia had done what they'd done. I wasn't entirely sure I was an alcoholic. But as I drank the chocolate milk, I gradually started to relax. I brushed my teeth and set my alarm. Sadly, I couldn't remember the last time I'd brushed my teeth before going to bed, and it was quite an unusual sensation. When I lay on the couch and pulled the blankets over me, my mind was running a hundred miles an hour.

Adrian came back. We said hi and she went to her room.

❖

The alarm woke me with a jolt. The first thing I noticed was I didn't have a headache and my stomach felt okay. Then I recalled what I'd done the night before. I hadn't had a drink. Huh. I had eaten a burrito and a cookie and drunk some hot chocolate and I had gone to sleep. I was tired but I felt okay.

I took a shower, made a piece of toast, and took it with me. The morning was gray and a little drizzly. Riding on the Muni downtown, I couldn't stop thinking about how I wasn't sickly or in pain. Just tired. I could deal with tired.

After the afternoon deliveries, I realized as I walked back to the office that I was going to face a choice. Jay's "I buy, you fly." Beer time.

"You go ahead," I said to Rob. "I'll start sorting for tomorrow."

He gave a quizzical look and left.

I pawed through all the envelopes, dividing the filings into piles according to which court they were destined for and tried with all my might not to think of Jay, Rob, and the servers in the next room downing Budweisers. *Just don't drink.*

Through the doorway, I could see them clutching their tall cans, but I turned away. *Don't think about it.*

Back at Adrian's, she came in and out, greeting me gently but not saying much.

Look at me, I wanted to shout. *Look, no vodka.*

I shuffled through the pamphlets and looked at the book that Talia had pressed into my hands. There was one piece that was called "Twenty Questions." I found a piece of paper and a pencil. I answered yes to all but three.

I called Laurie, and she answered on the third ring. Was she waiting for my call?

"Hi. It's Max."

"Hi, Max. How are you doing?" Damn, she sounded happy to hear from me. Her voice was low and had an affectionate undertone.

I told her about my day.

Laurie chuckled at my rueful description of my answers to the "Twenty Questions." But she turned serious when I told her about the SOP of my workplace.

"You've passed a serious test, Max. You ought to congratulate yourself. There will be more, but you successfully resisted your normal urge to drink."

That's true. That was way different for me. I felt unaccountably pleased with myself. *I didn't drink.*

I described my physical state. I just told her all kinds of stuff and she was encouraging. I liked Laurie more and more. She was kind and attentive, she was a terrific listener. I started wondering if she was single.

"I'm probably going to a meeting tomorrow evening. Would you like to come with me?"

"You and Talia?"

"Nope, just me."

Hmm. What did that mean? Well, I didn't have anything better to do unless I wanted to sit at home not drinking. There was Adrian, but something told me I maybe needed to be a few more days alcohol free until I approached her.

"Yeah, sure."

"I'll pick you up at six fifteen."

I fell asleep speculating about Laurie and her intentions and visualizing her blonde hair and clear blue eyes.

It was a church basement this time, but otherwise the ambience was almost identical. Boy, were these meetings ever depressing. Drab locations. The people, though, were—well, they were entirely too chirpy.

"Generally, if you are less than thirty days sober, you introduce yourself as a newcomer," Laurie said, not unkindly but with a small edge.

"I don't want to do that," I said flatly. Though I didn't want to admit it was embarrassing. And sounded asinine. Along with everybody saying their names plus they're alcoholic sounded cult-like.

"Okay. Did you read the newcomer's pamphlet I gave you?"

"Sure." I didn't add, *so what?* What I'd concluded was I was going to hang around long enough to get the alcohol thing under control. That shouldn't take long since clearly, I was already on my way. Two whole days, not a drop of vodka. What do you know?

"This program doesn't work unless you want it. If you want it to work, you have to be willing to do the work."

All right, now Laurie was starting to sound a touch holier than thou. What she and Talia had told me of themselves two nights ago, they had some similar experiences to me. That was helpful, but it didn't convince me I had to be just like them and do exactly what they did.

"Yeah." There wasn't much point in arguing, I could tell.

"Okay, so one of the things I learned early on was, when I was at meetings, take the cotton out of my ears and put it in my mouth."

"Uh-huh?" This sounded mildly offensive. But the meeting was starting, so we had to shut up.

Okay, I guessed I could listen. I was certainly more present than I'd been the night before. There was a different person speaking. This was a gay guy. I liked that he was funny. He told an absolutely hair-raising story. He was picked up for drunk driving and thrown in jail, like Talia, but the other people there figured out he was a fag and just hounded him mercilessly all night. He barely got out alive.

"But that didn't make me stop drinking. Oh no. I just stopped driving anywhere. I took cabs. Then I couldn't understand why the guys I was trying to pick up would shine me on. I was falling-down drunk. Not pretty." A little light of recognition flipped in my mind. I remembered some girl saying that—who?

It was Lily. Right. Maybe I was worse off than I thought.

Some girl came up to me after the meeting and introduced herself.

"Hi, I'm Tina."

"Hi, I'm Max."

"Hi, Max. how long have you been sober?" Geez, these people were nosy.

"Two days."

"Oh right, you're a newcomer." I supposed I was one whether or not I said I was.

"Have you gotten a sponsor?"

"A what?" More cultish crap, I thought.

"Someone to help you do the steps."

"Oh."

I asked Laurie about it after the meeting when we went out to coffee around the corner from the meeting.

"Sure. Let's see. Right now I'm your temporary sponsor."

What was that? Why temporary? I was a bit miffed.

Laurie said, "What do you think so far?"

"I don't know. I guess I have a problem with alcohol, and ending up in the hospital wasn't great. Also my roommate saying I couldn't stay unless I stop drinking."

"You're at step zero." Laurie grinned. "Step one is…" She recited the thing from the poster from memory. I didn't know whether to be impressed or uneasy.

She continued. "My girlfriend literally threw me out of the house and all my clothes after me. She said I was a disgusting, unreliable, lying bitch."

"Whoa, she was mad, huh?"

"Yep. It wasn't for a few months that I had to agree with her. I just thought she had to cool off and then she'd take me back 'cause I'm so charming. She always had taken me back before. Not that time. I was as hungover as hell and I had to go stay with one of my drinking buddies. But when I tried to get Lisa to let me come back home, she said, 'No, you're on your own. I'm through with you.'"

This was interesting. Laurie projected such an air of calm togetherness, it was hard to see her as a screwup.

She drank some coffee, and though she didn't exactly stare at me, she fixed me with a look so intense, it made me nervous.

"You think I'm telling you a story? Blowing smoke up your ass? I'm not. I drank for six more months until even my drinking buddy I was staying with couldn't stand me. I went to a rehab. It worked for me."

I didn't say it, but I wondered if she was merely trying to convince me she was the real deal and that would make me want to stick around this dopey so-called program. That's what they called it during the meetings, "the program." More cult-speak. It was like she could read my mind, and that bugged me.

"Look, Max. You're the only one who can decide what you want to do with your life. Right now, your life doesn't look so hot. You are on probation with your roommate, you have no money, you ended up in the hospital with an overdose, and your best friend died."

The reality that Chris was gone came rushing back into my thoughts, and I hated that she'd brought him up. She had a point, I conceded. Maybe.

Laurie said, "The way you get sober in AA is doing the steps. If I'm going to sponsor you, I've got some ground rules. Call me every day whether you feel like you're going to drink or not. Try to go to ninety meetings in ninety days. You have the meeting list, right? We'll meet once a week. We'll start with the first step."

Whoa. Was this high school or what? My head was starting to ache. But there were two things. One was I felt better physically than I had in years. Two, as annoying and bossy as Laurie was, I kind of liked her telling me what to do. She was hot.

"Okay. I think I got it. But why ninety meetings in ninety days?" That seemed excessive to me.

Laurie laughed and that irked me. "Because you drank every night, right?"

"Well. Yeah. But—"

"So then, since you're not drinking, you have time to go to meetings. The other reason is it immerses you in the program so you can start to incorporate it into your life."

"Right."

We hugged goodbye, and that was nice. As I went home, I talked to myself about it. What did I have to lose? I'd just give it a try and never mind my misgivings. At least I could spend time with Laurie.

It felt almost normal. *I* wouldn't have believed it if someone said to me I wouldn't have a single drink for three whole months. Not a one, no Valium either. Adrian had already taken care of that. There was none in the house and she wasn't dealing anymore. She hadn't let me back into her bed yet, but we were getting along fine and I had hope.

We talked about me being sober and she said, "Do you remember when we met? Parade day? You didn't drink, at least not until four o'clock in the afternoon." She chortled, which annoyed me somewhat.

"But honestly, Max, I liked that you. You were so happy, so open to me. You seemed like an honest and down-to-earth woman, someone I could be close to."

We were sitting in the kitchen, drinking coffee and smoking cigarettes.

Adrian said, "Can you believe it? I'm a stockbroker now."

"Well, I'm amazed, but not too much. I always knew you were smart with your BS in math. What changed?"

"It just got old, the drugs, the creepy and flaky people. I saw what was going on with you. It scared me. It was actually one of my customers who worked at the Pacific Stock Exchange and told me I could apply. So I thought why not. I have to start at six thirty in the morning." She grinned.

There were still random girls drifting in and out, Adrian admitted. Some things were the same.

"Do you think we'll ever sleep together again?" I asked. "I'm three months sober already."

"I don't think it's a good idea, Max, but I have to say the change in you is breathtaking. Phenomenal. You're more like that sweet, happy-go-lucky gal I met year before last."

That was all swell, but with my newfound sobriety, I was looking for more in my life. This sleeping on Adrian's couch was getting old. Real old.

The irritation of working at the messenger company actually increased the longer I was alcohol free. I assuaged it somewhat by taking pot breaks with Rob. I needed to find a new job, but going through the motions of applying for one, finding it first, then interviewing for it made me procrastinate.

Jay had cut way back on his coke habit, so that wasn't around to tempt me. Jay said, "Coke is God's way of telling you you're making too much money, since you end up having no money." Our wake-up lines had dwindled to once per month or less. I honestly didn't miss it that much. I most certainly didn't miss my hangovers.

I went to the meetings, mostly. If I didn't feel up to it, I didn't. There were times when I was absolutely exhausted. I heard from people that that was normal. I heard a lot of stuff like that from a lot of people. Some of it was helpful, like HALT, which stood for hungry, angry, lonely, tired. That means that you're more likely to want to drink if you're in one or more of those states. Find the appropriate remedies and you'll feel better.

But there were other things people said. "Clean and sober means NO drugs, including pot." Well, that was just ridiculous. I wasn't addicted to weed. I liked to smoke it every so often. So what? I never told Laurie I was smoking. It was none of her business. Besides, it was all I could do to keep up with her "suggestions." It was only those big blue eyes and earnest manner of hers that got to me and induced me to at least do some of them. I was usually busy picturing her naked, though, while she was talking and that was both a spur and a distraction. If only she weren't so serious all the time. If only we could have a drink together...oh wait.

Laurie told me, "The way this works is you do the twelve steps. That is, if you want to stay sober."

I was powerless over alcohol. That was clear, at least, and my life had been unmanageable. I would concede that. The whole God concept, though, eluded me. I'd stopped going to church after high school. I was a rational scientist. Educated. The Big Book—that was the bible of AA, so cutely named—said you *could* be an agnostic, but it seemed to imply that you'd believe in God after a while.

Meetings. Oh gosh, some days I'd walk away after inspired, uplifted. Other days I just wanted to scream. The only way AA *wasn't* a cult was that you could leave if you wanted to. No one was going to stop you. That was something. Otherwise, Jesus Christ. The dopey slogans: "One Day at a Time," "Easy Does It," "First Things First." Cunning, baffling, powerful. People actually said this crap out loud when they shared at meetings. Or in conversation, even. Cult robots.

I sat there, silently rating and judging everyone's share. My Higher Power—they meant God—this, my Higher Power that, my Higher Power doesn't want me to drink. Or my Higher Power—even worse, my "HP"—wants to me to be happy, joyous, and free. Yet another slogan. As though God was some sort of celestial personal trainer.

Or the converse: My disease wants me to fail. My disease doesn't want me to be sober.

Two things kept me from totally losing my mind: I wasn't drinking and I was fine. Two: Laurie. I was going to be sober enough one of these days to get into her jeans. Her perfectly fitting jeans over her clearly shapely legs. My libido was waking up again. With Adrian, it was more complicated. I wanted her magic touch. I wanted her to love me. I had thought she did love me. I would see.

Laurie. Well. Laurie was a challenge, and I do like challenges.

We sat in the usual booth in the usual café on Wednesday night and she wanted to talk about the steps. I wanted to talk about just about anything else.

We'd argued about the second step (the God step). And the third step—well, I didn't know what the fuck that meant. First, I had to wrap my mind around the second step.

Laurie said, "Look. AA doesn't demand that you believe in God. The books were written with the Judeo-Christian patriarchal God in mind, but that doesn't mean it has to be your concept."

I'd read the atheists and agnostics chapter in the Big Book and it hadn't helped. I didn't say that to Laurie, though.

"Okay. I'll read it."

"And do some writing on it and we'll talk about it next week."

I took a breath and asked Laurie, "Could we like go to a movie sometime? Not a date."

"Yeah, that would be fine." Ha. I knew it.

"How about Friday night?"

Laurie raised her eyebrows but nodded.

❖

I dressed carefully, as though I was going on a date. Damn it, I wasn't going out to clubs anymore, how was I going to meet women? Laurie was a find for sure. When she talked, I'd stare into her eyes, hoping I wasn't being too moony. Since I was supposed to listen to her, I didn't think she could tell.

As soon as we were seated, I made sure our arms and thighs were touching, and the feeling was electric. I wanted to jump out of my skin and I could barely concentrate on the movie.

Afterward, we walked along the Embarcadero and looked at the

Bay. I was in a fever trying to decide if I should attempt a kiss. I knew I was thinking too much. This had never happened while I was drinking. No thinking happening there. Then I recalled where that led. To all those one-night stands.

We stopped to stare over the water, and when we turned at the same time, I put my lips on hers. There was only a moment where I could enjoy the texture and she pulled away.

"Max, no. This is not the way this works. I cannot become romantically involved with you."

"Why not?"

"It's not that kind of relationship. If that's what you want, you're going to need to find a new sponsor."

"Okay," I said agreeably. "In that case, I will." I had no idea how to go about doing that.

"And even then, it may not be such a good idea for us to get involved. You're too new."

"Well, then. I'll go find a new sponsor and then we'll see. We can continue to see each other, right?"

Laurie was silent for such a long time I wanted to scream, but finally she said, "Yes, I'd like that."

I had a half-hearted intention of finding a new sponsor. I kept going to the meetings, usually with Laurie because I didn't want her to think I wasn't serious about staying sober.

At the Monday night women's meeting, I began to look for a new sponsor, one who might not be as demanding as Laurie. And no one Laurie knew. I had a feeling that if I managed to sleep with Laurie, it would get back to my sponsor and I'd be in trouble. AA had to be as gossipy and backbiting as any other bunch of lesbians.

Amanda fit the bill. She wasn't cute and she seemed, well, mousy and pliant.

At our first meeting over coffee, she said she wasn't into being bossy because "that doesn't work." Good enough for me. I showed her some writing dating from my days with Laurie and she nodded. Then she started to discuss me writing the fourth step. This was for sure not anything I had any plans to do. The whole concept of writing down all the stupid horrible crap I'd done, including what I'd done to Chris, was not appealing. I kept hearing people in meetings say that was how they stayed sober. I much preferred listening to all the tales of drinking and drugging. They were, at least, entertaining, and I could identify with what people said. I didn't want to drink, thank God or whatever.

Meanwhile, Laurie was a hard nut to crack. This whole idea of dating threw me into a major tizzy. I thought wining and dining a girl would be the process. So we'd skip the wining part and concentrate on the dining. Trouble was, I had no money. Laurie and I kept hanging out together and splitting what bills there were, and it all reeked of friendship and nothing further. Yet I could still sense a bit of yielding on Laurie's part. She at least was agreeable about us continuing to see each other. I was waiting for another chance at a kiss but I was taking it slow, as difficult as that was.

"Come on, let's go roller skating." I was attempting to wheedle her into this outing.

"Max, I haven't roller-skated since I was ten. I'm going to fall. A lot."

"So, I'll catch you." I, on the other hand, had skated frequently with Chris when we were in Cleveland. Those memories were sweet but still tainted by what happened later, so I pushed them away.

The roller-skating place was out in the suburbs, so Laurie drove us, another style-cramping aspect of our relationship.

When we'd laced on our skates and hit the rink, as I had hoped, she was hanging on to my arm, teetering on the edge of collapse. I furtively looked around, trying to judge how much touching was okay and what might get us harassed. I was reassured since there were a number of female couples, many of whom were clinging to each other as they skated, wobbling around the rink.

"Here you go," I said. "Hold my hand and get your balance."

She obeyed and off we went. As we speeded up, Laurie started to grin and then to laugh.

"This is great," she said and promptly tottered on the brink of collapse. I grabbed her around the waist.

"Steady there." And we looked at each other, and there, I was pretty sure I saw a little glint in her eye. I reluctantly let her loose when I was certain she had her balance back. There were no further mishaps. Regretfully, I let her go and we skated a few circuits.

"Coffee?" Laurie asked me once we were back in her car and headed up the freeway back to the City.

"Are you inviting me back to your place?"

There was beat of silence on her part, then she said, "Uh. Okay."

Eureka.

We sat in her living room, coffee cups in hand, not talking. It was abysmally awkward. I didn't know what to say or do. Without the helpful lubrication of vodka, I was like a rusty joint, I couldn't move.

"Laurie?" I had no idea what I was going to say, but luckily, she spared me the further embarrassment of trying to be articulate by pressing her mouth against mine. I was acutely self-conscious of my smoker's breath in a manner I'd never been when I was drinking. It was a great kiss, though, and as we progressed from lips to tongues to hair to breasts, I got hot. Good thing kissing still worked.

Laurie's breasts were phenomenal. I'd been secretly ogling them for weeks, and when we at last progressed to her bedroom and undressed each other, they didn't disappoint, and neither did the rest of her. What loomed large for me, though, was the old fear that I wouldn't orgasm with her. Was sobriety going to help me or inhibit me? I was going to find out. At least I had my old standby, the "it's not you, it's me" explanation. But I desperately wanted everything to work. Because who knew what was going to happen with Adrian, and I wanted a girlfriend.

It was terrifying how real sex was without booze. My senses reveled in Laurie's body even as anxiety bloomed in my mind about what was going to happen or not happen. Thinking this much was surely not helpful. I wrestled her onto her back right off and dived between her thighs. Surefire. And she did come without trouble. After that I calmed down somewhat, but it was short-lived. As she began to make love to me, I closed my eyes and tried to concentrate as though this was a math problem I needed to solve.

No dice. No amount of holding my breath or tightening my leg muscles was going to cut it. I was frigid, no doubt about it, except with Adrian. Every one of my nerves had gone into freeze frame. I had the distant impression that this was supposed to be pleasurable but it was like I was reading a book or something. I wasn't even in my body. I was outside it observing us and analyzing.

I tapped Laurie's arm—she was using her hand—and she looked up.

"Shall I try something different? Do you want to rest?" These words, spoken matter-of-factly in a neutral tone and heard in my cold, clear, alcohol-free state, were devastating.

"No," I said. "I'm fine."

She rolled to the side and touched my shoulder gently.

"You know, the first time you have sex sober isn't always the greatest."

That was an understatement. I truly wanted to disappear at that moment. There was no psychic cushion for this, as there had been when I was drinking.

Then nothing about sex seemed to matter other than doing it and getting my partner off. Now I found to my dismay it did. I wanted to sweep Laurie away, and having dynamite sex with her was part of the scenario.

"I better go," I said. If I couldn't vaporize myself, at least I could leave.

"Wait," Laurie said, grabbing my arm. I sank back down, slowly.

She propped herself up on a couple of pillows.

"I had been thinking and thinking about you and about this for a long time. I knew it wasn't a good idea but my body had other plans. I hope you're not going to drink over it."

Oh brother, now we're back to the "program." Swell.

"Nope. I'm not going to drink," I said with far more certainty than I felt.

"Let's get up and talk awhile."

"You know, I don't think I want to. If you don't mind, I'll go home."

"Yeah. Okay. If that's what you want." I noticed she didn't attempt to keep me there. She ended up driving me home.

I sat in the dark living room for a long time. If this was what sobriety was like, it sucked even worse than I thought it would.

Chapter Eight

It wasn't what I intended to do, but I ended blurting out to Amanda what happened. The disclosure habits taught by the program had clearly had an effect on me.

She fixed me with a disappointed glare. "That was not a good call."

"You're right. I admit it," I agreed but then she continued.

"There's a reason why we tell people not to get into or out of relationships during their first year of recovery. We're just not emotionally equipped to handle them. No wonder it didn't work."

Well, that was not the reason my "relationship" didn't work, dear Amanda, and I'm not going to deprive myself of sex just because you think I should. Who said anything about relationships anyhow?

I kept my thoughts to myself and nodded sadly. Maybe I could get another chance with Laurie. Maybe if we could try it a couple more times, I could relax. It was worth a try. Or maybe I was off probation with Adrian and...also possible.

The next time Laurie and I went out, though, as usual, after the Monday night women's meeting, she dropped the bomb on me.

"I don't think we ought to see each other anymore except as friends."

"What?" I asked, rather idiotically.

"I think you heard me. I'm not very good at this either, and you're messing up my mind and I don't want to drink."

"Yes, but...we could try again?" I couldn't have sounded more pathetic than if I was drunk and sorry.

"I don't think so."

Super. *Way to go, Maxy, you dimwit.*

Home and in a bad mood, I was brooding in the living room when Adrian strode in.

"Hey, girl, what's up?" She was cheerful and friendly enough. I suppose coming home and not coming upon me drunk and/or passed out was having a good effect on her mood and improved her opinion of me.

"Oh, you know, I sort of struck out with a girl."

"Oops, that's too bad. Wait a sec. I'll be back and you can tell me about it."

I didn't actually want to tell her about it, I wanted her to lick me to orgasm so I could forget about it. I wanted to touch that dusky golden brown skin again. Lust hit me so hard, I was shaking.

Adrian sat down with a beer in her hand. Nice. I stared at it.

"This okay?" she asked lightly.

"Oh sure. Sure." Now I could taste that beer, cold and crisp. One beer would be fabulous. Maybe two, max. Ha. *Max.*

"So what happened?"

"Oh, you know. The sex wasn't that good."

Adrian tipped the bottle up and I watched her throat move as she swallowed it. I began to sweat. "Bummer. What are you going to do?"

"Nothing, I guess." I spoke so softly it was almost a mutter.

"Max? Are you all right?"

No. Not even close.

I scooted over close to Adrian and put my hand on her leg. "Adrian?"

She picked up my hand and placed it back on my lap. "No. Max, this is not going to work for me. It's not good for you either."

"Adrian. Please." I guess the kindlier version of Adrian was done with.

She sat still and just stared at me.

I said, "Okay. All right then, I'm going out. Can you not be here when I get back? I want to be alone for a while."

"I need to remind you that I have to get up to go to work tomorrow. What do you expect me to do? Where do you think I'm going to sleep?"

I put on my coat. "I don't know, one of your many girlfriends' places?"

My whirlpool of thoughts and emotions included a lot of things:

killing Adrian, killing Laurie. Or giving each a piece of my mind. Oh, and also ripping Amanda too with her stupid advice about not getting into relationships. Screw all of them.

I walked around the block trying to calm myself. Fuck AA. What good had it ever done for me? I circled back around and ended up in front of the corner store where Ahmed sold me a pint of vodka. I'd just been paid, handily.

I went outside the store, leaned against the wall, unscrewed the cap, and took a long drink. The ninety-proof alcohol seared my throat, hit my stomach with a big silent splash, and then soared back up to my brain. Ah, I'd almost forgotten how good this felt. No, I hadn't forgotten, I'd just put it out of my mind so I could try and stay sober.

I sat down on the step of an apartment building. I couldn't go home since Adrian was probably still there. I drank about half the bottle and then hid it in my coat and staggered home anyhow. Fuck it.

The house was quiet. Adrian's bedroom door was closed. I flopped on the couch, took another pull, and closed my eyes. I wanted to not think, but no such luck.

I'd have to raise my hand as a newcomer again. *If* I went back.

Christ, all the AA-isms flooded through my mind, corrupting my enjoyment of the vodka I'd drunk. My brain issued the obvious observation: here I am drunk again. Then I was treated to a parade of faces; Adrian, Laurie, Amanda, Rob, then Chris. He stuck around and assumed the various poses in various situations from his life. The last one was in the hospital bed when he was dying. That's the last thing I saw before I passed out.

I woke up with a snap, swimming in nausea. I ran to the bathroom and threw up, then I crawled back to the couch, relieved I'd made in time. Oh God, I remembered what I'd done, and the shame almost made me upchuck again. But I fell unconscious again.

I woke up in gray light. The first thing I saw was a note on the coffee table. From Adrian.

You have two weeks to find a new place to live.

I couldn't face going to work. No way. I scrabbled for the phone and left a message, happy it was too early for anyone to in yet.

I wanted to die, but apparently that wasn't going to happen just yet. I tried to eat something but it didn't work. I wondered if Ahmed had any Pepto-Bismol and when he was going to open the store. Eight?

The bottle of vodka was still there in my coat pocket. I sat looking at it for a long time. "What have you ever done for me?" I asked the bottle of vodka or maybe the universe or God something. Great, I was talking to myself. I went to the kitchen, dumped it down the drain, and threw the empty in the recycling.

What would Laurie say? "Call someone" was what she would say. But I couldn't call her, no way. I didn't want to call Amanda either. I'd been given dozens of phone numbers at meetings but I had thrown them all away. My stomach did a forward roll.

I checked the clock in the kitchen. It said eight thirty. Ahmed would be open. I struggled into my jeans and shoes and, dizzy and queasy, I went out the door. The light hurt my eyes but I squinted and that helped.

I went in and sort of waved at Ahmed and he nodded a silent greeting. I didn't want to try and speak, so sleepwalked through the store trying to get my vision to clear enough so I could get what I needed. Saltines—good idea. Ginger ale? Right. There was an overpriced little bottle of Pepto-Bismol up front, and I snagged that.

"Not feeling well?" Ahmed asked as he rang me up.

"Nope. I think I've got the flu again," I croaked. He probably knew I didn't have the flu.

Back home, I treated my symptoms and asked myself what I was going to do. First, before I could think about anything, I had to feel better. I turned on the TV. Slack jawed, I watched the soap operas and the talk shows for a few hours. I dozed off again and when I woke up I was closer to being half alive. I munched on saltines and drank ginger ale.

Could I go back to AA? Likely. But I didn't want to. The prospect of talking about what I'd done was worse than my hangover. But that little teeny squeaky voice in my head said that was what I had to do. Or I could drink. That prospect was unappealing. There was nothing on the other side of drinking again except the same dreary round. Drink, hangover, recover, drink, etc. Blah.

Adrian's note was probably her final word: I was going to have to move. And go where? Also, I had a feeling I was going to get fired.

Something in Jay's tone when he answered the phone when I called in sick. Oddly, that didn't bother me as much as not having a place to live. I'd go back on welfare and food stamps. I put my head in my hands and tried to stop the thoughts from careening through.

"One day at time" was one of the stupid things I heard over and over in AA. Sometimes people said, "One thing at a time." The only coherent thought I could muster because I couldn't think of anything else at that moment was to go to a meeting. A meeting I'd never been to and where no one would know me.

I found the little meeting schedule book, and there was one at six p.m. at the Metropolitan Community Church on Eureka Street. Speaker discussion. In the Castro. I'd stuck to the women's meetings because it seemed like a good idea because, well, they were full of lesbians. This meeting was likely all gay guys. Once upon a time I used to like to hang out with gay guys. Like Chris. Chris was gone. I got a wave of grief to go along with my lingering nausea. Yay.

Well, hanging out with women in AA wasn't working out so well. I had no inclination to call Amanda. There was nothing wrong with her. Just…no. Okay then. Six o'clock. MCC Gay speaker/discussion.

I managed to sleep some more in the afternoon, and when I woke up I was able to eat some toast. But I was so tired, it seemed like an impossible task to walk five blocks to the MCC. As I walked, I rehearsed what I would say. What could I say? I'd fucked up. The only thing I kept a grip on was I wouldn't be kicked out if I said I'd drank again. I knew that much. AA has to take you in no matter what. And I was hopeful I could get some suggestions on where I could find a place to live. There were all these helpful things that AA people would do. I remembered how much AA got on my nerves, but then again, yes, the people in AA could be helpful. At this point, what choice did I have? As I walked, the answer came back clearly: none.

It felt like coming home when I walked into that room and took a seat in the back row. Yeah. This is me. Sad but true.

In a hot second, there was a tall black guy sitting next to me. He stuck out his hand.

"Hi, I'm Anthony."

"Hi, Max."

"Very good, Max. First time at this meeting?"

I didn't quite want to talk to anyone yet, I just wanted to sit and be quiet at the meeting and listen like Laurie always told me I should. No such luck. Here clearly was Mr. Gregarious.

"Will you read the steps?" Oh, bother, read the steps. I didn't want to, but something told me to say yes.

"Sure."

"Thanks." He made a note on the paper he carried with him. He was the meeting secretary, obviously.

The speaker, an older gay man, told his story. I'd heard similar versions before, but he at least incorporated some humor.

"I was drunk and I climbed out my window in order to get to the bedroom window of the guy upstairs who I had a major crush on. I thought I would show up at his window, ready to go, so to speak. How could he say no? Wrong. He did, and when I tried to get back in, the window had slammed shut and I couldn't open it. I couldn't go back to my crush's place, so I had to find someone else in the building to let me in."

Even in my defeated state, I had to laugh at the absurdity and the truth of the story. We do stupid shit when we drink.

His tone turned grave, though.

"Yeah, I did dumb stuff when I was drinking, but somewhere along the way, drinking wasn't fun anymore. I couldn't stop, but I couldn't get the right results anymore, the ones that would let me ignore everything. And thing is, you can't really ignore everything for any longer than you can stay drunk. Then reality comes rushing back in. Yet I kept on drinking. My mother cut off all contact with me, everyone did. I was utterly alone. I woke up one morning, came to is the more accurate description, and I knew I had to decide. I called AA."

He said more after that, but I was no longer listening. I was thinking about myself. What he'd described was exactly where I was. My night of drinking was not at all enjoyable. Not one minute of it. I saw myself sitting on the steps by the store sucking on my bottle of vodka like a street person. Pathetic *and* disgusting. I was going to be fired from my job, Adrian had finally truly kicked me out. What the fuck was I going to do? There was no Chris anymore. There was nobody and nothing that could help me. I didn't know what to do. All the AA rigmarole started floating through my thoughts again. I hated it, it sounded so inane, but what other choice did I have? The answer came back unequivocally: none. I couldn't bear the thought of drinking again.

The meeting had moved on to discussion, and I turned my attention to the room again. These guys were telling the same story and saying similar things to what I'd heard before. They talked about hope. As they talked, they said "life on life's terms." I don't know, they said a bunch of things, and some of it made sense. Or perhaps I was ready to hear it. Or at least some of it.

I had duly introduced myself as a newcomer. The clapping seemed so incongruous. What was there to applaud? I sat motionless. After the meeting broke up, Anthony was immediately at my side. He introduced himself again and made me make eye contact with him.

"How long since your last drink?" Here came the nosy questions, but somehow his expression was so gentle and so understanding, I answered him honestly.

"Yesterday."

"And how do you feel today?" I don't remember anyone ever asking me that in all the meetings I'd attended the last three months. They must have, but I didn't remember.

"Like shit," I said.

He grinned. "Right. What happened?"

Oh, crap, I had to talk. But somehow, I *wanted* to talk, I wanted to tell him what happened. I sketched out the previous couple days of my sorry life, including the fact that I'd been in AA before. He heard me out without interruption—another first, it seemed to me.

"More research," he said and chuckled.

"What do you mean?"

"You weren't convinced, so you had drink some more."

"Oh." Maybe that was true.

"So what do you want to do now? What do you *think* you ought to do?" I couldn't quite believe what I heard. Number one, he wasn't telling me what to do. He was asking me. Two, I hadn't a clue what I was going to do, that was why I was at a meeting.

I stuttered some, saying, "I'm not sure, but I have to get sober again. After that, I don't know. Find a new place to live."

"Any fool can get sober, *staying* sober is the trick," Anthony said. "It took me a long time to get that. And the way to stay sober is to be willing to suspend disbelief. I had to. I had all sorts of issues when I started."

"I'm not sure that AA is really for me. The God thing." I'd never admitted this out loud.

Anthony didn't launch into a lecture about Higher Power and all that nonsense, he just said, "Don't worry about that right now. I'm going to be your temporary sponsor. Are you ready, really ready to quit? Are you convinced?" His dark eyes bored into me.

It was somewhat intimidating, but I forced myself to hold his gaze. I said, "Yes."

"Okay then, let's go get you something to eat. We'll talk some more."

So we did the AA social thing, and I did feel better after eating a decent meal. Anthony told me more about himself. He had done a lot of disco, drugs, and dick, he said, but not proudly. He said it sort of like he was describing someone else's life, someone who he'd once admired but didn't anymore. It was just a story now. It was history.

I told him about my work situation and that I was expecting to be fired.

He said, "Well, that could happen, but you could try something."

"Like what?"

"Try telling the truth about what you did and where you are and how you're trying to get sober and could you have another chance. It might not work, but it might."

I was skeptical, to say the least, but if Anthony thought it might work, I guessed it was worth a try.

"What if I get fired anyhow?"

"One thing at a time. If you get fired, you'll deal with it."

I was dubious.

When we were on our way to Adrian's, he said, "I want you to start praying. I don't care what you believe or don't believe. Do the action. Make it simple, say thanks for being sober today. Ask the universe for help with your problems. No God involved."

I liked him so much I wanted to be honest and tell I didn't want to pray, but I kept my mouth shut. Okay. I would do what he said to do.

He hugged me and told me he would call me tomorrow. That was also different. I was always told to call someone and I never did.

I settled myself on the couch. As I prepared to go to sleep, I said what he told me to say to myself silently. Then I fell asleep.

❖

I woke up without the ringing of my alarm, and the first thing I noticed was I wasn't sick. I wasn't nauseated and headachy and stiff. Then I remembered. *Oh, didn't drink last night. This is what that's like when I don't drink and I'm not hungover.*

I found Jay first thing in the morning before anyone else was there. If I was going to get fired, I wanted to get it over with.

He swiveled in his old-fashioned desk chair with his hands clasped, his eyes closed and resting on his belt as I talked. His expression didn't change. My little speech was somewhat disjointed, but I didn't strategically omit anything, as I normally would.

Jay swiveled back toward me and opened his eyes.

"You were not drinking and then you got drunk, but now you are going to stop again?"

"Uh, right."

"Yep, I was thinking about firing you. It's unfair to Rob when you are so undependable." There was no excuse I could offer. "Yet when you didn't drink for three months, you were great."

"Thanks," I said weakly.

"Okay. You got it. Another chance, but the next time it happens, you're out with two weeks' notice."

"I really appreciate it, I do. Thank you." And the odd thing was, I was honest about that too.

Anthony called me and asked me how everything was, and I told him and he congratulated me, then immediately asked, "What meeting are you going to today, or have you already gone?"

"I wasn't planning on one because..."

"All right, I'm coming to pick you up and take you to a meeting. We'll talk more on the way."

As annoyed as I was at him, he'd been right about my job dilemma, so just maybe he might be right about everything else. In retrospect, I'd not believed that my previous contacts in AA had anything to teach me. They were all women. Was I sexist?

In the car, he said, "Ninety in ninety."

I said, "Yeah. I know."

"Will you commit to that?" He was not speaking unkindly, but he was stern.

"I don't want to and then disappoint you." I sounded so lame, and I knew this was the wrong thing to say as soon as it was out of my mouth.

"Max. This isn't about me. I'm not your dad that you have to obey or please. This is for you. It will help you if you think of what I'm suggesting as things that I have done myself and they work, and you can *choose* to do them to help yourself. If you don't want to, and I know you don't, no one does, not at first, do them anyway. It's like I told you to pray. You didn't want to. Fine, but it's the action that counts. It's going to the meeting that counts. Whether you want to or not. You can act your way into right thinking, but you can't think your way into right action. Your thoughts are what are going to lead you back to drinking. Your actions, as you repeat them, will finally move your thoughts in the right direction, and you'll want to drink less."

"Oh," was all I could think of as a response. No one had ever put it quite that way. In AA, I'd heard a lot of suggestions that seemed suspiciously like orders and made me want to rebel and not do a single thing. Or at least to not do everything. I wanted to pick and choose what I would do. And all I heard was what I ought to do and no explanation except for "that's what we do."

Anthony continued, "No alcoholic and no human wants to be told what to do. We rebel at 'you must,' 'you ought to,' 'you have to,' and worst of all, 'you should.' We're just humans like everyone else, but unlike normal people, our actions and thoughts can lead us to pick up alcohol and drugs and maybe *die.*"

The way he emphasized the last word scared me. I'd not thought of the possibility of dying, but I suppose ending up in the hospital having my stomach pumped wasn't what I'd thought of either. The way Anthony talked made sense, though his manner wasn't especially warm and fuzzy. He was sort of stern, like a parent, but it didn't bother me. Some of the dykes in AA talked me in a sort of "oh, you poor thing" manner that bugged me the same way their suggestions did. I could tell he cared about me, and he wasn't going through the motions. He said the steps were suggestions in the way that opening the ripcord when you were in a parachute was a suggestion. Oh, right.

I didn't truly want to stop drinking, not really until that moment. I realized I'd had in the back of my mind that I could drink again after I was feeling better for the short three months of my first leap into sobriety. The word "die" had a certain ring to it. I also thought of Chris but rapidly pushed the thought away.

We sat through the meeting and I kept hearing people say the same things. Maybe I'd heard them before, but I'd not really heard them. Laurie's saying about taking the cotton out of my ears came back to me. I didn't know what it was exactly but I knew I didn't want to die or be miserable.

After I made that leap, I started to hear other things.

Someone told a story, a parable, I suppose.

There was a man who was stuck in a deep hole in the ground and he couldn't get out of it. A preacher came along and told him, "Oh, I can pray over you and God will get you out." Someone else said to him, "I think you ought to try and build a ladder." A third person told him, "You just have to use positive thinking, that'll get you out." Finally, a fourth man came along and said, "I've been in this hole and I can tell you how I managed to get out of it."

I got it.

One guy in a meeting said, "You can save your ass or you can save your face, but not both. Pick one. I go for saving my ass." He'd been talking about the fear of asking for help or the denial of needing help. Right.

In the car with Anthony on the way back to Adrian's, I said, "I don't want to drink anymore."

Anthony grinned. "That's a good start. Keep telling yourself that and keep doing what we've been talking about. You don't have to suffer anymore, truly. You don't. Alcoholism is a disease, and one of its primary symptoms is you are convinced you don't have it. Congrats on getting over your denial."

PART III: WHAT IT'S LIKE NOW

CHAPTER ONE

Anthony gave me something called *Shame and Addiction* to read. I had to read it through twice before I could even start to make sense of it.

> *Shame and addiction are Siamese twins.*
> *Most of us come into recovery as innocents. In the rawness of hitting bottom and accepting the first step about powerlessness, we are like children hoping everything will be fixed now. The reality is that getting sober merely gets us to the starting gate. Eventually if we are true to our recovery, we will collide with the feelings we ran from for years.*

I looked up "shame" in the dictionary. It said, "the painful feeling of having done something dishonorable, improper, ridiculous, etc." Whoops, that hit home.

> *Recovery is not a destination, it is a journey.*

There was a lot more.

Anthony said, "The word 'admit' might remind you of what someone says who's guilty of doing something wrong. It actually means, 'recognize that which is true.'"

"Right. I am recognizing the truth of my powerlessness over substances because I used them when I didn't want to. I couldn't stop or predict what would happen when I did."

Anthony scrutinized me. "You have to be gut-level honest and really ready to face the truth about yourself, or this doesn't work or it won't work for long."

"I don't think I was ready when I tried before. I just didn't want to feel bad." I told Anthony all about my cavalier approach to AA, my petulance and the disingenuous way I tried to please women who were trying to help me. The secrets, the lies. And all the drugs and what happened to me at work. But I didn't say anything about Chris. I wasn't ready for that.

"And now?"

"Yes. I'm there."

"Good. We're going to be talking a lot about shame. And you as an alcoholic and an addict are riddled with it. You as a gay person are also unfairly subjected to much more shame than the average person. You get the difference between shame and guilt?"

"Yes, but I had to look them up," I said proudly, and he laughed.

"Okay, tell me."

"Guilt is specifically related to an act. Shame is the general feeling of unworthiness."

"That's right. Homophobia is designed to make us feel unworthy, ashamed of who we are."

"Yeah. It's awful."

"We have the double whammy of being ashamed of being alcoholics *and* being gay. Those two things are as an inseparable as shame and addiction."

I sat back in my chair. The café bustled around us. I was scarcely aware of the clink of cups and the chatter of other patrons. Anthony stayed silent, I think to give me the space to absorb what he said. I took it in, and at that moment, my life began to make sense to me. I knew that what I been living wasn't the life I wanted. I wanted something else.

❖

As Anthony said, going to meetings got easier. I dragged my tired, sorry ass to a meeting every day. Sometimes I went to one downtown at noon before I started my delivery route. The besuited business people in that meeting didn't give off the same disdainful air of the people in the law offices. They were, in fact, friendly in the manner that everyone at AA meetings is friendly. Alcoholism is a great democratizer.

At first, I was suspicious, but slowly I began to trust more. I still avoided women's meetings and stuck to either mixed gay meetings or straight meetings such as the noontime Financial District meeting. I couldn't say why, but going to these meetings made me less anxious and less bored. I suspected it was something to do with how I viewed women. I took a big leap and I told Anthony about it.

"Did you ever think that might be about your internalized homophobia, i.e., shame?"

I was shocked. "No. Never."

"Think about it. Think about how you used to drink and pick up sex partners."

"Oh." I hadn't told him about my difficulties with orgasms. That would have to wait for a bit. But the word "shame" popped into my consciousness when I thought about how I'd behaved. I couldn't stand to face my sex partners in daylight, I couldn't even pick someone up and attempt sex unless I was drunk. Adrian was the exception, but our relationship was a whole other level of dysfunction. I was going to tell Anthony all about it. Sometime.

I told him about my issues with the God stuff, and as usual, he was empathetic and told me what he'd done instead of telling me what to do. I was starting to recognize this pattern and it made me smile, but I came to realize exactly how shrewd Anthony was. He always threw stuff back at me. What did I think I had to do? What was really going on with me? He never told me what to do, so I couldn't rebel against him.

"I have to listen to other people talk about their concepts of God and use them to develop my own."

He grinned. "Bingo."

Within a month, I was able to stop saying I was a newcomer, which pleased me inordinately. I would look around at meetings thinking everyone looked so goddamn happy, it was impossible to picture them as a sloppy drunks, but that's how they described themselves, and I had no reason to doubt them.

❖

"Want to go around the corner?"

It was Rob asking me if I wanted to get high.

I was silent. I had gone ahead and done that those first three months I was sober, but now I was imbibing no consciousness-altering substances. None.

"No, thanks," I said before I could think about it too much. At that instant I wanted to get high, but I stopped myself.

Rob looked at me quizzically but only said, "Okay," turned on his heel, and left.

I sat in the office and ate the sandwich I'd brought. If nothing else, if I didn't smoke a joint, I wouldn't be tired when I came down. That was something to tell myself to stave off that sudden craving for the mellow peace of being high.

When I told Anthony my story, I hadn't left out the part where I continued to smoke dope even though I'd stopped drinking and taking drugs.

He said, "It doesn't seem like a big deal, but two things happen. The first is you give yourself permission for pot and then you can easily justify anything else as you did. The second is you cannot start learning how to get through life sober. This is not about deprivation, it's about finding other ways to cope."

It was gratifying to tell Anthony about my choice because it gave me a little glow of achievement. It wasn't that Anthony didn't say the things I'd heard before, but somehow, I had stopped being cynical and was doing the things he'd described to me that he had done that kept him sober. The list seemed endless, though, and Anthony wouldn't cut me a break or let me slack. He praised my page-and-a-half essay on the first step and promptly assigned me to read the second step and write a page or two on my belief in a Higher Power.

"But why do I have to write all this stuff down?" I heard the ghost of my old whiny tone, but he merely raised his left eyebrow. He could raise one eyebrow at a time; it mystified me.

"Because I say so." He laughed and added, "You are in need of direct adult supervision. Everyone is, including me."

I knew he was joking because his eyes twinkled, but underneath he was dead serious.

"Thinking and writing makes it clearer to you. The writing

prompts the thinking. Then you read it aloud to me. Those are the three elements."

"I don't know what to say because I don't believe in a Higher Power." I put the imaginary quotes around the phrase with my voice.

"Well, read some more. Listen to other people. I told you my story. The Higher Power just has to work for you."

With my job secure for the moment, the biggest issue I had was finding a place to live for which I could pay very little. It almost killed me, but I asked Anthony for help. I added, "I can't pay hardly anything but I could trade for labor, yard work, housework, or something."

"Hm. Let me think about it."

A couple days later, he called me and said he'd found something that might work. "I know a guy in the program who has an in-law apartment."

"A what?"

"In-law. Like a little place where your mother-in-law could live."

"Uh-huh."

"Here's his number. It's up to you to go talk to him. I told him about you."

This was a lot harder than I thought it would be. I'd have to negotiate with some strange guy. I was silent. I didn't want to whine but Anthony could read my mind even on the phone.

"Max. You can do this. It's scary, but you can do it."

"Right."

It turned out that this fellow, Rick, would let me stay for three months almost rent free but I'd have to help him fix the place up—painting and cleaning, and work in the garden, and generally be his slave. I thought about working my regular job and then doing all that as well, and it was daunting. I'd have a place to live and it would get me away from Adrian. I didn't want to separate from her, but I knew I had to.

I said yes. It was another leap into the unknown.

❖

Anthony would not let me off the hook about my Higher Power.

"I got nothing." I shrugged and gave him my best sheepish smile.

"Keep listening, reading, and thinking and it'll come to you," Anthony said. "Remember, this is for you, not for me. Whether or not you do it doesn't affect me either way other than I don't want you to drink. There are other ways to get sober, but this is the one I know. It works for a lot of other people as well, but there aren't shortcuts. The steps are in order for a reason."

I was as grouchy as I could be about it, but somehow, I had grasped that I had to try, and the act of trying was the main purpose.

A couple days later, I was sitting in the Financial District meeting where I heard one of the suits, an executive in an accounting firm of some kind, nobody I would even talk to, let alone want to listen to, open our meeting with the usual ten-minute share. And as a subject, he chose the second step. When he started to speak, I began to shut down, but by brute force I made myself listen as Anthony had instructed me. Keep an open mind.

Hal read a couple of sentences from the book on the steps.

"I used to think religion was a form of insanity, a socially acceptable form of insanity. I didn't have any religious background. God was also a social construct. I didn't have any need for it or him or whatever."

Okay. That was me.

Hal said, "I was a scotch drinker. Gallons of scotch. Oceans of scotch. The hangovers were brutal. My wife was going to leave me, my kids couldn't stand to be around me. 'I'll quit, honey. Tomorrow, I promise' and then I wouldn't, I'd just keep on drinking.

"I finally called the AA number and I went to a meeting, and I wore a three-piece suit. Can you imagine? I thought that I had to look good. The meeting was in the evening and no one else there was dressed up like me. I'd even shaved." The people seated around the table laughed along with Hal.

He continued, "There was an old guy there. He had to be seventy-something. After the meeting, he made a beeline for me. 'You're a smart guy, I bet,' he said. 'No one tells you what to do.' I was so foggy I was almost speechless. The old guy asked me, 'If you're so smart, how come you can't stop drinkin'?' He had me there. I mumbled something."

I let this seep into my brain. Okay. I was smart too. This Hal guy was clearly not a dummy even if he was a suit.

Hal said, quoting the old man he'd met, even making his voice sound scratchy and old, "'You probably think you're God.' 'No. I don't.' I was offended he'd think that. 'You act like you are, though. Everyone has to dance to your tune, do what you say, probably, you're always right.'"

Hal grinned. "When I thought about it, if I was honest, what he said was mostly true. I was a big shot. I told people how to handle their money, rich people with large amounts of money. So yeah, I thought I was fairly intelligent. Then the old guy says, 'You ain't God. You don't have any control over nothing.' Okay. He had my attention. So he goes, 'What's the definition of insanity?' I said I didn't know. 'Doing the same thing over and over and expecting different results.'"

Hal stopped and looked as though he might cry any second. Another surprise to me. He visibly teared up. The fancy haircut, three-piece-suit dude was about to cry. We waited until he got himself in hand.

"That was me. I drank every day and told my wife over and over that I was sorry, I'd change. And I never did. I just kept right on doing the same frigging thing.

"Then the old guy said to me, 'The second step says God can restore us to sanity. That's what you have to do. You have to believe even if you don't know what the hell you believe in. You have to believe you can be restored to sanity.'"

After Hal finished speaking, there were other people who talked, but I stopped listening to think about what Hal said and think about myself. I had to leave right away, but I snagged him when the meeting ended and told him my name.

"I am on the second step and I don't know what to do. I don't believe in God. I don't know what a Higher Power is."

"Me neither," Hal said and smiled. If I hadn't just heard him and saw him almost break down, I would never think someone who looked like him would have anything good to teach someone like me. That smile of his would look like a smirk and I'd be out of there.

Not this time. Hal was sweet and generous.

Hal said, "Faith is a funny thing. Faith in what? I don't know. For sure I have faith in AA. It gave me my life back. It saved my marriage. I chose to have faith that I'll be okay, that it will all work out. I *choose* that. I am restored to sanity."

I thanked him and went on to complete my afternoon work. I thought about how good it was not to be hungover and to have a job that let me be outside part of the time. And I thought about the second step. There was a lot of other stuff in the book about getting over being obstinate. When I had spoken with Anthony about how rational I was, science and all that, he said, "Contempt prior to investigation," and made me read the appendix in the Big Book that explained that concept.

That's what I was doing: investigating. When Anthony told me what he did in early sobriety and that it worked, I believed him. I believed Hal. I was investigating what it took to stay sober. It was like an experiment.

I went back to that meeting in the Financial District many times. Not only did I become very fond of Hal, it helped make sure I could get to a meeting during the day, and I was able to achieve my ninety meetings in ninety days.

When I finished work, I would spend an hour or so working on whatever Rick wanted me to do. I sanded, I painted. I learned how to stain a wood floor. I pulled weeds, I dug in the dirt. Then I would eat something quick and simple and I would go to sleep. Then I would wake up and do it over again. On weekends, I would meet with Anthony and go to more meetings. I never did exactly define what a Higher Power was. It wasn't me, as Hal had explained. I could say that I had faith that everything was going to work out. I was no longer walking through life in a perpetual state of dread that the sky was going to fall. Because it didn't. Or if it did, then I'd figure out what to do.

Rick let me make calls on his phone. Outgoing calls. I couldn't afford a phone. I had yet another mattress on the floor to sleep on. I saved money as much as I could. At some point, the in-law cottage would be ready for rental and I'd have to leave.

Oddly, none of this bothered me. I was fine. I no longer spent my days in a state of exhaustion and anxiety. Well, I was still exhausted, but it was a different kind of exhaustion, a good kind. It was like I had learned about how to sleep when I was tired and eat when I was hungry. I learned to be an adult.

One Saturday afternoon, as I sanded off the layer of old paint in the kitchen area of the in-law, the radio that Rick had given me played a song I'd heard before but that day suddenly struck me. It was the old tune "I Can See Clearly Now" by Johnny Nash.

What a great metaphor for getting sober. I can see what I never saw before. This made me smile. It was a bright day, full of sunshine.

I'd acquired a sheath of alcoholic fat around my abdomen that I shed in the first few months. Who knew that not drinking was better than a diet?

When I couldn't sleep, I read the AA literature, and it made me doze right off.

It was a strange sort of life—comforting and calm as anything. The most basic routines of life now gave me great joy instead of feeling like horrible tasks. I understood that when I was drinking and doing drugs, everything was hard. *Everything*. Starting with simply getting up in the morning every day. Not anymore.

But…there were the steps to complete.

As Anthony often reminded me, they're in order, and the only one we can do perfectly is the first, admitting we are powerless over alcohol.

"The steps *are* the spiritual experience," he said and added, "Religion is for people who are afraid of going to hell, spirituality is for those who have already been there." When Anthony said things like this, my mind no longer issued cynical comebacks. I believed him and I believed that I could do what he described. Anthony told me in detail how he performed each step and what it meant to him.

"You've overcome two hurdles, and it's essential you recognize how monumental that is." He said this after my Hal breakthrough, as I liked to call it.

I had fully embraced the reality that I was powerless over alcohol. I had more than enough evidence of it, and to my rational mind, nothing was better than evidence. I had a less comfortable relationship with the spirituality—the God stuff, as most people called it. But the more I heard doubt from other people, the easier it became to simply accept it instead of trying to intellectualize it. *I am not God.*

The AA sayings made more sense to me to the longer I stayed sober. They ceased being annoying clichés and began to sound like simple but profound pieces of advice.

When Anthony and I read about the third step together in the book, I reverted somewhat to skepticism and argumentativeness, but he was, as always, patient with me but acerbic.

"I'm willing," I said, protesting, wanting to be reassured that I was virtuous. I had completed the first and second steps, so I thought I was hot shit.

"What does this mean?" I asked him, referring to the description of "willingness" in the literature.

"You can say you're willing, but it means nothing unless you actually *do* the work. 'Faith without works is dead.'" That was yet another of Anthony's favorite AA-isms.

I pouted, still wanting more help.

Anthony grinned at me in his usual fashion. He was sympathetic, but he never cut me *any* slack.

"I'll know if you're willing. If you can consistently participate in your recovery, if you go to the meetings, call me, read the literature, and do the steps, I'll see that you're willing. Saying you are is all empty blather. Show me. That is what this is all about. I cannot produce willingness in you. It has to come from you. There is no shortcut. Write down all the ways you're willing to do the program. Then we'll dive right into your moral inventory." By that, he meant writing down everything that I'd done wrong. It seemed counterintuitive to all the talking about shame but…

I huffed and rolled my eyes, but I didn't object.

❖

During meetings over the next six months, I always sat across the room from Anthony rather than next to him so I could watch his face. He reacted to various people's shares in an amusing way. I couldn't laugh aloud, though sometimes it was difficult not to. The surprising thing was I *could* laugh. That had been missing from my life for a long, long time.

Anthony fitted his hands together in an oval shape. That meant he thought the person speaking was oversharing. Going into too much detail, rambling. I nodded slightly as our eyes met. The person going on and on about his mother at last stopped. Then the next person who shared said something so breathtaking I would think about it for days.

It was another revelation to me that I wasn't expected to like everybody in AA. When I started, I had the impression that I ought to. When I came to the program, I'd liked hardly anybody, but the reason for that became clear over time. I was judgmental, superior, and impatient. It was good to not be an asshole anymore.

As Anthony said, "If everyone around you is a jerk, it's time to take a good look at yourself. *You* might be the jerk. That's why we do inventories."

Ah yes, the fourth step: a searching and fearless moral inventory. I even hated the name of it. I sighed. I procrastinated. I rationalized. When I was supposed to be working on my fourth step inventory, I was doing nothing but making up reasons why I couldn't do it.

I told Anthony, "I'm having a hard time."

He cocked his eyebrow. "Have you a pencil? Piece of paper?"

I laughed even though I didn't want to. Anthony had no patience for my bullshit, for which he had a highly developed detector. As we went on, he was freer about letting me know he noticed when I tried to put one over on him. I loved him and I hated him.

"I don't want to think about how I acted with anyone."

I had already been forthcoming with him about my ways with women. Adrian, Annie, Lily, and all the rest of them. Anthony had chuckled. They were amusing stories, and I liked to make him laugh. He told me a few of his own: The visiting bodybuilder in the 1981 Gay Olympics. The parties in Pacific Heights mansions with closeted millionaires and bowls full of every drug you could name. I admit I salivated a bit when I heard that.

He was celibate now, even though he could have had a lover if he wanted one. He was so magnetic, every man who knew him was half in love with him. I didn't ask him why he was celibate. He would tell me if and when he wanted to. Anthony explained the concept of boundaries to me, and he demonstrated his grasp of the necessity of maintaining them.

"I think you might need to do a sex inventory," Anthony said.

"A what?" That term "sex inventory" alarmed me. I still didn't want to talk about my orgasm problem.

"Read page whatever in the *Twelve and Twelve*," Anthony said in his irksome way whenever I asked a question like this. "It tells you." He meant read the *Twelve Steps and Twelve Traditions.*

I read aloud what he showed me and then closed the book.

"Yeah. That's me." Selfish, elusive, cavalier. It was depressing to contemplate how big a bitch I'd been. Except with Adrian. She was the one who hurt me.

"Let's start with sex."

I reminded myself how much I wanted to not drink anymore. This inventory thing was key to being able to do that. As I listened in meetings, I heard a lot of people say how much they hated this part of the program.

I did it, I wrote their names down and then, in as much detail as I could remember, I described what I did or didn't do. It was horrifying to see it all laid out in detail in one place.

"I'm not trying to make you feel bad," Anthony said patiently. That was exactly what I thought he was doing with this insistence on inventory.

"You will not be able to move on with your life until you've dealt with the wreckage of your past. All your broken relationships and all your bad behavior. My part is to listen to you and tell you what sort of patterns I see."

"Right," I said, my teeth gritted. I read it all out for him.

"I'm a shit," I said, finally, after I'd finished. "There were a lot of women I mistreated."

"You could be a gay guy, the way you acted," he said. I laughed. I knew he was joking but I guess that was true. If only my sex partners had been men maybe it wouldn't have been so bad. But maybe not. Probably not.

"Are you afraid of women?" Anthony asked me. Was I? That seemed to be the case.

"How could I be afraid of women? I slept with a slew of them."

Anthony fixed me with his bullshit radar look. His eyes narrowed, the left eyebrow went up. I didn't want to answer, I didn't want to admit I was afraid of anything, let alone women.

"Yeah. Okay. Likely."

"It isn't sex, it's intimacy you're afraid of." Oh. That was almost certainly true.

"Or internalized homophobia. Otherwise known as shame."

Where was he going with this? Anthony was esoteric sometimes.

Not only was he deeply immersed in the program, he went to therapy and read all kinds of things. He would try to get me to read—the program literature, certainly, but other things as well.

"Anyhow, let's talk about Adrian. You wouldn't be able to tell if you liked someone or not because you were always drunk and then you got rid of them quickly. As fast as possible. Except Adrian. Why was she different? She was your drug dealer, of course. Handy gal to have around."

I hated Anthony's knowing grin, sometimes because he actually did seem to understand me more than I understood myself. But the other reason for Adrian, besides the drugs, still wasn't something I wanted to reveal. Anthony waited for me to answer his question. With everything we'd talked about, I was no longer able to lie to him. Even by omission.

"'Cause she's the only woman I ever had sex with where I could come. Like a supernova."

"I see. That's monumental," he said, almost in a whisper. "You could only get off with Adrian. You never cared about monogamy until you met her."

"No. I was the opposite of monogamous." I snorted. "Of course, there were no relationships to speak of. I wanted Lily to stick around, but only so I could say I had a girlfriend, and I was just annoyed she rejected me. For being an alcoholic, of course. But I wanted Adrian all to myself, and I was pissed that she didn't go along."

"Did you ask her?" Anthony wanted to know.

Another realization. "Nope. I didn't. I only tried to get her to keep me supplied with drugs. And she manipulated me around drugs all the time. I was her slave and I thought that was love."

"Of course she did. What's your part?" That was another question Anthony often asked, and I hated it.

I read from my list. "I let her. I was needy. I'm a drug addict and I wanted to keep having sex with her."

"Yep." Anthony leaned back. We were seated in a café as usual. He waited for what I would say next. That was another wonderful and profoundly irritating thing about him. He listened so hard it terrified me and then he waited for me to reach my own conclusions.

"I'm a fucking mess," I moaned.

"No more so than anyone else, Max my dear. No worse than any other alcoholic."

As I fell asleep that night, I noticed I felt better. As Anthony predicted, I was psychically lighter after writing all of it down and then telling him.

CHAPTER TWO

After the sex part of my inventory was done, it was easier for me to go on with the rest of it—my parents, my manager at Cal Genetics, etc. All except Chris. I still felt like my insides were being twisted into knots when I thought of him. I was beginning to grasp that if I wanted that sensation to stop every time I thought of him, I would have to do something about it. Not only did my memories bedevil me, the thing that killed Chris, AIDS, was killing other men as well. They talked about it in meetings. A lot.

Someone would say, "I was diagnosed last week." There was no further information needed or conveyed. That only meant one thing. The man meant he had AIDS.

"If I'm going to die, I want to die sober."

"My boyfriend is in the hospital."

"I talked to the doctor and he said…"

This was not helping me to get over Chris. It was making it worse. It was in my face all the time. Chris invaded my thoughts at odd times, and there was no longer any way to numb out, even temporarily. The downside of sobriety.

I started to be obsessed with reading about it. I, who never read a newspaper if I could avoid it, read the gay rags every week, and the news was not good.

"Who's Chris?" Anthony asked me when I told him I'd left one name off my fourth step inventory.

I told him about Chris. In the nine months since I'd come back to AA, I hadn't said his name aloud. Not speaking his name turned out to be not much of a relief because he was in my head and there were guys like him in the rooms of AA and they were not shy about sharing their situations.

After I was done telling the Chris story, I started to weep. Anthony moved to my side of the table. He didn't smile knowingly or crack a joke or spout any AA saying. He just put his arm around me and waited until I calmed down.

"You know what you have to do," he said kindly. "Let's give you two weeks on this inventory."

"If you say so."

I would sit on my bed in the in-law apartment and tap my pencil on my legal pad. Nothing was forthcoming. Or rather, there was too much. Worse than anything I had said to Chris was my abandonment of him, my utter inability to connect to him when he was sick. I never even went to his fucking funeral. I took a deep breath and said to myself, "Do this chronologically." There was my lack of gratitude for everything he'd helped me with. My failure to take responsibility when I worked at Cal Genetics. Or for paying rent. Then I got mad at him for kicking me out of the apartment. And I wrote down all the rest of it. I never expressed a single word of love or appreciation to him while he was alive. Our friendship seemed like it was one huge joke, but it wasn't.

Anthony listened impassively to my reading of the Chris inventory. I cried through the whole thing.

"Max," Anthony said, "you're much too hard on yourself. It's not your fault he got AIDS and died." This was, of course, Anthony's signature kind of bald statement of the truth—my truth, his truth. THE truth. I had come to love Anthony's utter lack of sentimentality, but this hurt too much. It *was* my fault.

"When you've done something wrong to someone and you keep beating yourself up about it, you are only compounding the problem. The first person you have to forgive is yourself, Max. Then you can work on forgiving other people."

"What am I supposed to do?" I asked, and I cried some more.

"We're still doing the steps. You have a ways to go, try to be less hard on yourself. You're evolving slowly. What you have to do will become clear to you in time. Easy does it and one day at a time." The AA-isms no longer irritated me, thank goodness.

I sniffed and blew my nose. "Yeah, yeah." I did feel better, though.

Somewhat. I didn't know how in the hell I could ever forgive myself for abandoning Chris.

❖

Rick and I reached an agreement where he let me stay in the in-law apartment at a reduced rent and in exchange for work that included gardening, cleaning his house, and helping at his interior design studio every other weekend. I grew inordinately proud of my gardening skills, and I would not ever have guessed that I would take such satisfaction in housecleaning and filing. I think it was being able to accomplish tasks successfully. I asked Anthony and he agreed.

"Everything you are able to do is repairing your self-esteem. The more you do in sobriety, the more it all seems possible, and your brain and your soul heal."

It was as predicted. I was mildly euphoric after I finished my inventories and told Anthony everything. It was a feeling close to what I used to feel after my third drink, a feeling I'd chased forever to no avail.

Yet.

I knew I had to find a way to get back to my profession. I didn't disdain the work I was doing for Rick, but it wasn't enough. I wanted to engage my intellect, which, along with everything else about me, had begun to function. I had no idea how to do that, but I constantly reminded myself to be patient.

The other black cloud in my sunny sky of happiness was my memories of Chris. They hurt, and I talked to Anthony about it and he was sympathetic, but it didn't help that much. I was still awash in regret. The clarity that my sobriety brought made me realize the awfulness in every detail. I was clear that I couldn't have prevented his death but I was unable to forget how utterly awful and non-supportive I'd been. I was absent when I should have been the most present. Anthony was trying to move me along to the next phase of my recovery—making amends. I was as filled with dread about this part as I'd ever been about the personal inventory, mostly because it wasn't at all clear how I could say I was sorry to someone who was dead. Not to mention say I was sorry to all the people I'd fucked over who were still alive, and that was a long list.

"You will know when you know," Anthony said in reference to how I would deal with my memories of Chris. How I hated that phrase. I wanted to know *now*. I hated uncertainty worse than anything, and I complained about it regularly to Anthony, who would merely smile and say something about faith.

❖

Another six months zipped by and it was 1986, and I celebrated two years of sobriety. Anthony let me slide on my step work, I think because he wasn't feeling particularly well. Neither of us voiced what the reason could be, but it was there anyhow. He asked me to go with him to get the test at the SF Department of Health. The US government had announced the test the previous year. There was now a way to discover whether or not you were positive without having to wait to get sick. Not that it particularly mattered since there was still no treatment for AIDS, let alone a cure.

"Why me?" I asked him as we rode downtown on Muni.

"Half of the people I know already took the test and they're positive, and they sure as shit don't want to go back to DPH. The other half are too freaked out and don't even want to talk about it, let alone get the test. They're in severe denial. None of this applies to you, and I didn't want to go by myself."

"It's really great you asked me," I said. I didn't mention that I was terrified he was going to test positive and I was going to lose him like I lost Chris.

Anthony stared vacantly out the window at the walls of the Muni Metro tunnel flying by.

"Hey," I whispered to Anthony, "that guy over there is cruising you." I hoped it would cheer him up.

"I already saw him," Anthony said, morosely. "Not only that, we've talked, gone to his apartment, taken our clothes off and done it, and I'm on my way back home. The entire scenario has played like a short film in my head."

"Wow." That was something. "Are you having sex at all or just fantasies?" I asked him. Our relationship had reached a depth of intimacy where nothing seemed off-limits, much as it once had been with Chris and me.

"Nada. It holds no appeal for me at the moment."

I lapsed into silence to contemplate that. I, of course, wasn't having any encounters anymore like the ones I used to have when I picked up girls in bars. Anthony had reminded me it was best to not get involved with anyone in my first year, and I willingly obeyed. Considering what had happened to me when I tried it, it was not difficult to avoid it. I was scared of women anyhow, and I was in no hurry to throw myself back into the dating pool.

We arrived at DPH and Anthony went to the lab to get his blood drawn while I waited. They'd notify him in a few days of the result.

He called me and asked me to come over to be with him while he opened the letter. It was something, to see the man I considered the anchor to which my recovery was tethered so vulnerable and scared. It simultaneously impressed me and terrified me. He'd asked me to support him, and I prayed I was up to the task.

We sat in his living room an Anthony slowly ripped open the envelope. His expression didn't change. He said nothing but only handed me the letter. It said he was positive. I looked up from the letter and into his face.

"You will not cry. I'm not going to. I expected it. I had all the symptoms of seroconversion. God knows I know them by heart. This is just confirmation."

Once upon a time, Chris had made a joke of going to the DPH to get tested for gonorrhea and meeting new tricks there. I guess that joke was truly over.

"What are you going to do now?" I asked him in a whisper.

"Go to a meeting," Anthony said. That's what we did.

❖

I made my list of people to whom I had to make amends. It was straightforward; all I had to do was look at the names of people in my fourth step inventories. It was a daunting list, but Anthony, predictably, told me to rank it in order of priority, with the easy ones first. I wasn't sure I'd be able to track down all the random women I had slept with, especially back in Cleveland. The most obvious amends were to women I'd met in San Francisco. The top of my list was Adrian, then came Lily, then the others.

Anthony's health was outwardly normal, but the constant threat of some sort of catastrophic infection hung over his head and it would never leave.

"I've got about twelve T cells." He meant the T-lymphocytes, the white blood cells whose number predicted the health and function of one's immune system. In a normal person, there were supposed to be about four hundred or more.

I read more about AIDS. I educated myself, and my technical background helped me to understand what I read. I became somewhat obsessed since I wanted to be helpful to Anthony. He was already quite the expert himself.

"A little self-interest goes a long way as motivation," he said. When I was around him and the other men in the program, I might as well have been listening to a bunch of research scientists and health experts. They discussed the medical aspects of AIDS, what someone thought was a protective diet, what each opportunistic infection was like, what treatments for those infections might work—you name it.

I worked on staying positive, as in optimistic. It wouldn't do me any good, or nor would it be any use to Anthony if I succumbed to despair. Normal life such as it was had to go on for him.

"I have to just stay in one day at a time or I'll lose my mind for sure," he said.

We reviewed my list of people who I had to apologize to, which ones I would see in person, which I would write letters to. The most problematic people were my former manager at Cal Genetics and, naturally, Chris. I saved them until last.

"Do you want to have a relationship with the person? Or just clean up the wreckage and go your separate ways?" Anthony asked.

"I'd like to still be friends with Adrian. The others maybe not." I didn't say I harbored a secret wish that Adrian might want to get back to together with me now that I was clean and sober. I kept that wish to myself even as I recognized that it was likely not a good thing not to disclose to Anthony. A girl is entitled to *some* secrets.

"A sincere 'I'm sorry for what I did' is extremely important. But it's more important that you commit to changing your behavior," he said.

"Well, for all those girls I fucked then fucked over, changing my behavior is a snap. I'm not having sex with *anyone*." This state of affairs, so to speak, was beginning to wear on me, so I was irritated. And that spurred me to want to see Adrian to see if there was anything possible.

"Hmm. You'll have plenty of chances in the future to amend your behavior. What are you going to say to Adrian?"

Ah, that was a good question. I was still pissed off at her for the other women and the drug stuff. But Anthony knew this.

"Remember, it's not what she did, it's what you did. It's not a clean amends if you have any reservations."

"I know, I know." I worked on my little speech to Adrian. Maybe she'd refuse to see me and I wouldn't have to worry about my lingering anger. But to my astonishment, she was happy to have me come over and talk to her.

She looked good, in fact better than good. Some of the old attraction came back, but I mentally crossed my fingers.

"Max, you look amazing," she said. "What happened?"

"I've been clean and sober for two years."

"That is wonderful. Really, I wouldn't have expected that, knowing you. You look so good."

"Thanks. I feel good. But I wanted to see you because I've got to talk with you about something important."

Her face changed. She was interested, even eager. She listened to my recitation of all the crappy aspects of our relationship. I made myself speak in a calm, even tone and stick to my mental script. I was dying to ask if she had a girlfriend, but I didn't. I remembered that she was quite averse to the concept as it was traditionally understood. That was part of what made her attractive to me until I became obsessed with her, and then came the other girls and threesome and all the rest of it. Gah.

She listened without comment to my entire spiel. When I stopped talking, she smiled.

"I never thought I'd hear those words out of your mouth. It's fine, really. I didn't treat you the best either. I took advantage of you. I'm sorry too."

"It's fine. I'm not here to get an apology from you, Adrian. But only to offer my own. I hope we can be friends."

She reached across the table and took my hand. Oops—a shiver of lust went through me. I must have recoiled slightly, her face fell.

"Oh, sorry." She pulled her hand back. "Invaded your space, I guess."

"It's okay. Are you still a stockbroker?"

"Yup. It's going well. I can afford this flat myself."

"So, no roommate? No…?"

"Nope. I have a few friends." The emphasis she put on "friends" told me what I needed to know. She hadn't changed.

"Uh-huh. Yeah."

I was at a loss for words. I didn't know what to say next. I stood up and said, "Thanks for seeing me."

We said our goodbyes and I walked out the door. I went over the scene in my mind, and the next time I saw Anthony I came clean.

"You know, my hopes evaporated. Insanity is doing the same thing over and over and expecting different results. I might have been able to sleep with Adrian, but I didn't want to. I wasn't looking for more hassles or dramas."

"Congratulations. The disappearance of your tolerance for drama is another sign of recovery. Excellent choice, Max. I'm proud of you."

He didn't say this stuff often, but when he did, I felt like I'd won an Oscar. Good thing, because within days or at most a week, Anthony would catch me in some boneheaded complaint and point it out. My ego didn't have a chance to get too large since he was always quick to puncture it even though he was nice about it.

I worked my way through my amends list until I came to the last two names: Sarah and Chris. Here I came to a full stop. Partially, it was my fear and procrastination. Anthony said procrastination was only fear in five syllables. He checked in with me about the list, but he never said anything else. He was waiting for me to work it out for myself. He did this more and more about every problem I discussed with him. He would listen and he would ask questions. As I answered his questions, the solution would come to me. It was an effective way to get me to think for myself. At first, I didn't like it because I wanted him to tell me via an example from his own life, but sometimes he only said he never had the experience. Or he'd tell me to go talk to someone else. Or I would work it out for myself.

One of our program friends, Cliff, would drag himself to the Friday night meeting, leaning on a cane, looking far older than his actual thirty-four years. He would not say much but sit and listen, his face sallow and his cheekbones sticking out. But when he spoke, it was to the point, befitting a man who had not much time left.

"When I die, I'm going to die sober. That's all I want," he once said. I'd watch Anthony's face when Cliff or someone like him spoke. He was somber. He never spoke much about AIDS except in the abstract. I guess it was how he kept the terror tamped down. But others were not so reticent—that is, if they had the strength to say anything, let alone physically come to a meeting. Sometimes we'd go to someone's house and take a meeting to him if he was too sick to get out of bed.

We heard through the AA grapevine that Cliff was likely in the hospital for the last time. Anthony and I arrived at SFGH to see Cliff and pay our respects while he was still conscious. The AIDS ward had different rules than other hospitals. You didn't have to be a relative to visit, for one thing. For a lot of gay men, there were no supportive family members, only their family of friends.

Sitting by Cliff's bed was someone we didn't know. Anthony and I both took Cliff's hands, squeezed them, and let him know we were there and who we were. He was able to nod but he couldn't talk. There was a faint ghost of smile on his lips.

The stranger said, "Nice to meet you. I'm Cliff's Shanti volunteer, Ted."

Anthony, who'd known Cliff for a few years, talked to him. He was practiced at making a conversation sound deceptively like small talk. This was only my second deathbed visit for an AA friend, and I was still not very good at it. It was hard for me to look at the person in the bed and try to talk to him like all this was normal. It was the memory of Chris in this state, of course, that haunted me. I was sure Anthony meant it to be helpful, and it was. Somewhat. It was in the guise of being *his* support that he was nudging me toward confronting my own fear and shame.

"What does that mean, Shanti volunteer?" I asked Ted.

"The Shanti Project is a support group for people with terminal illness. I'm an emotional support volunteer. Cliff is my client, so I've spent a lot of time with him, mostly just talking. I went to the doctor with him if he needed me to. And now, well, I'm just here if he needs me."

"I'm in AA with him and with Anthony."

Ted grinned. "Yeah. A lot of AA people come by."

"How did you start doing this?" I asked.

Ted grew serious. He looked down at Cliff for a moment, then he met my eye. "I had to do *something*. It wasn't doing me any good to only wait for the next friend to die. Or wait for my own death."

"Are you positive?" I asked him.

"Oh yes." There was beat of silence and both of us looked at Cliff anchored to his tubes and sensors, barely alive.

"Are you interested in Shanti? We always need more people. You can be practical support if you don't want to do what I do. Help guys with housework and stuff. It's not quite as heavy." Ted smiled.

"I don't know. Maybe." I wasn't willing to commit, and God knows, I didn't need any extra work in my life between my job and helping Rick.

Ted handed me a flyer, which I folded up and put in my pocket. Anthony and I stayed a while longer until a nurse came in and told the three of us we needed to let Cliff rest, so we left.

What Ted had to say stayed with me for days, but I wasn't sure why or what I thought about it. As Anthony always told me, "Sometimes you have to wait for the universe to reveal to you what you need to know." That was how he described the function of a Higher Power in his life. It was also another way he counseled me to have patience, something I still struggled with.

"So," Anthony said, "I half heard what you and Ted talked about. What do you think?"

Anthony was lying. He didn't half hear, he was completely aware of what Ted asked me and he wanted me talk to him about it.

"About what part?" I was being kind of passive-aggressive because I knew quite well what he meant.

Anthony's glare was skeptical. He didn't even have to say anything, I took his meaning.

"You mean the volunteer part?" It was starting to dawn on me what he might be getting at.

"Your amends to Chris," he said quietly. "I'm not so concerned with your amends to your old manager. You'll get to that. But you're more troubled by Chris. You remember our discussions about shame?"

"Yes. I remember."

"I have a suggestion for you, Max." Uh-oh.

"Perhaps you ought to make your amends to Chris by being a

Shanti volunteer. He's not here anymore, but there are more than enough like him around. It would be the epitome of a living amends."

"Right. I'm never going to see or talk to him again, but…"

"You know the important thing is to be able to forgive yourself aside from receiving forgiveness from other people you've hurt. You haven't forgiven yourself. Yet."

"Is that why you asked me to go to the hospital with you?" I asked dully.

"Partly. But more than that, I need you too."

That was the first time I'd ever heard Anthony say something like that.

"You do?"

His face was so sad at that moment, I almost started to weep.

"You're not going to die. At least not the way everyone else I know will die. You *will* die sometime. Not of alcoholism, thank goodness, probably old age. And that to me makes you precious. I can depend on you, Max."

I did start to cry then. Someone depended on me, and it was likely that I wouldn't let him down like I'd let Chris down.

"But back to you. You have to heal yourself, let go of the shame. I think this is the way to do it. You can make your amends to Chris and you can be free. I dislike telling you what to do, as you know. But this one time, I sort of am telling you what to do. Trust me on this one."

I couldn't speak, so I just nodded. Anthony was always right, damn it. Besides, Ted's explanation, *I have to do something*, resonated with me. I had both a more generalized feeling of obligation to help and an extremely specific deeply personal need to rectify my failure as Chris's friend to be even the tiniest bit present during his ordeal. I reminded myself that I'd been deep in the disease of alcoholism at the time. I was sober now, my disease was in remission, and I had a chance to make a different choice. Also, just possibly I could let go of that shame that Anthony and I so often discussed.

CHAPTER THREE

A s with everything else in life, it turned out to be more involved than it would appear. I decided to sign up for Shanti Project practical support because, well, I'm a practical woman and I thought I could handle that better than the feelings I would undoubtably experience if I were an emotional support volunteer.

I attended two consecutive weekends of nonstop volunteer training. Rick was gracious about letting me off my obligations when I told him what I was doing and why.

"Don't worry about it," he said. "I know where to find you."

We sat in a circle on the floor of the main Shanti Project offices, we ten volunteers, and we talked about life and death and we learned about all the ramifications of AIDS in a person's life. We talked about the deaths of relatives and loved ones and we talked about our own deaths. We learned about boundaries and we discussed empathy. We read a book called *On Death and Dying.*

There was a surprising variety to the Shanti volunteers. In my class, besides three gay men, there was a mother whose son had died, a retired grandfatherly straight guy, and two lesbians, including me.

In some exercises, we had to work in pairs, and I found myself assigned to the other lesbian in the class. Kendra was her name, and she was quiet but clearly strong willed. We started to talk during breaks. I'd not paid much attention to the lesbians in the program since my return, and I tended to hang out mostly with gay men. Some of the women in the meetings I attended I was friendly with, but I didn't get close. I was scared, I guess. One of these days I was going to have to face dating again. It was clear I wasn't going to be meeting women in the old manner I had employed, which hadn't worked out so well anyhow. But I wasn't in a hurry. Kendra elicited some familiar interest on my part, but I thought it was just because we were doing this thing together. I was attracted to her as a friend with a common interest.

In one scenario, one of us was blindfolded and the other had to feed the blindfolded one pudding. One of the many infections a person with AIDS, or PWA, as we were taught to call them, could contract rendered him blind. We would literally have to help a guy eat. It was an odd sensation to be blind and have someone literally spoon-feed you. Humility came to mind, something I was familiar with from my AA work. It didn't seem hard or embarrassing, but it was strange at first.

When I took off my blindfold and looked at Kendra, there was something about her face that moved me. She almost always had a grave, somber expression while we were training. Smiling wasn't something she did often. I guess the nature of what we were learning didn't lend itself to much humor. But along with her usual stillness came something else. I didn't know what it was, but I liked it. Maybe, just maybe there was a sliver of interest there. I didn't know and didn't want to pursue it. I pushed it away. It was enough for me that there might be something there. It fed my ego sufficiently.

We were pronounced ready by the Shanti staff and within a week came the notification of whom I'd be assigned to as a practical support volunteer and my volunteer support group. It turned out that people like us who were working with PWAs needed our own support. We needed to talk about how it affected us. This was all deeply familiar to me because of AA. I had indeed learned to express myself within a group. Kendra was assigned to my volunteer group, and that gave me pause. If nothing else, though, AA taught me to take one step at a time and not to get too far ahead of myself. It was called future tripping. It was one thing to make plans, but it was another to let go of what might happen. One must not be a prisoner of expectations and not assume anything. I knew this balancing act. Nonetheless, I experienced a little thrill about seeing Kendra once a week when our group met. The volunteer commitment was two years. Longer than that took too big a toll on a volunteer. When my client died, I would be assigned someone new.

My guy, Keith, lived a few blocks away from me on Sanchez Street in the Duboce Triangle. His needs weren't anything too outrageous. He needed some housecleaning and laundry twice a week. When I was discussing my assignment with my Shanti coordinator, I'd said, "I hope I don't have to cook much, 'cause I'm not much of a cook."

"Don't worry about that," he'd said kindly. "Most of these guys can barely eat."

❖

Keith lived all by himself in a studio apartment on the bottom floor of a Victorian near Duboce Park. He answered the door, shook my hand, then turned on his heel, walked back into his apartment, and flopped down on his couch. I took a seat on the daybed that was right angle to the couch. A large orange tabby cat stood up and stretched himself, then butted against my hand.

"That's Sebastian. Sebastian, be nice to her."

"I like cats, but I've never tried to take care of one."

"Oh Sebastian's got his own volunteer. Terry from PAWS comes over a couple times a week." Keith grinned. "I've got my team and then there's Sebastian's entourage, Terry and my friend Al, who's going to take Sebastian in when I'm gone. Sebastian doesn't know that yet because I don't want him to get an attitude."

And just like that, Keith stated in the most matter-of-fact terms what would surely be his fate.

He continued, "I've got my emotional support volunteer, Raoul. My doctor, my visiting nurse, and...now you." He gave me a brilliant smile. "I'm all set."

PAWS was the acronym for Pets Are Wonderful Support. AIDS organizations were an alphabet soup of acronyms and served hundreds of different purposes. Anthony put a lot of time in with the AIDS Emergency Fund, whose jars where pennies were collected graced the front counters of all the businesses in the Castro. The money was used to support housing for homeless PWAs. Someone had to pick up those monstrously heavy gallons of pennies and bring them back to AEF so they could be counted and then return the empties to their spots every week or more often.

"Where should I start?" I asked Keith.

"Oh, Sebastian, watch out, this is a live one. You best mind your p's and q's." He lit a cigarette and waved it in a grand way. I petted Sebastian and smiled back at Keith.

❖

"He's sort of sarcastic but sweet." That was how I described Keith to my support group. "I think he likes to make jokes so that he can avoid talking about anything heavy, like how sick he is."

I happened to be sitting next to Kendra in the circle, and as I spoke I went around looking at each person, and my gaze came to rest on Kendra. She listened intently, and her singular focus reminded me of Anthony. It wasn't until I finished speaking and was looking right at her that I noticed the gentle-but-something-else smile she wore.

When I looked in the mirror at home and I thought about Kendra at the same time, I stood up a little straighter and fussed with my hair. I wasn't sure, but I thought it might be a little shinier and a little thicker since I got sober. I already noted the change in my body as I lost weight. All the physical work I did with Rick gave some upper body definition to go along with the leg muscles I'd acquired at work. All of which, to my thinking, added up to healthy self-esteem rather than out-of-control ego. Anthony schooled me well in the manner humility could coexist with self-love. Balance was what it took, like everything else.

I contemplated the idea of Kendra and the idea of dating her, and it was equal parts terror and exhilaration. It was time, I realized. I couldn't hide out from intimacy with women forever. Well, I could, but it wouldn't be good for me and I didn't want to. During my long discussions with Anthony over my drunken antics in bars, his final pronouncement, the only one he made on that subject, was, "In recovery, you can learn to stop fearing intimacy, but it's going to take time and work. I don't see you being alone forever. You know that all those pickups were because you were looking for love? You just didn't call it that. You were running from that exactly like you ran from all other feelings. It's what we do."

Right. Again.

It was a good thing I was done with my check-in, because looking Kendra right in the face was dangerously close to rendering me speechless. What I thought was plainness at first was morphing over time. Each time we met, I noticed a new detail about her. One day it was her fine feathery light brown hair and how it conformed to the shape of her head and always looked well-trimmed. The next time was the way she sat cross-legged with her posture erect. I had to sit with my legs to the side to be comfortable. And so forth.

I listened to the rest of the group as attentively as I could, but Kendra's presence threatened to dilute my concentration. When she spoke about Jon Michael, her client, she sounded a little worried. He was a drinker. Not a falling-down drunk, but he was usually sipping chilled chardonnay in a beautiful glass. We all knew that drugs and alcohol weren't the best for PWAs. But who wants to begrudge a person who might die soon some pleasure? It was another tightrope we had to walk.

At last, the meeting was over, and somehow, Kendra and I sat still and began talking, trivia mostly. Someone was going to have to make the first move. The eternal lesbian dilemma.

I went for the tried and true program invite, the recovering alcoholic equivalent of "Hey, do you want to get a drink?"

"Would you like to go for coffee sometime?" I asked carefully.

Her eyes lit up "You know, I would really like that." She had lovely hazel and gray eyes, I noted.

"Great. Uh. This weekend?" It was a Tuesday night.

"I'm sorry. I'm out of town. Some other time?" Instant deflation.

"How about next weekend? Saturday at four?" I hoped I didn't sound too eager.

Anthony told me to try and consider dating an adventure rather than a chore to which I could apply my famous procrastinative tendencies.

My other looming recovery challenge was at the top of my mind along with Kendra and whether or not we were going to go out and all that implied—i.e., sex. I had one last major amends to make, and I was dreading it. Against all my self-protective instincts and in spite of my residual shame, I had to meet face-to-face with Sarah.

Anthony said, "There is no way around it, only through it." This was AA parlance for you gotta do what you gotta do if you want to feel better and grow. There is no standing still if you want to stay sober. I, of course, believed in the theory as I believed all of AA's prescriptions, but there was the problem of the actual follow-through. I told myself to stop thinking and act.

She'd agreed to meet me though she was clearly surprised when I called. And she accepted my somewhat cryptic "I have something I need to talk to you about in person" reason.

Sarah was a manager now. California Genetics had grown since I left. She had a bigger, better office. They were also in Berkeley, not Pacific Heights anymore. We made strained small talk for a few moments, then I cleared my throat.

"I'm here to say I'm sorry to you for how I acted when I worked for you." I recounted all the mistakes I made when I was hungover and my failure to take responsibility for anything. Her face didn't change while I talked. When I stopped talking, Sarah didn't say anything for a while, just swiveled her desk chair back and forth.

"Well, I knew something was wrong with you, but I didn't know what it was. Now I know. I appreciate you coming clean with all that. That's amazing. And you don't drink anymore?"

"Nope, not for a few years, and I hope to not ever again. It's not for me. Thank you very much for seeing me and letting me explain all that." I rose to leave.

"Wait a second," Sarah said. She had turned her chair to the side and was staring at a spot somewhere in the corner of her office. I resumed my seat, wondering what she wanted. I was mainly relieved to be done with my eighth and ninth steps, and I wished to leave and go enjoy that feeling.

"You weren't a bad employee all the time. There were moments you truly shone, like when you came up with the idea to shorten the protein assay down to six steps. And you designed the validation of the LPS assay and executed it."

"Oh really? Well. Thanks a lot." I barely remembered these two things.

"It was at the end there when you started to fall apart."

"Yes." I coughed. "I was drinking pretty heavy. Drugs too."

Sarah nodded. "I think I made the right decision, don't get me wrong."

"No, of course. I understand. I'm not here to make judgments about what you did or didn't do." I wasn't going to mention my utter fury and frustration with her.

"There's an opening in the Quality Assurance group for an analyst. We're in Phase Three trials and there is a lot of work. You should apply."

"Me? Apply?" I stuttered, simply taken off guard.

"Sure. Why not? I'll recommend you. The past is history. I can see you're a different person than you were three years ago. I can leave out that you were fired and why. You will have to sink or swim on your own, naturally. But I think you'll be okay."

I sat there, dumbfounded. And trying once again to not cry. I needed to leave, right away.

"Go over to HR and make an application. Tell them to route it to me, and I'll get into Thom's hands. He's the director of QA."

I shook Sarah's hand, walked out of her office and into the admin building, and followed her directions. I was so blown away it was hard to string coherent thoughts together. I couldn't wait to tell Anthony.

"Cash and prizes," he said, laughing. "I told you. The promises. I am so happy for you, for the amends. But also, see what good can come to you if you do the work? It's important to see results. Tangible results. We're only human. We can't exactly exist on spirituality alone. We need positive reinforcement. Even if you don't get the job, you got a big dose of yippee today."

I hugged him and his body felt warm, too warm.

"You okay?" I leaned back, locked eyes with him.

He disengaged. "Sure. Sure. Touch of fever. Not a big deal."

Keith turned over restlessly on his couch where he spent most of his time. Sebastian had the daybed with the window behind all to himself during the day.

"Max, honey, if I can get from my bed to my couch and to the can on my own, it means I'm still alive."

He was skeletal—his sweatpants hung on him and his T-shirt didn't hide his sunken chest—but verbally, he was certainly not dead.

"I'm not sure what Dr. Kildare has up his sleeve. I've got another new drug to take."

He was referring to his AIDS doc whose name, I knew, was Terrence Small but who, according to Keith, was "as gay as a goose." Camp was another one of his coping mechanisms. It probably predated his diagnosis but still came in handy.

Keith had swept a cigarette-holding hand over his living room coffee table, which held possibly one hundred pill bottles.

I didn't bother looking at the names of the drugs. It was none of my business. What *was* my business was removing everything from the coffee table and cleaning it off and then putting everything back.

Directly across from Keith on his sofa was the TV, tuned typically to VH1 or a cooking show. He loved music videos and he loved to critique them.

"You want anything to drink?" I asked him as I migrated to the kitchen to start cleaning.

"Coffee please, love."

I often made Keith a cup of instant coffee with two tablespoons of sugar. Microwaved. It was awful. But I was certainly familiar with the coffee-and-cigarette duo.

Keith called from the living room. "Every video Madonna does, she gets sluttier. I don't see the appeal. She thinks she's a diva. She's just a slut with better makeup."

Not a Madonna fan was Keith. He was into old-time torch singers or blues gals—Nina Simone, Eartha Kitt—but they weren't on VH1. But I think he just loved to criticize, and there was always plenty to criticize.

I brought him his cup of coffee and moved on to the bathroom. The laundry would be done soon and I'd go downstairs to pick it up. It was a blessing not to have to go to a Laundromat. He didn't have too many dirty clothes since he lived in his sweats all day every day.

After I finished with the cleaning, I sat down with him to smoke and shoot the breeze. He knew all about my life and he remembered an astonishing number of details.

In between kibitzing with me, watching VH1 and issuing commentary, he barked orders at Sebastian, who was most often in a seated pose on the daybed, staring vacantly. He had the laid-back friendliness of the orange tabby breed but he didn't do much and certainly not anything to draw Keith's oft spoken order, "Sebastian, get a grip." It wasn't long before I discerned it wasn't Sebastian that Keith was telling to get a grip, it was himself.

Keith rarely watched TV news, but one day, it was on when I arrived. Something caught my attention. The news person mentioned that Elizabeth Taylor was headlining a fundraiser for the AIDS Project Los Angeles. Chris would have been quite happy and proud to hear that. And at that moment, the thought of Chris didn't leave me with a stab of regret. I told Keith about Chris, and talking about him didn't hurt either. Keith listened soberly and he didn't make a joke. When I finished the story, he looked at me and said, "I had a feeling about you when we met. You weren't just doing this for the heck of it. It's personal, right?"

"Yep, it is, I guess." I began to tear up. Keith smiled sympathetically.

"You have some tears left. Good for you. I don't have any more. I'll enjoy yours vicariously."

I pulled myself together and said, "I might be going to back to the company I got fired from before I got sober."

"Ooh, girl." Keith grinned. It was a congratulatory "ooh, girl" rather than an admonishment. He had actually been in the program— one of my requests. I had told him all about me and my journey.

"Yeah. I'm going for an interview next week."

He waved his cigarette. "You'll be fine. Break a leg. You can just put the laundry away. That's all I need for right now. Thank you."

❖

The interview was relatively painless. I said I had to take some time off from biotech to account for being a legal messenger. The guy I was talking to didn't bat an eye. He took a lot of notes.

"I talked to Sarah Robinson," he said but didn't elaborate.

Three days after that he called me to say I could start whenever I was able. They say be careful what you ask for…

I said goodbye to Legal Partners, not without some sadness, but with far more joy than regret. It would be something to not be in a workplace with people using. At least I assumed that would be the case. The admin details had increased since my departure three years before, and it took the better part of a day to get situated. I wasn't as scared as I thought I would be. I'd told my new boss that I was a little rusty, but I was certain my skills would return with some practice. He shrugged, not concerned. He was an exceptionally laid-back guy for quality assurance, and I liked him. It could be I was truly better suited to getting along with male managers. Maybe it was my thing about women again. I seemed to have this twisted attraction-versus-repulsion response to them.

When I was working on my fourth step inventory, my memory

dredged up a painful episode from my teenage years. My gym teacher, whom I idolized—not a surprise—called me in to talk with her one day. And what she told me devastated me. The girls who I thought were my friends found me mean and sarcastic, not very friendly. I loved my girlfriends, worshipped them really. In retrospect, it was likely my adolescent sexual feelings surging up and I didn't know what they were or how to handle them, so I was defensive.

This sort of thing happened often enough. When I told Anthony, he shrugged and said, "Those things are going to surface as you get more recovered." I was growing concerned about *him*, though. He and I didn't meet as often as we had, but I was working at my new job and I was less raw and needy. He was having health issues and I think he didn't want me to worry.

His friend Liam kept me in the loop. I wasn't shocked when he called to tell me Anthony was in the hospital, Ward 5B of course.

"It's pneumocystis," Liam said grimly.

I went to visit and Anthony couldn't speak, of course, because he was on oxygen. But he wasn't on a ventilator. Liam said, "I'm his health care rep and he made me promise no ventilator because that would mean he's going to die. He has a DNR as well."

"What's a DNR?"

"Do Not Resuscitate."

Emotionally, I froze. I was two people really, the person who knew that I couldn't start crying and upset Anthony and the woman who'd lost her best friend to the exact same infection and who wanted to scream in terror. I kept myself together and talked to Liam dispassionately.

"Is his family aware?" I asked.

"Yep. He's estranged from them, he doesn't want them here."

"Is he going to die?" I asked, evenly.

"No one knows," Liam said as we stood side by side staring at Anthony. He coughed so hard and so long that I feared he would hurt himself. He was covered by a refrigerated electric blanket to keep his fever down, and his IV pumped powerful antibiotics into his body.

I swallowed.

You are being tested. You messed up with Chris. This time, it's different. You're not the same woman you were two and a half years ago.

"It depends on him," Liam said. "If he wants to live, he might live. If he wants to die, then…" He trailed off. From what I knew of Anthony, I was sure he wanted to live. He loved being clean and sober, he loved AA, he loved all the people like me whom he lived to help. It wasn't possible he would want to leave us. At least, that's what I told myself. I stared at his closed eyes. At least he still had some color, unlike Chris. He was still alive. I knew that in addition to not drinking or doing drugs, he was meticulous about his diet and he didn't smoke. I could only hope it would be enough to keep him alive. I left the hospital saying the Serenity Prayer over and over.

❖

Kendra and I kept our long-delayed coffee date.

She seemed subdued, but she was hard to read since she didn't normally show much emotion anyhow.

I asked her about her trip, and that elicited some animation.

I was so used to the program and asking everyone—or being asked—what was going on with them all the time and how they were feeling that I decided to be bold and do the same with her.

"Are you all right? You don't seem exactly happy at the moment."

She actually smiled, gratefully. That surprised me.

"No, basically, I'm fine. I was nervous about meeting you, that was one thing."

That admission astonished me.

"Why is that? I mean I am too, nervous I mean, but I'm new to dating. That's my excuse."

"You always act so competent. So together, like you know who you are and where you're going."

"Me?" Holy shit.

"Yeah. But it was my little attack of nerves, though I'm glad to hear you're nervous too. It makes me feel less lonely."

I wanted to explore this with her, but I also wanted to let her say what she wanted to say and be the good listener as I'd learned to be by emulating Anthony.

"Is there something else?" I asked.

"Well, I ran into my ex-girlfriend the other day. We'd not parted on bad terms exactly, but our interests had diverged. She'd turned into a hard-core separatist, and that's not me. So anyway, we were catching up and I told her about Shanti and the volunteer work I was doing."

I nodded for her to go on.

"She gave me an earful about how could I do this when I knew that if we were the ones who were sick, no faggots would lift a finger and they brought it on themselves, etc., etc. I only said that was not the way I looked at it, but what she said shook me."

I was shocked but not really surprised. I didn't hear that sort of talk from the lesbians I knew in AA, but they, like me, were sitting in meetings where AIDS was discussed frequently. I suppose I could understand where it came from. Gay guys weren't necessarily feminists—they mostly didn't understand women at all. Nor did they need to, most of the time.

"I can imagine. That's awful. I mean, there might be some truth to it, but I hope we don't ever have to put that idea to the test." I tried a smile on Kendra, and she lightened up. "I hope it doesn't discourage you from staying with Shanti."

"Oh no. Not at all. I've made a commitment."

"Me too. I have some issues I have to work through, and it's helping me with those."

"Oh? What sort of issues?" she asked, and since she looked truly interested and I wanted her to know about me, I told her about Chris and AA and making amends.

"Gosh. Congrats on being clean and sober. That's an accomplishment."

I bit my tongue because we don't view it recovery in that way, but I didn't want to start an argument with Kendra on our first date. It was just a compliment, so the best thing to do was accept it and move on.

"Thanks."

"I'm sorry about your friend. That must have been awful."

"It was." Damn, I was starting to tear up. "My AA sponsor is in the hospital with PCP and we don't know if he's going to make it."

She reached across the table and took my hand. I wanted to not let her and I wanted to revel in her touch at the same time.

"This is personal for you, isn't it? It's not abstract, it's not someone else's problem."

I pulled myself together and said, "Nope. It's not. I'm glad you see that."

She didn't take her hand away. She squeezed my hand and smiled ever so slightly.

We spent a few silent moments, then went on to chat about movies and the loveliness of autumn in San Francisco.

CHAPTER FOUR

I put on a fresh clean lab coat with the company name over the breast pocket, pulled latex gloves over my hands, and, new to me, put on safety glasses. This was apparently a recent addition to lab procedure.

With my notebook in hand, I gathered everything I needed and arranged it on the lab bench, which I'd covered with clean bench paper that I taped down. I remembered that the beauty of doing QC tests was following the directions and getting an expected result. Precision, concentration, consistency. Voilà—you get what you want, something you have confidence in and can be proud of.

I experienced a prickle of anxiety, but I talked to myself silently but firmly. *You are a trained laboratory person, an analyst. Take it slowly and be careful, and you'll be fine.*

And as the program always promised me, take the right steps, in the right order, and it will work. And it did. I sat at my desk basking in gratitude. The phone rang and it was Liam.

"He's awake. His fever's broken."

"He is? Gosh, that's great. I'll be over after work."

Muni was its usually laggardly self, but thank goodness for Ward 5B's relaxed visiting hours. I raced down the hall and there was Liam sitting next to Anthony's bed. Anthony's eyes were open. He looked weak but he was off oxygen.

I kissed and hugged him, and though he couldn't respond very well, I didn't care.

"You're back."

"I responded to the meds. Finally. My stupid immune system remembered what it was supposed to do."

"You helped it out by taking care of yourself."

He waved his hand slightly. "Eh. I think I was lucky, Max."

I looked at Liam, who was looking jubilant and very relieved. I wondered if there was something there. Anthony always dismissed the idea of having a boyfriend. *Too much trouble. I wouldn't want to get close and then die or he dies.*

People do it all the time. Why not be optimistic?

He said, *Optimism is not a luxury I can indulge in. Just like smart cocktails and coke. Can't indulge in them any more either.*

I sat with Liam and we three chatted. My relief at Anthony's recovery from pneumocystis was mixed with a sense of accomplishment. I'd have to tell Anthony about it later.

I was scraping grime out from under the legs of Keith's kitchen table when his doorbell rang. When I was there, I always answered the door so he could keep his place on the couch.

A young woman handed me an aluminum take-out container. "Here you go. Have a nice evening."

"Thanks."

I took it to Keith.

"What's this?" I asked him.

"Oh. Open Hand delivery. Open it."

It was a chicken breast, mashed potatoes, and green beans. It was still warm and it smelled terrific.

Keith took a drag on his smoke. "You can eat it. They bring one every evening now. I'm not hungry." He showed me a flyer describing the home delivery of nutritious meals to PWAs.

I usually ate something before I went over to Keith's but not always, and today I was hungry.

"Are you sure?"

He put his arm under his head and tapped his cigarette ash into the ashtray on his chest.

"Uh-huh. You're a growing girl. You go ahead."

He wouldn't let me save him anything, so I ate all of it. We watched VH1 and chatted while I ate.

A clip of the old sixties TV show *Hullabaloo* came on. It was Nancy Sinatra singing "These Boots Are Made for Walkin'." We laughed at the miniskirts and white disco boots as we watched the backup dancers kick in the air from their backs. Keith imitated them from his position on the couch while we sang along. When I came back for my second visit of the week, it was the same deal. He insisted I eat his Open Hand dinner so it wouldn't go to waste.

"I'm not up for eating right now. I tried yesterday and I upchucked it all."

"Did you talk to Dr. Kildare?"

"Raoul asked me the same thing. No." He tossed restlessly. I couldn't believe he'd asked for his usual cup of coffee if his stomach was upset. That wasn't even remotely appetizing for someone with an upset stomach.

"I will. Soon," he said.

It wasn't my job to bug him about health issues, so I didn't say anything else.

Two months after I started back at work at California Genetics, I moved into a studio apartment. It was the first time in my life that I had ever lived by myself and it was phenomenal, amazing. No roommates, no crazy family to bother me. Even if it was only a one-room place with a Murphy bed, it didn't matter. It was all mine. I could bring women home. That was a thought.

Kendra and I seemed to be on the same wavelength when it came to the progress of intimacy. We were taking it slow. I both wanted to get to the sex part and didn't want to. There was the memory of my disastrous encounter with Laurie to contend with. I had no assurance that sleeping with Kendra would turn out any better than sleeping with Laurie, but I sure wanted to do it more every time I saw her. It was a revelation how completely dissimilar the me of three years previously was to the me of the present. Even though I was technically sober when I had my encounter with Laurie, I might as well have been drinking for all the lack of consciousness I'd brought to it. I was now nothing *but* consciousness, but I had no idea if that was enough to get me to orgasm.

"I'm fine with the pace," Kendra said. "Yes, I want to. Sometime. Soon."

"Me too."

The first time we kissed, it was at her apartment after dinner. Unlike me, she was a good cook. She'd asked me sweetly and shyly to come over for pasta and salad. I watched her as she cooked and arranged and somewhat fussed over me, and it was endearing.

"Do you want flat or bubbly water?" Kendra asked brightly. "I hope you like vinaigrette."

"I'm fine," I said more than once.

When the time came for me to leave, I stood just outside her door, reluctant to actually leave and awkward about it. She finally leaned forward to kiss me gently on the lips.

"Thanks for coming over, Max."

"Thank you for dinner, it was great," I managed to say. That short, soft kiss was more compelling than any slobbery drunken lip-lock I'd ever had with anyone. I tried to remember what my kisses with Laurie had been like and I couldn't. Was I on some sort of autopilot when I was with her? I didn't know. I was going to have to discuss this with Anthony. His battle with pneumonia was over now and we could go back to our sponsor and sponsee relationship, which we'd had to put on hold when he was sick. He'd not said anything nor asked me to meet with him yet. I wanted to give him space to recover from his illness, but I was somewhat at sea. His battle with pneumonia had lasted several weeks.

Finally we spoke and I went to his apartment to meet with him, which wasn't our routine but that's what he asked me to do, so I went.

"Hi. How are you feeling?" I asked after our hug.

"I'm okay, still somewhat weak."

"Well, you look pretty good," I told him, and it was true. Except for the weight he'd lost, he looked okay.

"Looks may be deceiving," he said but didn't follow that up.

We enjoyed some small talk about people we knew from the program.

"I started dating someone," I said. And I updated him on where I was. He was attentive as always but he seemed muted, not quite present, and I didn't want to ask because I wasn't sure of our boundaries around it and also I thought he ought to tell me on his own. If it was something I needed to know, he would always tell me. Anthony was as forthcoming about his feelings as any person, man or woman, I'd ever met.

"What do you want to happen?" Anthony asked. "Are you in love with her?"

"No, I'm not in love with her. I want to sleep with her but I'm afraid to. I'm afraid it won't be good. That *I* won't be good."

He cocked his left eyebrow. "Lots of fear going on and not much faith."

"Right. You already know I'm afraid of women. I don't know how to relate to them."

"Max, it stands to reason that you are afraid to relate to women because you never related to anyone without alcohol. There's no more alcohol, so…"

"My armor is gone. I have no shield."

"That's true and that's a good thing, but you're not going to learn to relate unless you actually relate. What if you have sex and it isn't good the first time? You could try again or try it with a different woman. It's not the end of the world."

I laughed. "You always said alcoholics are people who want to commit suicide if they have a flat tire."

He smiled, though it wasn't much of a smile.

"We are completely unable to deal with failure. But that is your task, to learn how to take what happens, learn from it, move on. You don't know what's going happen until it happens."

"Uh-huh." It still irked me that he was always right, but as I pondered what he said, I became braver and less unsure of what I ought to do. We were never made uncomfortable sitting in silence together for some interval.

"Max, I'm not myself," Anthony said abruptly. "I'm not sure I can work with you anymore. I'm not certain I've anything left to give."

This startled and frightened me. Anthony was my rock, my support. In a lot of ways our relationship was far closer and more profound than the one I'd enjoyed with Chris. As my memories bubbled up, it became more obvious to me that Chris, though he'd been a loving and loyal friend to the extent he could be, was not actually all that dependable or good at being a friend. We were two immature kids thrown together.

"What makes you say that?"

"I'm probably going to die. This bout of pneumo was hard. As you know, most people don't get over it, and I'm glad I did, no mistake. But it brought home to me that it could happen again, and if it does, I probably won't survive."

It was harsh to hear even if I knew that it was the truth. Alcoholics in recovery are nothing if not realists.

"You once said something about optimism being a luxury to you."

"Yes, I did, and it's even truer now." He looked down at the floor. "I have an incurable disease, and I'm not talking about alcoholism. There is no cure for it, but there's also no treatment like we have for our alcoholism. We can't go to meetings and do steps to treat AIDS. There are no medical interventions, no pills, no operation."

"I know." I had nothing to say because he was right. I had no idea what it was like to just to wait to die, to be always wondering if the next infection would be the fatal one or if the virus would invade my brain and render me insane. That had happened to a few men we knew, and their last days alive they couldn't recognize anyone or even speak. Death from AIDS came in so many varieties, it was unpredictable. What was totally predictable was it would happen. Anthony was going to die. No amount of AA program could prevent it. What could I do to help him with that? Nothing.

"You're going through a tough time. I get that." I sounded so lame to myself I wanted to take back what I said immediately. Anthony only nodded, though.

"I still want you as my sponsor. I still need you. Whatever you can give me is okay. If we have to meet less or whatever, I'm okay."

"That would not be helpful to you. You should get someone else."

"I don't want anyone else right now. I'm fine with you."

"If you're sure, then okay."

I was relieved. If and when it happened, then I would deal with it at the time. Until then, it was up to me to stay in the good old one day at a time mode.

❖

I sat with Keith on the afternoon of the Saturday that I anticipated would finally be the day with Kendra. He'd greeted me with a mumbled hello and didn't, as he normally would, call after me when I went to the kitchen to tidy up, and for once, he didn't want a cup of his awful coffee.

I'd fairly flown through the chores and was ready for a chat. I sat on the end of the couch by his feet. He lit a cigarette and so did I.

"Today's the day, eh?" He grinned. "Ooh la la. Are you quivering with anticipation?" He drew out the word "anticipation" out. I recognized the *Rocky Horror Picture Show* line of Dr. Frank-N-Furter and laughed.

"I am," I said. He grinned lasciviously.

"What are you doing to get ready? Special underthings? A cologne? If you use cologne, don't overdo it. Are you going out?" He was talking as rapidly as he usually did but sounded a bit hoarse.

"No cologne. *Clean* underwear with no holes. We're lesbians, after all. We're not fancy."

"I see. Au naturel." He stubbed his cigarette out half smoked and put the ashtray on the coffee table. That was unusual.

"She's cooking for me, so we'll be at her place. When I used to do one-night stands, I always tried to go to the other woman's house so I could make up some excuse to leave right away in the morning."

"Oh, I know, we think we've gone home with Prince or Princess Charming and they're actually some ugly troll."

"Something like that. I never knew what to say to people, so I would just leave. Escape so I wouldn't have to relate. I was no prize myself."

"Excuse me." Keith turned on the couch, grabbed his wastebasket, and vomited in to it. A couple times.

He set it back down and wiped his mouth. "Sorry."

"No problem, let me take care of that."

I dumped it in the toilet and rinsed it out. Oddly, it scarcely affected me. It didn't seem at all weird. Keith was sick. I was more astonished that he could carry on a conversation while he was queasy. That was quite a trick. I would never have been be able to pull it off. I didn't want anyone around or anyone to talk to me if I was sick to my stomach.

I returned the wastebasket to its spot by his head and sat down again.

Keith said, "The nausea's gotten bad. I've progressed to not being able to eat anything. I'm seeing the doctor on Monday."

We resumed our talk about our impending evening, but I didn't stay very long and he didn't, as he often did, try to get me to stay longer. I left, hoping he would feel better. Perpetual nausea was no way to get through life.

❖

When she answered the door, Kendra was as outwardly calm as she always appeared. We exchanged a medium-heat kiss. When we broke, there was a little sparkle in her eye. The only sign I could see that this date was not as other dates was she rattled the glass of water on the coaster as she put it by my plate before dinner.

She'd asked me over when we'd seen each other at our Shanti volunteer support group meeting, the first one after our kissing date.

"I was hoping you'd let me cook dinner for you again next Saturday. If you're not busy, that is."

"I accept," I said heartily, and she beamed. That was how I knew this *might* be it. The day before I'd had a stern talk with myself, reiterating Anthony's advice to merely be in the moment and try not to have expectations. *Be open and be calm. It will be whatever it will be.* I didn't need to be afraid. I couldn't quite avoid sexual fantasies, but I didn't think Anthony would disapprove. Kendra had captured my imagination in the last couple months, and by the time I sat down at her tastefully set dining room table, I was primed.

For an alcoholic like me, it was unprecedented to approach a potential sexual encounter in such a deliberate fashion. I didn't think I'd read the signs wrong, but if I had, I had and there would, for me, be no self-recrimination. Disappointment perhaps, but that was it. I had finally, it seemed, embraced the often-repeated wisdom in AA that one cannot control other people, places, or things but can only control one's own feelings.

"I hope you like rice," Kendra said.

"I do. Did I already tell you I like your apartment?" It was simply decorated, sort of no frills, but comfortable and attractive, much like Kendra.

"No, but that's good."

It was an apartment, smallish but with some nice bay windows and a beveled glass panel in the main front door. Kendra had books in her living room and what looked some decent small sculptures. And it was clean. I shivered recalling how slovenly I became in the last year of my drinking, not that Adrian was that particular about housekeeping.

We ate broiled salmon with lemon and capers and asparagus, along with basmati rice, all cooked to perfection. Kendra's cooking resembled her personality: not fancy but well-executed. I smiled to myself at that thought. She drank exactly one glass of white wine. I didn't begrudge her that. I would have if I could have, just a little something to take the edge off. But that wasn't available to me. I had to rely on my inner peace, such as it was.

"How is Jon Michael doing?" I asked her in reference to her client.

"Back in the hospital again, this time for thrush." She meant the oral yeast infection that often plagued PWAs. It wasn't a problem unless you had a weakened immune system.

"He asked me if I had ever had a yeast infection and I said of course. Tad said 'I've got the same thing in my throat that you had in your cooch,' and I had to laugh."

I laughed too but I said, "At least the yeast infections we get don't threaten our lives."

"True." Kendra looked pensive and stayed quiet for a moment.

Then she said, "I wonder sometimes if I could be as brave as these guys are if I had a disease that was going to kill me."

"You would be, I'm sure. But I remind myself every day that I'm lucky to be healthy and sober."

"That's for sure. The healthy part goes for me as well. I'm happy you're sober too."

"If I wasn't I wouldn't be here, nor would you like me if you happened to meet me." This sort of popped into my head, and I hadn't meant to say it out loud but there it was.

Kendra looked unsure. "What makes you say that? I can't picture you drunk, by the way."

"Because when I was drinking, I hated myself and I hated everyone else, especially the women I ended up sleeping with." This was sliding into dangerous territory, i.e., the unstated but potential future of this pleasant dinner date, and I could sabotage the whole thing if I didn't watch out. I cursed my program tendency to speak in terms that are too honest for normal people. "Oversharing," Anthony would have admonished me.

Kendra's face clouded. "Is that right? How awful."

I needed to do some damage control.

"I'm sorry, I didn't mean that to come out so harshly. I don't hate myself anymore, and therefore I don't tend to hate women. I am still, however, made nervous by them."

Kendra scrutinized me closely. I tried to decide how much I could reveal and whether further revelations would reassure her, scare her more, or just put the kibosh on anything romantic happening.

I inhaled deeply and went with my gut feeling. "I have a history of exactly one relationship, and it was with someone I used with and it was screwed up. The first time I got sober, I induced someone to sleep with me and it turned out badly. I've not had any sort of sex since then. I'm not sure what sort of evening you were planning for, but I kind of hope and kind of suspect that we might end up in bed." I watched her reaction and her eyes got a little wide. I didn't know if that was good or bad.

I continued. "But if not, that's okay too. I'm not trying to put expectations on you."

"What do you want to happen?" Kendra asked. Fair question.

"I like you, I think you're great. I would like, if you're game, to sleep with you."

"But you haven't had sex in how long?"

"Three years."

"Holy smokes. That's a long time."

"And…other than that one disaster, I've never done it sober."

"Oh wow. And you want me to…with me…?" I couldn't tell if she was excited or dismayed by this idea.

"I do," I said. And come to think of it, it was a prospect that, until that moment, I'd not wanted to let into my consciousness because I was so busy tamping down my expectations so they wouldn't get all out of control.

Kendra stood up from the table and said, "Would you like some coffee?" This was a jarring change of subject, but I went with it.

"Sure. Decaf."

She strode into the kitchen and I took a chance and followed her.

"I'm sorry. Was that too much for you?"

"Not exactly, but I wanted a moment to collect myself. If you don't mind, would you please go and put some music on, and I'll be in with our coffees in a minute."

I backed off. "Absolutely." I busied myself searching for the perfect music. I gave up and just put in a cassette of someone I liked, Judy Collins.

I waited on the couch and Kendra returned carrying two cups.

"Max, you're a unique woman."

"Do you mean in a good way or a bad way?"

"Oh. In a good way. Your honesty is just a bit overwhelming, but after I took a moment to absorb what you were telling me, it made sense."

"Well, that's a relief." I laughed so we could both relax and lighten up.

Kendra took a sip of coffee, then carefully placed her cup on the table before us. She leaned over, put both her hands on either side of my face, and kissed me firmly. My blood pressure shot up, as did my breathing. She kept it up for a time. This was a much sexier kiss than she'd given me before, and I liked it.

When she broke off, she looked me at straight on and said, "I'd love to make love with you." That about knocked me over, with a hit of lust but more for her directness. It was refreshing, but somehow it was Kendra-like. Maybe my instincts about people weren't as bad as I thought they were. Maybe my now-clear mind was able to make correct judgments. Maybe I was about to get laid for real.

I didn't speak but nodded my agreement, and we proceeded to kiss a whole lot more and grew very warm. It occurred to me while we kissed and stroked each other's hair and shoulders and backs that this was how sex was supposed to feel. It wasn't this crazy, fuzzy, headlong drink-propelled sweat fest. It was undeniably arousing and exhilarating, but I noticed many more details that I would have surely missed when I was drunk. Kendra smelled like lavender soap and a little bit of lemon and coffee from our dinner. Her neck, thanks to our body heat, became moist. I squeezed her breasts and elicited a little whimper that made me feel the seam of my jeans in a pleasantly irritating way.

In my mind was the faint, distant warning question. *What if you can't come?* Amidst all these very pleasurable physical sensations, my brain couldn't keep quiet and let my autonomous nervous system take over. But at least I didn't have to listen to it. *Don't listen to your stupid mind. What did I learn in AA? Let it go. Whatever the it that is bothering me, LET IT GO. Surrender, Max, this is all about the feeling. Stay in your body.*

We were in bed, naked, and things were speeding along. If she wanted to take over, I wanted her to. I wasn't like I was before when I was drinking, I wasn't trying to prove anything. She had exquisite touch. She was assertive but not aggressive as her hands moved over my body restlessly. Freed of clothes, Kendra's body was more luscious than I would have guessed. Her breasts were nice sized and her butt round. I was hot and wet, no mistake, and I wanted her.

She probed between my thighs and murmured her approval when she felt how wet I was. She was grew bolder and stroked my clitoris. It was wonderful, and I strove to give myself over to the experience and her touch, but I involuntarily stiffened and she stopped.

"Are you okay? Too much or not enough?" This was such a thoughtful question I could have sobbed with gratitude.

Instead, I said, "I'm good. I'd like to go slow so I can feel everything." This was a better response than one making explicit that I was terrified I wasn't going to be able to orgasm.

She had made eye contact with me and smiled slightly and resumed stroking me, slowly but gradually increasing her speed and pressure.

"This good?" she asked.

"Yes, really really good." It was. I was losing myself, I didn't feel anxious. I could feel I was close, it was only going to take a moment. I tensed my legs and my abdomen. Then she was gone and I wanted to scream, "Wait. I'm almost there."

Then she was back, with her mouth this time, and with a couple of flicks of her tongue, my clit tightened, then I came suddenly. It seemed to last forever, and I'm pretty sure I screamed out loud for real. She refused to let me go, only staying still for a couple of moments, then beginning again, and I came again, harder. After that she let me rest.

I lay on my back, unbelieving, wrecked but triumphant. It had worked. My dismissal of my overactive mind had done the trick at last. I was free. The veil of alcohol was gone but I had conquered my anxiety. I had let myself go.

I couldn't very well stop us to tell Kendra all of this; it wasn't a good time for that and would be a real buzzkill in the moment.

I smiled. She would assume that was from bliss, and I didn't need to disabuse her. What I needed to do was show her as much pleasure as she'd shown me without being a show-off as I usually tended to do. *Not a command performance, nor is it about your ego. Just be nice.*

It turned out to be effortless. Kendra was a normal woman, unlike me. She was certainly responsive and unembarrassed about moving my hand around to suit her needs. She even said, "I tend to get overstimulated with oral, so your fingers are great."

Wow, so this was what you got when you had sex and you were sober: actual communication. Who knew? I didn't laugh aloud, and I'm sure happy Kendra couldn't read my mind.

We fell asleep and woke up for another round but then it was morning. Here would be my cue to manufacture some excuse for leaving right away. Not this time. I watched her sleep for a few minutes and then snuck out of bed and went to see if I could make coffee. It turned out to not be too difficult since she had a well-organized kitchen.

I waved a cup of coffee under her nose, which she wrinkled adorably, and she woke up. She kissed me sweetly and we drank our coffee with my hand buried in her crotch. This seemed to call for some more lovemaking. Sex in the morning—that was a new concept to me too. No dark of night, pitch black. The morning light was very bright and it was very real and I loved every minute. I was not speeding out the door, never to be heard from again.

"Well, kudos to you, Max. I'm happy for you. This is a milestone," Anthony said as he hugged me.

"It sure feels like one. It doesn't have to be such a big deal. Sex, that is."

He grinned. "Well. It *is* still a big deal, but I know what you mean. Meanwhile, what about everything else?"

That was a good question. Work was fine, it had ups and downs but I was finding that those peaks were not as high and the valleys weren't low. I could actually picture a line graph in my head.

"I'm just taking it one day at time. Like I'm supposed to. I'm a worker among workers, not better or worse than anyone else, especially not worse. It's remarkable how well I can function when I don't have booze or drugs in my system. I can think clearly, remember what I've done and see what I have to do."

"Marvelous. You have conquered the two biggest obstacles in your life. Nowhere to go but up."

I laughed and then I asked him, "What about you?"

Anthony was silent for some moments.

"I'm on a one day at time program myself. I don't know what's going to happen. I might live or…I might die. There is simply no way to tell. I decided that I may as well act like I'm going to live. I started seeing Liam. I am thinking of working again."

"Wow, that's terrific." And it was. I needed Anthony to be, if not optimistic, at least not pessimistic. I was aware that I could lose him—that possibility lurked on the fringes of my consciousness, but I didn't want to focus on it. I guessed I was learning to deal with uncertainty.

Keith's condition, on the other hand, was more problematic. He was looking more dragged out every time I saw him.

Right after my big date with Kendra, I went to see him.

"I hope it doesn't bother you." He was smoking a joint. "It helps with my nausea."

Given the choice between him throwing up and smoking weed, I'd take the weed-smoking.

"Raoul gets it for me. I know the program says you're not supposed to, but, well, I'm doing it so I don't upchuck. So I can eat."

"It doesn't bother me," I said, "but I definitely don't want any." I grinned to let him know it was cool, and it was.

The pot made him more talkative than he already was, which made me smile.

He leered. "How was your date? Is she a catch?"

"Yeah, I believe she is." I told him about it minus the sex part.

He was rarely serious, but this time he was. "You deserve the best. You deserve to be happy."

"Thanks. I think that's true. Finally, I can believe that."

"Did I ever show you the pictures from my drag days?"

"No, you have not. Can I see them?"

"I thought you'd never ask."

"Give me a half hour and I can stop when I put the laundry in."

The pictures were hilarious. In a couple, Keith had really immersed himself in his role.

"My drag name was Thelma Catalina. I won a couple contests."

"I bet you did. What's this one?"

It showed Keith not in a glamorous evening gown and lots of makeup but in a garishly printed number that looked suspiciously as though it might be polyester.

"Oh, that." He laughed evilly. "That was a special drag contest. We had to exemplify the tackiest of Middle America housewife but dressed up. No housedresses or capri pants. I describe this as 'Daly City bowling league awards dinner circa 1974.' I won second place." He beamed proudly.

"Is that…polyester?" I asked.

"Oh, listen to you. Close. Rayon." He cackled. "My makeup was from Kmart. But the high-end stuff."

"Did you go home with anyone that night?"

Keith often enjoyed recalling his tricks. He managed to remember more of his dissolute days than I did of mine.

"Oh, honey. You know I did. There's never a shortage of tacky queens and those who love them."

"Of which you were certainly one that evening."

He roared with laughter. I hadn't ever seen him so cheerful. I hope it wasn't all due to the marijuana.

"You know what they say, don't you?"

"No. What do *they* say?"

"Good girls go to heaven, bad girls go everywhere."

"That is so true. I was a bad girl once myself." I flashed on my barhopping one-night-stand days.

"And I'm certain you were a very good bad girl."

"As were you."

We went on to relive some of our bad good old days.

"I spent some time with the Barbary Coast Cloggers," Keith said, "A whole different kind of drag."

"Who were they?"

"Clogging—it's a type of dancing the hillbillies in Appalachia used to do. But we were on a whole other level."

"Good clean fun—that doesn't seem to fit with you."

"I beg your pardon, Max darling. It was athletic and musical. But after the show was over—ooh-wee."

"I think I get the picture."

It was time for me to go. I hugged him, leaving him on his couch to daydream about the good old days. He was exactly thirty-two years old, and he hadn't had that many good old days.

CHAPTER FIVE

There was more pressure at work than ever. Cal Genetics was in Phase III clinical trials. There were more patients and they had to be treated much more frequently, so there was a higher demand to release the product. I'd been assigned to DNA analysis, and while I was proud of that, it was a bigger challenge. The DNA part of the quality control was much more involved. I had to extract the DNA from the cells, label it with a radioactive tracer, then put it into a gel and expose it to x-ray film to visualize the DNA. There were more places to make a mistake or where something could go wrong and invalidate the results. It was also a two-day process.

I had extracted the DNA and started the part of labeling with phosphorus 32, the radioactive label. This involved injecting the hot solution into a plastic bag and incubating it for a couple of hours. I worked behind a plastic shield so I wouldn't expose myself to radiation. It was a bit awkward but still doable.

Once again, the clinical department had phoned, saying, "Can't you make it go faster? The patients are waiting with IVs in their arms." I assumed this was an exaggeration and metaphorical; I was better able to not internalize such statements and let them rattle me. Thom was also a blessing—he was a shield between the clinical research people and our group. Somehow he managed to put people off without making them mad. It was a gift.

I stood at my bench, safely suited up with my arms wrapped around the plastic shield. I held the plastic bag in my left hand and the syringe with the radioactive solution in my right. I tucked the syringe into the small hole I'd cut at the corner of the bag. At the moment I pressed the plunger, my left hand moved slightly and I sprayed the solution all over my glove and onto my shirt sleeve, which stuck out of my lab coat. I froze, willing myself not to panic or even to move until I could gather my thoughts. My training kicked into gear: call for help first.

"Mike?" I raised my voice so the guy on the other side of the lab could hear it.

He was at my side in less than a moment, his expression concerned.

"I've sprayed the hot label all over the place, including on me."

"Okay, okay. Don't worry. I can help you. Put everything down behind the shield. Take off your gloves."

I did as he said. My heart was pounding not only from the accident but from my thoughts already racing ahead to what the consequences would be.

Mike grabbed the Geiger counter and, beginning at my shoulders, scanned me from top to bottom. When he reached my left sleeve, the meter ticked loudly, showing where the contamination was.

"Take off your lab coat." He checked my wrist—no ticks, I had none on my skin.

He slowly scanned me all the way to my feet, then the bottom of my shoes. Clean. He had me step away while he ran the probe over the bench and the shield.

"Can you help me with the cleanup?"

"Yes, I can." I found a fresh lab coat and gloves and we gathered everything into the proper waste bags and cleaned the shield.

"I have to go report this to Thom."

"I'll come with you," Mike said.

Thom was philosophical about the botched test. He neither blamed me nor expressed any dismay at having to disappoint the folks in clinical and my fear dissipated.

"You'll have to start over, eh?" he asked.

"Yes, I will." And it meant I'd be staying very late. It was already midafternoon, and I had begun this early in the morning. The prospect didn't faze me in the least, I realized. I wasn't hungover and craving a drink after work. I'd be tired, that was all, and I'd have to go out and find something to eat. I'd miss my carpool's five p.m. on the dot departure and have to take BART home. None of it was terrible, merely necessary.

I went to my desk where I'd stowed some snacks and had something to eat and drank some water, then I returned to the lab.

On the BART ride, there wasn't much else to do except think. The train hurtled under the San Francisco Bay with me slouched in my seat, clutching my backpack. I'd passed another test. Not one devised by someone else, but entirely of my own making. I wasn't a screwup anymore, or at least I'd not screwed up so bad that I couldn't fix it. I didn't fall apart, I didn't dissolve in a puddle of anxiety, I did, as AA advises, "the next right thing." I wouldn't be drowning my sorrows in vodka. I'd would be going to sleep sober so I could wake up and be back at work early via another BART ride to finish my task.

"So what do *you* want to do?" I asked Kendra. We were trying to plan a date. We'd spend the night together a couple more times and all had gone well, but I was beginning to suspect that we didn't have all that much in common aside from Shanti. Like movies, for instance. I liked action movies, she didn't ("too violent"). I didn't care for fast food, she did. She liked to sleep in, I wanted to have sex fast then get up.

It wasn't that didn't like her, because I did, and she was certainly an improvement over all the women I'd had drunken sex with and then dismissed. I was ready for a relationship, but Kendra, it seemed, was not going to be the one. This was apparently what could happen when you dated like a normal person: you might want to stop dating the other woman. Would this make things awkward at the support group meetings? Maybe or maybe not. Which one of us was going to make the first move? Back to that question again. I chuckled to myself.

"We could get take-out and stay in," Kendra said. "And rent a movie."

"We could. But which movie? And what kind of food?"

She threw me a look. "We could compromise, you know."

"We could. I can do that."

In the end, we rented a comedy, *Risky Business*, and ate some sort of Chinese chicken thing. Later in bed while we made love, my mind wandered a bit, which was new, and I felt guilty about it. That was probably not a good sign.

The thing to do, of course, was talk to Anthony. After the last conversation where I begged him to keep being my sponsor, we'd met, we'd talked, it seemed to be as it was, but I wasn't sure. Were we going through the motions? Was I phoning it in with Kendra? I thought I might be. I didn't want to be a heel, but somehow I thought I ought to have more and stronger feelings. I ought to be head over heels, floating on a cloud, etc.

I described it all to Anthony and then sat back and waited to hear his wisdom.

"What do *you* think you should do?"

That bugged me. As often as I'd heard him say that, it struck me the wrong way.

"That's why I'm telling you. I *don't* know!"

"I think you do know and you don't want to say so. Max, you're not a newcomer anymore."

"You said 'What do you think you should do' all the time when I was new."

"And," he said complacently, "you figured it out."

"Yes, I suppose so." I was glum.

"You know yourself well enough now. You don't need reassurance from me. You did when you were new, but that's over now. In this case, you don't require direct adult supervision."

"I have to stop dating her. Cut the cord, end it."

"Is that what you want?" He was persistent, that was for sure.

"I don't want to hurt her feelings. I don't want to be a jerk."

"You're not being a jerk by being honest. Didn't those Al-Anon meetings I sent you to teach you anything?"

Anthony had made me go to some Al-Anon meetings. "After all," he said, "we have to deal with drunks all the time, and they have great advice." I did find them helpful, not nearly as much fun as AA but not a waste of time.

"Yeah." I wanted to fight with him. My tone was grudging. "What I think is after all those years being so awful to women, I don't want to be that way anymore."

Anthony smiled slightly. "And you don't have to be, and I submit that you are not that way. Here's a question."

Oh good, another question.

"Would it be better to string her along, drag your heels, be wishy-washy?"

"No."

"Well then, I think you have your answer. Max, we need to discuss our relationship."

Uh-oh.

"I told you I didn't think I had the ability to be your sponsor anymore a few months ago."

"I remember." I was despondent because I knew what was coming next.

"I thought some more about it and I think it's best if you find someone else. And I encourage you to find someone else."

I knew arguing with him wasn't the best path to take. "Okay."

"We're still friends, for sure."

"For sure." I hugged him to show him I was fine with it. I wasn't fine, but strangely I wasn't overwhelmingly sad either. He'd already floated the idea with me, so it wasn't a shock. It was a bleak prospect being left to fend for myself, but on the other hand, Anthony wouldn't likely say this unless he knew I could handle it.

"God doesn't give you anything you can't handle," the AA saying went. I wasn't positive I believed that, since I still didn't believe in God. I did, however, have enough time in the program to accept. *Acceptance is the key.*

❖

I invited Kendra out for dinner in order to break up with her. It was funny that I was willing to let go of someone and not have to be booted, like Adrian had to do to me. I probably owed Adrian a certain amount of gratitude for detaching from me, mess that I was. I hoped that Kendra could take as generous a view of what I was about to do.

The evening didn't start well, as we had to wait a half hour for a table and then the table service was slow. I was surprised to see that Kendra became impatient. Maybe that explained why we ate at her house so often; she didn't like restaurants and the all-over-the-map quality of service.

When the waiter arrived at last to take our order, she asked him a million questions about substitutions, source of ingredients. She brought up a peanut allergy, which she'd never mentioned to me before. All of it was leavened by her calm conversational tone, but it was still unnerving to the waiter, who was either new to the job or merely not good at handling difficult customers.

We completed our order at last and could turn our attention to one another. I had debated when to start the talk. Before entrées? During? Dessert? After the whole thing, take a walk and *then* talk? No time seemed like the right time. I settled on doing it when we were eating. I was not happy that things had begun so poorly. Kendra didn't seem exactly mad but she wasn't cheerful either.

The food arrived and we began to eat.

"How does it taste?" I asked.

She'd ordered fish, I had chosen roast chicken. This wasn't a super high-end restaurant, but I'd thought it would be decent. Good enough as a scene for a breakup.

"Eh, you know, it's okay."

"Do you need to send it back?"

"Oh no. I guess I'm not fond of anyone's cooking but my own." That was clear.

"Well, I understand, but since I don't cook at all, I thought it appropriate to take you out to dinner since you've cooked so often for me."

She raised her eyes from her plate and looked at me. "You don't have to do that."

"I know I don't *have* to. I wanted to." I tried on a slightly pleading tone, hoping to get her to modify her attitude somewhat. Probably not possible.

"There's no quid pro quo, Max. I don't need to be thanked."

Whoa, this was going downhill fast, and I hadn't even said anything about breaking up.

"I realize that, I am being nice."

She paused and put her fork down. "I'm sorry. Of course you're being nice. It's me who's making trouble because I'm not good with eating out."

"Why is that?" It was late in the game for nosy questions, but why not. I was curious.

"Oh, probably because my parents used to fight over the dinner table and my dad would accuse my mom of being a terrible cook and she'd get mad and he'd storm out. He was a drunk." Of course he was. "So, in some weird way, I have to be perfect at home cooking. Also, she would tell him if he hated her cooking so much, why don't we eat out, and when we did, he'd make a scene in the restaurant."

"Ouch. That's awful."

"Yes. As you can see, it has me rather screwed up."

No shit. "Well, that's understandable."

We continued eating in silence for a while. I grew more and more uneasy. How was I going to pull this off tonight? Was this the time? I didn't want to drag things out.

"Kendra, how do you feel about our relationship? Where do you think this is going?"

"I'm fine with it. I don't need to define anything." Noncommittal. Great.

"Um, well, I sort of do. And I've been thinking..." Dangerous phrase for an alcoholic, I'd heard. She likely didn't know that, though.

I paused, not sure how to say what I wanted to say. She looked at me suspiciously.

"And...?"

"I'm not certain we're well suited, and, I eh, wonder if we should keep seeing each other."

"Really?" She didn't say it in a friendly tone.

"How do you feel?"

"If you want to break up, just say so, Max."

This was why I didn't want to date. You got involved with someone and then you had to have hard conversations, like an adult. Yuck. Well, here I was, and I had to finish what I'd started.

"I don't necessarily want to break up but I feel, well, that we're not in a long-term relationship, it doesn't seem."

"I've had my doubts about you as well." Ack. That didn't sound good.

"What sort of doubts?"

"You know, are you right for me? Do we have chemistry?" Well, I thought we did, at least at first.

"We had some measure of it, I think." But then sex had gone by the wayside rather swiftly, and I'd always come up with a reason for it.

"Maybe. God, this is difficult, isn't it."

"Yes, but I don't want to make it this big emotional thing. I don't want us to have hard feelings."

"I don't have hard feelings. Do you?" This she said in a challenging fashion.

"No. I'm fine."

And at that precise moment, the waiter arrived and said with faux cheeriness, "Dessert?"

We stared at each other.

"No," I told him firmly. "Thanks."

As soon as he left, Kendra folded her arms.

"You might have warned me you were taking me out to break up with me."

"Eh. I wasn't sure how best to do it."

"This wasn't it. Now it seems like you bought me dinner to, I don't know, try to placate me."

"Yikes. No, not at all." That wasn't the reason, was it?

"Uh-huh. Well. I'm not sorry you want to stop seeing me. That's A-OK."

Don't try to fix her feelings! my Al-Anon training advised me.

It was a ride back home in a car filled with strained silence.

"I wish you well," I said as I exited the car. "Truly."

"Yeah. Thanks." She drove off without another word.

Keith was in the hospital again, so there had been no need to come over to see him. I'd stopped in briefly one time. His PAWS volunteer, Terry, took care of Sebastian while he was gone, and Raoul visited him in the hospital and gave me updates. Hospital visits were still not something I was good at it. I still had work to do overcoming that aversion.

I went over when he was back home.

"So that, as they say, was that." I told Keith all about Kendra. His face was sympathetic. "That is also why I never had any real relationships. That way I wouldn't have to end them." I was only half joking. The whole thing left me awash in ambivalence.

"Sure," Keith said. "Nothing ventured, nothing gained. Or lost."

"Right. What about you?"

"Oh, you know. Dr. Kildare mutters about this or that." He waved his cigarette.

"And?"

His smile was that of a Cheshire cat. "Well, I've got this."

He raised his T-shirt and there, embedded in his abdomen, was a needle with a rubber tube attached.

"What's this?"

"It's a feeding tube. I can't eat anything, I can't keep it down, so they gave me this. When the nurse comes over, she pumps some liquid nutrition into me and then cleans everything."

"Wow. So back to Dr. Kildare."

"Oh. New drugs. My T cells are practically zero. Anything that comes along will probably kill me."

He'd never said that explicitly, and it rattled me. I struggled to keep a straight face.

"Well, as long as you never go out."

"Sure. And don't you go getting sick," he said.

"I'll try not to." That was a terrifying thought. What if he caught something from me?

"Oh," I said, "I brought you the newspaper." I handed him the gay newspaper I picked up for him.

"Look at this." I opened it up and pointed out an article. Keith read through it, then tossed the paper aside.

"Is that what we're supposed to believe now? AIDS is psychological? We just need to have a better attitude toward life?"

The article was by a gay psychologist who stated that gay men were abandoned as children and they had undergone "psychoincubation" and developed AIDS. This unscientific dreck was being read by scared gay men. It was appalling.

I looked back at Keith, who was staring into space.

"Let's turn on VH1. Or are there any old movies on?"

"Doesn't matter. Go ahead. Whenever I watch TV, all the ads are about retirement plans, IRAs, and 401(k)s and all that. Nothing that matters to me."

I didn't know what to say to that, so I turned the TV on, tuned it to VH1, and got started on my cleaning chores.

❖

Seeing Kendra at the support group meetings turned out to be fine. Mostly we no longer sat next to one another; that was the only difference. It was odd to sit there in the circle and look across at her and not feel a thing. Easy come and easy go, like streetcars, the sober version, I guessed. And I wasn't trying to avoid her or being frightened of seeing her because of what I'd done. Minor awkwardness was tolerable.

At our support group meetings, we all reported slightly different versions of the same thing. Our clients got sicker, then they might get better for a time, then they became very sick. Then they died. I heard my fellow volunteers say that their clients would withdraw and simply were unable to interact with them any longer. Like ghosts. It was like they were dead before they died. I wondered how much longer Keith would hang on. He was still cheerful when I saw him, but his silences were getting longer. I didn't struggle to fill the voids with my own babble.

Anthony invited me over for a chat, saying he had something important to tell me.

While we drank hot chocolate, he explained that he was moving out of the City.

"Why?" I asked, aghast.

"It's time. Liam is going to rent a house in the Russian River and work at one of the resorts. I'm going with him. I need a break. It's not far away, Max, you can visit. Please look for a new sponsor. I hope you will consider that. And you'll be fine, I'm sure."

Easy for him to say. I was pissed off and really sad. At least I'd learned to name my emotions. The anger made me sad, not the other way around. I felt like I was being abandoned, though I knew that wasn't true. He was likely going to die sometime, and this was the dress rehearsal. Things always change, whether we want them to or not. Besides, along with AA, I still had my job by some miracle, and my Shanti work. Keith was hanging in there, though I suspected it wouldn't be for much longer.

Right after Anthony left for the Russian River, I got a phone call from Keith's friend Al to tell me Keith was back in the hospital.

"And I don't think he's coming home again," he added.

We met at Keith's apartment so he could let me in. I wanted to check and see if anything needed to be done. Sebastian had gone home with Terry, so he was fine. Al and I looked around. There were fecal stains on the blanket on the couch, so we washed the bedding and cleaned the bathroom. Then we drove over to SFGH.

"Oh, my goodness, look who's here, my entire entourage," he said as we each hugged and kissed him. Raoul was already there. Keith was clearly weak, but he grinned gamely.

"We went and tidied up your place to be ready for when you come home," I said. "I missed seeing Sebastian."

Keith blinked. His skin had the grayish cast to it that I was familiar with.

"I told Sebastian he was going to have to go with Terry and he had to get a grip. When Terry came to pick him up, he didn't give me so much as a backward glance. Ungrateful bitch." Keith's smile wasn't as good humored as I remembered.

"How is it, not smoking?" I asked.

"Oh, it's fine. You know, I sort of lost the taste for it."

Raoul said, "Is anyone reading to you?"

Keith waved an arm, "Sure." He lowered his voice. "You know, there is one nurse here. I seem to pay attention better if he reads to me. I miss my TV. My music videos." He was sadder than I had ever seen him. It really sucked to be in the hospital and not in his home.

"Is Dr. Kildare going to be around?" I asked. "Do I get to meet him?"

"I don't know. I'll see if Abel can find him."

"Who's Abel?" I asked.

Keith raised his eyebrows. Oh, he must be Keith's favorite nurse.

"Sharon McKnight did a show the other day. It was almost like being in a club. Almost."

Sharon McKnight was a locally famous cabaret singer who came to Ward 5B once a week to perform for the troops, so to speak. Ward 5B was definitely not a typical hospital ward in any fashion other than it was full of sick people. I had heard there was a waiting list to get in. SFGH was not a luxury place, it was the City's public hospital and the amenities were bare bones. It was the gay community, including the nurses and doctors who worked there, who did what they could to make the last days or weeks of the PWAs better.

"Tell me. Who are you seeing? Give me some good gossip." Keith touched my arm.

"Nobody. I'm pretty boring these days."

"Oh don't say that, Max, sweetie, you are *never* boring. I think someone will come along." This man was dying and he was worried about *my* love life. Talk about humility—mine, that is—it was spinning off the charts.

"Hey, I think Raoul wants to have a heart-to-heart with you. I'm going to step out." I squeezed his hand, and Al and I left the room. Al went to the cafeteria but I begged off. I wanted to be by myself with my feelings. I walked down the institutional beige hallway, tears in my eyes. No one even looked at me. I don't think tears were a rare sight in Ward 5B. I walked around for a bit, collecting my wits. There was a lot of activity, a lot of visitors milling in and out of rooms. They had no set hours; anyone was permitted to see their loved ones anytime.

I returned to Keith's room where Raoul sat beside him, holding his hand. I took up another chair next to him. It was mostly a matter of waiting now. His heart would stop, or he'd slip into a coma first and then his heart would stop. His body would just give up the fight and quit working.

I went to a meeting that evening, not having anything better to do. I worked the next day in a sort of mental equivalent of San Francisco's famous fog. In the evening, Raoul called me to say he was gone. It had been almost exactly one year that I'd been his practical support volunteer.

Keith's friends held a memorial for him. He, of course, had specified what he wanted done. He was cremated and we went out on the Blue & Gold Ferry to the Golden Gate Bridge to spread his ashes. Just as the ferry passed under the bridge, Al opened the box, and we watched him throw Keith's ashes into the Pacific. Unfortunately, the western wind of the Pacific blew everything back into our faces. We stood rooted in shock for a moment, then started to laugh and brush Keith's ashes off our our jackets. Al said, "As usual, Thelma, you still have the last laugh."

I was given his coffee table, the one I had cleaned so many times, and I put it in my small living room so I could see it every day.

❖

There's a saying in AA warning us to not mistake serenity for boredom. I wasn't in much danger of doing that. I was astonished that I had any serenity at all after the swift series of losses I'd undergone: Kendra, Anthony, Keith. At least I was no longer in mourning for Chris. I was at peace about him—my emotional debt was paid. I was sad about Keith, but I didn't need to push the emotions away. I could hear his voice in my head, and it comforted me. I didn't mind. He was always joking or camping or singing or telling me not worry. Whatever was going to happen to Anthony, I would have to wait and see.

I wouldn't have predicted that losing three people at the same time wouldn't devastate me. I used to think alcohol was my shield against, well, everything. I know now it doesn't work. I was awash in all sorts of feelings: loss, grief, sadness, uncertainty. They were like a tsunami, except I wasn't getting swept away. Recovery was a lifeboat, and I floated atop the waves and was delivered to the shore, safe and dry.

The Friday-night AA meeting at MCC was essentially one continual PWA support group along with the AA talk. There were more men getting sick. Those who weren't sick were worried, and fewer were in the denial that Anthony had once described to me.

Art came to the meeting, his first, after his lover died of a drug overdose.

"We were shooting meth every day. Yesterday morning, I woke up and he was dead in bed next to me." He stopped talking and we waited patiently for him to continue.

His voice broke and he said, "His heart stopped. Just stopped and he was gone. I don't want to end up like him. I want to be clean and sober for what time I have. It won't be long, I know. I don't think he'd want me to go like that."

Then a man named Tim spoke up. His story, if anything, was worse.

"Ralph contracted cytomegalovirus, CMV, and it invaded his brain. Even though Ralph doesn't talk to his parents, he was in the hospital and it looked like he was going to go soon, so I called them and told them. I told his mother who I was, and there was like this big silence on the other end of the phone. It was horrible having to deliver this news to her. She finally said something like, 'I see. Well, we'll be there in two days.'"

He paused to collect himself. "They arrived, but Ralph couldn't speak because he was on a ventilator. I tried to talk to his mom and dad. I had told his mother over the phone who I was, and I tried to be nice. His dad wouldn't even look at me, let alone talk to me. His mom, Agnes, barely could talk to me. They mostly just sat there and stared at him. They didn't touch him at all. I think they were afraid. He passed the next day. I'd already arranged a memorial service for him and I invited them, but they declined. They informed me they were coming over to the house to collect his stuff. I said that they could have his clothes and his family pictures and a couple other things. They took everything. They left me some furniture. Agnes told me she considered his death my fault. I didn't get angry, but I said he was diagnosed right when we met and I'd been taking care of him and I loved him as she did. She screamed at me not to try and compare myself to his family. They left and that was that."

He started crying for real, and someone put an arm around him, and the meeting went on. I was too sad to want to say anything. I couldn't believe someone's parents could be so cold, but then again that was homophobia for you. Tim would be cared for and loved by his real family, in AA and his friends, and he would stay sober, I hoped.

Some meetings were worse than others, but even in the face of all this tragedy, we had to soldier on. There were so many things to do. I could at least know I was participating even beyond Shanti. Chris would have been proud of me. I know if he'd been around, he would have broken through his denial and dived into service.

I walked down Castro Street on my way to the Eureka Valley Community Center, to a group called Our Boys Need Blood.

The Castro Street scene was much different than the one that had greeted me and Chris in 1981. The guys still hung out at Hibernia Beach but there were fewer of them. Many fewer. The clones didn't stride around showing off their muscles. There were skinny, stooped guys shuffling along with walkers and oxygen. A whole generation had aged into old men, but they weren't old, they were sick. Some of them had KS spots marring their once-handsome faces. The light poles and the bulletin boards were covered with fundraiser advertisements. There were still parties and discos, but they had a grim purpose. We had to raise money, a lot of it. The City of San Francisco did have services for PWAs, but it wasn't nearly enough and the gay community had to take up the slack. It was Thursday and I, like everyone else in the community, picked up the *Bay Area Reporter* and turned to the obituaries to see if I knew anyone who'd died the previous week. Often, I did. Some AA guy or someone's Shanti client.

I closed the newspaper and turned onto Collingwood Street. At least I could do what I could do. I didn't have to hide behind drugs or alcohol. I was taught in AA to be of service, and here was a golden opportunity for service. I was alive, and there was a reason for that. I had my life back to do with what I wanted.

The gym was covered with dozens of cots. Cyndi Lauper's "Time after Time" played on the loudspeaker. Fitting.

A tiny spark of inspiration flared in my head. Maybe I could meet someone here at blood donation? I scoped out the room and then saw a dark-haired, blue-eyed gal lying on a cot, calmly awaiting the nurse to prep her to give blood.

I took the cot right next to her and gave her a big grin.

"Hi, there, I'm Max."

"Hey, Max. I'm Trish."

And she lit up with a brilliant smile of her own exactly as if she'd been waiting for me to show up all along.

About the Author

Kathleen Knowles grew up in Pittsburgh, Pennsylvania, but has lived in San Francisco for more than thirty years. She finds the city's combination of history, natural beauty, and multicultural diversity inspiring and endlessly fascinating. Her first novel, *Awake Unto Me*, won the Golden Crown Literary Society Award for best historical romance novel of 2012. She lives with her spouse and their three pets atop one of San Francisco's many hills. When not writing, she works as a health and safety specialist at the University of California, San Francisco.

Books Available From Bold Strokes Books

All She Wants by Larkin Rose. Marci Jones and Tessa Dalton get more than they bargained for when their plans for a one-night stand turn into an opportunity for love. (978-1-63555-476-2)

Beautiful Accidents by Erin Zak. Stevie Adams doesn't believe in fate, not after losing her parents in a car crash. But she's about to discover that sometimes the best things in life happen purely by accident. (978-1-63555-497-7)

Before Now by Joy Argento. The instant Delaney Peyton and Jade Taylor meet, they sense a connection neither can explain. Can they overcome a betrayal that spans the centuries to reignite a love that can't be broken? (978-1-63555-525-7)

Breathe by Cari Hunter. Paramedic Jemima Pardon's chronic bad luck seems to be improving when she meets police officer Rosie Jones. But they face a battle to survive before they can find love. (978-1-63555-523-3)

Double-Crossed by Ali Vali. Hired thief and killer Reed Gable finds something in her scope that will change her life forever when she gets a contract to end casino accountant Brinley Myers's life. (978-1-63555-302-4)

False Horizons by CJ Birch. Jordan and Ash struggle with different views on the alien agenda and must find their way back to each other before they're swallowed up by a centuries-old war. Third in the New Horizons series. (978-1-63555-519-6)

Legacy by Charlotte Greene. In this paranormal mystery, five women hike to a remote cabin deep inside a national park—and unsettling events suggest that they should have stayed home. (978-1-63555-490-8)

Somewhere Along the Way by Kathleen Knowles. When Maxine Cooper moves to San Francisco during the summer of 1981, she learns that wherever you run, you cannot escape yourself. (978-1-63555-383-3)

Blood of the Pack by Jenny Frame. When Alpha of the Scottish pack Kenrick Wulver visits the Wolfgangs, she falls for Zaria Lupa, a wolf on the run. (978-1-63555-431-1)

Cause of Death by Sheri Lewis Wohl. Medical student Vi Akiak and K9 Search and Rescue officer Kate Renard must work together to find a killer before they end up the next targets. In the race for survival, they discover that love may be the biggest risk of all. (978-1-63555-441-0)

Chasing Sunset by Missouri Vaun. Hijinks and mishaps ensue as Iris and Finn set off on a road trip adventure, chasing the sunset, and falling in love along the way. (978-1-63555-454-0)

Double Down by MB Austin. When an unlikely friendship with Spanish pop star Erlea turns deeper, Celeste, in-house physician for the hotel hosting Erlea's show, has a choice to make—run or double down on love. (978-1-63555-423-6)

Party of Three by Sandy Lowe. Three friends are in for a wild night at billionaire heiress Eleanor McGregor's twenty-fifth birthday party. Love, lust, and doing the right thing, even when it hurts, turn the evening into one that will change their lives forever. (978-1-63555-246-1)

Sit. Stay. Love. by Karis Walsh. City girl Alana Brendt and country vet Tegan Evans both know they don't belong together. Only problem is, they're falling in love. (978-1-63555-439-7)

Where the Lies Hide by Renee Roman. As P.I. Camdyn Stark gets closer to solving the case, will her dark secrets and the lies she's buried jeopardize her future with the quietly beautiful Sarah Peters? (978-1-63555-371-0)

Beautiful Dreamer by Melissa Brayden. With love on the line, can Devyn Winters find it in her heart to stay in the small town of Dreamer's Bay, the one place she swore she'd never remain? (978-1-63555-305-5)

Create a Life to Love by Erin Zak. When sixteen-year-old Beth shows up at her birth mother's door, three lives will change forever. (978-1-63555-425-0)